…you take m… …r date, you'll win your bet.

"It …olates the spirit of it."

"It doesn't have to," Chase insisted. "Anyway, by the time I'm through with you, you'll be able to get any date you want."

She blinked. "Are you… are you Henry Higgins-ing me?"

He only had a vague knowledge of the old movie *My Fair Lady*, but he was pretty sure that was the reference. A man who took a grubby flower girl and turned her into the talk of the town.

"Yes," he said finally. "Yes, I am. Take me up on this, Anna Brown, and I will turn you into a woman."

* * *

Take Me, Cowboy
is part of the Copper Ridge series from
…SA TODAY bestselling author Maisey Yates

TAKE ME COWBOY

BY
MAISEY YATES

First Published in Great Britain 2016
By Mills & Boon, an imprint of HarperCollins*Publishers*
1 London Bridge Street, London, SE1 9GF

ISBN: 978-0-263-91855-7

51-0416

Our policy is to use papers that are natural, renewable and recyclable products and made from wood grown in sustainable forests. The logging and manufacturing processes conform to the legal environmental regulations of the country of origin.

Printed and bound in Spain
by CPI, Barcelona

Maisey Yates is a *USA TODAY* bestselling author of more than thirty romance novels. She has a coffee habit she has no interest in kicking and a slight Pinterest addiction. She lives with her husband and children in the Pacific Northwest. When Maisey isn't writing she can be found singing in the grocery store, shopping for shoes online and probably not doing dishes. Check out her website, www.maiseyyates.com.

To Nicole Helm, for your friendship, profane texts and love of farm animals in sweaters. My life would be boring without you.

One

When Anna Brown walked into Ace's bar, she was contemplating whether or not she could get away with murdering her older brothers.

That's really nice that the invitation includes a plus one. You know you can't bring your socket wrench.

She wanted to punch Daniel in his smug face for that one. She had been flattered when she'd received her invitation to the community charity event that the West family hosted every year. A lot less so when Daniel and Mark had gotten ahold of it and decided it was the funniest thing in the world to imagine her trying to get a date to the coveted fund-raiser.

Because apparently the idea of her having a date at all was the pinnacle of comedic genius.

I can get a date, jackasses.

You want to make a bet?

Sure. It's your money.

That exchange had seemed both enraging and empowering about an hour ago. Now she was feeling both humiliated and a little bit uncertain. The fact that she had bet on her dating prowess was…well, embarrassing didn't even begin to describe it. But on top of that, she was a little concerned that she had no prowess to speak of.

It had been longer than she wanted to admit since she'd actually had a date. In fact, it was entirely possible that she had never technically been on one. That quick roll in the literal hay with Corbin Martin hadn't exactly been a date per se.

And it hadn't led to anything, either. Since she had done a wonderful job of smashing his ego with a hammer the next day at school when she'd told her best friend, Chase, about Corbin's…limitations.

Yeah, her sexual debut had also been the final curtain.

But if men weren't such whiny babies, maybe that wouldn't have been the case. Also, maybe if Corbin had been able to prove to her that sex was worth the trouble, she would view it differently.

But he hadn't. So she didn't.

And now she needed a date.

She stalked across the room, heading toward the table that she and Chase, and often his brother, Sam, occupied on Friday nights. The lighting was dim, so she knew someone was sitting there but couldn't make out which McCormack brother it was.

She hoped it was Chase. Because as long as she'd known Sam, she still had a hard time making conversation with him.

Talking wasn't really his thing.

She moved closer, and the man at the table tilted his head up. Sam. Dammit. Drinking a beer and looking grumpy, which was pretty much par for the course with him. But Chase was nowhere to be seen.

"Hi," she said, plopping down in the chair beside him. "Bad day?"

"A day."

"Right." At least when it came to Sam, she knew the difficult-conversation thing had nothing to do with her. That was all him.

She tapped the top of her knee, looking around the bar, trying to decide if she was going to get up and order a drink or wait for someone to come to the table. She allowed her gaze to drift across the bar, and her attention was caught by the figure of a man in the corner, black cowboy hat on his head, his face shrouded by the dim light. A woman was standing in front of him looking up at his face like he was her every birthday wish come true.

For a moment the sight of the man standing there struck her completely dumb. Broad shoulders, broad chest, strong-looking hands. The kind of hands that made her wonder if she needed to investigate the potential fuss of sex again.

He leaned up against the wall, his forearm above his head. He said something and the little blonde he was talking to practically shimmered with excitement. Anna wondered what that was like. To be the focus of a man's attention like that. To have him look at you like a sex object instead of a drinking buddy.

For a moment she envied the woman standing there, who could absolutely get a date if she wanted one. Who would know what to wear and how to act if she were invited to a fancy gala whatever.

That woman would know what to do if the guy wanted to take her home after the date and get naked. She wouldn't be awkward and make jokes and laugh when he got naked because there were all these feelings that were so…so weird she didn't know how else to react.

With a man like that one…well, she doubted she would laugh. He would be all lean muscle and wicked smiles. He would look at her and she would… Okay, even in fantasy she didn't know. But she felt hot. Very, very hot.

But in a flash, that hot feeling turned into utter horror. Because the man shifted, pushing his hat back on his head and angling slightly toward Anna, a light from above catching his angular features and illuminating his face. He changed then, from a fantasy to flesh and blood. And she realized exactly who she had just been checking out.

Chase McCormack. Her best friend in the entire world. The man she had spent years training herself to never, ever have feelings below the belt for.

She blinked rapidly, squeezing her hands into fists and trying to calm the fluttering in her stomach. "I'm going to get a drink," she said, looking at Sam. *And talk to Ace about the damn lighting in here.* "Did you want something?"

He lifted his brow, and his bottle of beer. "I'm covered."

Her heart was still pounding a little heavier than usual when she reached the bar and signaled Ace, the establishment's owner, to ask for whatever pale ale he had on tap.

And her heart stopped altogether when she heard a deep voice from behind her.

"Why don't you make that two."

She whisked around and came face-to-chest with Chase. A man whose presence should be commonplace, and usually was. She was just in a weird place, thanks to high-pressure invitations and idiot brothers.

"Pale ale," she said, taking a step back and looking up at his face. A face that should also be commonplace. But it was just so very symmetrical. Square jaw, straight nose, strong brows and dark eyes that were so direct they bordered on obscene. Like they were looking straight through your clothes or something. Not that he would ever want to look through hers. Not that she would want him to. She was too smart for that.

"That's kind of an unusual order for you," she continued,

more to remind herself of who he was than to actually make commentary on his beverage choices. To remind herself that she knew him better than she knew herself. To do whatever she could to put that temporary moment of insanity when she'd spotted him in the corner out of her mind.

"I'm feeling adventurous," he said, lifting one corner of his mouth, the lopsided grin disrupting the symmetry she had been admiring earlier and somehow making him look all the more compelling for it.

"Come on, McCormack. Adventurous is bungee jumping from Multnomah Falls. Adventurous is not trying a new beer."

"Says the expert in adventure?"

"I'm an expert in a couple of things. Beer and motor oil being at the top of the list."

"Then I won't challenge you."

"Probably for the best. I'm feeling a little bit bloodthirsty tonight." She pressed her hands onto the bar top and leaned forward, watching as Ace went to get their drinks. "So. Why aren't you still talking to short, blonde and stacked over there?"

He chuckled and it settled oddly inside her chest, rattling around before skittering down her spine. "Not really all that interested."

"You seemed interested to me."

"Well," he said, "I'm not."

"That's inconsistent," she said.

"Okay, I'll bite," he said, regarding her a little more closely than she would like. "Why are you in the mood to cause death and dismemberment?"

"Do I seem that feral?"

"Completely. Why?"

"The same reason I usually am," she said.

"Your brothers."

"You're fast, I like that."

Ace returned to their end of the bar and passed two pints toward them. "Do you want to open a tab?"

"Sure," she said. "On him." She gestured to Chase.

Ace smiled in return. "You look nice tonight, Anna."

"I look…the same as I always do," she said, glancing down at her worn gray T-shirt and no-fuss jeans.

He winked. "Exactly."

She looked up at Chase, who was staring at the bartender, his expression unreadable. Then she looked back at Ace.

Ace was pretty hot, really. In that bearded, flannel-wearing way. Lumbersexual, or so she had overheard some college girls saying the other night as they giggled over him. Maybe *he* would want to be her date. Of course, easy compliments and charm aside, he also had his pick of any woman who turned up in his bar. And Anna was never anyone's pick.

She let go of her fleeting Ace fantasy pretty quickly.

Chase grabbed the beer from the counter and handed one to her. She was careful not to let their fingers brush as she took it from him. That type of avoidance was second nature to her. Hazards of spending the years since adolescence feeling electricity when Chase got too close, and pretending she didn't.

"We should go back and sit with Sam," she suggested. "He looks lonely."

Chase laughed. "You and I both know he's no such thing. I think he would rather sit there alone."

"Well, if he wants to be alone, then he can stay at home and drink."

"He probably would if I didn't force him to come out. But if I didn't do that, he would fuse to the furniture and then I would have all of that to deal with."

They walked back over to the table, and gradually, her

heart rate returned to normal. She was relieved that the initial weirdness she had felt upon his arrival was receding.

"Hi, Sam," Chase said, taking his seat beside his brother. Sam grunted in response. "We were just talking about the hazards of you turning into a hermit."

"Am I not a convincing hermit already?" he asked. "Do I need to make my disdain for mankind a little less subtle?"

"That might help," Chase said.

"I might just go play a game of darts instead. I'll catch up with you in a minute." Sam took a long drink of his beer and stood, leaving the bottle on the table as he made his way over to the dartboard across the bar.

Silence settled between Chase and herself. Why was this suddenly weird? Why was Anna suddenly conscious of the way his throat moved when he swallowed a sip of beer, of the shift in his forearms as he set the bottle back down on the table? Of just how masculine a sound he made when he cleared his throat?

She was suddenly even conscious of the way he breathed.

She leaned back in her chair, lifting her beer to her lips and surveying the scene around them.

It was Friday night, so most of the town of Copper Ridge, Oregon, was hanging out, drowning the last vestiges of the workweek in booze. It was not the end of the workweek for Anna. Farmers and ranchers didn't take time off, so neither did she. She had to be on hand to make repairs when necessary, especially right now, since she was just getting her own garage off the ground.

She'd just recently quit her job at Jake's in order to open her own shop specializing in heavy equipment, which really was how she found herself in the position she was in right now. Invited to the charity gala thing and embroiled in a bet on whether or not she could get a date.

"So why exactly do you want to kill your brothers today?" Chase asked, startling her out of her thoughts.

"Various reasons." She didn't know why, but something stopped her from wanting to tell him exactly what was going on. Maybe because it was humiliating. Yes, it was definitely humiliating.

"Sure. But that's every day. Why specifically do you want to kill them today?"

She took a deep breath, keeping her eyes fixed on the fishing boat that was mounted to the wall opposite her, and very determinedly not looking at Chase. "Because. They bet that I couldn't get a date to this thing I'm invited to and I bet them that I could." She thought about the woman he'd been talking to a moment ago. A woman so different from herself they might as well be different species. "And right about now I'm afraid they're right."

Chase was doing his best to process his best friend's statement. It was difficult, though. Daniel and Mark had solid asshole tendencies when it came to Anna—that much he knew—but this was pretty low even for them.

He studied Anna's profile, her dark hair pulled back into a braid, her gray T-shirt that was streaked with oil. He watched as she raised her bottle of beer to her lips. She had oil on her hands, too. Beneath her fingernails. Anna wasn't the kind of girl who attracted a lot of male attention. But he kind of figured that was her choice.

She wasn't conventionally beautiful. Mostly because of the motor oil. But that didn't mean that getting a date should be impossible for her.

"Why don't you think you can get a date?"

She snorted, looking over at him, one dark brow raised. "Um." She waved a hand up and down, indicating her body. "Because of all of this."

He took a moment to look at *all of that*. Really look. Like he was a man and she was a woman. Which they were, but not in a conventional sense. Not to each other.

He'd looked at her almost every day for the past fifteen years, so it was difficult to imagine seeing her for the first time. But just then, he tried.

She had a nice nose. And her lips were full, nicely shaped, her top lip a little fuller than her bottom lip, which was unique and sort of…not sexy, because it was Anna. But interesting.

"A little elbow grease and that cleans right off," he said. "Anyway, men are pretty simple."

She frowned. "What does that mean?"

"Exactly what it sounds like. You don't have to do much to get male attention if you want it. Give a guy what he's after…"

"Okay, that's just insulting. You're saying that I can get a guy because men just want to get laid? So it doesn't matter if I'm a wrench-toting troll?"

"You are not a wrench-toting troll. You're a wrench-toting woman who could easily bludgeon me to death, and I am aware of that. Which means I need to choose my next words a little more carefully."

Those full lips thinned into a dangerous line, her green eyes glittering dangerously. "Why don't you do that, Chase."

He cleared his throat. "I'm just saying, if you want a date, you can get one."

"By unzipping my coveralls down to my belly button?"

He tipped his beer bottle back, taking a larger swallow than he intended to, coughing as it went down wrong. He did not need to picture the visual she had just handed to him. But he was a man, so he did.

It was damned unsettling. His best friend, bare beneath a pair of coveralls unfastened so that a very generous wedge of skin was revealed all the way down…

And he was done with that. He didn't think of Anna that way. Not at all. They'd been friends since they were freshmen in high school and he'd navigated teenage boy hormones without lingering too long on thoughts of her breasts.

He was thirty years old, and he could have sex whenever he damn well pleased. Breasts were no longer mysterious to him. He wasn't going to go pondering the mysteries of *her* breasts now.

"It couldn't hurt, Anna," he said, his words containing a little more bite than he would like them to. But he was unsettled.

"Okay, I'll keep that in mind. But barring that, do you have any other suggestions? Because I think I'm going to be expected to wear something fancy, and I don't own anything fancy. And it's obvious that Mark and Daniel think I suck at being a girl."

"That's not true. And anyway, why do you care what they—or anyone else—think?"

"Because. I've got this new business…"

"And anyone who brings their heavy equipment to you for a tune-up won't care whether or not you can walk in high heels."

"But I don't want to show up at these things looking…" She sighed. "Chase, the bottom line is I've spent a long time not fitting in. And people here are nice to me. I mean, now that I'm not in school. People in school sucked. But I get that I don't fit. And I'm tired of it. Honestly, I wouldn't care about my brothers if there wasn't so much…truth to the teasing."

"They do suck. They're awful. So why does it matter what they think?"

"Because," she said. "It just does. I'm that poor Anna Brown with no mom to teach her the right way to do things and I'm just…tired of it. I don't want to be poor Anna Brown. I want to be Anna Brown, heavy equipment mechanic who can wear coveralls and walk in heels."

"Not at the same time, I wouldn't think."

She shot him a deadly glare. "I don't fail," she said, her eyes glinting in the dim bar light. "I won't fail at this."

"You're not in remote danger of failing. Now, what's the mystery event that has you thinking about high heels?" he asked.

Copper Ridge wasn't exactly a societal epicenter. Nestled between the evergreen mountains and a steel-gray sea on the Oregon Coast, there were probably more deer than people in the small town. There were only so many events in existence. And there was a good chance she was making a mountain out of a small-town molehill, and none of it would be that big of a deal.

"That charity thing that the West family has every year," she mumbled. "Gala Under the Stars or whatever."

The West family's annual fund-raising event for schools. It was a weekend event, with the town's top earners coming to a small black-tie get-together on the West property.

The McCormacks had been founding members of the community of Copper Ridge back in the 1800s. Their forge had been used by everyone in town and in the neighboring communities. But as the economy had changed, so had the success of the business.

They'd been hanging on by their fingernails when Chase's parents had been killed in an accident when he was in high school. They'd still gotten an invitation to the gala. But Chase had thrown it on top of the never-ending pile of mail and bills that he couldn't bring himself to look through and forgotten about it.

Until some woman—probably an assistant to the West family—had called him one year when he hadn't bothered to RSVP. He had been…well, he'd been less than polite.

Dealing with a damned crisis here, so sorry I can't go to your party.

Unsurprisingly, he hadn't gotten any invitations after that. And he hadn't really thought much about it since.

Until now.

He and Sam had managed to keep the operation and properties afloat, but he wanted more. He needed it.

The ranch had animals, but that wasn't the source of their income. The forge was the heart of the ranch, where they did premium custom metal- and leatherwork. On top of that, there were outbuildings on the property they rented out—including the shop they leased to Anna. They had built things back up since their parents had died, but it still wasn't enough, not to Chase.

He had promised his father he would take an interest in the family legacy. That he would build for the McCormacks, not just for himself. Chase had promised he wouldn't let his dad down. He'd had to make those promises at a grave site because before the accident he'd been a hotheaded jackass who'd thought he was too big for the family legacy.

But even if his father never knew, Chase had sworn it. And so he'd see it done.

In order to expand McCormack Iron Works, the heart and soul of their ranch, to bring it back to what it had been, they needed interest. Investments.

Chase had always had a good business mind, and early on he'd imagined he would go to school away from Copper Ridge. Get a degree. Find work in the city. Then everything had changed. Then it hadn't been about Chase McCormack anymore. It had been about the McCormack legacy.

School had become out of the question. Leaving had been out of the question. But now he saw where he and Sam were failing, and he could see how to turn the tide.

He'd spent a lot of late nights figuring out exactly how to expand as the demand for handmade items had gone down. Finding ways to convince people that highly customized iron details for homes and businesses, and handmade leather bridles and saddles, were worth paying more for.

Finding ways to push harder, to innovate and modernize while staying true to the family name. While actively butting up against Sam and his refusal to go out and make that happen. Sam, who was so talented he didn't have to pound horseshoe nails if he didn't want to. Sam, who could forget gates and scrollwork on staircases and be selling his artwork for a small fortune. Sam, who resisted change like it was the black plague.

He would kill for an invitation to the Wests' event. Well, not kill. But possibly engage in nefarious activities or the trading of sexual favors. And Anna had an invitation.

"You get to bring a date?" he asked.

"That's what I've been saying," she said. "Of course, it all depends on whether or not I can actually acquire one."

Anna needed a date; he wanted to have a chance to talk to Nathan West. In the grand tradition of their friendship, they both filled the gaps in each other's lives. This was—in his opinion—perfect.

"I'll be your date," he said.

She snorted. "Yeah, right. Daniel and Mark will never believe that."

She had a point. The two of them had been friends forever. And with a bet on the table her brothers would never believe that he had suddenly decided to go out with her because his feelings had randomly changed.

"Okay. Maybe that's true." That frown was back. "Not because there's something wrong with you," he continued, trying to dig himself out of the pit he'd just thrown himself into, "but because it's a little too convenient."

"Okay, that's better."

"But what if we made it clear that things had changed between us?"

"What do you mean?"

"I mean…what if…we built up the change? Showed people that our relationship was evolving."

She gave him a fierce side-eye. "I'm not your type."
He thought back to the blonde he'd been talking to only twenty minutes earlier. Tight dress cut up to the tops of her thighs, long, wavy hair and the kind of smile that invited you right on in. Curves that had probably wrecked more men than windy Highway 101. She was his type.

And she wasn't Anna. Barefaced, scowling with a figure that was slightly more…subtle. He cleared his throat. "You could be. A little less grease, a little more lipstick."

Her top lip curled. "So the ninth circle of hell basically."

"What were you planning on wearing to the fund-raiser?"

She shifted uncomfortably in her seat. "I have black jeans. But…I mean, I guess I could go to the mall in Tolowa and get a dress."

"That isn't going to work."

"Why not?"

"What kind of dress would you buy?" he asked.

"Something floral? Kind of…down to the knee?"

He pinched the bridge of his nose. "You're not Scarlett O'Hara," he said, knowing that with her love of old movies, Anna would appreciate the reference. "You aren't going dressed in the drapes."

Anna scowled. "Why the hell do you know so much about women's clothes?"

"Because I spend a lot of time taking them off my dates."

That shut her up. Her pale cheeks flamed and she looked away from him, and that response stirred…well, it stirred something in his gut he wished would go the hell away.

"Why do *you* want to go anyway?" she asked, still not looking at him.

"I want to talk to Nathan West and the other businessmen there about investment opportunities. I want to prove that Sam and I are the kind of people that can move in their circles. The kind of people they want to do business with."

"And you have to put on a suit and hobnob at a gala to do that?"

"The fact is, I don't get chances like this very often, Anna. I didn't get an invitation. And I need one. Plus, if you take me, you'll win your bet."

"Unless Dan and Mark tell me you don't count."

"Loophole. If they never said you couldn't recruit a date, you're fine."

"It violates the spirit of the bet."

"It doesn't have to," he insisted. "Anyway, by the time I'm through with you, you'll be able to get any date you want."

She blinked. "Are you… Are you Henry Higgins-ing me?"

He had only a vague knowledge of the old movie *My Fair Lady*, but he was pretty sure that was the reference. A man who took a grubby flower girl and turned her into the talk of the town. "Yes," he said thoughtfully. "Yes, I am. Take me up on this, Anna Brown, and I will turn you into a woman."

Two

Anna just about laughed herself off her chair. "You're going to make me a…a…a woman?"

"Why is that funny?"

"What about it *isn't* funny?"

"I'm offering to help you."

"You're offering to help me be something that I am by birth. I mean, Chase, I get that women are kind of your thing, but that's pretty arrogant. Even with all things considered."

"Okay, obviously I'm not going to make you a woman." Something about the way he said the phrase this time hit her in an entirely different way. Made her think about *other* applications that phrase occasionally had. Things she needed to never, ever, ever, ever think about in connection with Chase.

If she valued her sanity and their friendship.

She cleared her throat, suddenly aware that it was dry and scratchy. "Obviously."

"I just meant that you need help getting a date, and I need

to go to this party. And you said that you were concerned about your appearance in the community."

"Right." He wasn't wrong. The thing was, she knew that whether or not she could blend in at an event like this didn't matter at all to how well her business did. Nobody cared if their mechanic knew which shade of lipstick she should wear. But that wasn't the point.

She—her family collectively—was the town charity case. Living on the edge of the community in a run-down house, raised by a single father who was in over his head, who spent his days at the mill. Her older brothers had been in charge of taking care of her, and they had done so. But, of course, they were also older brothers. Which meant they had tormented her while feeding and clothing her. Anyway, she didn't exactly blame them.

It wasn't like the two of them had wanted to raise a sister when they would rather be out raising hell.

Especially a sister who was committed to driving them crazy.

She loved her brothers. But that didn't mean they always had an easy relationship. It didn't mean they didn't hurt her by accident when they teased her about things. She acted invulnerable, so they assumed that she was.

But now, beneath her coveralls and engine grease, she was starting to feel a little bit battered. It was difficult to walk around with a *screw you* attitude barely covering a raw wound. Because eventually that shield started to wear down. Especially when people were used to being able to lob pretty intense rocks at that shield.

That was her life. It was either pity or a kind of merciless camaraderie that had no softness to it. Her dad, her brothers, all the guy friends she had…

And she couldn't really blame them. She had never behaved in a way that would demonstrate she needed any softness. In fact, a few months ago, a few weeks ago even, the idea would have been unthinkable to her.

But there was something about this invitation. Something about imagining herself in yet another situation where she was forced to deflect good-natured comments about her appearance, about the fact that she was more like a guy than the roughest cowboys in town. Yeah, there was something about that thought that had made her want to curl into a ball and never unfurl.

Then, even if it was unintentional, her brothers had piled on. It had hurt her feelings. Which meant she had reacted in anger, naturally. So now she had a bet. A bet, and her best friend looking at her with laser focus after having just promised he would make her a woman.

"Why do you care?" He was pressing, and she wanted to hit him now.

Which kind of summed up why she was in this position in the first place.

She swallowed hard. "Maybe I just want to surprise people. Isn't that enough?"

"You came from nothing. You started your own business with no support from your father. You're a female mechanic. I would say that you're surprising as hell."

"Well, I want to add another dimension to that. Okay?"

"Okay," he said. "Multidimensional Anna. That seems like a good idea to me."

"Where do we start?"

"With you not falling off your chair laughing at me because I've offered to make you a woman."

A giggle rose in her throat again. Hysteria. She was verging on hysteria. Because this was uncomfortable and sincere. She hated both of those things. "I'm sorry. I can't. You can't say that to me and expect me not to choke."

He looked at her again, his dark eyes intense. "Is it a problem, Anna? The idea that I might make you a woman."

He purposefully made his voice deeper. Purposefully added a kind of provocative inflection to the words. She knew he was kidding. Still, it made her chest tighten. Made her heart flutter a little bit.

Wow. How *annoying*. She hadn't had a relapse of Chase Underpants Feelings this bad in a long time.

Apparently she still hadn't recovered from her earlier bit of mistaken identity. She really needed to recover. And he needed to stop being…Chase. If at all possible.

"Is it a problem for *you*?" she asked.

"What?"

"The idea that I might make you a soprano?"

He chuckled. "You probably want to hold off on threats of castration when you're at a fancy party."

"We aren't at one right now."

She was her own worst enemy. Everything that she had just been silently complaining about, she was doing right now. Throwing out barbs the moment she got uncomfortable, because it kept people from seeing what was actually happening inside of her.

Yes, but you really need to keep Chase from seeing that you fluttered internally over something he said.

Yes. Good point.

She noticed that he was looking past her now, and she followed his line of sight. He was looking at that blonde again. "Regrets, Chase?"

He winced, looking back at her. "No."

"So. I assume that to get a guy to come up and hit on me in a bar, I have to put on a dress that is essentially a red ACE bandage sprinkled with glitter?"

He hesitated. "It's more than that."

"What?"

"Well, for a start, there's not looking at a man like you want to dismember him."

She rolled her eyes. "I don't."

"You aren't exactly approachable, Anna."

"That isn't true." She liked to play darts, and hang out, and talk about sports. What wasn't approachable about that?

"I've seen men try to talk to you," Chase continued. "You shut them down pretty quick. For example—" he barreled on before she could interrupt him "—Ace Thompson paid you a compliment back at the bar."

"Ace Thompson compliments everything with boobs."

"And a couple of weeks ago there was a guy in here that tried to buy you a drink. You told him you could buy your own."

"I *can*," she said, "and he was a stranger."

"He was flirting with you."

She thought back on that night, that guy. *Damn.* He had been flirting. "Well, he should get better at it. I'm not going to reward mediocrity. If I can't tell you're flirting, you aren't doing a very good job."

"Part of the problem is you don't think male attention is being directed at you when it actually is."

She looked back over at the shimmery blonde. "Why would any male attention be directed at me when *that's* over there?"

Chase leaned in, his expression taking on a conspiratorial quality that did…things to her insides. "Here's the thing about a girl like that. She knows she looks good. She assumes that men are looking at her. She assumes that if a man talks to her, that means he wants her."

She took a breath, trying to ease the tightness in her chest. "And that's not…a turnoff?"

"No way." He smiled, a sort of lazy half smile. "Confidence is sexy."

He kind of proved that rule. The thought made her bristle.

"All right. So far with our lessons I've learned that I

should unzip my coveralls and as long as I'm confident it will be okay."

"You forgot not looking like you want to stab someone."

"Okay. Confident, nonstabby, showing my boobs."

Chase choked on his beer. "That's a good place to start," he said, setting the bottle down. "Do you want to go play darts? I want to go play darts."

"I thought we were having female lessons."

"Rain check," he said. "How about tomorrow I come by the shop and we get started. I think I'm going to need a lesson plan."

Chase hadn't exactly excelled in school, unless it was at driving his teachers to drink. So why exactly he had decided he needed a lesson plan to teach Anna how to be a woman, he didn't know.

All he knew was that somewhere around the time they started discussing her boobs last night he had become unable to process thoughts normally. He didn't like that. He didn't like it at all. He did not like the fact that he had been forced to consider her breasts more than once in a single hour. He did not like the fact that he was facing down the possibility of thinking about them a few more times over the next few weeks.

But then, that was the game.

Not only was he teaching her how to blend in at a function like this, he was pretending to be her date.

So there was more than one level of hell to deal with. Perfect.

He cleared his throat, walking down the front porch of the farmhouse that he shared with his brother, making his way across the property toward the shop that Anna was renting and using as her business.

It was after five, so she should be knocking off by now. A good time for the two of them to meet.

He looked down at the piece of lined yellow paper in his hand. His lesson plan.

Then he pressed on, his boots crunching on the gravel as he made his way to the rustic wood building. He inhaled deeply, the last gasp of winter riding over the top of the spring air, mixing with the salt from the sea, giving it a crisp bite unique to Copper Ridge.

He relished this. The small moment of clarity before he dived right into the craziness that was his current situation.

Chase McCormack was many things, but he wasn't a coward. He was hardly going to get skittish over giving his best friend some seduction lessons.

He pushed the door open but didn't see Anna anywhere.

He looked around the room, and the dismembered tractors whose various parts weren't in any order that he could possibly define. Though he knew that it must make sense to Anna.

"Hello?"

"Just up here."

He turned, looked up and saw Anna leaning over what used to be a hayloft, looking down at him, a long dark braid hanging down.

"What exactly are you doing up there?"

"I stashed a tool up here, and now I need it. It's good storage. Of course, then I end up climbing the walls a little more often than I would like. Literally. Not figuratively."

"I figured you would be finished for the day by now."

"No. I have to get this tractor fixed for Connor Garrett. And it's been a bigger job than I thought." She disappeared from view for a moment. "But I would like a reputation as someone who makes miracles. So I better make miracles."

She planted her boot hard on the first rung of the ladder and began to climb down. She was covered from head to toe in motor oil and dust. Probably from crawling around in this space, and beneath tractors.

She jumped down past the last three rungs, brushing dirt off her thighs and leaving more behind, since her hands were coated, too. "You don't exactly look like a miracle," he said, looking her over.

She held up her hand, then displayed her middle finger. "Consider it a miracle that I don't punch you."

"Remember what we talked about? Not looking at a guy like you want to stab him? Much less threatening actual bodily harm."

"Hey, I don't think you would tell a woman that you actually wanted to hook up with that she didn't look like a miracle."

"Most women I want to hook up with aren't quite this disheveled. Before we start anyway."

Much to his surprise, color flooded her cheeks.

"Well," she said, her voice betraying nothing, "I'm not most women, Chase McCormack. I thought you would've known that by now."

Then she sauntered past him, wearing those ridiculous baggy coveralls, head held high like she was queen of the dust bowl.

"Oh, I'm well aware of that," he said. "That's part of the problem."

"And now it's your problem to fix."

"That's right. And I have the lesson plan. As promised."

She whipped around to face him, one dark brow lifted. "Oh, really?"

"Yes, really." He held up the lined notepaper.

"That's very professional."

"It's as professional as you're gonna get. Now, the first order of business is to plant the seed that we're more than friends."

She looked as though he had just suggested she eat a handful of bees. "Do we really need to do that?"

"Yeah, we *really* need to do that. You won't just have

a date for the charity event. You're going to have a date every so often until then."

She looked skeptical. "That seems…excessive."

"You want people to believe this. You don't want people to think I'm going because of a bet. You don't want your brothers to think for one moment that they might be right."

"Well, they're going to think it for a few moments at least."

"True. I mean, they are going to be suspicious. But we can make this look real. It isn't going to be that hard. We already hang out most weekends."

"Sure," she said, "but you go home with other girls at the end of the night."

Those words struck him down. "Yes, I guess I do."

"You won't be able to do that now," she pointed out.

"Why not?" he asked.

"Because if I were with you and you went home with another woman, I would castrate you with nothing but my car keys and a bottle of whiskey."

He had no doubt about that. "At least you'd give me some whiskey."

"Hell no. The whiskey would be for me."

"But we're not really together," he said.

"Sure, Chase, but the entire town knows that if any man were to cheat on me, I would castrate him with my car keys, because I don't take crap from anyone. So if they're going to believe that we're together, you're going to have to look like you're being faithful to me."

"That's fine." It wasn't all that fine. He didn't do celibacy. Never had. Not from the moment he'd discovered that women were God's greatest invention.

"No booty calls," she said, her tone stern.

"Wait a second. I can't even call a woman to hook up in private?"

"No. You can't. Because then *she* would know. I have

pride. I mean, right now, standing here in this garage taking lessons from you on how to conform to my own gender's beauty standards, it's definitely marginal, but I have it."

"It isn't like you really know any of the girls that I…"

"Neither do you," she said.

"This isn't about me. It's about you. Now, I got you some things. But I left them in the house. And you are going to have to…hose off before you put them on."

She blinked, her expression almost comical. "Did you buy me clothes?"

He'd taken a long lunch and gone down to Main Street, popping into one of the ridiculously expensive shops that—in his mind—were mostly for tourists, and had found her a dress he thought would work.

"Yeah, I bought you clothes. Because we both know you can't actually wear this out tonight."

"We're going out *tonight*?"

"Hell yeah. I'm taking you somewhere fancy."

"My fancy threshold is very low. If I have to go eat tiny food on a stick sometime next month, I'm going to need actual sustenance in every other meal until then."

He chuckled, trying to imagine Anna coping with miniature food. "Beaches. I'm taking you to Beaches."

She screwed up her face slightly. "We don't go there."

"No, we haven't gone there. We go to Ace's. We shoot pool, we order fried crap and we split the tab. Because we're friends. And that's what friends do. Friends don't go out to Beaches, not just the two of them. But lovers do."

She looked at him owlishly. "Right. I suppose they do."

"And when all this is finished, the entire town of Copper Ridge is going to think that we're lovers."

Three

Anna was reeling slightly by the time she walked up the front porch and into Chase's house. The entire town was going to think that they were...*lovers*. She had never had a lover. At least, she would never characterize the guy she'd slept with as a lover. He was an unfortunate incident. But fortunately, her hymen was the only casualty. Her heart had remained intact, and she was otherwise uninjured. Or pleasured.

Lovers.

That word sounded...well, like it came from some old movie or something. Which under normal circumstances she was a big fan of. In this circumstance, it just made her feel...like her insides were vibrating. She didn't like it.

Chase lived in the old family home on the property. It was a large, log cabin–style house with warm, honey-colored wood and a green metal roof designed to withstand all kinds of weather. Wrought-iron details on the porch and the door were a testament to his and Sam's craftsmanship.

There were people who would pay millions for a home like this. But Sam and Chase had made it this beautiful on their own.

Chase always kept the home admirably clean considering he was a bachelor. She imagined that the other house on the property, the smaller one inhabited by Sam, wasn't quite as well kept. But she also imagined that Sam didn't have the same amount of guests over that Chase did. And by *guests*, she meant female companions. Which he would be cut off from for the next few weeks.

Some small, mean part of her took a little bit of joy in that.

Because you don't like the idea of other women touching him. It doesn't matter how long it's been going on, or how many women there are, you still don't like it.

She sniffed, cutting off that line of thinking. She was just a crabby bitch who was enjoying the idea of him being celibate and suffering a bit. That was all.

"Okay, where are my…girlie things?"

"You aren't even going to look at them until you scrub that grease off."

"And how am I supposed to do that? Are you going to hose me off?"

He clenched his jaw. "No. You can use my shower."

She took a deep breath, trying to dispel the slight fluttering in her stomach. She had never used Chase's shower before. She assumed countless women before her had. When he brought them up here, took their clothes off for them. And probably joined them.

She wasn't going to think about that.

"Okay."

She knew where his shower was, of course. Because she had been inside his bedroom casually, countless times. It had never mattered before. Before, she had never been about to get naked.

She banished that thought as she walked up the stairs

and down the hall to his room. His room was…well, it was very well-appointed, but then again, obviously designed to house guests of the female variety. The bed was large and full of plush pillows. A soft-looking green throw was folded up at the foot of it. An overstuffed chair was in the corner, another blanket draped over the back.

She doubted the explosion of comfort and cozy was for Chase's benefit.

She tamped that thought down, continuing on through the bathroom door, then locking it for good measure. Not that he would walk in. And he was the only person in the house.

Still, she felt insecure without the lock flipped. She took a deep breath, stripped off her coveralls, then the clothes she had on beneath them, and started the shower. Speaking of things that were designed to be shared…

It was enclosed in glass, and she had a feeling that with the door open it was right in the line of sight from the bed. Inside was red tile, and a bench seat that… She wasn't even going to think what that could be used for.

She turned and looked in the mirror. She was grubby. More than grubby. She had grease all over her face, all up under her fingernails.

Thankfully, Chase had some orange-and-pumice cleaner right there on his sink. So she was able to start scrubbing at her hands while the water warmed up.

Steam filled the air and she stepped inside the shower, letting the hot spray cascade over her skin.

It was a *massaging* showerhead. A nice one. She did not have a nice massaging showerhead in her little rental house down in town. Next on her list of Ways She Was Changing Her Life would be to get her own house. With one of these.

She rolled her shoulders beneath the spray and sighed. The water droplets almost felt like fingers moving over her tight muscles. And, suddenly, it was all too easy to imagine a man standing behind her, working at her muscles with his strong hands.

She closed her eyes, letting her head fall back, her mouth going slack. She didn't even have the strength to fight the fantasy, God help her. She'd been edgy and aroused for the past twenty-four hours, no denying it. So this little moment to let herself fantasize…she just needed it.

Then she realized exactly whose hands she was picturing.

Chase's. Tall and strong behind her, his hands moving over her skin, down lower to the slight dip in her spine, just above the curve of her behind…

She grabbed hold of the sponge hanging behind her and began to drag it ferociously over her skin, only belatedly realizing that this was probably what he used to wash himself.

"He uses it to wash his balls," she said into the space. Hoping that that would disgust her. It really should disgust her.

It did not disgust her.

She put the scrubber back, taking a little shower gel and squeezing it into the palm of her hand. Okay, so she would smell like a playboy for a day. It wasn't the end of the world. She started to rub the slick soap over her flesh, ignoring the images of Chase that were trying to intrude.

She was being a crazy person. She had showered at friends' houses before, and never imagined that they were in the shower stall with her.

But ever since last night in the bar, her equilibrium had been off where Chase was concerned. Her control was being sorely tested. She was decidedly unstoked about it.

She shut the water off and got out of the shower, grabbing a towel off the rack and drying her skin with more ferocity than was strictly necessary. Almost as though she was trying to punish her wicked, wicked skin for imagining what it might be like to be touched by her best friend.

But that would be crazy.

Except she felt a little crazy.

She looked around the room. And realized that her stupid friend, who had not wanted her to touch the nice clothing he had bought her, had left her without anything to wear. She couldn't put her sweaty, grease-covered clothes back on. That would negate the entire shower.

She let out an exasperated breath, not entirely certain what she should do.

"Chase?" she called.

She didn't hear anything.

"Chase?" She raised the volume this time.

Still no answer.

"Butthead," she muttered, walking over to the door and tapping the doorknob, trying to decide what her next move was.

She was being ridiculous. Just because she was having an increase of weird, borderline sexual thoughts about him, did not mean he was having them about her. She twisted the knob, undoing the lock as she did, and opened the door a crack. "Chase!"

The door to the bedroom swung open, and Chase walked in, carrying one of those plastic bags fancy dresses were stored in and a pair of shoes.

"I don't have clothes," she hissed through the crack in the door.

"Sorry," he said, looking stricken. At least, she thought he looked stricken.

She opened the door slightly wider, extending her arm outside. "Give them to me."

He crossed the room, walking over to the bathroom door. "You're going to have to open the door wider than that."

She already felt exposed. There was nothing between them. Nothing but some air and the towel she was clutching to her naked body. Well, and most of the door. But she still felt exposed.

Still, he was not going to fit that bag through the crack.

She opened the door slightly wider, then grabbed hold of the bag in his hand and jerked it back through. "I'll get the shoes later," she called through the door.

She dropped the towel and unzipped the bag, staring at the contents with no small amount of horror. There was… underwear inside of it. Underwear that Chase had purchased for her.

Which meant he had somehow managed to look at her breasts and evaluate their size. Not to mention her ass. And ass size.

She grabbed the pair of panties that were attached to a little hanger. Oh, they had no ass. So she supposed the size of hers didn't matter much.

She swallowed hard, taking hold of the soft material and rubbing her thumb over it. He would know exactly what she was wearing beneath the dress. Would know just how little that was.

He isn't going to think about it. Because he doesn't think about you that way.

He never had. He never would. And it was a damn good thing. Because where would they be if either of them acted on an attraction between them?

Up shit creek without a paddle or a friendship.

No, thank you. She was never going to touch him. She'd made that decision a long time ago. For a lot of reasons that were as valid today as they had been the very first time he'd ever made her stomach jump when she looked at him.

She was never going to encourage or act on the attraction that she occasionally felt for Chase. But she would take his expertise in sexual politics and use it to her advantage.

Oh, but those panties.

The bra wasn't really any less unsettling. Though at least it wasn't missing large swathes of fabric.

Still, it was very thin. And she had a feeling that a cool

ocean breeze would reveal the shape of her nipples to all and sundry.

Then again, maybe it was time all and sundry got a look at her nipples. Maybe if they had a better view, men would be a little more interested.

She scowled, wrenching the panties off the hanger and dragging them on as quickly as possible, followed closely by the bra. She was overthinking things. She was overthinking all of this. Had been from the moment Chase had walked into the barn. As evidenced by that lapse in the shower.

She had spent years honing her Chase Control. It was just this change in how they were interacting that was screwing with it. She was not letting this get inside her head, and she was not letting hot, unsettled feelings get inside her pants.

She pulled the garment bag away entirely, revealing a tight red dress slightly too reminiscent of what the woman he had been flirting with last night was wearing.

"Clearly you have a type, Chase McCormack," she muttered, beginning to remove the slinky scrap of material from the hanger.

She tugged it up over her hips, having to do a pretty intense wiggle to get it up all the way before zipping it into place. She took a deep breath, turned around. She faced her reflection in the mirror full-on and felt nothing but deflated.

She looked…well, her hair was wet and straggly, and she looked half-drowned. She didn't look curvy, or shimmery, or delightful.

This was the problem with tight clothes. They only made her more aware of her curve deficit.

Where the blonde last night had filled her dress out admirably, and in all the right places, on Anna this dress kind of looked like a piece of fabric stretched over an ironing board. Not really all that sexy.

She sighed heavily, trying to ignore the sinking feeling in her stomach.

Chase really was going to have to be a miracle worker in order to pull this off.

She didn't really want to show him. Instead, she found the idea of putting the coveralls back on a lot less reprehensible. At least with the coveralls there would still be some mystery. He wouldn't be confronted with just how big a task lay before him.

"Buck up," she said to herself.

So what was one more moment of feeling inadequate? Honestly, in the broad tapestry of her life it would barely register. She was never quite what was expected. She never quite fit. So why'd she expect that she was going to put on a sexy dress and suddenly be transformed into the kind of sex kitten she didn't even want to be?

She gritted her teeth, throwing open the bedroom door and walking out into the room. "I hope you're happy," she said, flinging her arms wide. "You get what you get."

She caught a movement out of the corner of her eye and turned her head, then recoiled in horror. It was even worse out here. Out here, there was a full-length mirror. Out here, she had the chance to see that while her breasts remained stunningly average, her hips and behind had gotten rather wide. Which was easy to ignore when you wore loose attire most days. "I look like the woman symbol on the door of a public restroom."

She looked over at Chase, who had been completely silent upon her entry into the room, and remained so. She glared at him. He wasn't saying anything. He was only staring. "Well?"

"It's nice," he said.

His voice sounded rough, and kind of thin.

"You're a liar."

"I'm not a liar. Put the shoes on."

"Do you even know what size I wear?"

"You're a size ten, which I know because you complain about how your big feet make it impossible for you to find anything in your size. And you're better off buying men's work boots. So yes, I know."

His words made her feel suddenly exposed. Well, his words in combination with the dress, she imagined. They knew each other a little bit too well. That was the problem. How could you impress a guy when you had spent a healthy amount of time bitching to him about your big feet?

"Fine. I will put on the shoes." He held them up, and her jaw dropped. "I thought you were taking me out to dinner."

"I am."

"Do I have to pay for it by working the pole at the Naughty Mermaid?"

"These are *nice* shoes."

"If you're a five-foot-two-inch Barbie like that chick you were talking to last night. I'm like…an Amazon in comparison."

"You're not an Amazon."

"I will be in those."

"Maybe that would bother some men. But you want a man who knows how to handle a woman. Any guy with half a brain is going to lose his mind checking out your legs. He's not going to care if you're a little taller than he is."

She tried her best to ignore the compliment about her legs. And tried even harder to keep from blushing.

"I care," she muttered, snatching the shoes from his hand and pondering whether or not there was any truth to her words as she did.

She didn't really date. So it was hard to say. But now that she was thinking about it, yeah. She was self-conscious about the fact that with pretty low heels she was eye level with half the men in town.

She finished putting the shoes on and straightened. It was like standing on a glittery pair of stilts. "Are you satisfied?" she asked.

"I guess you could say that." He was regarding her closely, his jaw tense, a muscle in his cheek ticking.

She noticed that he was still a couple of inches taller than her. Even with the shoes. "I guess you still meet the height requirement to be my dinner date."

"I didn't have any doubt."

"I don't know how to walk in these," she said.

"All right. Practice."

"Are you out of your mind? I have to *practice* walking?"

"You said yourself, you don't know how to walk in heels. So, go on. Walk the length of the room."

She felt completely awash in humiliation. She doubted there was another woman on the planet that Chase had ever had to instruct on walking.

"This is ridiculous."

"It's not," he said.

"All of women's fashion is ridiculous," she maintained. "Do you have to learn how to walk when you put on dress shoes? No, you do not. And yet, a full-scale lesson is required for me to go out if I want to wear something that's considered *feminine*."

"Yeah, it's sexist. And a real pain in the ass, I'm sure. It's also hot. Now walk."

She scowled at him, then took her first step, wobbling a bit. "I don't understand why women do this."

She took another step, then another, wobbling a little less each time. But the shoes did force her hips to sway, much more than they normally would. "Do you have any pointers?" she asked.

"I date women in heels, Anna. *I've* never walked in them."

"What happened to helping me be a woman?"

"You'll get the hang of it. It's like…I don't know, water-skiing maybe?"

"How is this like water-skiing?"

"You have to learn how to do it and there's a good likelihood you'll fall on your face?"

"Well, I take it all back," she said, deadpan. "These shoes aren't silly at all." She took another step, then another. "I feel like a newborn baby deer."

"You look a little like one, too."

She snorted. "You really need to up your game, Chase. If you use these lines on all the women you take out, you're bound to start striking out sooner or later."

"I haven't struck out yet."

"Well, you're still young and pretty. Just wait. Just wait until time starts to claim your muscular forearms and chiseled jawline."

"I figure by then maybe I'll have gotten the ranch back to its former glory. At that point women will sleep with me for my money."

She rolled her eyes. "It's nice to have goals."

In her opinion, Chase should have better goals for himself. But then, who was she to talk? Her current goal was to show her brothers that they were idiots and she could too get a date. Hardly a lofty ambition.

"Yes, it is. And right now my goal is for us not to miss our reservation."

"You made a…reservation?"

"I did."

"It's not like it's Valentine's Day or something. The restaurant isn't going to be full."

"Of course it won't be. But I figured if I made a reservation for the two of us, we could start a rumor, too."

"A rumor?"

"Yeah, because Ellie Matthews works at Beaches, and I believe she has been known to *service* your brother Mark."

Anna winced at the terminology. "True."

"I thought the news of our dining experience might make it back to him. Like I said, the more we can make this look organic, the better."

"No one ever need know that our relationship is in fact grown in a lab. And in no way GMO free," she said.

"Exactly."

"I don't have any makeup on." She frowned. "I don't have any makeup. At all."

"Right," he said. "I didn't really think of that."

She reached out and smacked him on the shoulder. "You're supposed to be my coach. You're failing me."

He laughed, dodging her next blow. "You don't need makeup."

She let out an exasperated sigh. "You're just saying that."

"In fairness, you did threaten to castrate me with your car keys earlier."

"I did."

"And you hit me just now," he pointed out.

"It didn't hurt, you baby."

He took a deep breath, and suddenly his expression turned sharp. "Believe me when I tell you you don't need makeup." He reached out, gripping her chin with his thumb and forefinger. His touch was like a branding iron, hot, altering. "As long as you believe it, everyone else will, too. You have to believe in yourself, Anna."

He released his hold on her, straightening. "Now," he said, his tone getting a little bit rougher, "let's go to dinner."

Chase felt like he had been tipped sideways and left walking on the walls from the moment that Anna had emerged from the bathroom at his house wearing that dress. Once she had put on those shoes, the feeling had only gotten worse.

But who knew that underneath those coveralls his best friend looked like that?

She had been eyeing herself critically, and his brain had barely been working at all. Because he didn't see anything to criticize. All he saw was the kind of figure that would make a man willingly submit to car key castration.

She was long and lean, toned from all the physical labor she did. Her breasts were small, but he imagined they would fit in a man's hand nicely. And her hips…well, using the same measurement used for her breasts, they would be about perfect for holding on to while a man…

Holy hell. He was losing his mind.

She was Anna. Anna Brown, his best friend in the entire world. The one woman he had never even considered going there with. He didn't want a relationship with the women he slept with. When your only criteria for being with a woman was orgasm, there were a lot of options available to you. For a little bit of satisfaction he could basically seek out any woman in the room.

Sex was easy. Connections were hard.

And so Anna had been placed firmly off-limits from day one. He'd had a vague awareness of her for most of his life. That was how growing up in a small town worked. You went to the same school from the beginning. But they had separate classes, plus at the time he'd been pretty convinced girls had cooties.

But that had changed their first year of high school. He'd ended up in metal shop with the prickly teen and had liked her right away. There weren't very many girls who cursed as much as the boys and had a more comprehensive understanding of the inner workings of engines than the teachers at the school. But Anna did.

She hadn't fit in with any of the girls, and so Chase and

Sam had been quick to bring her into their group. Over the years, people had rotated in and out, moved, gone their separate ways. But Chase and Anna had remained close.

In part because he had kept his dick out of the equation.

As they walked up the path toward Beaches, he considered putting his hand on her lower back. Really, he should. Except it was potentially problematic at the moment. Was he this shallow? Stick her in a tight-fitting dress and suddenly he couldn't control himself? It was a sobering realization, but not really all that surprising.

This was what happened when you spent a lot of time practicing no restraint when it came to sex.

He gritted his teeth, lifting his hand for a moment before placing it gently on her back. Because it was what he would do with any other date, so it was what he needed to do with Anna.

She went stiff beneath his touch. "Relax," he said, keeping his voice low. "This is supposed to look like a date, remember?"

"I should have worn a white tank top and a pair of jeans," she said.

"Why?"

"Because this looks… It looks like I'm trying too hard."

"No, it looks like you put on a nice outfit to please me."

She turned to face him, her brow furrowed. "Which is part of the problem. If I had to do this to please you, we both know that I would tell you to please yourself."

He laughed, the moment so classically Anna, so familiar, it was at odds with the other feelings that were buzzing through his blood. With how soft she felt beneath his touch. With just how much she was affecting him in this figure-hugging dress.

"I have no doubt you would."

They walked up the steps that led into the large white restaurant, and he opened the door, holding it for her. She looked at him like he'd just caught fire. He stared her down, and then she looked away from him, walking through the door.

He moved up next to her once they were inside. "You're going to have to seem a little more at ease with this change in our relationship."

"You're being weird."

"I'm not being weird. I'm treating you like a lady."

"What have you been treating me like for the past fifteen years?" she asked.

"A...bro."

She snorted, shaking her head and walking toward the front of the house where Ellie Matthews was standing, waiting for guests. "I believe we have a reservation," Anna said.

He let out a long-suffering sigh. "Yes," he confirmed. "Under my name."

Ellie's eyebrow shot upward. "Yes. You do."

"Under Chase McCormack and Anna Brown," Chase clarified.

"I know," she said.

Ellie needed to work on her people skills. "It was difficult for me to tell, since you look so surprised," Chase said.

"Well, I knew you were reserving the table for the two of you, but I didn't realize you were...reserving the table for *the two of you*." She was looking at Anna's dress, her expression meaningful.

"Well, I was," he said. "Did. So, is the table ready?"

She looked around the half-full dining area. "Yeah, I'm pretty sure we can seat you now."

Ellie walked them over to one of the tables by a side window that looked out over the Skokomish River where it fed into the ocean. The sun was dipping low over the water, the rays sparkling off the still surface of the slow-moving river. There were people milling along the wooden boardwalk that was bordered by docks on one side and storefronts on the other, before being split by the highway and starting again, leading down to the beach.

He looked away from the scenery, back at Anna. They had shared countless meals together, but this was different. Normally, they didn't sit across from each other at a tiny table complete with a freaking candle in the middle. Mood lighting.

"Your server will be with you shortly," Ellie said as she walked away, leaving them there with menus and each other.

"I want a burger," Anna said, not looking at the menu at all.

"You could get something fancier."

"I'll get it with a cheese I can't pronounce."

"I'm getting salmon."

"Am I paying?" she asked, an impish smile playing around the corners of her lips. "Because if so, you better be putting out at the end of this."

Her words were like a punch in the gut. And he did his best to ignore them. He swallowed hard. "No, *I'm* paying."

"I'll pay you back after. You're doing me a favor."

"The favor's mutual. I want to go to the fund-raiser. It's important to me."

"You still aren't buying my dinner."

"I'm not taking your money."

"Then I'm going to overpay for rent on the shop next month," she said, her tone uncompromising.

"Half of that goes to Sam."

"Then he gets half of it. But I'm not going to let you buy my dinner."

"You're being stubborn."

She leaned back in her chair, crossing her arms and treating him to that hard glare of hers. "Yep."

A few moments later the waiter came over, and Anna

ordered her hamburger, and the cheeses she wanted, by pointing at the menu.

"Which cheese did you get?" he asked, attempting to move on from their earlier standoff.

"I don't know." She shrugged. "I can't pronounce it."

They made about ten minutes of awkward conversation while they waited for their dinner to come. Which was weird, because conversation was never awkward with Anna. It was that dress. And those shoes. And his penis. That was part of the problem. Because, suddenly, it was actually interested in his best friend.

No, it is not. A moment of checking her out does not mean that you want to...do anything with her.

Exactly. It wasn't a big deal. It wasn't anything to get worked up about. Not at all.

When their dinner was placed in front of them, Anna attacked her sweet potato fries, probably using them as a displacement activity.

"Chase?"

Chase looked up and inwardly groaned when he saw Wendy Maxwell headed toward the table. They'd all gone to high school together. And he had, regrettably, slept with Wendy once or twice over the years after drinking too much at Ace's.

She was hot. But what she had in looks had been deducted from her personality. Which didn't matter when you were only having sex, but mattered later when you had to interact in public.

"Hi, Wendy," he said, taking a bite of his salmon.

Anna had gone very still across from him; she wasn't even eating her fries anymore.

"Are you… Are you on a date?" Wendy asked, tilting her head to the side, her expression incredulous.

Wendy wasn't very smart in addition to being not very nice. A really bad combination.

"Yes," he said, "I am."

"With Anna?"

"Yeah," Anna said, looking up. "The person sitting across from him. Like you do on a date."

"I'm just surprised."

He could see color mounting in Anna's cheeks, could see her losing her hold on her temper.

"Are you here by yourself?" Anna asked.

Wendy laughed, the sound like broken crystal being pushed beneath his skin. "No. Of course not. We're having a girls' night out." She eyed Chase. "Of course, that doesn't mean I'm going home with the girls."

Suddenly, Anna was standing, and he was a little bit afraid she was about to deck Wendy. Who deserved it. But he didn't really want to be at the center of a girl fight in the middle of Beaches.

That only worked in fantasies. Less so in real life.

But it wasn't Wendy whom Anna moved toward.

She took two steps, came to a stop in front of Chase and then leaned forward, grabbing hold of the back of his chair and resting her knee next to his thigh. Then she pressed her hand to his cheek and took a deep breath, making determined eye contact with him just before she let her lids flutter closed. Just before she closed the distance between them and kissed him.

Four

She was kissing Chase McCormack. Beyond that, she had no idea what the flying F-bomb she was doing. If there was another person in the room, she didn't see them. If there was a reason she'd started this, she didn't remember it.

There was nothing. Nothing more than the hot press of Chase's lips against hers. Nothing more than still, leashed power beneath her touch. She could feel his tension, could feel his strength frozen beneath her.

It was…intoxicating. Empowering.

So damn *hot.*

Like she was about to melt the soles of her shoes hot. About to come without his hands ever touching her body hot.

And that was unheard-of for her.

She'd kissed a couple of guys, and slept with one, and orgasm had never been in the cards. When it came to climaxes, she was her own hero. But damn if Chase wasn't about to be her hero in under thirty seconds, and with nothing more than a little dry lip-to-lip contact.

Except it didn't stay dry.

Suddenly, he reached up, curling his fingers around the back of her head, angling his own and kissing her hard, deep. With tongue.

She whimpered, the leg that was supporting her body melting, only the firm hold he had on her face, and the support of his chair, keeping her from sliding onto the ground.

The slick glide of his tongue against hers was the single sexiest thing she'd ever experienced in her life. And just like that, every little white lie she'd ever told herself about her attraction to Chase was completely and fully revealed.

It wasn't just a momentary response to an attractive man. Not something any red-blooded female would feel. Not just a passing anomaly.

It was real.

It was deep.

She was so screwed.

Way too screwed to care that they were making out in a fancy restaurant in front of people, and that for him it was just a show, but for her it was a whole cataclysmic, near-orgasmic shift happening in the region of her panties.

Seconds had passed, but they felt like minutes. Hours. Whole days' worth of life-changing moments, all crammed into something that probably hadn't actually lasted longer than the blink of an eye.

Then it was over. She was the one who pulled away and she wasn't quite sure how she managed. But she did.

She wasn't breathing right. Her entire body was shaking, and she was sure her face was red. But still, she turned and faced Wendy, or whichever mean girl it was. There were a ton of them in her nonhalcyon high school years and they all blended together. The who wasn't important. Only the what. The *what* being a kiss she'd just given to the hottest guy in town, right in front of someone who didn't think she was good enough. Pretty enough. Girlie enough.

"Yeah," she said, her voice a little less triumphant and a lot more unsteady than she would like, "we're here on a date. And he's going home with me. So I'd suggest you wiggle on over to a different table if you want to score tonight."

Wendy's face was scrunched into a sour expression. "That's okay, honey, if you want my leftovers, you're welcome to them."

Then she flipped her blond hair and walked back to her table, essentially acting out the cliché of every snotty girl in a teen movie.

Which was not so cute when you were thirty and not fifteen.

But, of course, since Wendy was gone, they'd lost the buffer against the aftermath of the kiss, and the terrible awkwardness that was just sitting there, seething, growing.

"Well, I think that started some rumors," Anna said, sitting back down and shoving a fry into her mouth.

"I bet," Chase said, clearing his throat and turning back toward his plate.

"My mouth has never touched your mouth directly before," she said, then stuffed another fry straight into her mouth, wishing it wasn't too late to stifle those ridiculous words.

He choked on his beer. "Um. No."

"What I mean is, we've shared drinks before. I've taken bites off your sandwiches. Literally sandwiches, not— I mean, whatever. The point is, we've germ-shared before. We just never did it mouth-to-mouth."

"That wasn't CPR, babe."

She made a face, hoping the disgust in her expression would disguise the twist low and deep in her stomach. "Don't call me babe just because I kissed you."

"We're dating, remember?"

"No one is listening to us talk at the table," she insisted.

"You don't know that."

Her heart was thundering hard like a trapped bird in her chest and she didn't know if she could look at him for another minute without either scurrying from the room like a frightened animal or grabbing him and kissing him again.

She didn't like it. She didn't like any of it.

It all felt too real, too raw and too scary. It all came from a place too deep inside her.

So she decided to do what came easiest. Exactly what she did best.

"I expected better," she told him, before taking a bite of her burger.

"What?"

"You're like a legendary stud," she said, after swallowing her food. "The man who every man wants to be and who every woman wants to be with. Blah, blah." She picked up another sweet potato fry.

"It wasn't good for you?" he asked.

"Six point five from the German judge. Who is me, in this scenario." She was a liar. She was a liar and she was a jerk, and she wanted to punch her own face. But the alternative was to show that she was breaking apart inside. That she had been on the verge of the kind of ecstasy she'd only ever imagined, and that she wanted to kiss him forever, not just for thirty seconds. And that was…damaging. It wasn't something she could admit.

"Six point five."

"Sorry." She lifted her shoulder and shoved the fry into her mouth.

They finished the rest of the dinner in awkward silence, which made her mad because things weren't supposed to be awkward between them. They were friends, dammit. She was starting to think this whole thing was a mistake.

She could bring Chase as her plus one to the charity thing without her brothers buying into it. She could lose the bet. The whole town could suspect she'd brought a friend because she was undatable and who even cared?

If playing this game was going to screw with their friendship, it wasn't worth it.

Chase paid the tab—she was going to pay the bastard back whether he wanted her to or not—and then the two of them walked outside. And that was when she realized her truck was back at his place and he was going to have to give her a ride.

That sucked donkey balls. She needed to get some Chase space. And it wasn't going to happen.

She wanted to go home and put on soft pajamas and watch *Seven Brides for Seven Brothers*. She needed a safe, flannel-lined space and the fuzzy comfort of an old movie. A chance to breathe and be vulnerable for a second where no one would see.

She was afraid Chase might have seen already.

They still didn't talk—all the way back out of town and to the McCormack family ranch, they didn't talk.

"My dirty clothes are in your house," she said at last, when they pulled into the driveway. "You can take me to the house first instead of the shop."

"I can wash them with mine," he said.

Her underwear was in there. That was not happening.

"No, I left them folded in the corner of the bathroom. I'd rather come get them. And put my shoes on before I try to drive home actually. How do people drive in these?" She tapped the precarious shoes against the floor of the pickup.

Chase let out a harsh-sounding breath. "Fine," he said. He sounded aggrieved, but he drove on past the shop to the house. He stopped the truck abruptly, throwing it into Park and killing the engine. "Come on in."

Now he was mad at her. Great. It wasn't like he needed

her to stroke his ego. He had countless women to do that. He had just one woman who listened to his bullshit and put up with all his nonsense, and in general stood by him no matter what. That was her. He could have endless praise for his bedroom skills from those other women. He only had friendship from *her*. So he could simmer down a little.

She got out of the truck, then wobbled when her foot hit a loose gravel patch. She clung tightly to the door, a very wussy-sounding squeak escaping her lips.

"You okay there, *babe*?" he asked, just to piss her off.

"Yeah, fine. Jerk," she retorted.

"What the hell, Anna?" he asked, his tone hard.

"Oh, come on, you're being weird. You can't pretend you aren't just because you're layering passivity over your aggression." She stalked past him as fast as her shoes would let her, walked up the porch and stood by the door, her arms crossed.

"It's not locked," he said, taking the stairs two at a time.

"Well, I wasn't going to go in without your permission. I have manners."

"Do you?" he asked.

"If I didn't, I probably would have punched you by now." She opened the door and stomped up the stairs, until her heel rolled inward slightly and she stumbled. Then she stopped stomping and started taking a little more consideration for her joints.

She was mad at him. She was mad at herself for being mad at him, because the situation was mostly her fault. And she was mad at him for being mad at her for being mad at him.

Mad, mad, *mad*.

She walked into the bathroom and picked up her stack of clothes, careful not to hold the greasy articles against her dress. The dress that was the cause of so many of tonight's problems.

It's not the dress. It's the fact that you kissed him and now you can't deal.

Rationality was starting to creep in and she was nothing if not completely irritated about that. It was forcing her to confront the fact that she was actually the one being a jerk, not him. That she was the one who was overreacting, and his behavior was all a response to the fact that she'd gone full Anna-pine, with quills out ready to defend herself at all costs.

She took a deep breath and sat down on the edge of his bed, trading the high heels for her sneakers, then collecting her things again and walking back down the stairs, her feet tingling and aching as they got used to resting flat once more.

Chase wasn't inside.

She opened the front door and walked out onto the porch.

He was standing there, the porch light shining on him like a beacon. His broad shoulders, trim waist…oh, Lord, his ass. Wrangler butt was a gift from God in her opinion and Chase's was perfect. Something she'd noticed before, but right now it was physically painful to look at him and not close the space between them. To not touch him.

This was bad. This was why she hadn't ever touched him before. Why it would have been best if she never had.

She had needs. Fuzzy-blanket needs. She needed to get home.

She cleared her throat. "I'm ready," she said. "I just… If you could give me a lift down to the shop, that would be nice. So that I'm not cougar food."

He turned slowly, a strange expression on his face. "Yeah, I wouldn't want you to get eaten by any mangy predators."

"I appreciate that."

He headed down the steps and got back into the truck,

and she followed, climbing into the cab beside him. He started the engine and maneuvered the truck onto the gravel road that ran through the property.

She rested her elbow on the armrest, staring outside at the inky black shadows of the pine trees, and the white glitter of stars in the velvet-blue sky. It was a clear night, unusual for their little coastal town.

If only her head was as clear as the sky.

It was full. Full of regret and woe. She didn't like that. As soon as Chase pulled up to the shop, she scrambled out, not waiting for him to put the vehicle in Park. She was heading toward her own vehicle when she heard Chase behind her.

"What are you doing?" she asked, turning to face him.

But her words were cut off by what he did next. He took one step toward her, closing the distance between them as he wrapped his arm around her waist and drew her up against his chest. Then, before she could protest, before she could say anything, he was kissing her again.

This was different than the kiss at the restaurant. This was different than…well, than any kiss in the whole history of the world.

His kiss tasted of the familiarity of Chase and the strangeness of his anger. Of heat and lust and rage all rolled into one.

She knew him better than she knew almost anyone. Knew the shape of his face, knew his scent, knew his voice. But his scent surrounding her like this, the feel of his face beneath her hands, the sound of that voice—transformed into a feral, passionate growl as he continued to ravish her—was an unknown. Was something else entirely.

Then, suddenly—just as suddenly as he had initiated it—the kiss was over. He released his hold on her, pushing her back. There was nothing but air between them now. Air and a whole lot of feelings. He was standing there, his hands planted on his lean hips, his chest rising and falling with each labored breath. "Six point five?" he asked, his tone challenging. "That sure as hell was no six point five, Anna Brown, and if you're honest with yourself, you have to admit that."

She sucked in a harsh, unsteady breath, trying to keep the shock from showing on her face. "I don't have to admit any such thing."

"You're a little liar."

"What does it matter?" she asked, scowling.

"How would you like it if I told you that you were only average compared to other women I've kissed?"

"I'd shut your head in the truck door."

"Exactly." He crossed his arms over his broad chest. "So don't think I'm going to let the same insults stand, honey."

"Don't *babe* me," she spat. "Don't *honey* me."

Triumph glittered in his dark eyes. The smugness so certain it was visible even in the moonlight. "Then don't kiss me again."

"You were the one who kissed me!" she shouted, throwing her arms wide.

"*This* time. But you started it. Don't do it again." He turned around, heading back toward his truck. All she could do was stand there and stare as he drove away.

Something had changed tonight. Something inside of her. She didn't think she liked it at all.

Five

"Now, I don't want to be insensitive or hurt your feelings, princess, but why are you being such an asshole today?"

Chase looked over at Sam, who was staring at him from his position by the forge. The fire was going hot and they were pounding out iron, doing some repairs on equipment. By hand. Just the way both of them liked to work.

"I'm not," Chase said.

"Right. Look, there's only room for one of us to be a grumpy cuss, and I pretty much have that position filled. So I would appreciate it if you can get your act together."

"Sorry, Sam, are you unable to take what you dish out every day?"

"What's going on with you and Anna?"

Chase bristled at the mention of the woman he'd kissed last night. Then he winced when he remembered the kiss. Well, *remembered* was the wrong word. He'd never forgotten it. But right now he was mentally replaying it, moment by moment. "What did you hear?"

Sam laughed. An honest-to-God laugh. "Do I look like I'm on the gossip chain? I haven't talked to anybody. It's just that I saw her leaving your house last night wearing a red dress and sneakers, and then saw her this morning when she went into the shop. She was pissier than you are."

"Anna is always pissy." Sam treated his statement to a prolonged stare. "It's not a big deal. It's just that her brothers bet her that she couldn't get a date. I figured I would help her out with that."

"How?"

"Well..." he said, hesitating about telling his brother the whole story. Sam wasn't looking to change the business on the ranch. He didn't care about their family legacy. Not like Chase did. But Chase had made promises to tombstones and he wasn't about to break them.

It was one of their main sources of contention. So he wasn't exactly looking forward to having this conversation with his older brother.

But it wasn't like he could hide it forever. He'd just sort of been hoping he could hide it until he'd shown up with investment money.

"That's an awfully long pause," Sam said. "I'm willing to bet that whatever you're about to say, I'm not going to like it."

"You know me well. Anna got invited to go to the big community charity event that the West family hosts every year. Now I want to make sure that we can extend our contract with them. Plus...doing horseshoes and gates isn't cutting it. We can move into doing details on custom homes. To doing art pieces and selling our work across the country, not just locally. To do that we need investors. And the West fund-raiser's a great place to find them. Plus, if I only have to wear a suit once and can speak to everyone in town that might be interested in a single shot? Well, I can't beat that."

"Dammit, Chase, you know I don't want to commit to something like that."

"Right. You want to continue on the way we always have. You want to shoe horses when we can, pound metal when the opportunity presents itself, build gates, or whatever else might need doing, then go off and work on sculptures and things in your spare time. But that's not going to be enough. Less and less is done by hand, and people aren't willing to pay for handcrafted materials. Machines can build cheaper stuff than we can.

"But the thing is, you can make it look special. You can turn it into something amazing. Like you did with my house. It's the details that make a house expensive. We can have the sort of clients who don't want work off an assembly line. The kind who will pay for one of a kind pieces. From art on down to the handles on their kitchen cabinets. We could get into some serious custom work. Vacation homes are starting to spring up around here, plus people are renovating to make rentals thanks to the tourism increase. But we need some investors if we're really going to get into this."

"You know I hate this. I don't like the idea of charging a ton of money for a…for a gate with an elk on it."

"You're an artist, Sam," he said, watching his brother wince as he said the words. "I know you hate that. But it's true."

"I hate that, too."

"You're talented."

"I hit metal with a hammer. Sometimes I shape it into something that looks nice. It's not really all that special."

"You do more than that and you know it. It's what people would be willing to pay for. If you would stop being such a nut job about it."

Sam rubbed the back of his neck, his expression shuttered. "You've gotten off topic," he said finally. "I asked you about Anna, not your schemes for exploiting my talents."

"Not really. The two are connected. I want to go to this

thing to talk to the Wests. I want to talk about investment opportunities and expanding contracts with other people deemed worthy of an invite. In case you haven't noticed, we weren't on that list."

"Yeah, I get that. But why would the lately not-so-great McCormacks be invited?"

"That's the problem. This place hasn't been what it was for a couple of generations, and when we lost Mom and Dad...well, we were teenagers trying to keep up a whole industry, and now we work *for* these people, not with them. I aim to change that."

"You didn't think about talking to me?" Sam asked.

"Oh, I did. And I decided I didn't want to have to deal with you."

Sam shot him an evil glare. "So you're going as Anna's date. And helping her win her bet."

"Exactly."

"And you took her out last night, and she went back to your place, and now she's mad at you."

Chase held his hands up. "I don't know what you're getting at—"

"Yes, you do." Sam crossed his arms. "Did you bang her?"

Chase recoiled, trying to look horrified at the thought. He didn't *feel* horrified at the thought. Which actually made him feel kind of horrified. "I did not."

"Is that why you're mad? Because you didn't?"

His brother was way too perceptive for a guy who pounded heavy things with other heavy things for a living.

"No," he said. "Anna is my friend. She's just a friend. We had a slight...altercation last night. But it's not that big a deal."

"Big enough that I'm worried with all your stomping around you're eventually going to fling the wrong thing and hit me with molten metal."

"Safety first," Chase said, "always."

"I bet you say that to your dates, too."

"You would, too, if you had any."

Sam flipped Chase the bird in response.

"Just forget about it," Chase said. "Forget about the stuff with the Wests, and let me deal with it. And forget about Anna."

When it came to that last directive, he was going to try to do the same.

Anna was dreading coming face-to-face with Chase again after last night. But she didn't really have a choice. They were still in this thing. Unless she called it off. But that would be tantamount to admitting that what had happened last night *bothered* her. And she didn't want to do that. More, she was almost incapable of doing it. She was pretty sure her pride would wither up and die if she did.

But Chase was coming by her shop again tonight, with some other kind of lesson in mind. Something he'd written down on that stupid legal pad of his. It was ridiculous. All of it was ridiculous.

Herself most of all.

She looked at the clock, gritting her teeth. Chase would be by any moment, and she was no closer to dealing with the feelings, needs and general restlessness that had hit her with the blunt force of a flying wrench than she had been last night.

Then, right on time, the door opened, and in walked Chase. He was still dirty from work today, his face smudged with ash and soot, his shirt sticking to his muscular frame, showing off all those fine muscles underneath. Yeah, that didn't help.

"How was work?" he asked.

"Fine. Just dealing with putting a new cylinder head on a John Deere. You?"

"Working on a gate."

"Sounds…fun," she said, though she didn't really think it sounded like fun at all.

She liked solving the puzzle when it came to working on engines. Liked that she had the ability to get in there and figure things out. To diagnose the situation.

Standing in front of a hot fire forging metal didn't really sound like her kind of thing.

Though she couldn't deny it did pretty fantastic things for Chase's physique.

"Well, you know it would be fine if Sam wasn't such a pain in the ass."

"Sure," she said, feeling slightly cautious. After last night, she felt like dealing with Chase was like approaching a dog who'd bitten you once. Only, in this case he had kissed her, not bitten her, and he wasn't a dog. That was the problem. He was just much too *much* for his own good. Much too much for her own good.

"So," she said, "what's on the lesson plan for tonight?"

"I sort of thought we should talk about…well, talking."

"What do you mean?"

"There are ways that women talk to men they want to date. I thought I might walk you through flirting."

"You're going to show me how to flirt?"

"Somebody has to."

"I can probably figure it out," she said.

"You think?" he asked, crossing his arms over his chest and rocking back on his heels.

His clear skepticism stoked the flames of her temper, which was lurking very close to the surface after last night. That was kind of her default. Don't know how to handle something? Don't know *what* you feel? Get angry at it.

"Come on. Men and women have engaged in horizontal naked kickboxing for millennia. I'm pretty sure flirting is a natural instinct."

"You're a poet, Anna," he said, his tone deadpan.

"No, I'm a tractor mechanic," she said.

"Yeah, and you talk like one, too. If you want to get an actual date, and not just a quick tumble in the back of a guy's truck, you might want to refine your art of conversation a little."

"Who says I'm opposed to a quick rough tumble in the back of some guy's truck?"

"You're not?" he asked, his eyebrows shooting upward.

"Well, in all honesty I would probably prefer my truck, since it's clean. I know where it's been. But why the hell not? I have needs."

He scowled. "Right. Well, keep that kind of talk to yourself."

"Does it make you uncomfortable to hear about my *needs*, Chase?" she asked, not quite sure why she was poking at him. Maybe because she felt so unsettled. She was kind of enjoying the fact that he seemed to be, as well. Really, it wouldn't be fair if after last night he felt nothing at all. If he had been able to one-up her and then walk away as though nothing had happened.

"It doesn't make me uncomfortable. It's just unnecessary information. Now, talking about your needs is probably something you shouldn't do with a guy, either."

"Unless I want him to fulfill those needs."

"You said you wanted to date. You want the kind of date who can go to these functions with you, right?"

"It's moot. You're going with me."

"This time. But be honest, don't you want to be able to go out with guys who belong in places like that?"

"I don't know," she said, feeling uncomfortable.

Truth be told, she wasn't all that comfortable thinking about her needs. Emotional, physical. Frankly, if it went beyond her need for a cheeseburger, she didn't really know how to deal with it. She hadn't dated in years. And she had been fine with that. But the truth of the matter was the only reason Mark and Daniel had managed to get to her when they had made this bet was that she was beginning to feel dissatisfied with her life.

She was starting a new business. She was assuming a new position in the community. She didn't just want to be Anna Brown, the girl from the wrong side of the tracks. She didn't just want to be the tomboy mechanic for the rest of her life. She wanted…more. It had been fine, avoiding relationships all this time, but she was thirty now. She didn't really want to be by herself. She didn't want to be alone forever.

Dear Lord, she was having an existential crisis.

"Fine," she said, "it might be nice to have somebody to date."

Marriage, family—she had no idea how she felt when it came to those things. But a casual relationship… That might be nice. Yes. That might be nice.

Last night, she had gone home and gotten under a blanket and watched an old movie. Sometimes, Chase watched old movies with her, but he did not get under the blankets with her. It would be nice to have a guy to be under the blanket with. Somebody to go home to. Or at least someone to call to come over when she couldn't sleep. Someone she could talk to, make out with. Have sex with.

"Fine," she said. "I will submit to your flirting lessons."

"All the girls submit to me eventually," he said, winking.

Something about that made her stomach twist into a knot. "Talking about too much information…"

"There," he said, "that was almost flirting."

She wrinkled her nose. "Was it?"

"Yes. We had a little bit of back and forth. There was some innuendo."

"I didn't make innuendo on purpose," she said.

"No. That's the best kind. The kind you sort of walk

into. It makes you feel a little dangerous. Like you might say the wrong thing. And if you go too far, they might walk away. But if you don't go far enough, they might not know that you want them."

She let out a long, frustrated growl. "Dating is complicated. I hate it. Is it too late for me to become a nun?"

"You would have to convert," he pointed out.

"That sounds like a lot of work, too."

"You can be pleasant, Anna. You're fun to talk to. So that's all you have to do."

"Natural to me is walking up to a hot guy and saying, 'Do you want to bone or what?'" As if she'd ever done that. As if she ever would. It was just…she didn't really know how to go about getting a guy to hook up with her any other way. She was a direct kind of girl. And nothing between men and women seemed direct.

"Fine. Let's try this," he said, grabbing a chair and pulling it up to her workbench before taking a seat.

She took hold of the back of the other folding chair in the space and moved it across from his, positioning herself so that she was across from him.

"What are you drinking?" he asked.

She laughed. "A mai tai." She had never had one of those. She didn't even know what it was.

"Excellent. I'm having whiskey, straight up."

"That sounds like you."

"You don't know what sounds like me. You don't know me."

Suddenly, she got the game. "Right. Stranger," she said, then winced internally, because that sounded a little bit more Mae West in her head, and just kind of silly when it was out of her mouth.

"You here with anyone?"

"I could be?" she said, placing her elbow on the workbench and tilting her head to the side.

"You should try to toss your hair a little bit. I dated this girl Elizabeth who used to do that. It was cute."

"How does touching my hair accomplish anything?" she asked, feeling irritated that he had brought another woman up. Which was silly, because the only reason he was qualified to give her these lessons was that he had dated a metric ton of women.

So getting mad about the thing that was helping her right now was a little ridiculous. But she was pretty sure they had passed ridiculous a couple of days ago.

"I don't know. It's cute. It looks like you're trying to draw my attention to it. Like you want me to notice."

"Which…lets you know that I want you in my pants?"

He frowned. "I guess. I never broke it down like that before. But that stands to reason."

She reached up, sighing as she flicked a strand of her hair as best she could. It was tied up in a loose bun and had fallen partway thanks to the intensity of the day's physical labor. Still, she had a feeling she did not look alluring. She had a feeling she looked like she'd been caught in a wind turbine and spit out the other end.

"Are you new in town?"

"I'm old in town," she said, mentally kicking herself again for being lame on the return volley.

"That works, too," Chase said, not skipping a beat. Yeah, there was a reason the man had never struck out before.

She started to chew on her lip, trying to think of what to say next.

"Don't chew a hole through it," he said, smiling and reaching across the space, brushing his thumb over the place her teeth had just grazed.

And everything in her stopped dead. His touch ignited her nerve endings, sending a brush fire down her veins and all through her body.

She hadn't been this ridiculous over Chase since she

was sixteen years old. Since then, she had mostly learned to manage it.

She pulled away slightly, her chair scraping against the floor. She laughed, a stilted, unnatural sound. "I won't," she said, her voice too loud.

"If you're going to chew on your lip," he said, "don't freak out when the guy calls attention to it or touches you. It looks like you're doing it on purpose, so you should expect a comment."

"Duh," she said, "I was. That was…normal."

She wanted to crawl under the chair.

"There was this girl Miranda that I—"

"Okay." She cut him off, growing more and more impatient with the comparisons. "I'm old in town, what about you?"

"I've been around."

"I bet you have been," she said.

"I'm not sure how I'm supposed to take that," he said, flashing her a lopsided grin.

"Right," she said, "because I don't know what I'm doing."

"Maybe this was a bad idea," he said. "I think you actually need to feel some chemistry with somebody if flirting's going to work."

His words were sharp, digging into her chest. *You actually had to feel some chemistry* to be able to flirt.

They had chemistry. She had felt it last night. So had he. This was his revenge for the six-point-five comment. At least, she hoped it was. The alternative was that he had really felt nothing when their lips attached. And that seemed…beyond unfair.

She had all this attraction for Chase that she had spent years tamping down, only to have it come roaring to the surface the moment she had begun to pretend there was more going on between them than just friendship. And then she had kissed him. And far from being a disappointment, he had superseded her every fantasy. The jackass. Then he had kissed her, kissed her because he was angry. Kissed her to get revenge. Kissed her in a way that had kept her awake all night long, aching, burning. And now he was saying he didn't have chemistry with her.

"It's just that usually when I'm with a girl it flows a little easier. The bar to the bedroom is a pretty natural extension. And all those little movements kind of lead into the other. The way they touch their hair, tilt their head, lean in for a kiss…"

Oh, that did it.

"The women that I usually hook up with tend to—"

"Right," she said, her tone hard. "I get it. They flip their hair and scrunch their noses and twitch at all the appropriate times. They're like small woodland creatures who only emerge from their burrows to satisfy your every sexual whim."

"Don't get upset. I'm trying to help you."

She snorted. "I know." Just then, she had no idea what devil possessed her. Only that one most assuredly did. And once it had taken hold, she had no desire to cast it back out again.

She was mad. Mad like Chase had been last night. And she was determined to get her own back.

"Elizabeth was good at flipping her hair. Miranda gave you saucy interplay like so." She stood up, taking a step toward him, meeting his dark gaze with her own. "But how did they do this?" She reached down, placing her hand between his thighs and rubbing her palm over the bulge in his jeans.

Oh, sweet Lord, there was more to Chase McCormack than met the eye.

And she had a whole handful of him.

Her brain was starting to scream. Not words so much as

a high-pitched, panicky whine. She had crossed the line. And there was no turning back.

But her brain wasn't running the show. Her body was on fire, her heart pounding so hard she was afraid it was going to rip a hole straight through the wall of her chest and flop out on the ground in front of him. Show him all its contents. Dammit, *she* didn't even want to see that.

But it was her anger that really pushed things forward. Her anger that truly propelled her on.

"And how," she asked, lowering herself slowly, scraping her fingernails across the line of his zipper, before dropping to her knees in front of him, "did they do this?"

Six

For one blinding second, Chase thought that he was engaged in some sort of high-definition hallucination.

Because there was no way that Anna had just put her hand…there. There was no way that she was kneeling down in front of him, looking at him like she was a sultry-eyed seductress rather than his best friend, still dirty from the workday, clad in motor-oil-smudged coveralls.

He blinked. Then he shook his head. She was still there. And so was he.

But he was so hard he could probably pound iron with his dick right about now.

He knew what he should do. And just now he had enough sense left in his skull to do it. But he didn't want to. He knew he should. He knew that at the end of this road there was nothing good. Nothing good at all. But he shut all that down. He didn't think of the road ahead.

He just let his brain go blank. He just sat back and watched as she trailed her fingers up the line of his zipper, grabbing hold of his belt buckle and undoing it, her movements clumsy, speaking of an inexperience he didn't want to examine too closely.

He didn't want to examine any of this too closely, but he was powerless to do anything else.

Because everything around the moment went fuzzy as the present sharpened. Almost painfully.

His eyes were drawn to her fingers as she pulled his zipper down, to the short, no-nonsense fingernails, the specks of dirt embedded in her skin. That should…well, he had the vague idea it should turn him off. It didn't. Though he had a feeling that getting a bucket of water thrown on him while he sat in the middle of an iceberg naked wouldn't turn him off at this point. He was too far gone.

He was holding his breath. Every muscle in his body frozen. He couldn't believe that she would do what it appeared she might be doing. She would stop. She had to stop. He needed her to stop. He needed her to never stop. To keep going.

She pressed her palm flat against his ab muscles before pushing her hand down inside his jeans, reaching beneath his underwear and curling her fingers around him. His breath hissed through his teeth, a shudder racking his frame.

She looked up at him, green eyes glittering in the dim shop light. She had a smudge of dirt on her face that somehow only highlighted her sharp cheekbones, somehow emphasized her beauty in a way he hadn't truly noticed it before. Yes, last night in the red dress she had been beautiful, there was no doubt about that. But for some reason, her femininity was highlighted wrapped in these traditionally masculine things. By the backdrop of the mechanic shop, the evidence of a day's hard work on her soft skin.

She tilted her chin up, her expression one of absolute challenge. She was waiting for him to call it off. Waiting for him to push her away. But he wasn't going to. He reached out, forking his fingers through her hair and tightening them, grabbing ahold of the loose bun that sat high on her head. Her eyes widened, her lips going slack. He didn't pull her away. He didn't draw her closer. He just held on tight, keeping his gaze firmly focused on hers. Then he released her. And he waited.

She licked her lips slowly, an action that would have been almost comically obvious coming from nearly anyone else. Not Anna.

Then she squeezed him gently before drawing her hand back. He should be relieved. He was not.

But her next move was not one he anticipated. She grabbed hold of the waistband of his jeans and underwear, pulling them down slowly, exposing him. She let out a shaky, shuddering breath before leaning in and flicking her tongue over the head of his arousal.

"Hell." He wasn't sure at first if he had spoken it out loud, not until he heard it echoing around him. It was like cursing in a church somehow, wrong considering the beauty of the gift he was about to receive.

Still, he couldn't think of anything else as she drew the tip of her tongue all the way down to the base of his shaft before retracing her path. She shifted, and that was when he noticed her hands were shaking. Fair enough, since he was shaking, too.

She parted her lips, taking him into her mouth completely, her lips sliding over him, the wet, slick friction almost too much for him to handle. He didn't know what was wrong with him. If it was the shock of the moment, if it was just that he was this base. Or if there was some kind of sick, perverted part of him that took extra pleasure in the fact that this was wrong. That he should not be letting his best friend touch him like this.

Because he'd had more skilled blow jobs. There was no

question about that. This didn't feel good because Anna was an expert in the art of fellatio. Far from it.

Still, his head was about to blow off. And he was about to lose all of his control. So there was something.

Maybe it was just her.

She tilted her head to the side as she took him in deep, giving him a good view of just what she was doing. And just who was doing it. He was so aware of the fact that it was Anna, and that most definitely added a kick of the forbidden. Because he knew this was bad. Knew it was wrong.

And not many things were off-limits to him. Not many things had an illicit quality to them. He had kind of allowed himself to take anything and everything that had ever seemed vaguely sexy to him.

Except for her.

He shoved that thought in the background. He didn't like to think of Anna that way, and in general he didn't.

Sure, in high school, there had been moments. But he was a guy. And he had spent a lot of time with Anna. Alone in her room, alone in his. He had a feeling that half the people who had known them had imagined they were getting it on behind the scenes. Friends with benefits, et cetera. In reality, the only benefit to their friendship had been the fact that they'd been there for each other. They had never been there for each other in this way.

Maybe that's what was wrong with him.

Of course, nothing felt wrong with him right now. Right now, pleasure was crackling close to the surface of his skin and it was shorting out his brain. All he could do was sit back and ride the high. Embrace the sensations that were boiling through his blood. The magic of her lips and tongue combined with a shocking scrape of her teeth against his delicate skin made him buck his hips against her even as he tried to rein himself in.

But he was reaching the end of his control, the end of himself. He reached down, cupping her cheek as she continued to pleasure him, as she continued to drive him wild, urging him closer to the edge of control he hadn't realized he possessed.

He felt like he lived life with the shackles off, but she was pushing him so much further than he'd been before that he knew he'd been lying to himself all this time.

He'd been in chains, and hadn't even realized it.

Maybe because of her. Maybe to keep himself from touching her.

She gripped him, squeezing as she tasted him, pushing him straight over the edge. He held on to her hair, harder than he should, as a wave of pleasure rode up inside of him. And when it crashed he didn't ride it into shore. Oh, hell no. When it crashed it drove him straight down to the bottom of the sea, the impact leaving him spinning, gasping for breath, battered on the rocks.

But dammit all, it was worth it. Right now, it was worth it.

He knew that any moment the feeling would fade and he would be faced with the stark horror of what he'd just done, of what he'd just allowed to happen. But for now, he was foggy, floating in the kind of mist that always blanketed the ocean on cold mornings in Copper Ridge.

And he would cling to it as long as possible.

Oh, dear God. What had she done? This had gone so far beyond the kiss to prove they had chemistry. It had gone so far past the challenge that Chase had thrown down last night. It had gone straight into Crazy Town, next stop You Messed Up the Only Friendship You Hadville.

In combination with the swirling panic that was wrapping its claws around her and pulling her into a spiral was the fuzzy-headed lingering arousal. Her lips felt swollen, her body tingling, adrenaline still making her shake.

She regretted everything. She also regretted nothing.

The contradictions inside her were so extreme she felt like she was going to be pulled in two.

One thing her mind and body were united on was the desire to go hide underneath a blanket. This was definitely the kind of situation that necessitated hiding.

The problem was, she was still on her knees in front of Chase. Maybe she could hide under his chair.

What are you doing? Why are you falling apart? This isn't a big deal. He has probably literally had a thousand blow jobs.

This one didn't have to be that big a deal. Sure, it was the first one she had ever given. But he didn't have to know that, either.

If she didn't treat it like a big deal, it wouldn't be a big deal. They could forget anything had ever happened. They could forget that in a moment of total insanity she had allowed her anger to push her over the edge, had allowed her inability to back down from a challenge to bring them to this place. And that was all it was—the fact that she was absolutely unable to deal with that blow to her pride. It was nothing else. It couldn't be anything else.

She rocked back on her heels, planting her hands flat on the dusty ground before rising to her feet. She felt dizzy. She would go ahead and blame that on the speed at which she had stood up.

"I think it's safe to say we have a little bit more chemistry than you thought," she said, clearing her throat and brushing at the dirt on her pants.

He didn't say anything. He just kept sitting there, looking rocked. And he was still exposed. She did her very best to look at the wall behind him. "I can still see your…"

He scrambled into action, standing and tugging his

pants into place, doing up his belt as quickly as possible. "I think we're done for the day."

She nodded. "Yeah. Well, *you* are."

She could feel the distance widening between them. It was what she needed, what she wanted, ultimately. But for some reason, even as she forced the breach, she regretted it.

"I don't… What just happened?"

She laughed, crossing her arms and cocking her hip out to the side. "If you have to ask, maybe I didn't do a very good job." The bolder she got, the more she retreated inside. She could feel herself tearing in two, the soft vulnerable part of her scrambling to get behind the brash, bold outward version that would spare her from any embarrassment or pain.

"You're…okay?"

"Why wouldn't I be okay?"

"Because you just…"

She laughed. Hysterically. "Sure. But let's not be ridiculous about it. It isn't like you punched me in the face."

Chase looked stricken. "Of course not. I would never do that."

"I know. I'm just saying, don't act like you punched me in the face when all I did was—"

"There's no need to get descriptive. I was here. I remember."

She snorted. "You should remember." She turned away from him, clenching her hands into fists, hoping he didn't notice that they were shaking. "And I hope you remember it next time you go talking about us not having chemistry."

"Do you *want* us to have chemistry?"

She whirled around. "No. But I have some pride. You were comparing me to all these other women. Well, compare that."

"I…can't."

She planted her hands on her hips. "Damn straight."

"We can't… We can't do this again," he said, shaking his head and walking away.

For some reason, that made her feel awful. For some reason, it hurt. Stabbed like a rusty knife deep in her gut.

"I don't want to do it again. I mean, you're welcome, but I didn't exactly get anything out of it."

He stopped, turning to face her, his expression tense. "I didn't ask you to do anything."

"I'm aware." She shook her head. "I think we're done for tonight."

"Yeah. I already said that."

"Well," she said, feeling furious now, "now I'm saying it."

She was mad at herself. For taking it this far. For being upset, and raw, and wounded over something that she had chosen to do. Over his reaction, which was nothing more than the completely predictable response. He didn't want her. Not really.

And she knew that. This evening's events weren't going to change it. An orgasm on the floor of the shop she rented from him was hardly going to alter the course of fifteen years of friendship.

An orgasm. Oh, dear Lord, what had she done? She really had to get out of here. There was no amount of bravado left in her that would save her from the meltdown that was pending.

"I have to go."

She was gone before he had a chance to protest. He should be glad she was gone. If she had stayed, there was no telling what he might have done. What other stupid bit of nonsense he might have committed.

He had limited brainpower at the moment. All of his blood was still somewhere south of his belt.

He turned, surveying the empty shop. Then, in a fit of rage, he kicked something metal that was just to the right of the chair. And hurt his foot. And probably broke the thing. He had no idea if it was important or not. He hoped it wasn't. Or maybe he hoped it was. She deserved to have some of her tractor shit get broken. What had she been thinking?

He hadn't been able to think. But it was a well-known fact that if a man's dick was in a woman's mouth, he was not doing much problem solving. Which meant Chase was completely absolved of any wrongdoing here.

Completely.

He gritted his teeth, closing his eyes and taking in a sharp breath. He was going to have to figure out how to get a handle on himself between now and the next time he saw Anna. Because there was no way things could continue on like this. There weren't a whole lot of people who stuck around in his world. There had never been a special woman. After the death of his and Sam's parents, relatives had passed through, but none of them had put down roots. And, well, their parents, they might not have chosen to leave, but they were gone all the same. He couldn't afford to lose anyone else. Sam and Anna were basically all he had.

Which meant when it came to Sam's moods and general crankiness, Chase just dealt with it. And when it came to Anna…no more touching. No more… No more of any of that.

For one second, he allowed himself to replay the moment when she had unzipped his pants. When she had leaned forward and tasted him. When that white-hot streak of release had undone him completely.

He blinked. Yeah, he knew what he had been thinking. That it felt good. Amazing. Too good to stop her. But physical pleasure was cheap. A friendship like theirs represented years of investment. One simply wasn't worth sacrificing the other for. And now that he was thinking clearly he realized that. So that meant no more. No more. Never.

Next time he saw her, he was going to make sure she knew that.

Seven

Anna was beneath three blankets, and she was starting to swelter. If she hadn't been too lazy to sit up and grab hold of her ice-cream container, she might not be quite so sweaty.

The fact that she was something of a cliché of what it meant to be a woman behind closed doors was not lost on her. Blankets, old movies, Ben & Jerry's. But hey, she spent most of the day up to her elbows in engine grease, so she supposed she was entitled to a few stereotypes.

She reached her spoon out from beneath the blankets and scraped the top of the ice cream in the container, gathering up a modest amount.

"Oklahoma!" she sang, humming the rest of the line while taking the bite of marshmallow and chocolate ice cream and sighing as the sugar did its good work. Full-fat dairy products were the way to happiness. Or at least the best way she knew to stop from obsessing.

Her phone buzzed and she looked down, cringing when

she saw Chase's name. She swiped open the lock screen and read the message.

In your driveway. Didn't want to give you a heart attack.

Why are you in my dr—

She didn't get a chance to finish the message before there was a knock on her front door.

She closed her eyes, groaning. She really didn't want to deal with him right now. In fact, he was the last person on earth she wanted to deal with. He was the reason she was currently baking beneath a stack of blankets, seeking solace in the bosom of old movies.

Still, she couldn't ignore him. That would make things weirder. He was still her best friend, even if she had—Well, she wasn't going to think about what she had. If she ignored him, it would only cater to the weirdness. It would make events from earlier today seem more important than they needed to be. They did not need to be treated as though they were important.

Sure, she had never exactly done *that* with a man. Sure, she hadn't even had sexual contact of any kind with a man for the past several years. And sure, she had never had that kind of contact with Chase. But that was no reason to go assigning meaning. People got ribbons and stickers for their first trips to the dentist. They did not get them for giving their first blow job.

She groaned. Then she rolled off the couch, pushing herself into a standing position before she padded through the small living area to the entryway. She jerked the door open, pushing her hair out of her face and trying to look casual.

Too late, she realized that she was wearing her pajamas. Which were perfectly decent, in that they covered every inch of her body. But they were also baggy, fuzzy and covered in porcupines.

All things considered, it just wasn't the most glorious of moments.

"Hello," she said, keeping her body firmly planted in the center of the doorway.

"Hi," he returned. Then he proceeded to study her pajamas.

"Porcupines," she informed him, just for something to say.

"Good choice. Not an obvious one."

"I guess not. Considering they aren't all that cuddly. But neither am I. So maybe it's a more obvious choice than it originally appears."

"Maybe. We'll have to debate animal-patterned pajama philosophy another time."

"I guess. What exactly did you come here to debate if not that?"

He stuffed his hands in his pockets. "Nothing. I just came to…check on you."

"Sound of body and mind."

"I see that. Except you're in your pajamas at seven o'clock."

"I'm preparing for an evening in," she said, planting her hand on her hip. "So pajamas are logical."

"Okay."

She frowned. "I'm fine."

"Can I come in?"

She was frozen for a moment, not quite sure what to say. If she let him come in…well, she didn't feel entirely comfortable with the idea of letting him in. But if she didn't let him in, then she would be admitting that she was uncomfortable letting him in. Which would betray the fact that she actually wasn't really all that okay. She didn't want to do that, either.

No wonder she had avoided sexual contact for so long. It introduced all manner of things that she really didn't want to deal with.

"Sure," she said finally, stepping to the side and allowing him entry.

He just stood there, filling up the entry. She had never really noticed that before. How large he was in the small space of her home. Because he was Chase, and his presence here shouldn't really be remarkable. It was now.

Because things had changed. She had changed them. She had kissed him the other day, and then…well, she had changed things.

"There. You are in," she said, moving away from him and heading back into the living room. She took a seat on the couch, picking up the remote control and muting the TV.

"Movie night?"

"Every night is movie night with enough popcorn and a can-do attitude."

"I admire your dedication. What's on?"

"Oklahoma!"

He raised his brows. "You haven't seen that enough times?"

"There is no such thing as seeing a musical too many times, Chase. Multiple viewings only enhance the experience."

"Do they?"

"Sing-alongs, of course."

"I should have known."

She smiled, putting a blanket back over her lap, thinking of it as a sort of flannel shield. "You should know these things about me. Really, you should know everything about me."

He cleared his throat, and the sudden awkwardness made her think of all the things he didn't know about her.

And the things that he did know. It hit her then—of course, right then, as he was standing in front of her—just how revealing what had happened earlier was.

Giving a guy pleasure like that…well, a woman didn't do that unless she wanted him. It said a lot about how she felt. About how she had felt for an awfully long time. No matter that she had tried to quash it, the fact remained that she did feel attraction for him. Which he was obviously now completely aware of.

Silence fell like a boulder between them. Crushing, deadly.

"Anyway," she said, the transition as subtle as a landslide. "Why exactly are you here?"

"I told you."

"Right. Checking on me. I'm just not really sure why."

"You know why," he said, his tone muted.

"You check on every woman you have…encounters with?"

"You know I don't. But you're not every woman I have encounters with."

"Still. I'm an adult woman. I'm neither shocked nor injured."

She was probably both. Yes, she was definitely perilously close to being both.

He shifted, clearly uncomfortable. Which she hated, because they weren't uncomfortable with each other. Ever. Or they hadn't been before. "It would be rude of me not to make sure we aren't…okay."

She patted herself down. "Yes. Okay. Okay?"

"No," he said.

"No? What the hell, man? I said I'm fine. Do we have to stand around talking about it?"

"I think we might. Because I don't think you're fine."

"That's bullshit, McCormack," she said, rising from the couch and clutching her blanket to her chest. "Straight-up bullshit. Like you stepped in a big-ass pile somewhere out there and now you went and dragged it into my house."

"If you were fine, you wouldn't be acting like this."

"I'm sorry, how did you want me to act?"

"Like an adult, maybe?" he said, his dark brows locking together.

"Um, I am acting like an adult, Chase. I'm pretending that a really embarrassing mistake didn't happen, while I crush my regret and uncertainty beneath the weight of my caloric intake for the evening. What part of that isn't acting like an adult?"

"We're friends. This wasn't some random, forgettable hookup."

"It is so forgettable," she said, her voice taking on that brash, loud quality that hurt her own ears. That she was starting to despise. "I've already forgotten it."

"How?"

"It's a penis, Chase, not the Sistine Chapel. My life was hardly going to be changed by the sight of it."

He reached forward, grabbing hold of her arm and drawing her toward him. "Stop," he bit out, his words hard, his expression focused.

"What are you doing?" she asked, some of her bravado slipping.

"Calling you on *your* bullshit, Anna." He lowered his voice, his tone no less deadly. She'd never seen Chase like this. He didn't get like this. Chase was fun, and light. Well, except for last night when he'd kissed her. But even then, he hadn't been quite this serious. "I've known you for fifteen years. I know when your smile is hiding tears, little girl. I know when you're a whole mess of feelings behind that brick wall you put up to keep yourself separate from the world. And I sure as hell know when you aren't fine. So don't stand there and tell me that it didn't change anything, that it didn't mean anything. Even if you gave out BJs every day with lunch—and I know you don't—that would have still mattered because it's *us*. And we don't do that. It changed something, Anna, and don't you dare pretend it didn't."

No. *No*. Her brain was screaming again, but this time she knew for sure what it was saying. It was all denial. She didn't want him to look at her as if he was searching for something, didn't want him to touch her as if it was only the beginning of something more. Didn't want him to see her. To see how scared she was. To see how unnerved and affected she was. To see how very, very not brave she was beneath the shield she held up to keep the world out.

He already knows it's a shield. And you're already screwed ten ways, because you can't hide from him and you never could.

He'd let her believe she could. And now he'd changed his mind. For some reason it was all over now. Well, she knew why. It had started with a dress and high heels and ended with an orgasm in her shop. He was right. It had changed things.

And she had a terrible, horrible feeling more was going to change before they could go back to normal.

If they ever could.

"Well," she said, hearing her voice falter. Pretending she didn't. "I don't think anything needs to change."

"Enough," he said, his tone fierce.

Then, before she knew what was happening, he'd claimed her lips again in a kiss that ground every other kiss that had come before it into dust, before letting them blow away on the wind.

This was angry. Intense. Hot and hard. And it was happening in her house, in spite of the fact that she was holding a blanket and *Oklahoma!* was on mute in the background. It was her safe space, with her safe friend, and it was being wholly, utterly invaded.

By him.

It was confronting and uncomfortable and scary as hell. So she responded the only way she could. She got mad, too.

She grabbed hold of the front of his shirt, clinging to him tightly as she kissed him back. As she forced her tongue between his lips, claiming him before he could stake his claim on her.

She shifted, scraping her teeth lightly over his bottom lip before biting down. Hard.

He growled, wrapping his arms around her waist. She never felt small. Ever. She was a tall girl with a broad frame, but she was engulfed by Chase right now. His scent, his strength. He was all hard muscle against her, his heart thundering beneath her hands, which were pinned between their bodies.

She didn't know what was happening, except that right now, kissing him might be safer than trying to talk to him.

It certainly felt better.

It let her be angry. Let her push back without saying anything. And more than that…he was an amazing kisser. He had taken her from zero to almost-there with one touch of his lips against hers.

He slid his hand down her back, cupping her butt and bringing her up even harder against him so she could feel him. All of him. And just how aroused he was.

He wanted her. Chase wanted her. Yes, he was pissed. Yes, he was…trying to prove a point with his tongue or whatever. But he couldn't fake a hard-on like that.

She was angry, but it was fading. Being blotted out by the arousal that was crackling in her veins like fireworks.

Suddenly, she found herself being lifted off the ground, before she was set down on the couch, Chase coming down over her, his expression hard, his eyes sharp as he looked down at her.

He pressed his hand over her stomach, pushing the hem of her shirt upward.

She should stop him. She didn't.

She watched as his strong, masculine hand pushed her shirt out of the way, revealing a wedge of skin. The contrast alone was enough to drive her crazy. Man, woman. Innocuous porcupine pajamas and sex.

Above all else, above anything else, there was Chase. Everything he made her feel. All of the things she had spent years trying *not* to feel. Years running from.

She couldn't run. Not now. Not only did she lack the strength, she lacked the desire. Because more than safety, more than sanity, she wanted him. Wanted him naked, over her, under her, *in* her.

He gripped the hem of her top and wrenched it over her head, the movement sudden, swift. As though he had reached the end of his patience and had no reserve to draw upon. That left her in nothing more than those ridiculous baggy pajama pants, resting low on her hips. She didn't have anything sexier underneath them, either.

But Chase didn't look at all disappointed. He didn't look away, either. Didn't have a faraway expression on his face. She wasn't sure why, but she had half expected to look up at him and be able to clearly identify that he was somewhere else in his mind, with someone else. But he was looking at her with a sharp focus, a kind of single-mindedness that no man, no *one*, had ever looked at her with before.

He knew. He knew who she was. And he was still hot for her. Still hard for her.

"You are so hot," he said, pressing his hand flat to her stomach and drawing it down slowly, his fingertips teasing the sensitive skin beneath the waistband. "And you don't even know it, do you?"

Part of her wanted to protest, wanted to fight back, because that was what she did. Instead, everything inside of her just kind of went limp. Melted into a puddle. "N-no."

"You should know," he said, his voice low, husky. A shot of whiskey that skated along her nerves, warming her, sending a kick of heat and adrenaline firing through her blood. "You should know how damn sexy you are. You're the kind of woman who could make a man lose his mind."

"I could?"

He laughed, but it wasn't full of humor. It sounded tortured. "I'm exhibit A."

He shifted his hips forward, his hard length pressing up against that very aroused part of her that wanted more of him. Needed more of him. She gasped. "Soon," he said, the promise in his words settling a heavy weight in her stomach. Anticipation, terror. Need.

He continued to tease her, his fingertips resting just above the line of her panties, before he began to trail his hand back upward. He rested his palm over her chest, reaching up and tracing her lower lip with his thumb.

She darted her tongue out, sliding the tip of it over his skin, tasting salt, tasting Chase. A flavor that was becoming familiar.

Then she angled her head, taking his thumb into her mouth and sucking hard. His hips arched forward hard, his cock making firm contact, sending a shower of sparks through her body as he did.

"You're going to be the death of me," he said, every word raw, frayed.

"I might say the same about you," she said, her voice thick, unrecognizable. She didn't know who she was right now. This creature who was a complete and total slave to sexual sensation. Who was so lost in it, she could feel nothing else. No sense of self-preservation, no fear kicking into gear and letting her know that she needed to put her walls up. That she needed to go on the defense.

She was reduced. She had none of that. And she didn't even care.

"You're a miracle," he said, tracing the line of her collarbone with the tip of his tongue. "A damn *miracle*, do you know that?"

"What?"

"The other day I told you you didn't look like a miracle. I was a fool. And I was wrong. Every inch of you is a miracle, Anna Brown."

Those words were like being submerged in warm water, feeling it flow over every inch of her, a kind of deep, soul-satisfying comfort that she really, really didn't want. Or rather, she didn't *want* to want it. But she did, bad enough that she couldn't resist.

But it was all a little too heavy. All a little too much. Still, she didn't have the strength to turn him away.

"Kiss me."

She said that instead of *get the hell out of my house*, and instead of *we can't do this*, because it was all she had strength for. Because she needed that kiss. And maybe, just maybe, if they didn't talk, she could make it through.

Chase—gentleman that he was—obliged her.

He angled his head, reaching up to cup her breast as he did, his mouth crashing down on hers just as his palm skimmed her nipple. She gasped, arching up against him, the combination of sensations almost too much to handle.

Yeah, she did not remember sex being like this. Granted, it had been a million years, but she would have remembered if it had come anywhere close to this. And her conclusion most certainly wouldn't have been that it was vaguely boring and a little bit gross. Not if it had even been in the same ballpark as what she was feeling now.

There was no point in comparing. There was just flat out no comparison.

He kissed her, long, deep and hard; he kissed her until she couldn't breathe. Until she thought she was going to die for wanting more. He kissed her until she was dizzy. And when he abandoned her mouth, she nearly wept. Until he lowered his head and skimmed his tongue over one hardened bud, until he drew it between his lips and sucked hard, before scraping her sensitized flesh with his teeth.

She arched against him, desperate for more. Desperate for satisfaction. Satisfaction he seemed intent on withholding.

"I'm so close," she said, panting. "Just do it now." Then it would be over. Then she would have what she needed, and the howling, yawning ache inside of her would be satisfied.

"No," he said, his tone authoritative.

"What do you mean no?"

"Not yet. You're not allowed to come yet, Anna. I'm not done."

His words, the calm, quiet command, made everything inside of her go still. She wanted to fight him. Wanted to rail against that cruel denial of her needs, but she couldn't.

Not when this part of him was so compelling. Not when she wanted so badly to see where complying would lead.

"We're not done," he said, tracing her nipple with the tip of his tongue, "until I say we are." He lifted his head so that their eyes met, the prolonged contact touching something deep inside of her. Something that surpassed the physical.

He kissed her again, and as he did, he pulled his T-shirt over his head, exposing his incredible body to her.

Her mouth dried, and other parts of her got wet. Very, very wet.

"Oh, sweet Lord," she said, pressing her hand to his chest and drawing her fingertips down over his muscles, his chest hair tickling her skin as she did.

It was a surreal moment. So strange and fascinating. To touch her best friend like this. To see his body this way, to know that—right now—it wasn't off-limits to her. To know that she could lean forward and kiss that beautiful, perfect dip just next to his hip bone. Suddenly, she was seized with the desire to do just that. And she didn't have to fight it.

She pushed against him, bringing herself into a sitting position, lowering her head and pressing her lips to his heated skin.

"Oh, no, you don't," he said, his voice rough. He took hold of her wrist, drawing her up so that she was on her knees, eye to eye with him on the couch. "We're not finishing it like that," he said.

"Damn straight we aren't," she said. "But that doesn't mean I didn't want to get a little taste."

"You give way too much credit to my self-control, honey."

"You give too much credit to mine. I've never..." She stared at his chest instead of finishing her sentence. "It's like walking into a candy store and being told I can have whatever I want. Restraint is not on the menu."

"Good," he said, leaning in, kissing her, nipping her lower lip. "Restraint isn't what I want."

He wrapped his arm around her, drawing her up against him, her bare breasts pressing against his hard chest, the hair there abrading her nipples in the most fantastic, delicious way.

And then he was kissing her again, slow and deep as his hand trailed down beneath the waistband of her pants, cupping her ass, squeezing her tight. He pushed her pants down over her hips, taking her panties with them, leaving her completely naked in front of him.

He stood up, taking his time looking at her as he put his hands on his belt buckle.

Nerves, excitement, spread through her. She didn't know where to look. At the harsh, hungry look on his face, at the beautiful lines of muscle on his perfectly sculpted torso. At the clear and aggressive arousal visible through his jeans.

So she looked at all of him. Every last bit. And she didn't have time to feel embarrassed that she was sitting there naked as the day she was born, totally exposed to him for the first time.

She was too fascinated by him in this moment. Too fascinated to do anything but stare at him.

This was Chase McCormack. The man that women lost their minds—and their dignity—over on a regular basis. This was Chase McCormack, the sex god who could—and often did—have any woman he pleased.

She had known Chase McCormack, loyal friend and confidant, for a very long time. But she realized that up until now, she had never met *this* Chase McCormack. It was a strange, dizzying realization. Exhilarating.

And she was suddenly seized by the feeling that right now, he was hers. All hers. Because who else knew both sides of him? Did anyone?

She was about to.

"Get your pants off, McCormack," she said, impatience overriding common sense.

"You don't get to make demands here, Anna," he said.

"I just did."

"You want to try giving orders? You have to show me you can follow them." His eyes darkened, and her heart hammered harder, faster. "Spread your legs," he said, his words hard and uncompromising.

She swallowed. There was that embarrassment that she had just been so proud she had bypassed. But this was suddenly way outside her realm of experience. It was one thing to sit there in front of him naked. It was quite another to deliberately expose herself the way he was asking her to. She didn't move. She sat there, frozen.

"Spread your legs for me," he repeated, his voice heavy with that soft, commanding tone. "Or I put my clothes on and leave."

"You wouldn't," she said.

"You don't know what I'm capable of."

That was true. In this scenario, she really didn't know him. He was a stranger, except he wasn't.

Actually, if he had been a stranger, all of this would've been a lot easier. She could have spread her legs and she wouldn't have worried about how she looked. Wouldn't have worried about the consequences. If a stranger saw her do something like that, was somehow unsatisfied and then walked away, well, what did it matter? But this was Chase. And it mattered. It mattered so very much.

His hands paused on his belt buckle. "I'm warning you, Anna. You better do as you're told."

For some reason, that did not make her want to punch him. For some reason, she found herself sitting back on the couch, obeying his command, opening herself to him, as adrenaline skittered through her system.

"Good girl," he said, continuing his movements, pushing his jeans and underwear down his legs and exposing his entire body to her for the first time. And then, it didn't matter so much that she was sitting there with her thighs open for him. Because now she had all of him to look at.

The light in his eyes was intense, hungry, and he kept them trained on her as he reached down and squeezed himself hard. His jaw was tense, the only real sign of just how frayed his control was.

"Beautiful," he said, stroking himself slowly, leisurely, as he continued to gaze at her.

"Are you just going to look? Or are you going to touch?" She wasn't entirely comfortable with this. With him just staring. With this aching silence between them, and this deep, overwhelming connection that she felt.

There were no barriers left. There was no way to hide. She was vulnerable, in every way. And normally she hated it. She kind of hated it now. But that vulnerability was wrapped in arousal, in a sharp, desperate need unlike anything she had ever known. And so it was impossible to try to put distance between them, impossible to try to run away.

"I'm going to do a lot more than look," he said, dropping down to his knees, "and I'm going to do a hell of a lot more than touch." He reached out, sliding his hands around to her ass, drawing her forward, bringing her up toward his mouth.

"Chase," she said, the short, shocked protest about the only thing she managed before the slick heat of his tongue assaulted that sensitive bundle of nerves at the apex of her thighs. "You don't have to…"

He lifted his head, his dark eyes meeting her. "Oh, I know I don't have to. But you got to taste me, and I think turnabout is fair play."

"But that wasn't…"

"What?"

"It's just that men…"

"Expect a lot more than they give. At least some of them. Anyway, as much as I liked what you did for me—and don't get me wrong, I liked it a lot—you have no idea how much pleasure this gives me."

"How?"

He leaned in, resting his cheek on her thigh. "The smell of you." He leaned closer, drawing his tongue through her slick folds. "The taste of you," he said. "You."

And then she couldn't talk anymore. He buried his face between her legs, his tongue and fingers working black magic on her body, pushing her harder, higher, faster than she had imagined possible. Yeah, making out with Chase had been enough to nearly give her an orgasm. This was pushing her somewhere else entirely.

In her world, orgasm had always been a solo project. Surrendering the power to someone else, having her own pleasure not only in someone else's hands but in his complete and utter control, was something she had never even thought possible for her. But Chase was proving her wrong.

He slipped a finger deep inside of her as he continued to torture her with his wicked mouth, then a second, working them in and out of her slick channel while he teased her with the tip of his tongue.

A ball of tension grew in her stomach, expanded until she couldn't breathe. "It's too much," she gasped.

"Obviously it's not enough yet," he said, pushing her harder, higher.

And when the wave broke over her, she thought she was done for. Thought it was going to drag her straight out to sea and leave her to die. She couldn't catch her breath as pleasure assaulted her, going on and on, pounding through her like a merciless tide, battering her against the rocks, leaving her bruised, breathless.

And when it was over, Chase was looming over her, a condom in his hand.

She felt like a creature without its shell. Sensitive, completely unprotected. She wanted to hide from him, hide from this. But she couldn't. How could she? The simple truth was, they still weren't done. They had gone only part of the way. And if they didn't finish this, she would always wonder. He would, too.

She imagined that—whether or not he admitted it—was why he had come here tonight in the first place.

They had opened the lid on Pandora's box. And they couldn't close it until they had examined every last dirty, filthy sin inside of it.

Even though she thought it might kill her, she knew that they couldn't stop now.

He tore open the condom, positioning the protection over the blunt head of his arousal, rolling it down slowly.

She was transfixed. The sight of his own hand on his shaft so erotic she could hardly stand it.

She would pay good money to watch him shower, to watch his hands slide over all those gorgeous muscles. To watch him take himself in hand and lead himself to completion.

Oh, yeah. That was now her number-one fantasy. Which was a problem, because it was a fantasy that would never be fulfilled.

Don't think about that now. Don't think about it ever.

He leaned in, kissing her, guiding her so that she was lying down on the couch, then he positioned himself between her legs, testing the entrance to her body before thrusting forward and filling her completely.

She closed her eyes tight, unable to handle the feeling of being invaded by him, both in body and in her soul.

"Look at me," he said.

And once more, she was completely helpless to do anything other than obey.

She opened her eyes, her gaze meeting his, touching her down deep, where his hands never could.

And then he kissed her, soft, gentle. That kind of tenderness that had been missing from her life for so long. The kind that she had always been too embarrassed to ask for from anyone. Too embarrassed to show that she needed. That she desperately craved.

But Chase knew. Because he was Chase. He just knew.

He flexed his hips again, his pelvis butting up against her, sending a shower of sparks through her body. There was no way she was ready to come again. Except he kept moving, creating new sensations inside of her, deeper than what had come before.

It shouldn't be possible for her to have another orgasm now. Not after the first one had stripped her so completely. But apparently tonight, nothing was impossible.

There was something different about this. About the two of them, working toward pleasure together. This wasn't just her giving it out to him, or him reciprocating. This was something they were sharing.

She focused on pieces of him. The intensity in his eyes. The way the tendons in his neck stood out, evidence of the control he was exerting. She looked at his hand, up by her head, grabbing hold of one of the blankets she had been using, clinging tightly to it, as though it were his lifeline.

She looked down at his throat, at the pulse beating there.

All these close, intimate snapshots of this man that she knew better than anyone else.

Her chest felt heavy, swollen, and then it began to expand. She was convinced that she was going to break apart. All of these feelings, all of this pleasure. It was just too much. She couldn't handle it.

"Please," she begged. "Please."

He released his grip on the blanket to grasp her hips, holding her steady as he pounded harder into her, as he pounded them both toward release. Toward salvation. It was too much. It needed to end. It was all she could think. She was begging him inside. *End it, Chase. Please, end it.*

Orgasm latched on to her throat like a wild beast, gripping her hard, violently, shaking her, pleasure exploding over her. Ugly. Completely and totally beyond control.

And then Chase let out a hoarse cry, freezing above her as he thrust inside her one last time, shivering, shaking as his own release took hold.

They were captive to it together. Powerless to do anything but wait until the savage beast was finished having its way. Until it was ready to move on.

And when it was over, only the two of them were left.

Just the two of them. Chase and Anna. No clothes, no shields.

She remembered the real reason she hadn't had sex since that first time. It had nothing to do with how good or bad it had felt. Nothing to do with what a jerk she'd been after.

It had been this. This feeling of being unable to hide. But with the other guy, it had been easy to regroup. Easy to pretend she felt nothing.

She couldn't do that with Chase. She was defenseless.

And for the first time in longer than she could remember, a tear slid down her cheek.

Eight

He couldn't swear creatively enough. He had just screwed his best friend's brains out on a couch in her living room. On top of what might be the world's friendliest, most nonsexual-looking blanket. With a Rodgers and Hammerstein musical on the TV in the background.

And then she had started crying. She had started crying, and she had wiggled out from beneath him and gone into the bathroom. Leaving him alone.

He had been sitting there by himself for a full thirty seconds attempting to reconcile all of these things.

And then he sprang into action.

He got up—still bare-ass naked—and walked down the hall. "Anna!" He didn't hear anything. And so he pounded on the bathroom door. "Anna!"

"I'm in the bathroom, dumbass!" came the terse, watery reply.

"I know. That's why I'm knocking on the bathroom door."

"Go away."

"No. I'm not going to go away. You need to talk to me."

"I don't want to talk."

"Anna, dammit, did I hurt you?"

He got nothing in return but silence. Then he heard the lock rattle, and the door opened a crack. One green eye looked up at him, accusing. "No."

"Why are you hiding?" He studied the eye more closely. It was red-rimmed. Definitely still weeping a little bit.

"I don't know," she said.

"Well…you had me convinced that I… Anna, it happened really fast."

"Not *that* fast. Believe me, I've had faster."

"You wanted all of that…? I mean…"

She laughed. Actually laughed, pushing the door open a little bit wider. "After my emphatic… After all the *yes-ing*… You can honestly ask whether or not I wanted it?"

"I have a lot of sex," he said. "I don't see any point in beating around the bush there. And women have had a lot of reactions to the sex. But I can honestly say none of them have ever run away crying. So, yeah, I'm feeling a little bit shaky right now."

"You're shaky? I'm the one that's crying."

"And if I was alone in this…if I pushed you further than you wanted to go…I'm going to have to ask Sam to fire up the forge and prepare you a red-hot poker so you can have your way with me in an entirely different manner."

"I wanted it, Chase." Her tone was muted.

"Then why are you crying?"

"I'm not very experienced," she said.

"Well, I mean, I know you don't really hook up."

"I've had sex once. One other time."

He was stunned. Stunned enough that he was pretty sure Anna could have put her index finger on his chest, given a light push and knocked him flat on his ass. "Once."

"Sure. You remember Corbin. And that whole fiasco.

Where I kind of made fun of his…lack of…attributes and staying power in the hall at school. And…basically ensured that no guy would ever touch me ever again."

"Right." He remembered that.

"Well, I didn't really get what the fuss was about."

"But you… I mean, you've had…"

"Orgasms? Yes. Almost every day of my life. Because I am industrious, and red-blooded, and self-sufficient."

He cleared his throat, trying to ignore the shot of heat that image sent straight through his blood. Anna. Touching herself.

What the hell was happening to him? Well, there was nothing happening. It had damn well *happened.* On the couch in Anna's living room.

He could never look at her again without seeing her there, obeying his orders. Spreading her thighs for him so that he could get a good look at her. Yeah, he could never unsee that. Wasn't sure if he wanted to. But where the hell did he go from here? Where did they go?

There were a lot of women he could have sex with, worry-free. Anna wasn't one of them. She was a rare, precious thing in his life. Someone who knew him. Who knew all about how affected he and Sam had been by the loss of their parents.

Someone he never had to explain it to because she'd been there.

He didn't like explaining all that. So the solution was keep the friends that were there when it happened, and make sure everyone else was temporary.

Which meant Anna couldn't be temporary. She was part of him. Part of his life. A load-bearing wall on the structure that was Chase McCormack. Remove her, and he would crumble.

That was why she had always stayed a friend. Why he had never done anything like this with her before. It wasn't because of her coveralls, or her don't-step-on-the-grass demeanor. Or even because she'd neatly neutered the reputation of the guy she'd slept with in high school.

It was because he needed her friendship, not her body.

But the problem was now he knew what she looked like naked.

He couldn't get that image out of his head. And he didn't even want to.

Same with the image of all her self-administered, industrious climaxes.

Damn his dirty mind.

"Okay," he said, taking a step away from the door. "Why don't you come out?"

"I'm naked."

"So am I."

She looked down. "So you are."

"We need to talk."

"Isn't it women who are supposed to require conversation after basic things like sex?"

"I don't know. Because I never stick around long enough to find out. But this is different. This is you and me, Anna, and I will be damned if I let things get messed up over a couple of orgasms."

She chewed her lower lip. She looked…well, she looked young. And she didn't look too tough. It made him ache. "They were pretty good ones."

"Are you all right?"

"I'm fine. It's just that all of this is a little bit weird. And I'm not really experienced enough to pretend that it isn't."

"Right." The whole thing about her having been with only one guy kind of freaked him out. Made him feel like he was responsible for some things. Big things, like what she would think of sex from this day forward. And then there was the bone-deep possessiveness. That he was the first one in all this time… He should hate it. It should scare him. It should not make him feel…triumph.

He was triumphant, dammit. "Why haven't you slept with anyone else?"

She lifted a shoulder. "I told you. I didn't really think my first experience was that great."

"So you just never…"

"I'm also emotionally dysfunctional, in case you hadn't noticed."

A shocked laugh escaped his lips. "Right. Same goes."

"I don't know. Sex kind of weirds me out. It's a lot of closeness."

"It doesn't have to be," he pointed out. It felt like a weird thing to say, though, because what they'd done just now had been the epitome of closeness.

"It just all feels…raw. And…it was good. But I think that's kind of why it bothered me."

"I don't want it to bother you."

"Well, the other thing is it was *you*. You and me, like you said. We don't do things like this. We hang out, we drink beer. We don't screw."

"Turns out we're pretty compatible when it comes to the screwing." He wasn't entirely sure this was the time to make light of what had just happened. But he was at sea here. So he had to figure out some way to talk to her. He figured he would make his best effort to treat her like he always did.

"Yeah," she said, finally pushing her way out of the bathroom. "But I'm not really sure there's much we can do with that."

He felt like he was losing his grip on something, something essential, important. Like he was on a rope precariously strung across the canyon, trying to hang on and not fall to his doom. Not fall to *their* doom, since she was right there with him.

What she was saying should feel like safety. It didn't. It felt like the bottom of the damn canyon.

"I don't know if that's the way to handle it."

"You don't?" she asked, blinking.

Apparently. He hadn't thought that statement through before it had come out of his mouth. "Yeah. Look, you kissed me yesterday. You gave me…oral pleasure earlier. And now we've had sex. Obviously, this isn't going away. Obviously, there's some attraction between us that we've never really acknowledged before."

"Or," she said, "someone cast a spell on us. Yeah, we drank some kind of sex potion. Makes you horny for twenty-four hours and then goes away."

"Sex potion?"

"It's either that or years of repressed lust, Chase. Pick whichever one makes you most comfortable."

"I would go with sex potion if I thought such a thing existed." He took a deep breath. "You know there's a lot of people that think men and women can't just be friends. And I've always thought that was stupid. Maybe this is why. Maybe it's because eventually, something happens. Eventually, the connection can't just be platonic. Not when you've spent so long in each other's company. Not when you're both reasonably attractive and single."

She snorted. "*Reasonably* attractive. What happened to me being a *damn miracle*?"

"I was referring to myself when I said reasonably. I'd hate to sound egotistical."

"Honestly, Chase, after thirty years of accomplished egotism, why worry about it now?"

He looked down at her. She was stark naked, standing in front of him, and he felt like he was in front of the pastry display case at Pie in the Sky. He wanted to sample everything, and he didn't know where to start.

But he couldn't do anything about that now. He was

trying to make amends. Dropping to his knees in front of her and burying his face between her legs probably wouldn't help with that.

He could feel his dick starting to wake up again. And since he was naked he might as well just go ahead and shout his intentions at her, because he wouldn't be able to hide them.

He couldn't look at her and not get hard, though. A new development in their relationship. But then, so was standing in front of each other without clothes.

"You're beautiful," he said, unable to help himself.

She wasn't as curvy as the women he usually gravitated toward. Her curves were restrained, her waist slim, with no dramatic sweep inward, just a slow build down to those wide, gorgeous hips that he now had fantasies about grabbing hold of while he pumped into her from behind. Her breasts were small but perfection in his mind. More would just be more.

He couldn't really imagine how he had ever looked at her face and found it plain. He had to kick his own ass mentally for that. He had been blind. Someone with unrefined, cheap taste. Who thought that if you stuck rhinestones and glitter on something, that meant it was prettier. But that wasn't Anna. She was simple, refined beauty. Something that only a connoisseur might appreciate. She was like a sunset over the ocean in comparison to a gaudy ballroom chandelier. Both had their strong points. But one was real, deep. Priceless instead of expensive.

That was Anna.

Something about those thoughts made a tightening sensation start in his gut and work its way up to his chest.

"Maybe what happened was just inevitable," he said, looking at her again.

"I can't really disprove that," she said, shifting uncomfortably. "You know, since it happened. I really need to put my clothes on."

"Do you have to?"

She frowned. "Yes. And you do, too. Because if we don't..."

"We'll have sex again."

The words stood between them, stark and far too true for either of their liking.

"Probably not," she said, sounding wholly unconvinced.

"Definitely yes."

She sighed heavily. "Chase, you can have sex with anyone you want. I'm definitely hard up. If you keep walking around flashing that thing, I'm probably going to hop on for a ride, I'll just be honest with you. But I understand if I'm not half as irresistible to you as you are to me."

Anger roared through him, suddenly, swiftly. And just like earlier, when she'd thrown her walls up and tried to drive a wedge between them, he found himself moving toward her. Moving to break through. He growled, backing her up against the wall, almost sighing in relief when his hardening cock met up with her soft skin, when her small breasts pressed against his chest. He grabbed hold of her hands, drawing them together and lifting them up over her head. "Let's get one thing straight, Anna," he said. "You are irresistible to me. If you weren't irresistible to me, I would still be at home. I never would have come here. I never would have kissed you. I never would have touched you. Don't you dare put yourself down. If this is because of your brothers, because of your dad..."

She closed her eyes, looking away from him. "Don't. It's not that."

"Then what is it? Why don't you think you can have this?"

"There's nothing to have. It's just sex. You mean the world to me. And just because I'm...suddenly unable to handle my hormones, I'm not going to compromise our friendship."

"It doesn't have to compromise it," he said, lowering his voice.

"What are you suggesting? We can't have a relationship with each other. We don't have those kinds of feelings for each other. A relationship is more than sex. It's romance and all kinds of stuff that I'm not even sure I want."

"I don't want it, either," he said. "But we're going to see each other. Pretty much every day. Not just because of the stupid bet. Not just because of the charity event. I'd call all that off right now if I thought it was going to ruin our friendship. But the horse has left the stable, Anna, well and truly. It's not going back in." He rolled his hips forward, and she gasped. "See what I mean? And if you were resistible? Then sure, I would tell you that we could just be done. We could pretend it didn't happen. But you're not. So I can't."

She opened her eyes again, looking up at him. "Then what are we doing?"

"You've heard of friends with benefits. Why can't we do that? I mean, I would never have set out to have that relationship. Because I don't think it's very smart. But… it's a little bit late for smart."

"Friends with benefits. As in…we stay friends by day and we screw each other senseless by night?"

Gah. That about sent him over the edge. "Yeah."

"Until what? Until…"

"Until you get that other date. Until the charity thing. As long as we're both single, why not? You're working toward the relationship stuff. You said you didn't want to be alone anymore. So, maybe this is good in the meantime. I know you're both industrious and red-blooded, and can get those orgasms all by yourself." He rolled his hips again and, much to his satisfaction, a small moan of pleasure escaped her lips. "But are they this good?"

"No," she said, her tone hushed.

"This is possibly the worst idea in the history of the world. But hell, you wanted to get some more experience… I'm offering to give it to you." The moment he said the words he wanted to bite his tongue off. The idea of giving Anna more experience just so she could go and do things with other men? That made him see red. Made him feel violent. Jealous. Things he never felt.

But what other option was there? He couldn't keep her. Not like this. But he couldn't let her go now.

He was messed up. *This* was messed up.

"I guess… I guess that makes sense. You know, until earlier today I'd never even given a guy a blow job."

"You're killing me," he said, closing his eyes.

"Well, I don't want you to die. You just offered me your penis for carnal usage. I want you alive."

"So that's it? My penis has now become the star of the show. Wow, how quickly our friendship has eroded."

"Our friendship is still solid. I think it just goes to prove how solid your dick is."

"With romantic praise like that, how are you still single?"

"I have no idea. I spout sonnets effortlessly."

He leaned forward, kissing her, a strange, warm sensation washing over him. He was kissing Anna. And it didn't feel quite as rushed and desperate as all the other times before it. A decision had been made. This wasn't a hasty race against sanity. This wasn't trying to get as much satisfaction as possible squeezed into a moment before reality kicked in. This was…well, in the new world order, it was sanctioned.

Instantly, he was rock hard again, ready to go, even though it'd been only a few minutes since his last orgasm. But there was one problem. "I don't have a condom," he said, cursing and pushing himself away from her. "I don't suppose the woman who has been celibate for the past thirteen years has one?"

"No," she said, sagging against the wall. "You only carry one on you?"

"Yeah. I'm not superhuman. I don't usually expect to get it on more than once in a couple of hours."

"But you were going to with me?"

He looked down at his very erect cock. "Does this answer your question?"

"Yeah."

"Well, then." He let out a heavy sigh.

"You could stay and watch...*Oklahoma!* with me."

He nodded slowly. He should stay and watch *Oklahoma!* with her. If he didn't, it kind of made a mockery of the whole friends-with-benefits thing. Because, before the sex, he would have stayed with her to watch a movie, of course. To hang out, because she was one of his favorite people on earth to spend time with. Even if her taste in movies was deeply suspect.

Of course, he didn't particularly want to stay now, because she presented the temptation that he could not give in to.

"Unless you have to work early tomorrow."

"I really do," he said.

"Thank God."

His eyebrows shot up. "You want to get rid of me?"

"I don't really want to hang out with you when I know I can't have you."

"I felt the same way, but I didn't want to say it. I thought it seemed kind of offensive."

Strangely, she smiled. "I'm not offended. I'm not offended at all. I kind of like being irresistible."

Instead of leaving, he knew that he could drive down to the store and buy a box of condoms. And he seriously considered it. The problem with that was there had to be some boundaries. Some limits. He was pretty sure being so horny and desperate that you needed to buy condoms right away instead of just waiting until you had protection on hand probably didn't fit within the boundaries of friends with benefits.

"I'll see you tomorrow, then."

She nodded. "See you tomorrow."

Nine

By the time Anna swung by the grocery store in the afternoon, she was feeling very mature, and very proud of herself. She was having a no-strings sexual relationship with her friend. And she was going to buy milk, cheese and condoms. Because she was mature and adult and completely fine with the whole situation. Also, mature.

She grabbed a cart and began to slowly walk up and down the aisles. She was not making sure that no one she knew was around. Because, of course, she wasn't at all embarrassed to be in the store looking for milk, cheese and—incidentally—prophylactics. She was *thirty*. She was entitled to a little bit of sexual release. Anyway, no one was actually watching her.

She swallowed hard, trying to remember exactly which aisle the condoms were in. She had never bought any. Ever. In her entire life.

She had been extremely tempted to make a dash to the store last night when Chase had discovered he didn't have any more protection, but she had imagined that was just a little bit too desperate. She was going to be nondesperate about this. Very chill. And not like a woman who was a near virgin. Or like someone who was so desperate to jump her best friend's bones it might seem like there were deeper emotions at play. There were not.

The strong feelings she had were just…in her pants. Pants feelings. That's it.

Last night's breakdown had been purely because she was unaccustomed to sex. Just a little post-orgasmic release. That's all it was. The whole thing was a release. Post-orgasmic tears weren't really all that strange.

She felt bolstered by that thought.

She turned down the aisle labeled Family Planning and made her way toward the condoms. Lubricated. Extra-thin. Ribbed. There were options. She had to stand there and seriously ponder ribbed. She should have asked Chase what he had used last night. Because whatever that had been had been perfect.

"Anna." The masculine voice coming from her left startled her.

She turned and—to her utter horror—saw her brother Mark standing there.

"Hi," she said, taking two steps away from the condom shelf, as though that would make it less obvious why she was in the aisle. Whatever. They were adults. Neither of them were virgins and they were both aware of that.

Still, she needed some distance between herself and anything that said "ribbed for her pleasure" when she was standing there talking to her brother.

"Haven't seen you in a couple days."

"Well, you pissed me off last time I saw you."

He lifted a shoulder. "Sorry."

He probably was, too.

"Hey, whatever. I win your bet."

His brows shot up. "I heard a rumor about you and Chase McCormack kissing at Beaches, but I was pretty sure that..." His eyes drifted toward the condoms. *"Really?"*

Dying of embarrassment was a serious risk at the moment, but she was caught. Completely and totally caught. And as long as she was drowning in a sea of horror...well, she might as well ride the tide.

If he needed proof her date with Chase was real, she imagined proof of sex was about the best there was.

She took a fortifying breath. "Really," she said, crossing her arms beneath her breasts. "It's happening. I have a date. I have more than a date. I have a whole future full of dates because I have a relationship. With Chase. You lose."

"I'm supposed to believe that you and McCormack are suddenly—" his eyes drifted back to the condoms again *"—that."*

"You don't have to believe it. It's true. He's also going to be my date to the charity gala that I'm invited to. I will take my payment in small or large bills. Thank you."

"I'm not convinced."

"You're not convinced?" She moved closer to the shelf and grabbed a box of condoms. "I am caught in the act."

"Convenient," he said, grabbing his own box.

She made a face. "It's not convenient. It happened."

"You're in love with him?"

The question felt like a punch to the stomach. She did not like it. She didn't like it at all. More than that, she had no idea what to say. *No* seemed...wrong. *Yes* seemed worse. And she wasn't really sure either answer was true.

You can't love Chase.

She couldn't not love him, either. He was her friend, after all. Of course she wasn't in love with him.

Her stomach twisted tight. No. She did not love him. She didn't do love. At all. Especially not with him. Because he would never...

"You look like you just got slapped with a fish," Mark said, and, to his credit, he looked somewhat concerned.

"I… Of course I love him," she said. That was a safe answer. It was also true. She did love him. As a friend. And… she loved his body. And everything about him as a human being. Except for the fact that he was a man slut who would never settle down with any woman, much less her.

Why not you?

No. She was not thinking about this. She wasn't thinking about any of this.

"Tell you what. If you're still together at the gala, you get your money."

"That isn't fair. That isn't what we agreed on."

He lifted a shoulder. "I know. But I also didn't expect you to grab your best friend and have him be your date. That still seems suspicious to me, regardless of…purchases."

"You didn't put any specifications on the bet, Mark. You can't change the rules now."

"We didn't put any specifications on it saying I couldn't."

"Why do you care?"

He snorted. "Why do you care?"

"I have pride, jackass."

"And I don't trust Chase McCormack. If you're still together at the gala, you get your money. And if he hurts you in any way, I will break his neck. After I pull his balls off and feed them to the sharks."

It wasn't very often that Mark's protective side was on display. Usually, he was too busy tormenting her. Their childhood had been rough. Their father didn't have any idea how to show affection to them, and as a result none of them were very good at it, either. Still, she never doubted that—even when he was a jerk—Mark cared about her.

"That's not necessary. Chase is my best friend. And now…he's more. He isn't going to hurt me."

"Sounds to me like he has the potential to hurt you worse than just about anybody."

His words settled heavily in the pit of her stomach. She should be able to brush them off. Because she and Chase were in a relationship. She and Chase were friends with benefits. And nothing about that would hurt at all.

"I'll be fine."

"If you need anything, just let me know."

"I will."

He lifted the condom box. "We'll pretend this didn't happen." Then he turned and started to walk away.

"Pretend what didn't happen?" She pulled her own box of condoms up against her chest and held it tightly. "See? I've already forgotten. Mostly because I can't afford therapy. At least not until you pay me the big bucks at the gala."

"We'll see," he said, walking out of sight.

She turned, chucking the box into her cart and making her way quickly down to the milk aisle. Chase wasn't going to hurt her, because Mark was wrong. They were only friends, and she quashed the traitorous flame in her stomach that tried to grow, tried to convince her otherwise.

She wasn't going to get hurt. She was just going to have a few orgasms and then move on.

That was her story, and she was sticking to it.

"I'm taking you dancing tonight," Chase said as soon as Anna picked up the phone.

"Did you bump your head on an anvil today?"

He supposed he shouldn't be that surprised to hear Anna's sarcasm. After last night—vulnerability, tears—he'd had a feeling that she wasn't going to be overly friendly today. In fact, he'd guessed that she would have transformed into one of the little porcupines that were on her pajamas. He had been right.

"No," he said. "I'm just following the lesson plan. I said I was taking you out, and so I am."

"You know," she said, her voice getting husky, "I'm curious about whether or not making me scream was anywhere on the lesson plan."

His body jolted, heat rushing through his veins. He looked over his shoulder at Sam, who was working steadily on something in the back of the shop. It was Anna's day off, so she wasn't on the property. But he and Sam were in the middle of a big custom job. A gate with a lot of intricate detail, with matching work for the deck and interior staircase of the home. Which meant they didn't get real time off right now.

"No," he returned, satisfied his brother wasn't paying attention, "that wasn't on the lesson plan. But I'm a big believer in improvisation."

"That was improvisation? In that case, it seems to be your strength."

The sarcasm he had expected. This innuendo, he had not. They'd both pulled away hard last night, no denying it. It would have been simple to go out and get more protection and neither of them had.

But damn, this new dynamic between them was a lot to get used to. Still, for all that it was kind of crazy, he knew what he wanted. "I'd like to show you more of my strengths tonight."

"You're welcome to improvise your way on over to my bed anytime." There was a pause. "Was that flirting? Was that *good* flirting?"

He laughed, tension exiting his body in a big gust. He should have known. He wasn't sure how he felt about this being part of the lesson. Not when he had been on the verge of initiating phone sex in the middle of a workday with his brother looming in the background. But keeping it part of the lesson was for the best. He didn't need to lose his head. This was Anna, after all. He was walking a very fine line here.

On the one hand, he knew keeping a clear line drawn in the sand was the right thing to do. They weren't just going to be able to slide right back into their normal relationship. Not after what had happened. On the other hand, Anna was…Anna. She was essential to him. And she wasn't jaded when it came to sexual relationships. Wasn't experienced. That meant he needed to handle her with care. And it would benefit him to remember that he couldn't play with her the way he did women with a little more experience. Women who understood that this was sex and nothing more.

It could never be meaningless sex with Anna. He couldn't have a meaningless conversation with her. That meant that whatever happened between them physically would change things, build things, tear things down. That was a fact. A scary one. Taking control, trying to harness it, label it, was the only solution he had. Otherwise, things would keep happening when they weren't prepared. That would be worse.

Maybe.

He cleared his throat. "Very good flirting. You got me all excited."

"Excellent," she said, sounding cheerful. "Also, I bought condoms."

He choked. "Did you?"

"They aren't ribbed. I wasn't sure if the one you used last night was."

"No," he said, rubbing the back of his neck and casting a side eye at his brother. "It wasn't."

"Good. I was looking for a repeat performance. I didn't want to get the wrong thing. Though maybe sometime we should try ribbed."

Sometime. Because there would be more than once.

More than last night. More than tonight. "We can try it if you want."

"I feel like we might as well try everything. I have a lot of catching up to do."

"Dancing," he said, trying to wage a battle with the heat that was threatening to take over his skull. "Do you want to go dancing tonight?"

"Not really. But I can see the benefit. Seeing as there will be dancing at the fund-raiser. And I bet I'm terrible at dancing."

"Great. I'm going to pick you up at seven. We're going to Ace's."

"Then I'll be ready."

He hung up the phone and suddenly realized he was at the center of Sam's keen focus. That bastard had been listening in the entire time. "Hot date tonight?" he asked.

"Dancing. With Anna," he said meaningfully. The meaning being *with Anna and not with you.*

"Well, then, you wouldn't mind if I tagged along." Jerkface was ignoring his meaning.

"I would mind."

"I thought this was just about some bet."

"It is," he lied.

"Uh-huh."

"You don't want to go out. You want to stay home and eat a TV dinner. You're just harassing me."

Sam shrugged. "I have to get my kicks somewhere."

"Get your own. Get laid."

"Nope."

"You're a weirdo."

"I'm selective."

Maybe Sam was, maybe he wasn't. Chase could honestly say that his brother's sex life was a mystery to him. Which was fine. Really, more than fine. Chase had a reputation,

Sam…did not. Well, unless that reputation centered around being grumpy and antisocial.

"Right. Well, you enjoy that. I'm going to go out."

"Chase," Sam said, his tone taking on a note of steel. "Don't hurt her."

Those words poked him right in the temper. "Really?"

"She's the best thing you have," Sam said, his voice serious. "You find a woman like that, you keep her. In whatever capacity you can."

"She's my best friend. I'm not going to hurt her."

"Not on purpose."

"I don't think you're in any position to stand there and lecture me on interpersonal relationships, since you pretty much don't have any."

"I have you," Sam said.

"Right. I'm not sure that counts."

"I have Anna. But if you messed things up with her, I won't have her, either."

Chase frowned. "You don't have feelings for her, do you?" He would really hate to have to punch his brother in the face. But he would.

"No. Not like you mean. But I know her, and I care about her. And I know you."

"What does that mean?"

Sam pondered that for a second. "You're not her speed."

"I'm not trying to be." He was getting ready to punch his brother in the face anyway.

"I'm just saying."

"You're just saying," he muttered. "Go *just say* somewhere else. A guy whose only friends are his younger brother and that brother's friend maybe shouldn't stand there and make commentary on relationships."

"I'm quiet. I'm perceptive. As you mentioned, I am an artist."

"You can't pull that out when it suits you and put it away when it doesn't."

"Sure I can. Artists are temperamental."

"Stop beating around the bush. Say what you want to say."

Sam sighed. "If she offers you more than friendship, take it, dumbass."

"Why would you think that she would ever offer that? Why would you think that I want it?"

He felt defensive. And more than a little bit annoyed. "She will. I'm not blind. Actually, being antisocial has its benefits. It means that I get to sit back and watch other people interact. She likes you. She always has. And she's the kind of good… Chase, we don't get good like that. We don't deserve it."

"Gee. Thanks, Sam."

"I'm not trying to insult you. I'm just saying that she's better than either of us. Figure out how to make it work if she wants to."

Everything in Chase recoiled. "She doesn't want to. And neither do I." He turned away from Sam, heading toward the door.

"Are you sleeping with her yet?"

Chase froze. "That isn't any of your business."

"Right. You are."

"Still not your business."

"Chase, we both have a lot of crap to wade through. Which is pretty obvious. But if she's standing there willing to pull you out, I'm just saying you need to take her up on her offer."

"She has enough crap of her own that she's hip deep in, Sam. I don't need her taking on mine."

Sam rubbed his hand over his forehead. "Yeah, that's always the thing."

"Anyway, she doesn't want me. Not like that. I mean,

not forever. This is just a…physical thing." Which was way more information than his brother deserved.

"Keep telling yourself that if it helps you sleep at night."

"I sleep like a baby, Sam." He continued out the door, heading toward his truck. He had to get back to the house and get showered and dressed so that he could pick up Anna. And he was not going to think about anything his brother had said.

Anna didn't want forever with him.

That thought immobilized him, forced him to imagine a future with Anna, stretching on and on into the distance. Holding her, kissing her. Sleeping beside her every night and waking up with her every morning.

Seeing her grow round with his child.

He shut it down immediately. That was a fantasy. One he didn't want. One he couldn't have.

He would have Anna as a friend forever, but the "benefits" portion of their relationship was finite.

So, he would just enjoy this while it lasted.

Ten

She looked like a cliché. A really slutty one. She wasn't sure she cared. But in her very short denim skirt and plaid shirt knotted above the waistline she painted quite the picture.

One of a woman looking to get lucky.

"Well," she said to her reflection—her made-up reflection, compliments of her trip to the store in Tolowa today, as was everything else. "You *are* looking to get lucky."

Fair. That was fair.

She heard the sound of a truck engine and tires on the gravel in her short little driveway. She was renting a house in an older neighborhood in town—not right in the armpit of town where she'd grown up, but still sort of on the fringe—and the yard was a little bit…rustic.

She wondered if Chase would honk. Or if he would come to the door.

Him coming to the door would feel much more like a date. A real date.

A *date* date.

Oh, Lord, what were they doing?

She had flirted with him on the phone, and she'd enjoyed it. Had wanted—very much—to push him even harder. Trading innuendo with him was...well, it was a lot more fun than she'd imagined.

There was a heavy knock on the door and she squeaked, hopping a little bit before catching her breath. Then she grabbed her purse and started to walk to the entry, trying to calm her nerves. He'd come to the door. That felt like A Thing.

You're being crazy. Friends with benefits. Not boyfriend.

The word *boyfriend* made her stomach lurch, and she did her best to ignore it. She jerked the door open, watching his face intently for his response to her new look. And she was not disappointed.

"Damn," he said, leaning forward, resting his forearm on the doorjamb. "I didn't realize you would be showing up dressed as Country Girl from My Dirtiest Dreams."

She shouldn't feel flattered by that. But she positively glowed. "It seemed fair, since you're basically the centerfold of *Blacksmith Magazine*."

He laughed. "Really? How would that photo shoot go?"

"You posing strategically in front of the forge with a bellows over your junk."

"I am not getting my *junk* near the forge. The last thing I need is sensitive body parts going up in flames."

"I know I don't want them going up in flames." She cleared her throat, suddenly aware of a thick blanket of awkwardness settling over them. She didn't know what to do with him now. Did she...not touch him unless they were going to have sex? Did she kiss him if she wanted to or did she need permission?

She needed a friends-with-benefits handbook.

"Um," she began, rather unsuccessfully. "What exactly are my benefits?"

"Meaning?"

"My benefits additional to this friendship. Do I…kiss you when I see you? Or…"

"Do you want to kiss me?"

She looked up at him, all sexy and delicious looking in his tight black T-shirt, cowboy hat and late-in-the-day stubble. "Is that a trick question? Because the only answer to 'Do I want to kiss a very hot guy?' is yes. But not if you don't want to kiss me."

He wrapped his arm around her waist, drawing her up against him before bending down to kiss her slowly, thoroughly. "Does that help?"

She let out a long, slow breath, the tension that had been strangling her since he'd arrived at her house leaving her body slowly. "Yes," she said, sighing. "It does."

"All right," he said, extending his hand. "Let's go."

She took hold of his hand, the warmth of his touch flooding her, making her stomach flip. She let him lead her to the truck, open her door for her. All manner of date-type stuff. The additional benefits were getting bound up in the dating lessons and at the moment she wasn't sure what was for her and what was for the Making Her Datable mission.

Then she decided it didn't matter.

She just clung to the good feelings the whole drive to Ace's.

When they got there, she felt the true weight of the spectacle they were creating in the community. Beaches was one thing. Them being together there had certainly caused a ripple. But everyone in Copper Ridge hung out at Ace's.

Sierra West, whose family was a client of both her and Chase, was in the corner with some other friends who were involved with local rodeo events. Sheriff Eli Garrett was over by the bar, along with his brother, Connor, and their wives, Sadie and Liss.

She looked the other direction and saw Holly and Ryan Masters sitting in the corner, looking ridiculously happy. Holly and Ryan had both grown up in foster care in Copper Ridge and so had been part of the town-charity-case section at school. Though Holly was younger and Ryan a little older, so she'd never been close friends with them. Behind them was Jonathan Bear, looking broody and unapproachable as usual.

She officially knew too many damn people.

"This town is the size of a postage stamp," she muttered as she followed Chase to a table where they could deposit their coats and her purse.

"That's good," he said. "Men are seeing you attached. It's all part of changing your reputation. That's what you want."

She grunted. "I guess." It didn't feel like what she wanted. She mostly just wanted to be alone with Chase now. No performance art required.

But she was currently a dancing monkey for all of Copper Ridge, so performance art was the order of the evening.

She also suddenly felt self-conscious about her wardrobe choice. Wearing this outfit for Chase hadn't seemed bad at all. Wearing it in front of everyone was a little much.

The jukebox was blaring, and Luke Bryan was demanding all the country girls shake it for him, so Anna figured—regardless of how comfortable she was feeling—it was as good a time as any for them to get out on the dance floor.

The music was fast, so people weren't touching. They were just sort of, well, *shaking it* near each other.

She was just standing there, looking at him and not shaking it, because she didn't know what to do next. It felt weird to be here in front of everyone in a skirt. It felt weird to be dancing with Chase. It felt weird to not touch him. But it would be weirder to touch him.

Hell if she knew what she was doing here.

Then he reached out, brushing his fingers down her arm. That touch, that connection, rooted her to the earth. To the moment. To him. Suddenly, it didn't matter so much what other people around them were doing. She moved in slightly, and he put his hand on her hip.

Then, before she was ready, the song ended, slowing things down. And now she really didn't know what to do. It seemed that Chase did, though. He wrapped his arm around her waist, drawing her in close, taking hold of her hand with his free one.

Her heart was pounding hard. And she was pretty sure her face was bright red. She looked up at Chase, his expression unreadable. He was not bright red. Of course he wasn't. Because even if this relationship was new for him, this kind of situation was not. He knew how to handle women. He knew how to handle sex feelings. Meanwhile, she was completely unsure of what to do. Like a buoy floating out in the middle of the ocean, just bobbing there on her own.

Her breathing got shorter, harder. Matching her heartbeat. She couldn't just dance with him like this. She needed to not be in front of people when she felt these things. She felt like her arousal was written all over her skin. Well, it was. She was blushing like a beacon. She could probably guide ships in from the sea.

She looked at Chase's face again. There was no way to tell what he was thinking. His dark gaze was shielded by the dim lighting, his jaw set, hard, his mouth in a firm line. That brief moment of connection that she'd felt was gone now. He was touching her still, but she had no idea what he was feeling.

She looked over to her left and noticed that people were

staring. Of course they were. She and Chase were dancing and that was different. And, of course, a great many of the stares were coming from women. Women who probably felt like they should be in her position. Like she didn't belong there.

And they could all see how much she wanted it. That she wanted him more than he wanted her. That she was the one who was completely and totally out of control. Needing him so much she couldn't even hide it.

And they all knew she didn't deserve it.

She pulled away from him, looking around, breathing hard. "I think… I just need a break."

She crossed the room and went back to their table, grabbing her purse and making her way over to the bar.

Chase joined her only a few moments later. "What's up?"

She shook her head. "Nothing."

"We were dancing, and then you freaked out."

"I don't like everybody watching us."

"That's the point, though."

That simple statement stabbed her straight through the heart. "Yeah. I know." That was the problem. He was so conscious of why they were doing this. This whole thing. And she could so easily forget. Could so easily let down all the walls and shields that she had put in place to protect her heart. And just let herself want.

She hated that. Hated craving things she couldn't have. Affection she could never hope to earn.

Her mother had left. And no amount of wishing that she would come back, no amount of crying over that lost love, would do anything to fix it. No amount of hoping her father would drop that crusty exterior and give her a hug when she needed it would make it happen. So she just didn't want. Or at least, she never let people see how much she wanted.

"I know," she said, her tone a little bit stiffer than she would like.

She was bombing out here. Failing completely at remaining cool, calm and unaffected. She was standing here in public, hemorrhaging needs all over the place.

"What's wrong?"

"I need a drink."

"Why don't we leave?"

She blinked. "Just…leave?"

"If you aren't having fun, then there's no point. Let's go."

"Where are we going?"

He grabbed her hand and started to lead her through the bar. "Somewhere fun."

She followed him out into the night, laughing helplessly when they climbed into the truck. "People are going to talk. That was all a little weird."

"Let them talk. They need something to do."

He started the engine and backed out of the parking lot, turning sharply and heading down the road, out of town.

"Where are we going?"

"Somewhere I bet you've never been."

"You don't know my life, Chase McCormack. You don't know where I've been."

"I do know your life, Anna Brown."

She gritted her teeth, because, of course, he did. She said nothing as they continued to drive up the road. And still said nothing when he turned onto a dirt road that forked into a narrower dirt road as it went up the mountain.

"What are we doing?" she asked again.

Just then, they came to a flat, clear area. She couldn't see anything; there were no lights except for the headlights on the truck, illuminating nothing but the side of another mountain, thick with evergreens.

"I want to make out with you. This is where you go do that."

"We're adults," she said, ignoring the giddy fluttering in her stomach. "We have our own bedrooms. And beds. We don't need to go make out in a car."

"*Need* is not the operative word here. We're expanding experiences and stuff." He flicked the radio on, country music filling the cab of the truck. "Actually, I think before we make out—" he opened the driver's-side door "—we should dance."

Now there was nobody here. Which meant there was no excuse. Actually, this made her a lot more emotional. She did not like that. She didn't like the superpower that Chase seemed to have of reaching down inside of her, past all the defenses, and grabbing hold of tender, emotional things.

But she wasn't going to refuse, either.

It was dark out here. At least there was that.

Before she had a chance to move, Chase was at her side of the truck, opening her door. He extended his hand. "Dance with me?"

She was having a strange out-of-body experience. She wasn't sure who this woman was, up in the woods with only a gorgeous man for company. A man who wanted to dance with her. A man who wanted to make out with her.

She unbuckled, accepting his offered hand and popping out of the truck. He spun her over to the front of the vehicle, the headlights serving as spotlights as the music played over the radio. "I'm kind of a crappy dancer," he said, pulling her in close.

"You don't seem like a crappy dancer to me."

"How many men have you danced with?"

She laughed. "Um, counting now?"

"Yeah."

"One."

He chuckled, his breath fanning over her cheekbone.

So intimate to share the air with him like this. Shocking. "Well, then, you don't have much to compare it to."

"I guess not. But I don't think I would compare either way."

"Oh, yeah? Why is that?"

"You're in a league of your own, Chase McCormack, don't you know?"

"Hmm. I have heard that a time or two. When teachers told me I was a unique sort of devil, sent there to make their lives miserable. Or all the times I used to get into it with my old man."

"Well, you did raise a lot of hell."

"Yeah. I did. I continue to raise hell, in some fashion. But I need people to see a different side of me," he said, drawing her even tighter up against him. "I need for them to see that Sam and I can handle our business. That we can make the McCormack name big again."

"Can you?" she asked, tilting her head up, her lips brushing his chin. The stubble there was prickly, masculine. Irresistible. So she bit him. Just lightly. Scraping her teeth over his skin.

He gripped her hair, pulling her head back. The sudden rush of danger in the movements sending a shot of adrenaline through her blood. This was so strange. Being in his arms and feeling like she was home. Like he was everything comforting and familiar. A warm blanket, a hot chocolate and a musical she'd seen a hundred times.

Then things would shift, and he would become something else entirely. A stranger. Sex, sin and all the things she'd never taken the time to explore. She liked that, too.

She was starting to get addicted to both.

"Oh, I can handle myself just fine," he said, his tone hard.

"Can you handle me?" she asked.

He slid his hand down to cup her ass, his eyes never

leaving hers as they swayed to the music. "I can handle you. However you want it."

"Hard," she said, her throat going dry, her words slightly unsteady. She wasn't sure what had possessed her to say that.

"You want it hard?" he asked, his words sounding strangled.

"Yes," she said.

"How else do you want it?" he asked, holding her against him, moving in time with the beat. She could feel his cock getting hard against her hip.

"Aren't you the one with the lesson plan?"

"You're the one in need of the education," he said.

"I don't want tonight to be about that," she said, and she was as sure about that as she'd been about wanting it hard and equally unsure about how she knew it.

"What do you want it to be about?"

"You," she said, tracing the sharp line of his jaw. "Me. That's about it."

"What do you want from me?" he asked.

Only everything. She shied away from that thought. "Show me what the fuss is about."

"I did that already."

Something hot and possessive spiked in her blood. Something she never could have anticipated, because she hadn't even realized that it lived inside of her. "No. Something you don't give other women, Chase. You're my friend. You're…more to me than one night and an orgasm. You're right. I could have gotten that from a lot of guys. Well, maybe not the orgasm. But sex for sure. My coveralls aren't that much of a turnoff. And you could have any woman. So give me you. And I'll give you me. Don't hold back."

"You're…not very experienced."

She stretched up on tiptoes, pressing her lips to his. "Did I ask for a gentleman? Or did I ask for hard?"

He tightened his grip on her hair, and this time when she looked up at his face, she didn't see a stranger. She saw Chase. The man. The whole man. Not divided up into parts. Not Her Friend Chase or Her Lover Chase, but just…Chase.

He was all of these things. Fun and laid-back, intense and deeply sexual. She wanted it all. She craved it all. As hard as he could. As much as he could. And still, it would never, ever be enough.

"Go ahead," she said, "take me, cowboy."

She didn't have to ask twice.

He propelled them both backward, pressing her up against the truck, kissing her deeply, a no-holds-barred possession of her mouth. She hadn't even realized kissing like this existed. She wasn't entirely sure what she had thought kissing was for. Affection. A prelude to sex. This was something else entirely. This was a language all its own. Words that didn't exist in English. Words that she knew Chase would never be able to say.

And her body knew that. Understood it. Responded. As surely as it would have if he had spoken.

She was drowning. In this, in him. She hadn't expected emotion to be this…fierce. She hadn't really expected emotion at all. She hadn't understood. She really had not understood.

But then she didn't have the time to think about it. Or the brainpower. He tugged on her hair, drawing her head to the side before he pressed his lips to her tender neck, his teeth scraping along the sensitive skin before he closed his lips around her and sucked hard.

"You want it hard?" he asked, his voice rough. "Then we're going to do it my way."

He grabbed hold of her hips, turning her so that she

was facing the truck. "Scoot just a little bit." He guided her down to where the cab of the truck ended and the bed began. "Grab on." She curved her fingers around the cold metal, a shiver running down her spine. "You ever do it like this?" he asked.

She laughed, more because she was nervous than because she thought the question was funny. "Chase, before you I had never even given a guy a blow job. Do you think I've ever done this before?"

"Good," he said, his tone hard, very definitely him. "I like that. I'm a sick bastard. I like the fact that no other man has ever done this to you before. I should feel guilty." He reached around and undid the top button on her top. "But I'm just enjoying corrupting you."

He undid another button, then another. She wasn't wearing a bra underneath the top. Because, frankly, when you were as underendowed as she was, there really wasn't any point. Also, it made things a little bit more easy access. Though that wasn't something she had thought about until just now. Until Chase undid the last button and left her completely bare to the cool night air.

"I'm kind of enjoying being corrupted."

"I didn't tell you you could talk."

She shut her mouth, surprised at the commanding tone he was taking. Not entirely displeased about it. He cupped her breasts, squeezing them gently before moving his hands down her stomach, bringing them around her hips. Then he tugged her skirt down, leaving her in nothing but her boots and her underwear.

"We'll leave the boots on. I wouldn't want you to step on anything sharp."

She didn't say anything. She bit her lip, eagerly anticipating what he might do next. He slipped his hand down between her thighs, his fingertips edging beneath her panties. He stroked his fingers through her folds, a harsh growl escaping his lips. "You're wet for me," he said—not a question.

She nodded, closing her eyes, trying to keep from hurtling over the edge as soon as his fingertips brushed over her. But it was a pretty difficult battle she was waging. Just the thought of being with Chase again was enough to take her to the precipice. His touch nearly pushed her over immediately.

He gripped her tightly with his other hand, drawing her ass back up against his cock as he teased her between her legs with his clever fingers. He slipped one deep inside of her, continuing to toy with her with the edge of his thumb while he thrust in and out of her slowly. He added a second finger, then another. And she was shaking. Trembling with the effort of holding back her climax.

But she didn't want it to end like this. Didn't want it to end so quickly. Mostly, she just didn't want him to know that with one flick of his fingertip over her sensitized flesh he could make her come so hard she wouldn't be able to see straight. Because at the end of the day it didn't matter how much she wanted him; she still had her pride. She still rebelled against the idea of revealing herself quite so easily.

She probably already had. Here she was, mostly naked, out underneath the stars. Here she was, telling him she wanted just the two of them, that she wanted it hard. Probably there were no secrets left. Not really. There were all sorts of unspoken truths filling in the silences between them, but she felt like they were easy enough to read, if he wanted to look at them.

He might not. She didn't really want to. Yet it didn't make them go away.

But she could ignore them. She could focus on this. On his touch. On the dark magic he was working on her body, the spell that was taking her over completely.

He swept her hair to the side, pressing a hot kiss to the

back of her neck. And then there was no holding back. Climax washed over her like a wave as she shuddered out her release.

"Good girl," he whispered, kissing her again before moving away for a moment. He pushed her panties down her legs, helping her step out of them, then he kissed her thigh before straightening.

She heard him moving behind her. But she didn't change her position. She stood there, gripping the back of the truck. Dimly, she was aware the radio was still on. That they had a sound track to this illicit encounter in the woods. It added to the surreal, out-of-body quality.

But then he was back with her, touching her, kissing her, and it didn't feel so surreal anymore. It was too raw. Too real. His voice, his scent, his touch. He was there. There was no denying it. This wasn't fantasy. Fantasy was gauzy, distant. This was sharp, so sharp she was afraid it would cut right into her. Dangerous. She wanted it. All of it. And she was afraid that in the end there would be nothing of her left. At least nothing that she recognized. That his friendship wouldn't be something that she recognized. But they'd gone too far to turn back, and she didn't even want to anymore. She wanted to see what was on the other side of this. Needed to see what was on the other side.

He reached up, bracing his hand on the back of her neck, holding her hip with the other as he positioned himself at the entrance to her body. He pressed the blunt head of his erection against her, sliding in easily, thrusting hard up inside her. She gasped as he went deeper than he had before. This was almost overwhelming. But she needed it. Embraced it.

His hold was possessive, all-encompassing. She felt like she was being consumed by him completely. By her desire for him. Warmth bloomed from where he held her, bled down beneath the surface of her skin, hemorrhaged in her chest.

"I fantasized about this," he said, the words seeming to scrape along his throat. Rough, raw. "Holding you like this. Holding on to your hips as I did this to you."

She couldn't respond. She couldn't say anything. His words had grabbed ahold of her, squeezing her throat tight, making it impossible for her to speak. He had fantasized about her. About this.

This position should feel less personal. More distant. But it didn't. That made it… It made it exactly what she had asked for. This was for her. And this was him. What he wanted, not just the next item on a list of things she needed to learn. Not just a set routine that he had with women he slept with.

He slid his hand down along the line of her spine, pressing firmly, the impression of his possession lingering on her skin. Then he held both of her hips tight, his blunt fingertips digging into her skin. He thrust harder into her, his skin slapping against hers, the sound echoing in the darkness. She gripped the truck hard, lowering her head, a moan escaping her lips.

"You wanted hard, baby," he ground out. "I'll give it to you hard."

"Yes," she whispered.

"Who are you saying yes to?" There was an edge to his words, a desperation she hadn't imagined he would feel, not with her. Not over this.

"Chase," she said, closing her eyes tight. "Yes, Chase. Please. I need this. I need you."

She needed all of him. And she suddenly realized why those thoughts about having someone to spend her nights with had seemed wrong. Because at the end of the day when she thought of sharing evenings with someone, when she thought of curling up under a blanket with someone, of watching *Oklahoma!* with someone for the hundredth time, it was Chase. It was always Chase. And that meant no other man had ever been able to get close enough to her. Because he was the fantasy. And as long as he was the fantasy, no one else had a place.

And now, now after this, she was ruined forever. Because she would never be able to do this with another man. Ever. It would always be Chase's hand she imagined on her skin. That firm grip of his that she craved.

He flexed his hips, going harder into her, then slipped his fingers around between her thighs again, stroking her as he continued to fill her. Then he leaned forward, biting her neck as he slammed into her one last time, sending them both over the edge. He growled, pulsing inside of her as he found his release. The pain from his teeth mingled with the all-consuming pleasure rolling through her in never-ending waves, pounding over her so hard she didn't think it would ever end. She didn't think she could survive it.

And when it passed, it was Chase who held her in his arms.

There was no denying it. No escaping it. And she was scraped raw. As stripped as she'd been after their first encounter, she was even more exposed now. Because she had read into all those empty, unspoken things. Because she had finally realized what everything meant.

Her asking him for help. Her kissing him. Her going down on him.

Her not having another man in her life in any capacity.

It was because she wanted Chase. All of Chase. It was why everything had come together for her tonight. Why she'd realized she couldn't compartmentalize him.

She wasn't ready to think the words yet, though. She couldn't. She did her very best to hold them at bay. To stop herself from thinking the things that would crumble her defenses once and for all.

Instead, she released her hold on the truck and turned to face him, looping her arms around his neck, pressing her bare body against his, luxuriating in him.

"That was quite the dance lesson," she said finally.

"A lot more fun than it would have been in Ace's." He slid his hand down to her butt, holding her casually. She loved that. So much more than she should.

"Yeah, we would have gotten thrown out for that."

"But can you imagine the rumors?"

"Are they really rumors if everyone has actually seen you screw?"

"Good question," he said, leaning forward and nipping her lower lip.

"You're bitey," she said.

"And you like to be bitten."

She couldn't deny it. "I guess I should… I mean, I have to work tomorrow."

"Me, too," he said, sounding regretful.

She wanted so badly to ask him to stay with her. But he wasn't bringing it up. And she didn't know if the almighty Chase McCormack actually *slept* with the women he was sleeping with.

So she didn't ask.

And when he dropped her off at her house, leaving her at her doorstep, she tried very, very hard not to regret that.

She didn't succeed.

Eleven

The best thing about having her own shop was working alone. Some people might find it lonely; Anna found it a great opportunity to run through every musical number she knew. She had already gone through the entirety of *Oklahoma!* and was working her way through *Seven Brides for Seven Brothers.*

Admittedly, she wasn't the best singer in the world, but in her own shop she was the best singer around.

And if the music helped drown out all of the neuroses that were scampering around inside of her, asking her to deal with her Chase feelings, then so much the better. She didn't want to deal with Chase feelings.

"When you're in love, when you're in love, there is no way on earth to hide it," she sang operatically, the words echoing off the walls.

She snapped her mouth shut. That was a bad song. A very bad song for this moment. She was not… She just wasn't going to think about it.

She turned her focus back to the tractor engine she currently had in a million little pieces. At least an engine was concrete. A puzzle she could solve. It was tactile, and most of the time, if she could just get the right parts, find the source of the problem, she could fix it. That wasn't true with much of anything else in life. That was one reason she found a certain sort of calm in the garage.

Plus, it was something her father knew how to do. He was his own mechanic, and weekends were often spent laboring over his pickup truck, getting it in working order so that he could drive it to work Monday. So she had watched, she had helped. It was about the only way she had been able to connect with her gruff old man. It was still about the only way she could connect with him.

It certainly wasn't through musicals. It could never have been a desire to be seen differently by other kids at school. A need to look prettier for a boy that she liked.

So she had chosen carburetors.

"But it can't be carburetors forever." Well, it could be. In that she imagined she would do this sort of work for the rest of her life. She loved it. She was successful at it. She filled a niche in the community that needed to be filled. But…it couldn't be the only thing she was. She needed to do more than fill. She needed to…be filled.

And right now everything was all kind of turned on its head. Or bent over the back of a pickup truck. Her cheeks heated at the memory.

Yeah, Chase had definitely come by his reputation honestly. It wasn't difficult to see why women lost their ever-loving minds over him.

That made her frown. Because she didn't like to think that she was just one of the many women losing their minds over him because he had a hot ass and skilled hands. She had known about the hot ass for years. It hadn't made her lose her mind. In fact, she didn't really think she had lost her mind now. She knew exactly what she was doing. She frowned even more deeply.

Did she know what she was doing? They had stopped and had discussions, made conscious decisions to do this friends-with-benefits thing. Tricked themselves into thinking that they were in control of this. Or at least that's what she had been doing. But as she had been carried away on a wave of emotion last night, she had known for an absolute fact that she wasn't in control of any of this.

"Doesn't mean I'm going to stop."

That, at least, was the absolute truth. He would have to be the one to call it off.

Just the thought made her heart crumple up into a little ball.

"Quitting time yet?"

She turned to see Chase standing in the doorway. This was a routine she could get used to. She wanted to cross the space between them and kiss him. And why not? She wasn't hiding her attraction to him. They weren't hiding their association.

She dropped her ratchet, wiped her hands on her coveralls and took two quick steps, flinging herself into his arms and kissing him on the lips. She wasn't embarrassed until about midway through the kiss, when she realized she had been completely and totally enthusiastic and hadn't hidden any of it. But he was holding on to her, and he was kissing her back, so maybe it didn't matter. Maybe it was okay.

When they parted, he was smiling.

Her heart felt tender, exposed. But warm, like it was being bathed in sunlight. Something to do with that smile of his. With that easy acceptance of what she had offered.

"I think it's about time to quit," she said.

"I like your look," he said, gesturing to her white tank top, completely smeared with grease and dirt, and her coveralls, which were unbuttoned and tied around her waist.

"Really?"

"Last night you were my dirty country girl fantasy and today you're a sexy mechanic fantasy. Do you take requests? Around Christmas you could go for Naughty Mrs. Claus."

She rolled her eyes, grabbing the end of her tank top and knotting it up just under her breasts. "Maybe more like this? Though I think I'm missing the breast implants."

His smile turned wicked. "Baby, you aren't missing a damn thing."

Her heart thundered harder, a rush of adrenaline flowing through her. "I didn't think this was your type. Remember? You had to give me a makeover."

"Yeah, that was stupid. I actually think I just needed to get knocked upside the head."

"Did I…knock you upside the head?"

"Yeah." He wrapped his arms around her bare waist, his fingertips playing over her skin. "You're pretty perfect the way you are. You never needed a dress or high heels. I mean, you're welcome to wear them if you want. I'm not going to complain about that outfit you wore last night. But all that stuff we talked about in the beginning, about you needing to change so that people would believe we were together… I guess everyone is just going to have to believe that I changed a little bit."

"Have you changed?" she asked, brushing her thumb over his lower lip. A little thrill skittered down her spine. That she could touch him like this. Be so close to him. Share this kind of intimacy with a man she had had a certain level of emotional intimacy with for years and years.

It was wonderful. It also made her ache. Made her feel like her insides were being broken apart with a chisel. And she was willingly submitting to it. She didn't know quite what was happening to her.

Are you sure you don't?

"Something did," he said, his dark eyes boring into hers.

"You know," she said, trying to tamp down the fluttering that was happening in her chest, "I think it's only fair that I give you a few lessons."

"What kind of lessons?" he asked, his gaze sharpening.

"I'm not sure you know your way around an engine quite the way you should," she said, smiling as she wiggled out of his hold.

"Oh, really?"

She nodded, grabbing hold of a rag and slinging it over her shoulder before picking up her ratchet again. "Really."

"Is this euphemistic engine talk?"

"Do you think I'm expressing dissatisfaction with the way you work under my hood?"

He chuckled. "You're really getting good at this flirting thing."

"I am. That was good. And dirty."

"I noticed." He moved behind her, sweeping her hair to the side and kissing her neck. "But if you're implying that I didn't do a very good job…I would have to clear my good name."

"I was talking about literal engines, Chase. But if you really want to try to up your game, I'm not going to stop you."

"What's that?" he asked, reaching past her and pointing to one of the parts that were spread out on the worktable in front of her.

"A cylinder head. I'm replacing that and the head gasket on the engine. And I had to take a lot of things apart to get to it."

"When do you need to have it done?"

"Not until tomorrow."

"So you don't need me to play the part of lovely assistant while you finish up tonight?"

"I would like you to assist me with a few things," she

said, planting her hand at the center of his chest and pushing him lightly. The backs of his knees butted up against the chair that was behind him and he sat down, looking up at her, a predatory smile curving his lips.

"Is this going to be a part of my lesson?"

"Yeah," she said, "I thought it might be."

Last night had been incredible. Last night, he had given her something that felt special. Personal. Now she wanted to give him something. To show him what was happening inside of her, because she could hardly bring herself to think it. She wanted… She just wanted. In ways that she hadn't allowed herself to want in a long time. More. Everything.

"What exactly are you going to teach me?"

"Well, I could teach you all the parts of the tractor engine. But we would be here all night. And it would just slow me down. Someday, we can trade. You can give me some welding secrets. Teach me how to pound steel."

"That sounds dirty, too."

"Lucky me," she said, stretching her arms up over her head, her shirt riding up a little higher. She knew what she wanted to do. But she also felt almost petrified. This was… well, this was the opposite of protecting herself. This was putting herself out there. Risking humiliation. Risking doing something wrong while revealing how desperately she wanted to get it right.

But she wanted to give him something. And honestly, there was no bigger gift she could give him than vulnerability. To show him just how much she wanted him.

She swayed her hips to the right, then moved them back toward the left in a slow circle. She watched his face, watched the tension in his jaw increase, the sharpness in his eyes get positively lethal. And that was all the encouragement she needed. She'd seen enough movies with lap dances that she had a vague idea of how this should go. Maybe her idea was the PG-13-rated version, but she could improvise.

He moved his hand over the outline of his erection, squeezing himself through the denim as she continued to move. Maybe it wasn't rhinestones and a miniskirt, but he didn't seem to mind her white tank top and coveralls. He was still watching her with avid interest as she untied the sleeves from around her waist and let the garment drop down around her feet. She kicked it off to the side, revealing her denim cutoff shorts underneath it.

"Come here," he said, his voice hard.

"I'm not taking orders from you. You have to be patient."

"I'm not feeling very patient, honey."

"What's my name?"

"Anna," he ground out. "Anna, I'm not feeling very patient."

"Not enough women have made you wait. You're getting spoiled."

She slid her hand up her midsection, her own fingertips combined with the electric look on Chase's face sending heat skittering along her veins. She let her fingers skim over her breast, gratified when his breath hissed through his teeth.

"Anna..."

"You know me pretty well, don't you? But you didn't know all this." She moved her hand back down, over her stomach, her belly button, sliding her fingers down beneath the waistband of her shorts, stroking herself where she was wet and aching for him. His fingers curled around the edge of the chair, his knuckles white, the cords on his neck standing out, the strength it was taking him to remain seated clear and incredibly compelling.

"Take them off," he said.

"Didn't I just tell you that you're not in charge?"

"Don't play games with me."

"Maybe patience is the lesson you need to learn."

"I damn well don't," he growled.

She turned around, facing away from him, taking a deep breath as she unsnapped her shorts and pushed them down her hips, revealing the other purchase she had made at the store yesterday. A black, lacy thong, quite unlike any other pair of underwear she had ever owned. And she had slipped it on this morning hoping that this would be the end of her day.

"Holy hell," he said.

She knew that she was not the first woman to take her clothes off for him. Much less the first woman to reveal sexy underwear. But that only made his appreciation for hers that much sweeter. She swayed her hips back and forth before dropping down low, and sweeping back up. It felt so cheesy, and at the same time she was pretty proud of herself for pulling it off.

When she turned to face him, his expression was positively feral.

Her shirt was still knotted beneath her breasts, and now she was wearing work boots, a thong and the top. If Chase thought the outfit was a little bit silly, he certainly didn't show it.

She moved over to the chair, straddling him, leaning in and kissing him on the lips. "I want you," she said.

She had said it before. But this was more. Deeper. This was the truth. Her truth, the truest thing inside of her. She wanted Chase. In every way. Forever. She swallowed hard, grabbing hold of his T-shirt and tugging it up over his head. She licked her lips, looking at his body, at his chest, speckled with just the right amount of dark hair, at his abs, so perfectly defined and tempting.

She reached between them, undoing his belt and jerking it through the loops, before tugging his pants and underwear down low on his hips. He put his hand on her backside, holding her steady as she maneuvered herself so that she was over him, rubbing up against his arousal. "I would never have considered doing something like this before last week. Not with anyone. It's just you," she said, leaning in and kissing his lips lightly. "You do this to me."

He shuddered beneath her, her words having the exact effect she hoped they would. He liked feeling special, too.

He took hold of her hand, drawing it between them, curving her fingers around him. "And you do this to me. You make me so hard, it hurts. I've never wanted a woman like this before. Ever."

She flexed her hips, squeezed him tighter, trapping him between her palm and the apex of her thighs. "Why? Why do you want me like this?"

It was important to know. Essential.

"Because it's you, Anna. There's this idea that having sex with a stranger is supposed to be exciting. Because it's dirty. Because it's wrong. Maybe because it's unknown? But I've done that. And this is… You're right. I know you. Knowing you like this… Your face is so familiar to me, your voice. Knowing what it looks like when I make you come, how you sound when I push you over the edge, baby, there's nothing hotter than that."

His words washed over her, everything she had never known she needed. This full, complete acceptance of who she was. Right here in her garage. The mechanic, the woman. The friend, the lover. He wanted her. And everything that meant.

She didn't even try to keep herself from feeling it now. Didn't try to keep herself from thinking it.

She loved him. So much. Every part of him, with every part of her. Her friend. The only man she really wanted. The only person she could imagine sharing her days and nights and blankets and musicals with.

And that realization didn't even make her want to pull

away from him. Didn't make her want to hide. Instead, she wanted to finish this. She wanted to feel connected to him. Now that she was in, she was in all the way. Ready to expose herself completely, scrape herself raw, all for him.

She rose up so that she was on her knees, tugged her panties down her hips and maneuvered herself so that she was able to dispense with them completely before settling over him, grabbing hold of his broad shoulders as she sank down onto his hardened length.

He swore, the harsh word echoing in the empty space. "Anna, I need to get a condom."

She pulled away from him quickly, hovering over him as he lifted his hips, grabbing his wallet and pulling out a condom with shaking hands, taking care of the practicalities quickly. She was trembling, both with the adrenaline rush that accompanied the stupidity of her mistake and with need. With regret because she wished that he was still inside of her even though it wouldn't be responsible at all.

Soon, he was guiding her back onto him, having protected them both. Thankfully, he was a little more with it than she was.

He gripped her tightly, guiding her movements at first, helping her establish a rhythm that worked for them both.

He moved his hands around, brushing his fingertips along the seam of her ass before teasing her right where their bodies were joined. She gasped, grabbing hold of the back of the chair, flexing her hips, chasing her own release as he continued to touch her. To push her higher.

She slid her hands up, cupping his face, holding him steady. She met his gaze, a thrill shooting down her spine. "Anna," he rasped, the words skating over her skin like a caress, touching her everywhere.

Pleasure gripped her, low and tight, sending her over the edge. She held his face as she shuddered out her orgasm and chanted his name, endlessly. Over and over again.

And when it was over, he held her to him, kissing her lips, whispering words against her mouth that she could barely understand. She didn't need to. The only words she understood were the ones she most needed to hear.

"Stay with me tonight."

Twelve

They dressed and drove across the property in Chase's truck. His heart was still hammering like crazy, and he had no idea what the hell he was doing. But then, it was Anna. She wasn't some random hookup. He wanted her again, and having her spend the night seemed like the best way to accomplish that.

He ignored the little terror claws that wrapped themselves around his heart and squeezed, and focused instead on the heavy sensation in his gut. In his dick. He wanted her, and dammit, he was going to have her.

The image of her dancing in front of him in the shop… that would haunt him forever. And it was his goal to collect a few more images that would make his life miserable when their physical relationship ended.

That was normal.

He parked the truck, then got out, following Anna mutely up the steps. When they got to the door, Anna paused.

"I don't...have anything with me. No porcupine pajamas."

Some of the tension in his chest eased. "You won't need pajamas in my bed," he said, his voice low, almost unrecognizable even to himself.

Which was fair enough, since this whole damn situation was unrecognizable. Saying this kind of stuff to Anna. Seeing her like this. Wanting her like this.

She was a constant. She was stability. And he felt shaky as hell right now.

"I've never spent the night with anyone," she blurted.

The words hit him hard in the chest. Along with the realization that this was a first for him, too. He knew it, logically. But for some reason it hadn't seemed momentous when he'd issued the invitation. Because it was Anna and sleeping with her had seemed like the most natural thing on earth. He liked talking to her, liked kissing her, liked having sex with her, and he didn't want her to leave. So the obvious choice was to ask her to stay the night.

Now it was hitting him, though. What that usually meant. Why he didn't do it.

But it was too late to take the invitation back, and anyway, he didn't know if he wanted to.

"I haven't, either," he said.

She blinked. "You...haven't? I mean, I had a ten-minute roll in the hay—literally—with a loser in high school, so I know why I've never spent the night with anyone. But you...you do this a lot."

"Are you calling me a slut?"

"Yes," she said, deadpan. "No judgment, but yeah, you're kind of slutty."

"Well, you don't have to spend the night with someone when you're done with them. I guess that's why I haven't. Because I am kind of slutty, and it has nothing to do with liking the person I'm with. Just..."

Oblivion. The easiest, most painless connection on earth with no risk involved whatsoever.

But he wasn't going to say that.

Anna wasn't oblivion. Being with her was like…being inside his own skin, really in it, and feeling it, for the first time since he was sixteen.

Like driving eighty miles per hour on the same winding road that had killed his parents, daring it to come for him, too. He'd felt alive then. Alive and pushing up against the edge of mortality as hard as he could.

Then he'd backed way off the gas. And he'd backed way off ever since.

This was the closest thing to tasting that surge of adrenaline, that rush he'd felt since the day he'd basically begged the road to take him, too.

You're a head case.

Yes, he was. But he'd always known that. Anna hadn't, though.

"Just?" she asked, eyebrows shooting up. She wasn't going to let that go, apparently.

"It's just sex."

"And what is this?" she asked, gesturing between the two of them.

"Friendship," he said honestly. "With some more to it."

"Those benefits."

"Yeah," he said. "Those."

He shoved his hands in his pockets, feeling like he'd just failed at something, and he couldn't quite figure out what. But his words were flat in the evening air. Just sort of dull and resting between them, wrong and weird, but he didn't know what to do about it.

Because he didn't know what else to say, either.

"Want to come inside?" he asked finally.

"That is where your bed is," she said.

"It is."

They made their way to the bedroom, and somehow it all felt different. He could easily remember when she'd been up here just last week, walking in those heels and that dress. When he'd been overwhelmed with the need to touch her, but wouldn't allow himself to do so.

He could also remember being in here with her plenty of times before. Innocuous as sharing the space with any friend.

How? How had they ever existed in silences that weren't loaded? In moments that weren't wrapped in tension. In isolation that didn't present the very tempting possibility of chasing pleasure together. Again and again.

This wasn't friendship plus benefits. That implied the friendship remained untouched and the benefits were an add-on. Easy to stick there, easy to remove. But that wasn't the case.

Everything was different. The air around them had changed. How the hell could he pretend the friendship was the same?

"I'm just—" She smiled sheepishly and pulled her shirt up over her head. "Sorry." Then she unhooked her bra, tossing it onto the floor. He hadn't had a chance to look at her breasts the last time they'd had sex. She'd kept them covered. Something that had added nicely to the tease back in the shop. But he was ready to drop to his knees and give thanks for their perfection now.

"Why are you apologizing for flashing me?"

"Because. In the absence of pajamas I need to get comfortable now." She stripped her shorts off, and her underwear—those shocking black panties that he simply hadn't seen coming, much like the rest of her—and then she flopped down onto his bed. He didn't often bring women back here.

Sometimes, depending on the circumstances, but if they had a hotel room, or their own place available, that was his preference. So it was a pretty unusual sight in general. A naked woman in his room. Anna, in this familiar place—naked and warm and about as inviting as anything had ever been—was enough to make his head explode.

His head, and other places.

"You never have to apologize for being naked." He stripped his shirt off, then continued to follow her lead, until he was wearing nothing.

He lay down beside her, not touching her, just looking at her. This was hella weird. If a woman was naked, he was usually having sex with her, bottom line. He didn't lie next to one, simply looking at her. Right now, Anna was something like art and he just wanted to admire her. Well, that wasn't *all* he wanted. But it was what he wanted right now. To watch the soft lamplight cast a warm glow over her curves, to examine every dip and hollow on the map of her figure. To memorize the rosy color of her nipples, the dark hair at the apex of her thighs. The sweet flare of her hips and the slight roundness of her stomach. She was incredible. She was Anna. Right now, she was his.

That thought made his stomach tighten. How long had it been since something was his?

This place would always be McCormack, through and through. The foundation of the forge and the business… it was built on his great-grandfather's back, carried down by his grandfather, handed to their father.

And he and Sam carried it now.

This ranch would always be something they were bound to by blood, not by choice. Even if given the choice, he could probably never leave. Their family… It didn't feel like their family anymore. It hadn't for a lot of years.

It was two of them, him and Sam. Two of them trying so damn hard to push this legacy back to where it had been. To make their family extend beyond these walls, beyond these borders. To fulfill all of the promises he'd made to his dad, even though the old man had never actually heard them.

Even though Chase had made them too late.

And so there was something about that. Anna, this moment, being for him. Something that he chose, instead of something that he'd inherited.

"I like when you look at me like that," she said, her voice hushed.

"I like when you take control like you did back in the shop. I like seeing you realize how beautiful you are," he said. It was true. He was glad that she knew now. And pissed that she was going to take that knowledge and work her magic on some other man with her newfound power. He wanted to kill that man.

But he could never hope to take his place, so he wouldn't.

"You're the first person who has made me feel like it all fit. And maybe it's because you're my friend. Maybe it's because you know me," she said.

"I don't follow."

"I had to be tough," she said, her tone demonstrating just that. "All my life I've had to be tough. My brothers raised me, and they did a damn good job, and I know you think they're jerks, and honestly a lot of the time they are. But they were young boys who were put in charge of taking care of their kid sister. So they took care of me, but they tortured me in that way only brothers can. Probably because I tortured them in ways that most little sisters could never dream. They didn't go out in high school. They had to make sure I was taken care of. They didn't trust my dad to do it. He wasn't stable enough. He would go out to the bar and get drunk, and he would call needing a ride home. They handled things so that I didn't have to. And I never felt like I could make their lives more difficult by showing how hard it was for me."

She shifted, sighing heavily before she continued. "And

then there was my dad. He didn't know what to do with a daughter. As pissed as he was that his wife left, I think in some ways he was relieved, because he didn't have to figure out how to fit a woman into his life anymore. But then I kind of started becoming a woman. And he really didn't know what to do. So I learned how to work on cars. I learned how to talk about sports. I learned how to fit. Even though it pushed me right out of fitting when it came to school. When it came to making friends."

He knew these things about Anna. Knew them because he'd absorbed them by being in her house, being near her, for fifteen years. But he'd never heard her say them. There was something different about that.

"You've always fit with me, Anna," he said, his voice rough.

"I know. And even though we've never talked about this, I'm pretty sure somehow you knew all of it. You always have. Because you know me. And you accept me. Not very many people know about the musicals. Because it always embarrassed me. Kind of a girlie thing."

"I guess so," he said, the words feeling inadequate.

"Also, it was my thing. And…I never like anyone to know how much I care about things. I… My mom loved old musicals," she said, her voice soft. "Sometimes I wonder what it would be like to watch them with her."

"Anna…"

"I remember sneaking out of my room at night, seeing the TV flickering in the living room. She would be watching *The Sound of Music* or *Cinderella. Oklahoma!* of course. And I would just hang there in the hall. But I didn't want to interrupt. Because by the end of the day she was always out of patience, and I knew she didn't want any of the kids to talk to her. But it was kind of like watching them with her." Anna's eyes filled with tears. "But now I just wish I had. I wish I had gone in and sat next to her. I wish I had risked her being upset with me. I never got the chance. She left, and that was it. So, maybe she would've been mad at me, or maybe she wouldn't have let me watch them with her. But at least I would've had the answer. Now I just wonder. I just remember that space between us. Me hiding in the hall, and her sitting on the couch. She never knew I was there. Maybe if I'd done a better job of connecting with her, she wouldn't have left."

"That's not true, Anna."

"She didn't have anyone to watch the movies with, Chase. And my dad was so… I doubt he ever gave her a damn scrap of tenderness. But maybe I could have. I think… I think that's what I was always trying to do with my dad. To make up for that. It was too late to make her stay, but I thought maybe I could hang on to him."

Chase tried to breathe past the tightness in his chest, but it was nearly impossible. "Anna," he said, "any parent that chooses to leave their child…the issue is with them. It was your parents' marriage. It was your mom. I don't know. But it was never you. It wasn't you not watching a movie with her, or irritating her, or making her angry. There was never anything you could do."

She nodded, a tear tracking down her pale cheek. "I do know that."

"But you still beat yourself up for it."

"Of course I do."

He didn't have a response to that. She said it so matter-of-factly, as though there was nothing else but to blame herself, even if it made no sense. He had no response because he understood. Because he knew what it was like to twist a tragedy in a thousand different ways to figure out how you could take it on yourself. He knew what it was like to live your life with a gaping hole where someone you loved should be. To try to figure out how you could have stopped the loss from happening.

In the years since his parents' accident he had moved beyond blame. Not because he was stronger than Anna, just because you could only twist death in so many different directions. It was final. And it didn't ask you. It just was. Blaming himself would have been a step too far into martyrdom.

Still, he knew about lingering scars and responses to those scars that didn't make much sense.

But he didn't know what it was like to have a parent choose to leave you. God knew his parents never would have chosen to abandon their sons.

As if she'd read his mind, Anna continued. "She's still out there. I mean, as far as I know. She could have come back. Anytime. I just feel like if I had given her even a small thing…well, then, maybe she would have missed me enough at some point. If she'd had anything back here waiting for her, she could have called. Just once."

"You were you," he said. "If that wasn't enough for her…fuck her."

She laughed and wiped another tear from her face. Then she shifted, moving closer to him. "I appreciate that." She paused for a moment, kissing his shoulder, then she continued. "It's amazing. I've never told you that before. I've never told anyone that before. It's just kind of crazy that we could know each other for so long and…there's still more we don't know."

He wanted to tell her then. About the day his parents died. About the complete and total hole it had torn in his life. She knew to a degree. They had been friends when it happened. He had been sixteen, and Sam had been eighteen, and the loss of everything they knew had hit so hard and fast that it had taken them out at the knees.

He wanted to tell her about his nightmares. Wanted to tell her about the last conversation he'd had with his dad.

But he didn't.

"Amazing" was all he said instead.

Then he leaned over and kissed her, because he couldn't think of anything else to do, couldn't think of anything else to say.

Liar.

A thousand things he wanted to tell her swirled around inside of him. A thousand different things she didn't know. That he had never told anybody. But he didn't want to open himself up like that. He just… He just couldn't.

So instead, he kissed her, because that he could do. Because of all the changes that existed between them, that was the one he was most comfortable with. Holding her, touching her. Everything else was too big, too unknown to unpack. He couldn't do it. Didn't want to do it.

But he wanted to kiss her. Wanted to run his hands over her bare curves. So he did.

He touched her, tasted her, made her scream. Because of all the things that were happening in his life, that felt right.

This was…well, it was a detour. The best one he'd ever taken, but a detour all the same. He was building the family business, like he had promised his dad he would do. Or like he should have promised him when he'd had the chance. He might never have been able to tell the old man to his face, but he'd promised it to his grave. A hundred times, a thousand times since he'd died.

That was what he had to do. That was on the other side of making love with Anna. Going to that benefit with her all dressed up, trying to help her get the kind of reputation she wanted. To send her off with all her newfound skills so that she could be with another man after.

To knuckle down and take the McCormack family ranch back to where it had been. Beyond. To make sure that Sam used his talents, to make sure that the forge and all the work their father had done to build the business didn't go to waste.

To prove that the fight he'd had with his father right before he died was all angry words and teenage bluster. That what he'd said to his old man wasn't real.

He didn't hate the ranch. He didn't hate the business. He didn't hate their name. He was their name, and damn him for being too young and stupid to see it then.

He was proving it now by pouring all of his blood, all of his sweat, all of his tears into it. By taking the little bit of business acumen he had once imagined might get him out of Copper Ridge and applying it to this place. To try to make it something bigger, something better. To honor all the work their parents had invested all those years.

To finish what they started.

He might not have ever made a commitment to a woman, but this ranch, McCormack Iron Works...was his life. That was forever.

It was the only forever he would ever have.

He closed those thoughts out, shut them down completely and focused on Anna. On the sweet scent of her as he lowered his head between her thighs and lapped at her, on the feel of her tight channel pulsing around his fingers as he stroked them in and out. And finally, on the tight, wet clasp of her around him as he slid home.

Home. That's really what it was.

In a way that nowhere else had ever been. The ranch was a memorial to people long dead. A monument that he would spend the rest of his life building.

But she was home. She was his.

If he let her, she could become everything.

No.

That denial echoed in his mind, pushed against him as he continued to pound into her, hard, deep, seeking the oblivion that he had always associated with sex before her. But it wasn't there. Instead, it was like a veil had been torn away and he could see all of his life, spreading out before him. Like he was standing on a ridge high in the mountains, able to survey everything. The past, the present, the future. So clear, so sharp it almost didn't seem real.

Anna was in all of it. A part of everything.

And if she was ever taken away…

He closed his eyes, shutting out that thought, a wave of pleasure rolling over him, drowning out everything. He threw himself in. Harder than he ever had. Grateful as hell that Anna had found her own release, because he'd been too wrapped up in himself to consider her first.

Then he wrapped his arms around her, wrapped her up against him. Wrapped himself up in her. And he pushed every thought out of his mind and focused on the feeling of her body against his, the scent of her skin. Feminine and sweet with a faint trace of hay and engine grease.

No other woman smelled like Anna.

He pressed his face against her breasts and she sighed, a sound he didn't think he'd ever get tired of. He let everything go blank. Because there was nothing in his past, or his future, that was as good as this.

Thirteen

Chase woke in a cold sweat, his heart pounding so heavily he thought it would burst through his bone and flesh and straight out into the open. His bed was empty. He sat up, rubbing his hand over his face, then forking his fingers through his hair.

It felt wrong to have the bed empty. After spending only one night wrapped around Anna, it already felt wrong. Not having her… Waking up in the morning to find that she wasn't there was… He hated it. It was unsettling. It reminded him of the holes that people left behind, of how devastating it was when you lost someone unexpectedly.

He banished the thought. She might still be here. But then, she didn't have any clean clothes or anything, so if she had gone home, he couldn't necessarily blame her. He went straight into the bathroom, took a shower, took care of all other morning practicalities. He resisted the urge to look at his phone, to call Anna's phone or to go downstairs and see if maybe she was still around. He was going to get through all this, dammit, and he was not going to behave as though he were affected.

As though the past night had changed something fundamental, not just between them, but in him.

He scowled, throwing open the bedroom door and heading down the stairs.

He stopped dead when he saw her standing there in the kitchen. She was wearing his T-shirt, her long, slim legs bare. And he wondered if she was bare all the way up. His mouth dried, his heart squeezing tight.

She wasn't missing. She wasn't gone. She was cooking him breakfast. Like she belonged here. Like she belonged in his life. In his house. In his bed.

For one second it made him feel like he belonged. Like she'd been the missing piece to making this his, to making it more than McCormack.

He felt like he was standing in the middle of a dream. Standing there looking at somebody else's life. At some wild, potential scenario that in reality he would never get to have.

Right in front of him was everything. And in the same moment he saw that, he imagined the hole that would be left behind if it was ever taken away. If he ever believed in this, fully, completely. If he reached out and embraced her now, there would be no words for how empty his arms would feel if he ever lost her.

"Don't you have work?" he asked, leaning against the doorjamb.

She turned around and smiled, the kind of smile that lit him up inside, from his head, down his toes. He did his very best not to return the gesture. Did his best not to encourage it in any way.

And he cursed himself when the glow leached out of her face. "Good morning to you, too," she said.

"You didn't need to make breakfast."

"*Au contraire.* I was hungry. So breakfast was needed."

"You could've gone home."

"Yes, Grumpy-Pants, I could have. But I decided to stay here and make you food. Which seemed like an adequate thank-you for the multiple orgasms I received yesterday."

"Bacon? You're trying to pay for your orgasms with bacon?"

"It seemed like a good idea at the time." She crossed her arms beneath her breasts and revealed that she did not, in fact, have anything on beneath the shirt. "Bacon is a borderline orgasmic experience."

"I have work. I don't have time to eat breakfast."

"Maybe if you had gotten up at a decent hour."

"I don't need you to lecture me on my sleeping habits," he bit out. "Is there coffee?"

"It's like you don't know me at all." She crossed the room and lifted a thermos off the counter. "I didn't want to leave it sitting on the burner. That makes it taste gross."

"I don't really care how it tastes. That's not the point."

She rested her hand on the counter, then rapped her knuckles against the surface. "What's going on?"

"Nothing."

"Stop it, Chase. Maybe you can BS the other bimbos that you sleep with, but you can't do it to me. I know you too well. This has nothing to do with waking up late."

"This is a bad idea," he said.

"What's a bad idea? Eating bacon and drinking coffee with one of your oldest friends?"

"Sleeping with one of my oldest friends. It was stupid. We never should've done it."

She just stood there, her expression growing waxen, and as the color drained from her face, he felt something even more critical being scraped from his chest, like he was being hollowed out.

"It's a little late for that," she pointed out.

"Well, it isn't too late to start over."

"Chase…"

"It was fun. But, honestly, we accomplished everything we needed to. There's no reason to get dramatic about it. We agreed that we weren't going to let it affect our friendship. And it…it just isn't working for me."

"It was working fine for you last night."

"Well, that was last night, Anna. Don't be so needy."

She drew back as though she had been slapped and he wanted to punch his own face for saying such a thing. For hitting her where he knew it would hurt. And he waited. Waited for her to grow prickly. For her to retreat behind the walls. For her to get angry and start insulting him. For her to end all of this in fire and brimstone as she scorched the earth in an attempt to disguise the naked pain that was radiating from her right now.

He knew she would. Because that was how it went. If he pushed far enough, then she would retreat.

She closed the distance between them, cupping his face, meeting his eyes directly. And he waited for the blow. "But I feel needy. So what am I going to do about that?"

He couldn't have been more shocked than if she had reached up and slapped him. "What?"

"I'm needy. Or maybe…wanty? I'm both." She took a deep breath. "Yes, I'm both. I want more. Not less. And this is… This is the moment where we make decisions, right? Well, I've decided that I want to move forward with this. I don't want to go back. I can't go back."

"Anna," he said, her name scraping his throat raw.

"Chase," she said, her own voice a whisper in response.

"We can't do this," he said.

He needed the Anna he knew to come to his rescue now. To laugh it all off. To break this tension. To say that it didn't matter. To wave her hand and say it was all whatever and they could forget it. But she wasn't doing that.

She was looking at him, her green eyes completely earnest, vulnerability radiating from her face. "We need to do this. Because I love you."

Anna could tell that her words had completely stunned Chase. Fair enough, they had shocked her just as much. She didn't know where all of this was coming from. This strength. This bravery.

Except that last night's conversation kept echoing in her mind. When she had told him about her mother. When she had told him about how she always regretted not closing the distance between them. Always regretted not taking the chance.

That was the story of her entire life. She had, from the time she was a child, refused to make herself vulnerable. Refused to open herself up to injury. To pain. So she pretended she didn't care. She pretended nothing mattered. She did that every time her father ignored her, every time he forgot an important milestone in her life. She had done it the first time she'd ever had sex with a guy and it had made her feel something. Rather than copping to that, rather than dealing with it, she had mocked him.

All of her inner workings were a series of walls and shields, carefully designed to keep the world from hitting the terrible, needy things inside of her. Designed to keep herself from realizing they were there. But she couldn't do it anymore. She didn't want to do it anymore. Not with Chase. She didn't want to look back and wonder what could have been.

She wanted more. She needed more. Pride be damned.

"I do," she said, nodding. "I love you."

"You can't."

"I'm pretty sure I can. Since I do."

"No," he said, the word almost desperate.

"No, Chase, I really do. I mean, I have loved you since

I was fifteen years old. And intermittently thought you were hot. But mostly, I just loved you. You've been my friend, my best friend. I needed you. You've been my emotional support for a long time. We do that for each other. But things changed in the past few days. You're my…everything." Her voice broke on that last word. "This isn't sex and friendship, it isn't two different things, this is all the things, combined together to make something so big that it fills me completely. And I don't have room inside my chest for shields and protection anymore. Not when all that I am just loves you."

"I can't do this," he bit out, stepping away from her.

"I didn't ask if you could do this. This isn't about you, not right now. Yes, I would like you to love me, too, but right now this is just about me saying that I love you. Telling you. Because I don't ever want to look back and think that maybe you didn't know. That maybe if I had said something, it could have been different." She swallowed hard, battling tears. "I don't know what's wrong with me. Unless it's a movie, I almost never cry, but you're making me cry a lot lately."

"I'm only going to make you cry more," he said. "Because I don't know how to do this. I don't know how to love somebody."

"Bull. You've loved me perfectly, just the way I needed you to for fifteen years. The way that you take care of this place, the way that you care for Sam… Don't tell me that you can't love."

"Not this kind. Not this… Not this."

"I'm closing the gap," she said, pressing on, even though she could see that this was a losing battle. She was charging in anyway, sword held high, chest exposed. She was giving it her all, fighting even though she knew she wasn't going to walk away unscathed. "I'm not going to wonder what would've happened if I'd just been brave enough to do it. I would rather cut myself open and bleed out. I would rather risk my heart than wonder. So I'm just going to say it. Stop being such a coward and love me."

He took another step back from her and she felt that gap she was so desperate to close widening. Watched as her greatest fear started to play out right before her eyes. "I just… I don't."

"You don't or you won't?"

"At the end of the day, the distinction doesn't really matter. The result is the same."

She felt like she was having an out-of-body experience. Like she was floating up above, watching herself get rejected. There was nothing she could do. She couldn't stop it. Couldn't change it. Couldn't shield herself.

It was…horrible. Gut-wrenching. Destructive. Freeing.

Like watching a tsunami racing to shore and deciding to surrender to the wave rather than fight it. Yeah, it would hurt like hell. But it was a strange, quiet space. Past fear, past hope. All she could hear was the sound of her heart beating.

"I'm going to go," she said, turning away from him. "You can have the bacon."

She had been willing to risk herself, but she wouldn't stand there and fall apart in front of him. She would fall apart, but dammit, it would be on her own time.

"Stay and eat," he said.

She shook her head. "No. I can't stay."

"Are we going to… Are we going to go to the gala together still?"

"No!" She nearly shouted the word. "We are not going to go together. I need to… I need to think. I need to figure this out. But I don't think things can be the same anymore."

It was his turn to close the distance between them. He grabbed hold of her arms, drawing her toward him, his expression fierce. "That was not part of the deal. It was friends plus benefits, remember? And then in the end we could just stop with the benefits and go back to the friendship."

"We can't," she said, tears falling down her cheeks. "I'm sorry. But we can't."

"What the hell?" he ground out.

"We can't because I'm all in. I'm not going to sit back and pretend that it didn't really matter. I'm not going to go and hide these feelings. I'm not going to shrug and say it doesn't really matter if you love me or not. Because it does. It's everything. I have spent so many years not wanting. Not trying. Hiding how much I wanted to be accepted, hiding how desperately I wanted to try to look beautiful, how badly I wanted to be able to be both a mechanic and a woman. Hiding how afraid I was of ending up alone. Hiding under a blanket and watching old movies. Well, I'm done. I'm not hiding any of it anymore. And you know what? Nothing's going to hurt after this." She jerked out of his hold and started to walk toward the front door.

"You're not leaving in that."

She'd forgotten she wasn't exactly dressed. "Sure I am. I'm just going to drive straight home. Anyway, it's not your concern. Because I'm not your concern anymore."

The terror that she felt screaming through her chest was reflected on his face. Good. He should be afraid. This was the most terrifying experience of her life. She knew how horrible it was to lose a person you cared for. Knew what kind of void that left. And she knew that after years it didn't heal. She knew, too, you always felt the absence. She knew that she would always feel his. But she needed more. And she wasn't afraid to put it all on the line. Not now. Not after everything they had been through. Not after everything she had learned about herself. Chase was the one who had told her she needed more confidence.

Well, she had found it. But there was a cost.

Or maybe this was just the cost of loving. Of caring,

deeply and with everything she had, for the first time in so many years.

She strode across the property, not caring that she was wearing nothing more than his T-shirt, rage pouring through her. And when she arrived back at the shop she grabbed her purse and her keys, making her way to the truck. When she got there, Chase was standing against the driver's-side door. "Don't leave like this."

"Do you love me yet?"

He looked stricken. "What do you want me to say?"

"You know what I want you to say."

"You want me to lie?"

She felt like he had taken a knife and stabbed her directly through the heart. She could barely breathe. Could barely stand straight. This was… This was her worst fear come true. To open herself up so completely, to make herself so entirely vulnerable and to have it all thrown back in her face.

But in that moment, she recognized that she was untouchable from here on out. Because there was nothing that could ever, ever come close to this pain. Nothing that could ever come close to this risk.

How had she missed this before? How had she missed that failure could be such a beautiful, terrible, freeing experience?

It was the worst. Absolutely the worst. But it also broke chains that had been binding her for years. Because if someone had asked her what she was so afraid of, this would have been the answer. And she was in it. Living it. Surviving it.

"I love you," she repeated. "This is your chance. Listen to me, Chase McCormack, I am giving you a chance. I'm giving you a chance to stop being so afraid. A chance to walk out of the darkness. We've walked through it together for a long time. So I'm asking you now to walk out of it with me. Please."

He backed away from the truck, his jaw tense, a muscle there twitching.

"Coward," she spat as he turned and walked away from her. Walked away from them. Walked back into the damned darkness.

And she got in her truck and started the engine, driving away from him, driving away from the things she wanted most in the entire world.

She didn't cry until she got home. But then, once she did, she was afraid she wouldn't stop.

Fourteen

She was going to lose the bet. That was the safest thought in Anna's head as she stood in her bedroom the night of the charity event staring at the dress that was laid across her bed.

She was going to have to go there by herself. And thanks to the elaborate community theater production of their relationship everyone would know that they had broken up, since Chase wouldn't be with her. She almost laughed.

She was facing her fears all over the place, whether she wanted to or not.

Facing fears and making choices.

She wasn't going to be with Chase at the gala tonight. Wasn't going to win her money. But she had bought an incredibly slinky dress, and some more makeup. Including red lipstick. She had done all of that for him. Though in many ways it was for her, too. She had wanted that experience. To go, to prove that she was grown-up. To prove that she had transcended her upbringing and all of that.

She frowned. Was she really considering dressing differently just because she wasn't going to be with Chase?

Screw that. He might have filleted her heart and cooked it like those hideous charred Brussels sprouts cafés tries to pass off as a fancy appetizer, but he *wasn't* going to take his lessons from her. She had learned confidence. She had learned that she was stronger than she thought. She had learned that she was beautiful. And how to care. Like everything inside her had been opened up, for better or for worse. But she would never go back. No matter how bad it hurt, she wouldn't go back.

So she wouldn't go back now, either.

As she slipped the black dress over her curves, laboring over the makeup on her face and experimenting with the hairstyle she had seen online, she could only think how much harder it was to care about things. All of these things. It had been so much easier to embrace little pieces of herself. To play the part of another son for her father and throw herself into activities that made him proud, ignoring her femininity so that she never made him uncomfortable.

All of these moments of effort came at a cost. Each minute invested revealing more and more of her needs. To be seen. To be approved of.

But there were so many other reasons she had avoided this. Because this—she couldn't help but think as she looked in the mirror—looked a lot like trying. It looked a lot like caring. That was scary. It was hard.

Being rejected when you had given your best effort was so much worse than being rejected when you hadn't tried at all.

This whole being-a-woman thing—a whole woman who wanted to be with a man, who loved a man—it was hard. And it hurt.

She looked at her reflection, her eyes widening. Thanks to the smoky eye shadow her green eyes glowed, her lips looking extra pouty with the dark red color on them. She looked like one of the old screen legends she loved so much. Very Elizabeth Taylor, really.

This was her best effort. And yes, it was only a dress, and this was just looks, but it was symbolic.

She was going to lay it all on the line, and maybe people would laugh. Because the tractor mechanic in a ball gown was too ridiculous for words. But she would take the risk. And she would take it alone.

She picked up the little clutch purse that was sitting on her table. The kind of purse she'd always thought was impractical, because who wanted a bag you had to hold in your hand all night? But the salesperson at the department store had told her it went with her dress, and that altogether she looked flawless, and Anna had been in desperate need of flattery. So here she was with a clutch.

It *was* impractical. But she *did* look great.

Of course, Chase wouldn't be there to see it. She felt her eyes starting to fill with tears and she blinked, doing her best to hold it all back. She was not going to smear her makeup. She had already put it all out there for him. She would be damned if she undid all this hard work for him, too.

With that in mind, Anna got into her truck and drove herself to the ball.

"Hey, jackass," Sam shouted from across the shop. "Are you going to finish with work anytime today?"

Okay, so maybe Chase had thrown himself into work with a little more vehemence than was strictly necessary since Anna had walked out of his life.

Anna. Anna had walked out of his life. Over something as stupid as love.

If love was so stupid, it wouldn't make your insides tremble like you were staring down a black bear.

He ignored his snarky internal monologue. He had been

doing a lot of that lately. So many arguments with himself as he pounded iron at the forge. That was, when he wasn't arguing with Sam. Who was getting a little bit tired of him, all things considered.

"Do I look like I'm finished?" he shouted back.

"It's nine o'clock at night."

"That's amazing. When did you learn to tell time?"

"I counted on my fingers," Sam said, wandering deeper into the room. "So, are we just going to pretend that Anna didn't run out of your house wearing only a T-shirt the other morning?"

"I'm going to pretend that my older brother doesn't Peeping Tom everything that happens in my house."

"We live on the same property. It's bound to happen. I was on my way here when I saw her leaving. And you chasing after her. So I'm assuming you did the stupid thing."

"I told her that I couldn't be in a relationship with her." That was a lie. He had done so much more than that. He had torn both of their hearts out and stomped them into the ground. Because Sam was right, he was an idiot. But he had made a concerted effort to be a safe idiot.

How's that working for you?

"Right. Why exactly?"

"Look, the sage hermit thing is a little bit tired. You don't have a social life, I don't see you with a wife and children, so maybe you don't hang out and lecture me."

"Isn't tonight that thing?" Sam seemed undeterred by Chase's rudeness.

"What thing?"

"The charity thing that you were so intent on using to get investors. Because the two of us growing our family business and restoring the former glory of our hallowed ancestors is so important to you. And exploiting my artistic ability for your financial gain."

"Change of plans." He grunted, moving a big slab of iron

that would eventually be a gate to the side. "I'm just going to keep working. We'll figure this out without schmoozing."

"Who are you and what have you done with my brother?"

"Just shut up. If you can't do anything other than stand there looking vaguely amused at the fact that I'm going through a personal crisis, then you can go straight to hell without passing Go or collecting two hundred dollars."

"I'm not going to be able to afford Park Place anyway, because you aren't out there getting new investors."

"I'm serious, Sam," Chase shouted, throwing his hammer down on the ground. "It's all fine for you because you hold everyone at a distance."

Sam laughed. The bastard. "*I* hold everyone at a distance. What do you think you do? What do you think your endless string of one-night stands is?"

"You think I don't know? You think I don't know that it's an easy way to get some without ever having to have a conversation? I'm well aware. But I don't need you standing over there so entertained by the fact that..."

"That you actually got your heart broken?"

Chase didn't have anything to say to that. Every single word in his head evaporated like water against molten metal. He had nothing to say to that because his heart was broken. But Anna wasn't responsible. It was his own fault.

And the only reason his heart was broken was because he...

"Do you know what I said to Dad the day that he died?"

Sam froze. "No."

No, he didn't. Because they had never talked about it. "The last thing I ever said to him was that I couldn't wait to get away from here. I told him I wasn't going to pound iron for the rest of my life. I was going to get away and go to college. Make something real out of myself. Like this wasn't real."

"I didn't realize."

"No. Because I didn't tell you. Because I never told anybody. But that's why I needed to fix this. It's why I wanted to expand this place."

"So it isn't really to harness my incredible talent?"

"I don't even know what it's for anymore. To what? To make up for what I said to a dead man. And for promises that I made at his grave… He can't hear me. That's the worst thing."

Sam stuffed his hands in his pockets. "Is that the only reason you're still here?"

"No. I love it here. I really do. I had to get older. I had to put some of my own sweat into this place. But now…I get it. I do. And I care about it because I care about it, not just because they cared about it. Not just because it's a legacy, but because it's worth saving. But…"

"I still remember that day. I mean, I don't just remember it," Sam said, "it's like it just happened yesterday. That feeling… The whole world changing. Everything falling right down around us. That's as strong in my head now as it was then."

"How many times can you lose everything?" Chase asked, making eye contact with his brother. "Anna is everything. Or she could be. It was easy when she was just a friend. But…I saw her in my house the other morning cooking me breakfast, wearing my T-shirt. For a second she made me feel like…like that house was our house, and she could be my…my everything."

"I wouldn't even know what that looked like for me, Chase. If you find that…grab it."

"And if I lose it?"

"You'll have no one to blame but yourself."

Chase thought back to the day his parents died. That was a kind of pain he hadn't even known existed. But, as guilty as he had felt, as many promises as he had made at his father's grave site, he couldn't blame himself for their death. It had been an accident. That was the simple truth.

But if he lost Anna now… Pushing her away hadn't been an accident. It was in his control. Fully and absolutely. And if he lost her, then it was on him.

He thought of her face as she had turned away from him, as she had gotten into her truck.

She had trusted him. His prickly Anna had trusted him with her feelings. Her vulnerability. A gift that he had never known her to give to anybody. And he had rejected it. He was no better than he had been as an angry sixteen-year-old, hurtling around the curves of the road that had destroyed his family, daring it to take him, too.

Anna, who had already endured the rejection of a mother, the silent rejection of who she was from her father, had dared to look him in the face and risk his rejection, too.

"I'll do it," Sam said, his voice rough.

"What?"

"I'm going to start…pursuing the art thing to a greater degree. I want to help. You missed this party tonight and I know it mattered to you…"

"But you hate change," Chase reminded him.

"Yeah," Sam said. "But I hate a lot of things. I have to do them anyway."

"We're still going to have to meet with investors."

"Yeah," Sam replied, stuffing his hands in his pockets. "I can help with that. You're right. This is why you're the brains and I'm the talent."

"You're a glorified blacksmith, Sam," Chase said, trying to keep the tone light because if he went too deep now he might just fall apart.

"With talent. Beyond measure," Sam said. "At least my brother has been telling me that for years."

"Your brother is smart." Though he currently felt anything but.

Sam shrugged. "Eh. Sometimes." He cleared his throat. "You discovered you cared about this place too late to ever let Dad know. That's sad. But at least Dad knew you cared about him. You know he never doubted that," Sam said. "But, damn, bro, don't leave it too late to let Anna know you care about her."

Chase looked at his brother, who was usually more cynical than he was wise, and couldn't ignore the truth ringing in his words.

Anna was the best he'd ever had. And had been for the past fifteen years of his life. Losing her…well, that was just a stupid thing to allow.

But the thing that scared him most right now was that it might already be too late. That he might have broken things beyond repair.

"And if it is too late?" he asked.

"Chase, you of all people know that when something is forged in fire it comes out the other side that much stronger." His brother's expression was hard, his dark eyes dead serious. "This is your fire. You're in it now. If you let it cool, you lose your chance. So I suggest you get your ass to wherever Anna is right now and you work at fixing this. It's either that or spend your life as a cold, useless hunk of metal that never became a damn thing."

It had not gone as badly as she'd feared. It hadn't gone perfectly, of course, but she had survived. The lowest point had been when Wendy Maxwell, who was still angry with Anna over the whole Chase thing, had wandered over to her and made disparaging comments about last season's colors and cuts, all the while implying that Anna's dress was somehow below the height of fashion. Which, whatever. She had gotten the dress on clearance, so it probably was. Anna might care about looking nice, but she didn't give a rat's ass about fashion.

She gave a couple of rat's asses about what had happened next.

Where's Chase?

Her newfound commitment to honesty and emotions had compelled her to answer honestly.

We broke up. I'm pretty upset about it.

The other woman had been in no way sympathetic and had in fact proceeded to smug all over the rest of the conversation. But she wasn't going to focus on the low.

The highs had included talking to several people whom she was going to be working with in the future. And getting two different phone numbers. She had made conversation. She had felt…like she belonged. And she didn't really think it had anything to do with the dress. Just with her. When you had already put everything out there and had it rejected, what was there to fear beyond that?

She sighed as she pulled into her driveway, straightening when she saw that there was a truck already there.

Chase's truck.

She put her own into Park, killing the engine and getting out. "What are you doing here, McCormack?" She was furious now. She was all dressed up, wearing her gorgeous dress, and she had just weathered that party on her own, and now he was here. She was going to punch his face.

Chase was sitting on her porch, wearing well-worn jeans and a tight black T-shirt, his cowboy hat firmly in place. He stood up, and as he began to walk toward her, Anna felt a raindrop fall from the sky. Because of course. He was here to kick her while she was down, almost certainly, and it was going to rain.

Thanks, Oregon.

"I came to see you." He stopped, looking her over, his jaw slightly slack. "I'm really glad that I did."

"Stop checking me out. You don't get to look at me like that. I did not put this dress on for you."

"I know."

"No, you don't know. I put this dress on for me. Because I wanted to look beautiful. Because I didn't care if anybody thought I was pretty enough, or if I'm not fashionable enough for Wendy the mule-faced ex-cheerleader. I did it because I cared. I do that now. I care. For me. Not for you."

She started to storm past him, the raindrops beginning to fall harder, thicker. He grabbed her arm and stopped her, twirling her toward him. "Don't walk away. Please."

"Give me a reason to stop walking."

"I've been doing a lot of thinking. And hammering."

"Real hammering, or is this some kind of a euphemism to let me know you're lonely?"

"Actual hammering. I didn't feel like I deserved anything else. Not after what happened."

"You don't. You don't deserve to masturbate ever again."

"Anna…"

"No," she said. "I can't do this. I can't just have a little taste of you. Not when I know what we can have. We can be everything. At first it was like you were my friend, but also we were sleeping together. And I looked at you as two different men. Chase, my friend. And Chase, the guy who was really good with his hands. And his mouth, and his tongue. You get the idea." She swallowed hard, her throat getting tight. "But at some point…it all blended together. And I can't separate it anymore. I just can't. I can't pull the love that I feel for you out of my chest and keep the friendship. Because they're all wrapped up in each other. And they've become the same thing."

"It's all or nothing," he said, his voice rough.

"Exactly."

He sighed heavily. "That's what I was afraid of."

"I'm sorry if you came over for a musical and a look at my porcupine pajamas. But I can't do it."

He tightened his hold on her, pulling her closer. "I knew it was going to be all or nothing."

"I can even understand why you think that might not be fair—"

"No. When you told me you loved me, I knew it was everything. Or nothing. That was what scared me so much. I have known… For a lot of years, I've realized that you were one of the main supports of my entire life. I knew you were one of the things that kept me together after my parents died. One of the only things. And I knew that if I ever lost you…it might finish me off completely."

"I'm sorry. But I can't live my life as your support."

"I know. I'm not suggesting that you do. It's just…when we started sleeping together, I had the same realization. That we weren't going to be able to separate the physical from the emotional, from our friendship. That it wasn't as simple as we pretended it could be. When I came downstairs and saw you in my kitchen…I saw the potential for something I never thought I could have."

"Why didn't you think you could have that?"

"I was too afraid. Tragedy happens to other people, Anna. Until it happens to you. And then it's like…the safety net is just gone. And everything you never thought you could be touched by is suddenly around every corner. You realize you aren't special. You aren't safe. If I could lose both my parents like that…I could lose anybody."

"You can't live that way," she said, her heart crumpling. "How in the world can you live that way?"

"You live halfway," he said. "You let yourself have a little bit of things, and not all of them. You pour your commitment into a place. Your passion into a job, into a goal of restoring a family name when your family is already gone. So you can't disappoint them even if you do fail." He took a deep breath. "You keep the best woman you know as a friend, because if she ever became more, your feelings for her could consume you. Anna… If I lost you…I would lose everything."

She could only stand there, looking at him, feeling like the earth was breaking to pieces beneath her feet. "Why did you—"

"I wanted to at least see it coming." He lowered his head, shaking it slowly. "I was such an idiot. For a long time. And afraid. I think it's impossible to go through tragedy like I did, like we did, and not have it change you. I'm not sure it's even possible to escape it doing so much as defining you. But you can choose how. It was so easy for me to see how you protected yourself. How you shielded yourself. But I didn't see that I was doing the same thing."

"I didn't know," she said, feeling stupid. Feeling blind.

"Because I didn't tell you." He reached up, drawing his thumb over her cheekbone, his expression so empty, so sad. Another side of Chase she hadn't seen very often. But it was there. It had always been there, she realized that now. "But I'm telling you now. I'm scared. I've been scared for a long time. And I've made a lot of promises to ghosts to try to atone for stupid things I said when my parents were alive. But I've been too afraid to make promises to the people that are actually still in my life. Too afraid to love the people that are still here. It's easier to make promises to ghosts, Anna. I'm done with that.

"You are here," he said, cupping her face now, holding her steady. "You're with me. And I can have you as long as I'm not too big an idiot. As long as you still want to have me. You put yourself out there for me, and I rejected you. I'm so sorry. I know what that cost you, Anna, because I know you. And please understand I didn't reject you because it wasn't enough. Because you weren't enough. It's because you were too much, and I wasn't enough. But I'm going to do my best to be enough for you now. Now and forever."

She could hardly believe what she was hearing, could hardly believe that Chase was standing there making declarations to her. The kind that sounded an awful lot like love. The kind that sounded an awful lot like exactly what she wanted to hear. "Is this because I'm wearing a dress?"

"No." He chuckled. "You could be wearing coveralls. You could be wearing nothing. Actually, I think I like you best in nothing. But whatever you're wearing, it wouldn't change this. It wouldn't change how I feel. Because I love you in every possible way. As my friend, as my lover. I love you in whatever you wear, a ball gown or engine grease. I love you working on tractors and trying to explain to me how an engine works and watching musicals."

"But do you love my porcupine pajamas?" she asked, her voice breaking.

"I'm pretty ambivalent about your porcupine pajamas, I'm not going to lie. But if they're a nonnegotiable part of the deal, then I can adjust."

She shook her head. "They aren't nonnegotiable. But I probably will irritate you with them." Then she sobbed, unable to hold her emotions back any longer. She wrapped her arms around his neck, burying her face in his skin, breathing his scent in. "Chase, I love you so much. Look what we were protecting ourselves from."

He laughed. "When you put it that way, it seems like we were being pretty stupid."

"Fear is stupid. And it's strong."

He tightened his hold on her. "It isn't stronger than this."

Not stronger than fifteen years of friendship, than holding each other through grief and pleasure, laughter and pain.

When she had pulled up and seen his truck here, Anna Brown had murder on her mind. And now, everything was different.

"Remember when you promised you were going to make me a woman?" she asked.

"Right. I do. You laughed at me."

"Yes, I did." She stretched up on her toes and kissed his lips. "Chase McCormack, I'm pretty sure you did make me a woman. Maybe not in the way you meant. But you made me feel…like a whole person. Like I could finally put together all the parts of me and just be me. Not hide any of it anymore."

He closed his eyes, pressing his forehead against hers. "I'm glad, Anna. Because you sure as hell made me a man. The man that I want to be, the man that I need to be. I can't change the past, and I can't live in it anymore, either."

"Good. Then I think we should go ahead and make ourselves a future."

"Works for me." He smiled. "I love you. You're everything."

"I love you, too." It felt so good to say that. To say it and not be afraid. To show her whole heart and not hold anything back.

"I bet that I can make you say you love me at least a hundred more times tonight. I bet I can get you to say it every day for the rest of our lives."

She smiled, taking his hand and walking toward the house, not caring about the rain. "I bet you can."

He led her inside, leaving a trail of clothes in the hall behind them, leaving her beautiful dress on the floor. She didn't care at all.

"And I bet—" he wrapped his arm around her waist, then laid her down on the bed "—tonight I can make you scream."

"I'll take that bet," she said, wrapping her legs around his hips.

And that was a bet they both won.

* * * * *

"Things are never going to be strictly business between us, Gabi.

The past is always going to be there along with that one question."

Don't ask.

Don't do it.

"What question?"

Kingsley leaned in even closer, and she had to fight the urge to bolt away from him. But she wouldn't let him know he was getting to her. She had to stand firm. He was just a man.

No.

He was more than a man. He was her own personal demon. One that she hadn't exorcised because she'd never been able to see him as anything other than a hot fantasy. They'd barely dated before they'd slept together, and then everything had fallen apart.

She couldn't let him continue to dominate every moment they had together.

"If that one night together was a fluke," he said.

He leaned in closer. So close that she'd barely have to incline her head for their lips to brush.

* * *

His Baby Agenda
is part of Mills & Boon Desire's No. 1 bestselling series, Billionaires and Babies: Powerful men… wrapped around their babies' little fingers

HIS BABY AGENDA

BY

KATHERINE GARBERA

First Published in Great Britain 2016
By Mills & Boon, an imprint of HarperCollins*Publishers*
1 London Bridge Street, London, SE1 9GF

ISBN: 978-0-263-91855-7

51-0416

Our policy is to use papers that are natural, renewable and recyclable products and made from wood grown in sustainable forests. The logging and manufacturing processes conform to the legal environmental regulations of the country of origin.

Printed and bound in Spain
by CPI, Barcelona

USA TODAY bestselling author **Katherine Garbera** is a two-time MAGGIE® Award winner who has written more than seventy books. A Florida native who grew up to travel the globe, Katherine now makes her home in the Midlands of the UK with her husband, two children and a very spoiled miniature dachshund. Visit Katherine on the web at www.katherinegarbera.com, or catch up with her on Facebook and Twitter.

This book is dedicated to Courtney and Lucas.
No mother could be prouder of her children
than I am of you.

Thank you to my wonderful editor, Charles,
for his insights and knowing the right questions
to ask in order to make my manuscripts better.
Thank you also to my dear friend Eve Gaddy,
who is always available to chat about my plot
when I run into problems.

One

The intercom buzzed and Gabriella de la Cruz put down her cup of tea to pick up the phone. "Yes, Melissa?"

"There is someone here to see you," her assistant said. To Gabi's ears Melissa sounded excited, the way she'd been that time she'd won five hundred dollars on a scratch-off lottery card. She could only guess that another one of the celebrities Melissa was always cyberstalking had dropped by looking for a nanny.

Gabi had started her nanny service seven years ago after a very successful run as a live-in nanny for the Hollywood director Malcolm Jeffers. Mal and his wife had sung Gabi's praises and suggested she start her own business when their kids were old enough to no longer need a nanny.

"I have an appointment in thirty minutes," Gabi said. "Can you ask them to come back?"

"I think you'll want to see *him*," Melissa said.

Doubtful. She was busy; it seemed as though everyone wanted something from her at this time of year. Her parents wanted her to make more time for them and come over to their place this weekend. Her clients were anxious about summer and instead of dealing with the nannies who worked in their homes year-round, they were calling her about activities, vacations and travel documents. Her clientele couldn't just nip down to Disneyland or Legoland for the weekend. They all wanted to go someplace exotic, which was a big headache.

"Who is it?" she asked at last. Melissa wasn't going to just tell him to go away. And Gabi needed to get back to writing the column she was working on for a national parenting magazine.

"It's Kingsley Buchanan. The former NFL quarterback, agent to the best athletes in the world."

Kingsley.

Of course when she was having a bad day he'd have to walk back into her life. Heck, even just his name sent a shiver through her. She wanted to pretend it was one of dread, but her pulse had picked up and she'd sat up a little straighter.

"I don't have the time," she said, hanging up the phone.

Let's face it; she didn't owe him more than that. He'd been her first lover—well, one-night stand might be more accurate given that he'd left her in the morning and been arrested before lunch. She'd only been alone with him one time after that. An ill-fated jailhouse visit when he'd told her she'd been naive to think there was more between them than what she'd gotten.

Idiot.

She wasn't sure if she meant him or herself.

Why was he here?

Why did she care?

She reached up to push her hair behind her ear and then pulled her laptop closer, staring at the screen and pretending she was reading the email her mother had sent about the first communion of her cousin Guillermo's daughter in Spain this summer. But she wasn't.

Why was Kingsley here?

Her door opened without a knock and she glanced up to see broad shoulders filling the doorway. She caught her breath. Of course she'd seen him on television in the past ten years—just occasionally—before she quickly changed the channel. But damn, time had been good to him.

His thick dark brown hair, longer on the top, was artfully styled; it must have had some sort of product in it to keep it in place. His eyes were still blue, but in her mind they seemed icier than they had been in college. His jaw was hard, square and stubbornly set, his beard neatly trimmed.

"Can I help you?"

"That's why I'm here," he said, walking into the room as if he owned it, closing the door behind him.

"I believe I asked Melissa to schedule you an appointment for later in the week. I'm booked solid."

"Surely you can make time for an old friend," he said.

But there was nothing friendly in his manner as he walked over to her desk and perched his hip on the edge of it. He did casual the way a tiger hunting its prey did it. She tried to convince herself she bore no resemblance to a mouse as she looked up at him.

Take control.

That was what she'd learned after years of dealing with recalcitrant parents and children.

She stood up and held her hand out to him. Time to put this on a business footing. She'd shake his hand and walk him back to the door and then gently tell him goodbye.

Solid plan.

She was a genius.

"It's wonderful to see you again, Kingsley. But I'm afraid I really don't have time this morning."

He took her hand in his but didn't shake it. He held it loosely, stroking his thumb over her knuckles and making goose bumps spread up her arm. His amused look as she pulled her hand free made her want to do something to jar him.

But she wasn't young and impulsive. He'd been the one to show her that being impetuous was the path to disaster. She stepped away from him.

"Why are you here?" she asked at last. "I think we've said all that needed to be said."

"I'm looking for a nanny," he said.

"I'm afraid my business only caters to real children, not those stuck in men's bodies."

He gave a bark of laughter and shook his head. "I'd forgotten that there was always a little edge to you."

He had no idea.

"You don't know me," she said carefully. "And really, I can see we have nothing further to discuss, so if you wouldn't mind leaving."

"But I would mind," he said. "I'm not one of your naughty clients who you can *firmly control with your calm tones*."

She tipped her head to the side to study him. How

did he know about her techniques? She'd written those very words last month in her column. Why was he here?

"For the last time, Kingsley, why are you here?"

"I told you, Gabriella, I need you."

The way he said her name, letting it roll off his tongue as his tone deepened, weakened her resolve to get him out of her office quickly. And he'd said he needed her...the words she'd been waiting ten years to hear.

"Too bad. I don't want to give the impression of being a clingy woman who doesn't know when a lover has had enough."

Kingsley had known coming back to California would be difficult, but he'd never shied away from obstacles. Experience had taught him that anything that didn't kill him made him stronger. He knew it was a cliché, but a decade ago he'd spent a rough six months being treated as a murderer before being cleared of charges. Rumors had swirled that his father had bought off the grand jury, but in the end there was no evidence and they'd had to let both him and the other suspect—his best friend, Hunter Carruthers—go. But that reputation had followed him into the NFL and he'd always been considered dangerous by his teammates and a publicity liability by his coaches and managers.

Over the years he'd learned to bury his emotions, beneath a layer of ice so that no one could rattle him. But all that seemed to be out the window now that he was in the same room as Gabi de la Cruz once again.

She'd grown into her beauty. Her caramel-colored hair was thick and long, falling past her shoulders in smooth waves. Her eyes were still deep brown, but instead of revealing every emotion she felt, they were cautious. She watched him warily—something he knew he deserved—as if he were about to pounce on her.

He'd be lying if he said she didn't still turn him on.

She'd always been different from other women, which was why he'd been quick to distance himself from her after Stacia Krushnik had been found dead. But that was the past. A past that really didn't concern Gabi, thanks to the heartless way he'd sent her from his life. He was back in California for revenge and he needed someone to keep his son protected from the shit storm that he suspected he and Hunter Carruthers were about to unleash.

"I'm not here for a lover, Gabi. I'm here because I need a nanny for my son."

"Your son?" she asked.

"Yes," he said. He'd followed her through the years via newspaper articles and online social media; it was a hit to his ego that she hadn't done the same. "Conner is three and desperately in need of a nanny."

He'd confused her.

Good. Finally, he felt as though the advantage was swinging back toward him.

She brushed past him; the subtle scent of her flowery perfume surrounded him as she sat down behind her desk. She reached for a piece of monogrammed paper and drew it toward her.

"Conner is three?" she asked. "What kind of nanny are you looking for?"

"You. I have spoken to Mal and he said you were the best. And I've read your parenting articles—I like your theories on child rearing."

"Thank you," she said, bowing her head slightly. "Why don't you have a seat while we discuss this?"

"I'm comfortable here," he said.

She gave him a tight smile. He bit the inside of his mouth to keep from smiling back. He was unnerving her. He liked it.

"Will your wife be part of the interview process for the nanny?" Gabi asked.

"She's dead."

"Oh," she said, looking up at him. "I'm sorry, Kingsley."

"It's okay," he said. "Conner doesn't remember her at all. It happened when he was six months old."

"What have you been doing for child care up to now?" she asked.

He'd been using his assistant, Peri, but she'd gotten married last month and was retiring. "My assistant. How soon can you start?"

"I can't."

"What?"

"I don't nanny anymore. I have a couple of nannies that are coming off assignments in the next week or so. I can set up some interviews for you, and I'd like to meet your son myself. Where is he?"

"With Hunter," Kingsley said. Hunter and he had been a great duo on the field in college, and after Stacia's death, Hunter had stopped playing football, being the second son of a privileged family. Hunter hadn't needed to work, so he had spent the past few years building his reputation as a playboy. Plus the stigma of being charged with the "Frat House Murder" hadn't helped.

"Um…we need to talk about that. He's got a wild reputation. I can't place one of my nannies in your home if he's going to be there."

"He won't be a problem," Kingsley said. "I don't want one of your nannies. I want you, Gabi."

"I can't."

"Why not?"

"I'm not in the field anymore."

"I'll make it worth your while," he said. If there was one thing he'd learned from his father, Jeb Buchanan, it was that everyone had a price. Many people believed his father had bought Kingsley's freedom and the silence of witnesses. But Jeb had a strong sense of justice and no one, not even his wayward younger son, could escape that. His father still wasn't convinced that Kingsley was innocent in Stacia's death.

But after Kingsley was done with his revenge, there would be no doubt as to who was responsible for her death.

"I can't be bought."

"No? What if I offered to fund the new playground you have been trying to get built?" he asked.

Gabi wouldn't do it for herself, but he remembered her soft heart and how she'd do anything for a good cause. He wondered if that had changed.

She chewed her lower lip and looked down at the paper in front of her.

It hadn't.

His gut was still right on the money when it came to this woman.

"We are talking a six-figure sum, Kingsley. Is my being a nanny to Conner worth that much?"

It was. He needed her to watch over his son and he needed her recollections of that party the night Stacia had died. Once he had her living under his roof, he'd be able to get the answers he needed.

There were certain parts of the night that didn't add up. And everyone he and Hunter had spoken to had a different version of the events. So whether it took six figures or nine, it didn't matter. He needed to put the ghosts of the past to rest. And Gabi was the only woman who could help him do that.

"Yes," he said. "I'll need you in my home by this evening. I've left my address with your assistant."

"I've agreed to be Conner's nanny, but that's it. I'm not living in," she said.

"For the amount I'm paying, I think you are," he said.

He stood up and starting walking to the door. He'd accomplished what he'd set out to do. It was time to get back to the rest of his day.

Arrogant bastard.

Gabi got up from her desk and dashed around in front of Kingsley before he could get to the door. She pressed her back against it and gave him a hard look.

She knew it was important to establish right this moment that he wasn't in charge. No matter how much it might seem otherwise.

"We're not finished yet."

"I can't imagine what else we have to discuss," he said.

He didn't stop as she'd thought he would. Instead he came right up until barely an inch of space separated them and put his hands on the door on either side of her head.

He surrounded her. She could see the flecks of green in his icy-blue eyes and the scar on his left eyebrow that she'd noticed the first time he'd kissed her. Her lips felt dry. Her breath got shallower and she wanted to smack herself in the forehead. *Don't react to him.*

This was Kingsley Buchanan—lover and leaver. Not a man she was interested in.

But her body said otherwise.

Every nerve inside her reacted to him as if she didn't

know he was bad news. As if she hadn't just agreed to live in his house… It was a deal with the devil.

Sure, she'd been battling with the county commissioners for the last eighteen months trying to get that park and playground built. And Kingsley's offer was too good to pass up. But he didn't own her. She had to stay in control.

Except his cologne smelled so good.

"We have a lot to discuss," she said. Her voice sounded thready and breathy to her own ears.

Ugh.

"Like what?"

"I'm not living in your house."

"Nonnegotiable."

She frowned at him.

"Everything is."

"Not that. I travel a lot with my job and I work from my home office. I need 24-7 care for Conner."

"I can't work 24-7 for you. I have to run this business," she said.

"I will give you an office in my home and if your office hours are flexible, I'm willing to work with your schedule to give you the time you need. But you must live in my house."

No, she thought. She couldn't do it. But there was something persuasive about him and she felt her resolve weakening. He was a client; she'd keep it all business.

"Okay. We can try it out. But if I feel like it's not working, then we will have to figure out something else."

"I'm sure it will work."

Of course he was.

"Was that all?" he asked.

All?

He leaned in closer and she felt the brush of his breath over her mouth. Her lips parted and she realized that she was never going to be all business with him. There was no way.

"No."

"No?"

"I need some resolution to the past," she said. "You can't be this close to me."

"You're the one blocking the door with your body."

She narrowed her eyes at him. He had a point, but he was still crowding her and he had been since he came into her office. "I mean it. Our arrangement is strictly business."

His left hand shifted on the door and she felt his fingers in her hair. Her scalp tingled and sensation spread slowly downward. "Things are never going to be strictly business between us, Gabi. The past is always going to be there along with that one question."

Don't ask.

Don't do it.

"What question?"

He leaned in even closer and she had to fight the urge to bolt away from him. But she wouldn't let him know he was getting to her. She had to stand firm. He was just a man.

No.

He was more than a man. He was her own personal demon. One that she hadn't exorcised because she'd never been able to see him as anything other than a hot fantasy. They'd barely dated before they'd slept together and then everything had fallen apart.

She couldn't let him continue to dominate every moment they had together.

"If that one night together was a fluke," he said.

He leaned in closer. So close that she'd barely have to incline her head for their lips to brush. Sure, she remembered their night together, but it had become hazy over the years, tinged with regret and anger. She wanted to take back something that she hadn't realized Kingsley had stolen until this moment, a part of her womanhood that he'd damaged when he'd left her.

She put her hands on his shoulders and went up on tiptoe, so they were eye to eye. He was impossible to read. He'd always been hard, but now there was a new layer of ice in his gaze. A new barrier that she couldn't see past.

For her own sanity, she had to keep this strictly business. She was twenty-eight and finally felt that she was getting her life on track. She wouldn't let a man like Kingsley derail that.

"Oh, I thought you meant if I'd still want you," she said, trying to turn the tables on him.

"Do you?"

She dashed to the side, ducking out from under his arm. "I've sort of outgrown bad boys."

"Have you?"

"All girls do when they grow up," she said. "Melissa will send over a contract. Good day, Kingsley."

Two

Kingsley wasn't sure if he'd won or lost the battle with Gabi. She'd always had the unique ability to throw him. Even in college before…everything had gone crazy, she'd rattled him. But the past ten years had changed him. And though he'd enjoyed flirting with her—hell, he was a red-blooded male, of course he enjoyed flirting with her—that wasn't why he was back in California, and he had to stay focused.

He got in his Porsche 911, driving a little over the speed limit as he headed to his new home. The mansion he'd purchased was perched on a cliff above the Pacific with a path to the beach that he intended to use frequently with his son. He'd been working hard—well, running from his past was more like it—since he'd left California. Now he was back and he knew one thing: he couldn't raise his son in a world where he had had to face that kind of stigma.

It was one thing that Stacia's death had left Kingsley mired in scandal. But he wouldn't let it touch Conner.

His phone rang, blasting out "Bad to the Bone." He hit the answer button on his hands free.

"What's up, Hunter? Is Conner okay?"

"He's fine, the little devil. I'm worn-out. I think he's got the makings of a running back," Hunter said. "Did she agree?"

Hunter wasn't the playboy the media made him out to be. Kingsley knew they'd still be best friends even if they hadn't been linked together in Stacia's murder. He was closer to Hunter than he was to his own brother.

"Yes, she did. I didn't mention anything about Stacia. I want to get Gabi out to my house so I can be subtle about the questioning," he said.

"Hey, it's your plan. I'm happy enough to let you set the pace. I just want to get some answers," Hunter said.

Hunter could barely remember the entire night. And that was a little worrying, since his friend hadn't been a big drinker in college. One theory they had was that someone had put a drug in Stacia's drink—she and Hunter had been dating—and that Hunter had ingested some of it over the course of the night.

"When will you be home? I've got a meeting with Tristan Sabine in forty-five minutes."

"I'll be there in twenty," Kingsley said. Tristan was one of the founders of a chain of nightclubs called Seconds. In fact, Gabi's cousin Gui was another owner. Hunter had recently purchased a franchise of the club and opened it in San Francisco, to much success.

"Sounds great," Hunter said. "I'm glad we're back here. It's way past time we got some answers and gave Stacia's ghost some peace."

And themselves, Kingsley thought. They'd never

been able to live with Stacia's murder or the fact that it had never really been solved.

He disconnected the call and concentrated on the traffic, but his mind wasn't really on the past or the drive. Gabi dominated his thoughts the same as she had back in college.

She'd changed.

Really, idiot?

But that was the best he could do. She had changed. It wasn't just maturing—it was more than that. There was a level of confidence that hadn't been in her at eighteen. A level of self-assurance that enabled her to stand her ground with him.

He admired that.

He wished…hell, there wasn't a day that had gone by in the past ten years that he hadn't regretted what he'd said when she'd come to see him in jail. Regretted it only insomuch as he knew he'd hurt her. He didn't regret that he'd gotten her out of the jailhouse before the press had descended. He'd kept her safe from the scandal that had rained down around him and Hunter.

But now…

The woman she was today could handle things that the girl she'd been hadn't been able to. That didn't mean he still wouldn't protect her. He had to get his revenge and keep Conner and Gabi from being hit with the fallout. That was going to take all of the skills he'd learned on and off the football field. Things such as faking out the rushers, keeping the press from seeing past his smile and definitely winning.

He pulled to a stop in the big circle drive in front of his house. The front door opened just as he shut off his car and stepped out of it.

Conner came running down the steps, laughing.

"Daddy!"

Kingsley scooped up his son and kissed the top of his head. Conner had Kingsley's own blue eyes, but Jade's reddish-blond hair.

"Get back here, imp," Hunter said, skidding to a halt in the doorway.

"Um, why was my son running outside?" Kingsley asked.

"'Cause he's spoiled," Hunter said.

"I am," Conner said.

Kingsley was pretty sure that Conner had no idea what spoiled meant, but he and Hunter were very close and Conner almost always agreed with his favorite "uncle."

"What's that got to do with anything?"

"Nothing. He's quick. I turned my back for a second..."

Kingsley laughed. His son had caught him like that as well. Hunter was right; he'd make a good running back one day. But only if Kingsley cleared up this mess with Stacia's murder. He didn't want Conner facing questions about his father in the pressroom someday.

Kingsley walked into the house carrying his son. He put him down when they were in the foyer.

"You heading out?" Kingsley asked.

"Yes. I'm going to stay at my place in Malibu for the next few weeks, but if you get any information I'll come back."

"Sounds good. I'll keep you posted. I've got Gabi moving in here and I think I should have something to go on soon."

"Good. The sooner we get to the bottom of the Stacia situation the better."

Hunter left and Kingsley watched his friend go until Conner tugged on his hand.

"Who's Stas?"

"An old friend of Daddy's. Good news, Con, we've got a new nanny coming to live with us."

"Like Peri?"

Nothing like Peri. For one thing, Kingsley had never gotten excited by the prospect of Peri living in his house. He tried to tell himself that he was only feeling that way because he could finally get to work on figuring out the past, but he knew it was lie.

He wanted more than that one night with Gabi. He wanted to know that what he remembered of their embrace had been real, and he wanted in his own mixed-up way to somehow make things up to her for their one-night stand.

Gabi paced her office for a few minutes after Kingsley left. She wasn't sure how it had happened but somehow she was back to being a nanny. A live-in nanny to a three-year-old she'd never met in the house of the only man she'd never been able to forget.

Ugh!

"Melissa, please draw up a contract for Mr. Buchanan," Gabi said as she walked into her assistant's office.

"I bet you're glad I let him in," Melissa said. "He is even hotter in person than he is on TV."

Yes, he was. There was no way a television could capture the force of his presence. But then, the meeting today hadn't taught her anything new.

"He did agree to fund the playground I've been lobbying for in town. And he wants me to start tonight."

"You? You don't work directly for clients anymore," Melissa said. "What happened in your office?"

This was what came of being too friendly with your

staff. Melissa felt comfortable asking her anything she wanted.

"We used to know each other," Gabi admitted. "He offered to fund the playground if I took charge of his son and worked out of his home. This is going to take a lot of effort between you and me to make this happen. Because for the amount he's paying—he wants me there today."

Melissa put her elbows on her desk, leaning forward. "Oh, my God. Did he make you an indecent proposal? Are you going to be his mistress?"

"What? No! Where do you get these ideas?"

"I read a lot and watch a lot of soap operas," Melissa said with a wink. "So no to the bargaining with your body?"

She shook her head. "Definitely no. Just the playground and the stipulation that I live and work from his house. Which means that you are going to have to run things at this office. Think you can handle it?"

"Yes. You know I can."

Gabi did know. "It'll mean a raise for you, and I'm thinking that you will be my assistant manager. We will probably need to hire another assistant for you."

"Thank you, Gabi. I won't let you down," Melissa said.

"I know you won't."

"I'm going to call the county commissioners and get an exact figure on the budget for the park. I want you to draw up our regular contract for a live-in nanny service and in place of the fees reference the addendum. I'll work on that."

"You said you have to be there tonight?"

Gabi kept her expression serene only after years of

training, but inside she grimaced. Kingsley had doubled her workload for the day. "Yes. If I send you the dimensions of my new office, will you order me some furniture?"

"Yes. Are you sure about this?" Melissa asked. "We still have our fund-raising plan to get the play area built. I think we could do it without you having to jump through hoops."

Gabi was grateful to have Melissa not just as her assistant but also as her friend. "It would take years to raise that kind of money. This is easier. Besides, I could use some new material for my parenting column. All of my experience is several years old now."

"Always look on the bright side?"

"It's worked so far," Gabi said.

She reentered her office and felt a little better about the encounter with Kingsley. Then she got down to business. She left a message for Rupert Green, the county commissioner who was her contact on the playground. Then she texted Kingsley asking for the dimensions of her office, which he immediately texted back, also assuring her that he would furnish the space. She almost told him that she would do it herself, but she still had to pack her office and her personal belongings so she decided to let him handle it.

She managed to stay busy enough the entire day not to allow herself to think until she was driving out to Kingsley's house. Butterflies danced in her stomach and she had that stupid tingling in her body that she knew was from excitement. How could she be excited?

Kingsley.

She knew it would be useless to deny it. They had unfinished business between them. Ten years might have passed, but when he'd walked into her office today she'd felt like a college freshman again, starstruck by her first sight of the handsome quarterback.

But she'd learned that the golden boy wasn't untouchable. So why…

She shook her head. Was it possible that she was still crushing on him? That Kingsley Buchanan still had a hold over her despite the way he'd treated her? Not just ten years ago but today, arrogantly waltzing back into her life and making her feel again.

Awakening desires and passions she'd shoved to the darkest part of her soul in an attempt to never be that vulnerable again.

She had to remember that. How exposed he'd made her feel. She was stronger now. She had to be.

And there was little Conner to think about. She knew next to nothing about the boy, only that he was three and that Kingsley had used some of her methods with the toddler.

Great.

She was doing the very thing she'd warned nannies not to do for years. Going in blind.

She could justify it to Melissa by saying Kingsley was funding a playground that an economically disadvantaged community desperately needed. She could justify it to her mom by saying that getting back in the field would give her a better perspective for running her business.

But justifying it to herself just felt hollow. Like a lie. As she pulled to a stop in front of Kingsley's Spanish-style mansion, she admitted that she was here for one reason and one reason alone.

Kingsley had asked and she'd been unable to say no.

* * *

Kingsley had tried to get furniture that mirrored the stuff he'd seen in Gabi's office earlier but it turned out some of her pieces, such as the settee, were one of a kind. So he'd had to settle for some substitutions. All in all he was happy with the stuff he'd managed to get here on such short notice.

He was working under the desk connecting the computer and printer cords while his son lay on the floor nearby coloring.

Seven years younger than his older brother, Kingsley had been an "accident." His parents had gone back to work and sort of moved into a new phase of their lives when he was born. He'd been left in the care of his nanny most of the time. And he wasn't complaining about that. But he'd never had much of a chance to just hang out with his father. Kingsley did his best to make sure that he and Conner did have plenty of time together.

"Daddy? How's this?" Conner brought a piece of copy paper that he'd been drawing on with his crayons over to him. The brightly colored scribbles were Conner's version of the view from their backyard. Kingsley had three of the images framed and hanging on his own office wall.

When he'd brought Conner into the office he was setting up for Gabi, his son had insisted on making her a picture—or rather, a "picter," as he said it.

"Looks good. I bet she'll love it."

Someone cleared her throat and Kingsley glanced up to see Gabi standing in the doorway. "The housekeeper let me in and told me where to find you."

He let his gaze skim over her from the floor up. She'd changed into a pair of white jeans that hugged her slim legs and a pretty turquoise blouse that was made out of some sort of flowing fabric. She had pulled her long caramel-colored hair back into a ponytail and wore a pair of flat sandals on her feet.

She squatted down, smiling at Conner. "Can I see your picture?"

"Yes."

He walked over to her with that toddler gait of his, sometimes speedy and a little unsteady. He handed her the photo and then went even closer, putting his hand on Gabi's knee as he pointed to the picture.

Kingsley swallowed as a rush of emotion he didn't want to define swamped him. Sometimes he got a punch of joy in the heart just watching Conner.

"This is the ocean and the sky. This is Daddy and Unca Hun."

"Unca Hun?"

"Hunter," Kingsley said.

"Of course. I'm Gabi," she said, turning her attention back to Conner. "I'm here to help your daddy take care of you."

"Like Peri."

Gabi glanced over at Kingsley and then turned back to the little boy. "Just like Peri. Did you help your daddy set up my office?"

He nodded and Gabi stood up, holding the paper loosely in her left hand. She held her right hand out to Conner.

Conner wasn't always good with strangers. There had been only a few people close to him since he'd been born. Pretty much Hunter and Peri. Then there were Kingsley's parents, who doted on Conner, but Jade's parents lived in Brazil and only saw Conner for a month each summer when they came to visit.

Kingsley took Gabi's hand and led her over to the desk. She looked at the surface, arching one eyebrow at him as she came to her monogrammed stationery.

"How did you do all this?"

"I have my ways," he said. He was pleased with himself because he'd surprised her. It was important to ensure that Gabi was happy here, because he needed her to watch over Conner. He'd even sort of justified it to Hunter by saying that he needed her recollections of the night that Stacia had died. But deep inside he knew he'd gone through all of this effort on her office and in her bedroom because he'd wanted to show off a little.

To let Gabi see the life he'd made for himself. To hopefully dispel the image she might have been carrying of him for all these years—the image of him in handcuffs behind a glass wall.

"Time for dinner, Conner," Kingsley said. "Let's go find Mrs. Tillman while Gabi gets settled into her office. I'll be back shortly to give you the tour."

She nodded. "I have some boxes in my car that I need to bring in."

"I'll help once I get Conner settled."

"Bye," Conner said as he and Kingsley left the office. They headed down the hallway, Conner running ahead of Kingsley, as he was wont to do.

And when they entered the kitchen, he found Mrs. Tillman putting Conner's plate on the large farmhouse-style table in the corner of the breakfast nook. It had a built-in padded bench, which Conner scrambled up onto.

Kingsley usually made it a point to eat with Conner when he was home, but tonight their schedule was slightly messed up. So Conner would be eating alone. Kingsley planned to dine with Gabi tonight to bring her up to speed on all the details of Conner's schedule. And because he wanted to get to know her again.

"Do you still need me to stay until bedtime?" Mrs. Tillman asked.

"Yes. I want to give Gabi time to settle in. Did you have a chance to introduce yourselves?"

"We did. I put her suitcase in her bedroom and after Conner's bath I will unpack it."

"That's okay, Mrs. Tillman," Gabi said from the doorway, a large brown box in her arms. "I can do it. Kingsley, do you have a hand truck I can use to bring my other office boxes in?"

"No, but I can help you carry them," he said.

"I don't want to disturb you," she said. "I can make a couple of trips."

She turned away and he realized it was too late—she'd already disturbed him and there was no coming back from that.

"Go on, Kingsley. I'll watch the scamp finish his dinner," Mrs. Tillman said.

"Is that okay, Con?"

"Yes."

Kingsley ruffled his son's hair and got to his feet, following after Gabi.

Three

"Everything Is Awesome" was blasting from the room next to hers. She had an idea that Conner was in there, but she doubted he was alone. She'd done a good job of avoiding being alone with Kingsley. But she had to admit it had been harder than she'd expected.

He'd followed her to her car and if Hunter hadn't called just then perhaps she would have found herself on the patio under the moonlit sky having dinner with this complicated man from her past. But Hunter had saved her from that. She'd escaped into the house and then into a shower and avoided Kingsley for the rest of the night.

But at 6:00 a.m. everything didn't feel awesome. As the nanny, she knew she needed to check on Conner. So she jumped out of bed and walked into his room. He was sitting quietly in his bed with a book open on his lap.

She turned the volume down on his radio before walking over to his toddler bed.

"Morning, kiddo. What are you doing?"

"Reading. Peri likes it if we start the morning quiet," he said softly.

"I'm not Peri," Gabi said, sitting on the edge of his bed and glancing over at the book. It was a picture book—*One Fish Two Fish Red Fish Blue Fish* by Dr. Seuss. She smiled as she noticed that he was rubbing his finger over the pictures and not really reading. But then he was only three, a little young for true reading.

"Do you like this one?" she asked.

"Yes. Daddy took me fishing in summer."

"Did you catch a red or blue fish?"

He laughed at her. "Nope. They were brown."

She ruffled his hair. "They usually are."

His room was neat and she noticed that someone had laid his clothes out for the day on a chair facing the window. She suspected that Conner had opened the curtains because they were only parted nearest the floor.

"What do you want to do today?"

He looked up at her, and it was odd seeing the innocence in a pair of eyes that reminded her very strongly of Kingsley. King had never been that innocent. Never.

"Can we go to the beach? Daddy and I walk in the morning after breffest."

She smiled and nodded. "Where do we eat breakfast?"

"In the kitchen with Mrs. Tillman. I have to finish my book first," he said.

"Want to read it to me?" she asked.

He nodded. "Uncle Hun taught me a rap."

Hunter was seemingly full of surprises. She chastised herself for thinking that. To be honest, she'd never really known Hunter, just his reputation, which prior to Stacia's death had been one of a charming Romeo, playful, sexy and fun. It was only afterward that she'd started to have doubts about him.

"I'd love to hear it."

Conner grinned up at her and then pushed the covers down and stood up on his bed. "Gimme a beat."

She had no idea how to beatbox. She wasn't too sure she'd have the nerve to ever try doing this if her audience was anyone other than a toddler, but he was waiting for her and she didn't want to let him down.

She made some beat noises and heard laughter from the door behind her.

"Finally we find the one thing that Gabi can't do," Kingsley said from the doorway. His hair was damp, presumably from his shower, and he had on a pair of faded jeans and a faded Buffalo Bills T-shirt. His feet were bare.

"Daddy, can you gimme a beat?"

Kingsley nodded. Gabi pretended not to notice how his shirt clung to his thickly muscled arms or the way he walked over to the bed.

Conner started jumping and rapping Dr. Seuss's timeless story. She had to admit she fell a little in love with Conner, and that cold lump in the pit of her stomach that had to do with old bitterness and resentment started to loosen.

For the first time since she left the jailhouse ten years ago she felt a spark of something like real emotion. She'd never been able to let a man get close to her after what Kingsley had done. Caution should be her watchword, but instead she wanted to throw it to the wind and find a little of the innocence she'd seen in Conner's eyes in her own life and in Kingsley's.

* * *

Every morning since his son was born Kingsley had woken with the desire to put the past to rest. This morning was no exception. As he'd lain in his bed watching the small bit of sun shining in through the crack in his blinds and realizing he was back in California, he'd felt the familiar anger and determination rise inside him.

He needed answers and if he were being totally honest, revenge against whomever had killed Stacia and set Hunter and him up. But rapping with his son and Gabi first thing in the morning brought peace to some long-forgotten part of his soul. A part he thought had died a long time ago.

As Conner finished rapping about the fish and did his "gangsta" pose, Gabi applauded. The little boy looked as if he'd swallowed the sun. He wasn't immune to Gabi, either.

Kingsley's entire life had been set on course by the actions of someone else. His silver-spoon existence had been taken away but he'd done his best to claw his way back, and having Conner made it all the more important that he succeed. But when he stood here near Gabi he had a glimpse of a life that might have been. Something he could have had if life hadn't been so cruel.

Damn. He was feeling sorry for himself and he couldn't tolerate that.

"I can get Conner ready if you want to get dressed and then we can go have breakfast."

"Yippee!" Conner said, dancing around.

"Okay, but isn't this my job?" she asked.

Kingsley nodded. "We need to get your schedule figured out. I have a meeting this afternoon with a potential client and I have to fly out for a few days after that.

But we can discuss that over breakfast. I did promise you'd have time to do your work, as well."

Gabi crossed her arms under her breasts. He was trying to ignore how sexy she looked in a sleeveless navy blue T-shirt and a pair of long, flowing pajama pants. But he wasn't doing a great job. Frankly, he knew that it was a cliché to hit on his son's nanny, but in this case he'd known Gabi way before she'd been Conner's nanny.

Still, he knew that hitting on her wasn't going to go over well. And he was smoother than that. Really, he was. No matter how kissable she looked. In fact, she looked like the woman he remembered from college. She wasn't wearing any makeup and the tough, businesslike facade she had worn yesterday was gone, leaving in its place a woman he wanted to cuddle up to.

"Why are you staring at me?" she asked as Conner went over to his closet to find his beach shoes.

"Because I want to kiss you."

"You aren't going to act on that, because the contract I sent over prohibits fraternization between the nanny and anyone in the house."

"That's why I struck that clause out. Whatever happens between us started a long time ago."

Conner came back out of his closet.

"We can discuss this later. You aren't going to get your way every time we negotiate."

"We'll see," he said.

Gabi walked away and Kingsley watched as she firmly closed the door between her room and Conner's.

"I like her," Conner said.

"Me, too," Kingsley admitted to his son. He helped Conner change and then supervised him brushing his teeth and washing his face.

He was always struck by how quickly Conner was

growing. It wasn't that long ago that Kingsley would have had to do both chores for him. But now he was independent enough to do them himself.

"Daddy?"

"Yes?"

"Are you ready for breffest?"

"Yeah, Con, I am. Let's go." Kingsley reached out to his son and felt that tiny hand grip his so securely. Whatever went down in the next few months it was paramount to Kingsley that Conner—and by extension, Gabi—was protected. Obviously, some stray sparks had burned her when Stacia died. Finding Stacia's real killer, clearing his name once and for all and making sure that justice was served…that was a tall order. But one that King and Hunter felt sure they were up to.

Hunter had heard that their old football coach had retired and was living in Carmel not too far from Kingsley's new home. Hunter planned to visit the old man and see what he remembered. The party where Stacia was killed had been held at his home on campus.

"What time are you leaving today?" Gabi asked as he entered the kitchen. He noticed that she had a bowl of cereal and fresh fruit prepared for Conner.

Conner scampered up onto the bench seat and started eating.

"Not until this afternoon."

"I need to run back to my office and sign some papers and I'd like to bring my assistant out here so she knows how to get here. It was a little complicated and Melissa isn't the best with her GPS."

Kingsley was irritated. He wanted Gabi here. That was what he'd paid for, but he was aware of how well saying something like that would go over. He needed her and he was willing to let her go for now. "Okay, but I want lunch, just you and me. Mrs. Tillman will watch Conner. We need to get a few details settled before I leave."

"What details?"

"We can discuss it at lunch," he said. He wanted to be alone with Gabi. He didn't question it. He'd been operating by his gut for a long time and it hadn't let him down—except for that one night with Stacia.

He was determined to put the past to rest and to make things up to Gabi. But he knew deep inside that it was her icy exterior that made him want to do it. He wanted to crack through it and find the young woman who'd been so in love with him that she'd come to visit him in jail.

Gabi had done her best to avoid Kingsley and she felt like a coward. But standing on the threshold of the terrace in the sun with the gorgeous view of the Pacific in the background, she was almost glad she was here. She'd come out here not just to be a nanny to Conner, but also to put the past to rest for once. Her mother was always keen to point out that she kept all men at arm's length.

She dated.

She was a woman and had needs and got tired of her own company, so of course she'd been out on dates and even hooked up occasionally. But she had yet to be with a man for more than one night, and she had studied enough psychology to recognize that pattern for what it was. Kingsley had left a part of her scarred when he'd rejected her.

So she was here in part to heal. To somehow bring closure to that one-night stand they'd had and hopefully make it possible for her to have a real relationship and give her mom those grandkids she was desperate for.

"I wasn't sure you'd come."

"Why not? I like to eat just as much as the next person."

"This isn't just about the meal. You've been avoiding being alone with me since you moved into my house," he said.

He wore a pair of perfectly tailored dress pants and a button-down shirt that had been cut to his size. Kingsley wore his wealth well. And she had to admit that she admired him for it. She was sick of seeing men in baggy jeans on the streets. Kingsley took pride in his appearance and she liked it.

She'd worn a sleeveless sheath dress in turquoise that her mother had told her brought out her eyes. Her mom spent a lot of her time making sure Gabi was presentable to the world.

Kingsley led the way to the table and held a chair out for her. She sort of regretted missing dinner last night. She'd feigned sleepiness and gone to bed early. But she'd needed time to shore up her barriers. To focus on what was important—the kids who'd get the playground that his fee was paying for. Conner, who needed a nanny focused on the job of caring for him and not his superhot dad. And rebuilding her shattered feminine self-worth. That was why she'd stayed away, but today, with the sun shining and Kingsley sitting next to her looking as though he'd stepped out of one of her dreams, it was hard to remember any of that.

"Why are you back in California?" she asked. Get to know him. Wasn't that the first thing every *Cosmo* quiz told a woman to do? It was also what she had decided she needed to help herself get over him.

"I wanted Conner to grow up with the sea and the sun. Plus, my parents haven't forgiven me for..."

"Stacia?" she asked. She wasn't going to pretend he didn't have that in his past. It was the incident that defined them as a couple. Three weeks of dating culminating in a one-night stand. And she suspected she needed some closure on that, as well. "What did happen that night?"

"I don't... Are you sure you want to talk about it?" he asked.

"Yes. I thought... Well, that doesn't matter. I remember that you took me home and stayed until my roommate came back and then you left. What happened next?"

He rubbed the back of his neck and took a long sip of his sparkling water before he put his elbows on the table and leaned forward. "I took a long walk around the campus. I didn't want to go back to the frat house or the party. I needed to think."

"What about?"

"You, Gabi. You were a freshman and I was a senior. My life was on track at that point. You know the draft was my next goal, but then you came along and things sort of changed."

"How?"

"You were different and it made me think about something other than football for a while," he said.

She wanted to believe him. There was no reason for him to lie to her at this moment, but if that was the truth, why had he been so cruel to her at the jailhouse?

"Yeah, right. Listen, we both know I was just some dewy-eyed coed that you saw as an easy score," she said. "You don't have to put a different spin on it. I was more than willing to go with you that night."

"Believe what you will, but that night was special for me. You were different," he said.

"Then why were you so mean when I came to visit you?" she asked. There had been no reason for that.

"I was protecting you. I had no clear memories of the night before. I only knew that I'd been found with Stacia and Hunter and that she had been killed. The cops were trying to implicate me in some sort of twisted sex game, and I wanted you as far from that as I could get you," he said.

She swallowed hard. "Really?"

"Would I lie about that? I certainly didn't leave you and go back to the party to kill Stacia."

"What did happen? Do you know?"

"I don't," he said. "We've never found out anything other than they had no evidence to prosecute Hunter and me. Both of us can't recall the night that clearly. What about you? Do you remember anything from that night?" he asked.

"Just being into you and around you," she said. She tipped her head to the side to study him. Stacia's death was still like a fresh wound to Kingsley. Gabi could tell by the way he was talking about it. Hear it in the anger in his voice.

"If you can remember anything from that night that seemed odd," he said, "I'd like to know about it."

"Why?"

"Hunter and I have been piecing together stories and memories of that night. Hunter and Stacia were serious about each other. He blames himself for her death."

"Did he kill her?"

"No. He didn't," Kingsley said. "Enough about that. Tell me about your business. How did you go from college to being a nanny?"

She put her hand on his and squeezed it. That knot of anger that had been deep inside her since the moment she'd woken to hear that her lover had been arrested for killing another woman eased. It had been a long time in coming, but she finally felt as if she was seeing Kingsley as the man he could be.

She didn't trust herself. Didn't know if she ever would be able to again, but there was a little bit of hope inside her now.

Four

Talking about the night Stacia died always made Kingsley feel anger and resentment. He'd had it all until then. He'd felt untouchable—in part thanks to his family's money. School had come easily to him and he'd been on the dean's list every semester. He hadn't won the Heisman Trophy, but he had been mentioned as a first-round draft pick. His life had been, well, charmed, and he'd taken it for granted.

He'd slept with Gabi, knowing that she came from a good family. He had imagined she'd be the perfect accoutrement for the idyllic life he pictured for himself. One where he outshone his older brother, where after he'd won the Super Bowl he'd retire and have the perfect family. He figured he'd play hard and when Gabi graduated he'd think about settling down with her.

But after the arrest those plans had disappeared. He'd been shocked that he hadn't been able to talk the cops out of arresting both him and Hunter. It had been inconceivable that anyone would think Hunter would have killed Stacia. Despite his name, Hunter didn't really have a killer instinct. Which is how they'd ended up being labeled the Frat House Killers.

Sitting in the sun with Gabi just reinforced his need for revenge. To find out who had killed Stacia and make them pay for the plans they'd interrupted, for the life they'd taken. And the years they'd lived with the stigma of being murderers.

Gabi pushed her sunglasses up to the top of her head and leaned forward.

"You look scary. Is that your don't-sack-me face?"

He forced a smile because he could tell that was what she wanted, but this lunch simply reinforced all he'd lost. If he hadn't been accused of murder, maybe he would have married better. Maybe Conner's mother would still be alive if he hadn't been so…uninterested in anything except making enough money so he could go after his revenge.

"Yeah. You'd be amazed at what it takes to stop a three-hundred-pound linebacker."

"I shudder to think of facing someone like that. I'm sorry I brought up Stacia. I can tell that it still bothers you," she said.

"Her killer was never brought to justice. Someone thought that Hunter and I would take the fall for them. They were wrong," he said.

"Maybe the cops will find that person," Gabi said.

Doubtful. Especially since most of them believed he and Hunter had gotten off because of their family money. But he didn't want to get into that with Gabi. He needed to know if she remembered anything else about that night. Hunter thought someone might have drugged them before Stacia was killed. Gabi was still on campus after the party, so she might have heard something along those lines. But for right now he wanted to enjoy this lunch.

He'd had some hot dreams about Gabi last night. Maybe it was the fact that they'd only had that one night together or maybe it was because she was under his roof again, but he wanted her. He wanted to see if the kiss, the sex he remembered with her had been real. Or just another illusion that would be shattered by reality.

"You're staring again."

"I'm wondering what it would be like to kiss you," he said.

She flushed under her tan and licked her lips. Her mouth had fascinated him from the first moment he'd met her. Her lips were full and lush. She'd never worn lipstick in college and now she wore something that made her lips shimmer but didn't add color to them.

"Well, stop wondering. I'm in your house to be a nanny, not to assuage your curiosity."

He threw his head back and laughed. "Assuage?"

"Yes, got a problem with it?"

"Not at all. It's just that I figured since you worked with kids—"

"I'd talk like a toddler?" she asked.

He shook his head. She rattled him and made his legendary charm disappear. It was unnerving and at the same time exciting. She was still different from every other woman he'd ever known.

"My curiosity still needs to be assuaged."

She shook her head and lifted the cloche off the plate in front of her. "I have to get to my meeting, so let's eat."

"Don't like talking about kissing me?" he asked.

He took his lid off as well and saw that Mrs. Tillman

had prepared fish tacos. His favorite. Gabi took a bite and chewed carefully.

Hell, he needed to kiss her and take her to his bed. Get over this odd infatuation he had with her. What else could he call watching her chew and thinking it was cute?

He took a bite of his taco, glad as hell that Hunter had gone to Malibu for a few weeks. He didn't want his friend to see him mooning over Gabi.

Was that what he was doing?

"So, while you are gone, is it okay to ask your housekeeper to watch Conner if I need to have a conference call?" she asked. "I will do my writing and paperwork either while Conner is having his nap or at night while he's sleeping. But I'm in the middle of placing two nannies with some rather high-profile clients and I don't want to lose their business."

"Yes, that will be fine. She's not interested in being a full-time nanny but will help out as needed."

"Great. Now, when will you be back?"

"In a week. Do you feel like you can handle Conner?"

"Certainly. He seems pretty well adjusted. You've done a good job with raising him," she said.

"I had some excellent advice," he said. "I bought your book."

She shook her head. "Lots of people have bought my book and still have kids that are out of control. You seem to actually listen to him, which is key."

"Well, I like my son," Kingsley said.

"That's a good thing."

"I like you, too," he said.

"Don't. We have a business relationship."

"I know that. But what's to preclude us from having more?"

"Common sense," she said.

Maybe it was being back in Cali or just being around Gabi, but he felt young again. Free in a way he hadn't been since their one night together. She made him want to be the man who had dreams. Not the man who was focused on vengeance.

But the dreamer was gone. And he was a taker now.

He wanted Gabi.

She kept him at arm's length, which was one thing he wasn't going to allow. She was part of the reason he was here. Not just revenge.

Okay, that wasn't entirely true. But now that she was under his roof, his focus was changing. He still craved revenge on whoever had set Hunter and him up, but he also desperately wanted Gabi.

It was her fault.

She sat across from him in the midday California sun, watching him as though she wanted more, too.

Maybe she'd been waiting, too. Waiting for him to come back into her life.

Yeah, right.

Hell.

What if she was involved with someone? Why wouldn't she be?

"Do you have a boyfriend?" he asked. "Is that why you are busy espousing common sense?"

She shook her head. "So the only reason a woman wouldn't want to throw away her professionalism with you is because she's involved with someone else?"

"This feels like a trap," he said. "I just wanted to know if there was a man in your life."

"There are a lot of them," she said.

That didn't fit with the woman he thought he knew. But then he had to admit that reading her column and her book didn't give him any special insight into her personal life.

"Fair enough."

She laughed in a very kind way. It was something he hadn't heard in a long time. Women didn't usually laugh around him.

"What?"

"You are so transparent."

"Am I?"

"Yes."

"What do you see?" he asked her. He had the feeling she was toying with him and that feeling of being free took him again. It had been a long time since anyone had teased him.

"I see a man who wants to kiss me."

"I told you that," he said.

"But you aren't the kind of man who'd poach so you want to know if I'm taken."

"What's wrong with that?"

"Nothing. It makes me like you a little bit more."

That sounded like a good thing, but with Gabi he wasn't sure. "Thanks."

"Don't sound scared. It is a good thing. You came into my office trying to get your own way instead of asking the way most people would. So why are you being so polite about this?" she asked.

Damn.

Of course she'd see what few others did. He rubbed the back of his neck and the feeling of freedom slipped away. The chains of the past were once again wrapped around his neck and ankles. Tying him to that one night, that one event. He didn't want to tell her that it was the fact that Stacia had been raped that night that had also stayed with him. The DNA evidence had been inconclusive and he had no memory of sleeping with anyone other than Gabi, but he wanted to give no woman the chance to say he'd taken her against her will.

"Let's just say consent is a biggie in my book," he said.

"It is in mine, too. But one kiss, Kingsley—I wouldn't begrudge that."

"If I took it you might later," he said.

She put her hand on his. "Do you know why I'm afraid to let go of common sense?"

He had a few thoughts on the matter—she might not want to kiss him, which, given the sexual attraction he felt around her, he hoped wasn't the case. She might have a boyfriend, but he was beginning to think that wasn't the case, either. But the real reason? Only Gabi knew that. She protected her secrets behind her pretty brown eyes like an armed security guard.

"Not really."

"You make me forget all of the caution I carefully built into myself over the last ten years. You make me want to be the freshman girl who took a senior football player back to her dorm room. And that's not smart. And this is the tricky part—I usually think of myself as a smart woman, so kissing you…well, that would be dumb."

He realized she was talking and rationalizing to keep herself safe. Hell, he didn't blame her, but every male instinct he had was saying she was his. He'd claimed her that night all those years ago and he wanted her back again.

But he had a son.

He had a mission in California.

He owed Hunter and himself a chance to clear their names.

Something he knew he couldn't do if he took Gabi to his bed again. She cluttered his mind. She made him want things he had lived a long time without.

But one kiss?

Surely, one kiss wouldn't do that much damage.

One kiss.

"One kiss," he said.

"What?"

"One kiss. That's all I'm asking for. What could it hurt? We are both wondering if our memories are right and if that fire between us was really as scorching hot as we remember."

"Are we?" she asked, but she took her sunglasses off her head, set them on the table next to her plate and put her hands on the armrests of her chair as if she were about to stand.

"Yes. You know it and I do, too. Common sense isn't going to withstand curiosity," he said.

"You're right," she admitted, standing up and walking over to him.

He scooted his chair back and before he could stand, she sat on his lap, wrapping her arms around him and tangling her hands in the hair at the back of his neck. Last time she'd been in his arms she'd been a girl, scared and unsure. This time she was a woman and knew what she wanted.

"One kiss, Kingsley. Better make it count."

He intended to.

Gabi knew she'd dared him to kiss her. Okay, so maybe she thought that way she'd be able to say he'd forced her into it later, though she knew that wasn't true.

There weren't many things she truly wanted for herself but Kingsley was one of them. There was no denying that despite the coldhearted way he'd dumped her at the police station she still wanted him. Still wanted this embrace.

She wanted to tell herself that he'd been so cruel that night because he'd been trying to protect her, but deep inside she had to admit that even if he hadn't, he was still hot. Still the one man she looked at and felt the kind of sexual longing that made her forget common sense and reason. He made her want to act like… well, like this.

Sitting on his lap in the midafternoon California sun for the entire world to see. Except there wasn't anyone else around. It was just the two of them.

She'd never really had Kingsley to herself during their brief courtship. He'd been big man on campus and everywhere they'd gone people knew him, had high-fived him and wanted to talk to him.

This was different.

He was different.

Hell, so was she. She'd been different for a long time now. But suddenly his mouth moved over hers and she forgot all of that.

Forgot to think and to worry.

Forgot to justify this because his mouth felt so good, so right as he parted his lips and his tongue slipped over her teeth.

She tightened her fingers on his shoulders. God, the man was still solid muscle.

But then his bespoke suits had already sort of hinted at that and she'd seen him in that tight T-shirt last night. He was fit. He always had been and she wanted to tear off his shirt and see the body beneath his clothes.

She shut her eyes as he put his hands on either side of her face and deepened the kiss. Everything feminine inside her clenched and then released. It felt as if her blood flow was heavier in her veins and her heart was racing. She heard the sound of her heart beating in her ears like the distant call of warning drums.

She knew she should tear her mouth from his, get up and walk away, but instead she brought her hands closer to his neck, brushed her fingers over his short beard and then ran her fingers over his jaw.

She wanted this kiss to last forever.

She needed to keep tasting him to somehow figure out if this was just another sort of dream that she was having. Like the foggy memories of their night together. This felt too good. Too intense. It couldn't be real. No man kissed like this.

No man had this kind of power over her.

She pulled back, opened her eyes and looked up at Kingsley. His eyes were half-closed, but she saw the fabulous blue of his irises.

He was her Achilles' heel. He was the one person who could make her behave in a way that she knew better. For some reason he'd always found his way around her will and with no great effort.

Why?

What kind of hold did he have over her?

And why the hell was it still there? She thought ten years would have dulled his magnetism, but that wasn't the case. If anything he was more captivating now. His kiss was more thorough than it had been in college.

She leaned closer to him. Put her arms around his shoulders and rested her cheek on it. She didn't want to look at him. Didn't want to kiss him again. And there was a very real worry that she would do just that.

"Kingsley."

"Gabriella," he said. Just her name in that low tone fanned the fires already burning deep inside her. She shook her head, pushed herself upright and started to get off his lap, but he put his hands on her waist.

She knew she could have escaped and dammit, she didn't want to. She liked the feel of him holding her. Keeping her close.

"That cannot happen again," she said at last.

"Not good enough?" he asked, arching one eyebrow arrogantly at her.

He knew it was plenty good enough. The bastard.

"I think we both know it couldn't get much better."

"Unless we were both naked," he said.

She bit her lower lip, tasted him on her and closed her eyes. How was she going to live in his house and not give in to this temptation again?

She'd never in all of her years of nannying been tempted by a father. Never thought about maybe hooking up with one. But Kingsley wasn't just a client to her. She knew Kingsley. Remembered what he looked like naked, and dammit if she wasn't ready to see him that way again. She knew she had a responsibility to Conner. And she'd be the best nanny that little boy ever had.

And there was only one way to do that. She pushed herself to her feet and walked back around to her side of the table. No more flirting.

No more giving in to her stupid curiosity.

No more kissing Kingsley.

He was still just watching her as she plucked her sunglasses off the table and put them on.

"Well, that was interesting."

Interesting? That was one way to describe it. Gabi thought it was dangerous, intoxicating, and she knew she was going to have to be on her guard every moment to prevent a repeat performance.

"I guess."

"You guess?"

She shrugged. She was trying to walk a fine line here. Professionalism had failed as a barrier to keep him at arm's length and it didn't seem as though dares were working well, either. It was only the stiff formal behavior her mother had drummed into her that kept her sitting there smiling as if nothing was wrong when inside she was on fire and felt that she'd made a very dangerous misstep.

Five

His phone rang. He hit the ignore button when he saw it was Hunter. Gabi gave him a quizzical look.

"It's Hunter. I'll call him later."

"You two are pretty close, aren't you?" she asked. She was sipping delicately at her water.

There was nothing sexy about drinking water, but somehow there was when she did it. He couldn't tear his eyes from her mouth as she put the glass back on the table and licked her lips.

She'd hidden her big brown eyes from him with her sunglasses and he wondered what she was thinking. This Gabi was very good at hiding what she felt. She wasn't at all like the hot-tempered girl he remembered. The one who'd let him have it if he as much as looked at another girl. She had told him she deserved a man who wasn't playing the field and if he didn't agree he could hit the road.

"So you never said if you were dating anyone," he said.

"Would I have kissed you if I were?"

He shrugged. He didn't think so, but why make assumptions? He wanted to hear from her own lips that she was single—and available to him.

"I don't know. It's been ten years."

"Fair enough. I have changed a bit, but not about that. I believe if you commit yourself to a relationship then you honor it."

"Me, too."

She arched one eyebrow at him. "Don't say that if you don't mean it. It was just a kiss—"

"It was more than a kiss, Gabi. It was a reaffirmation that there is still something white-hot between us."

She bit her lower lip. "Damn."

"What?"

"I was hoping that you didn't feel it, too."

"I'd have to be dead not to have felt it," he said. "Why did you want that?"

"Because I'm Conner's nanny. I'm here as a professional in your home, not to date you," she said. "I've never been tempted to mix business and pleasure and I'm not sure it's a wise idea now."

"I don't think it's a dumb idea," he said, trying for his most charming grin.

She shook her head. "That's because you're a man."

"Hey, that's not fair."

"But it's true."

He had to grin at her. She made him feel alive again. Something that he usually only experienced with Conner and his very small inner circle of employees and friends—Peri, Mrs. Tillman and Hunter.

Was this real, or was he feeling something from the past for Gabi?

She'd believed in his innocence back then and that had meant a lot to him.

"I think we can both handle this. I trust you to be a good nanny to Conner whatever happens between us."

"I'm not sure, Kingsley. How would you feel about maybe giving this a break until I'm not living in your home? I have to set a good example for the women who work for me. I have a strict no-fraternization policy," she said.

He had another glimpse of the woman Gabi was now. He had sort of seen those differences in the articles she'd written and in her office. She was a success in a business she'd built from the ground up. She came from a very wealthy family who were related to the Spanish royals, so she'd never needed to work. Yet she did.

She worked hard.

He didn't want to do anything that would harm her reputation or call her ethics into question.

But he wanted her.

He had been searching his entire adult life for a woman who could make him feel this way, and no other one had. He knew that he had another agenda and that his focus should be on clearing his and Hunter's names. Making whoever was responsible for Stacia's death pay. But sitting here in the Cali sun with Gabi made all that seem distant.

Suddenly getting revenge on the real killer wasn't as important as making sure he could kiss Gabi again and hold her in his arms. Make love to her until they both forget everything except the way it felt to be wrapped around each other.

His phone beeped and he saw it was a text message from Hunter.

WTF. Are you really romancing the nanny? I thought we decided that we'd fix the past.

Damn.

He glanced at Gabi.

"I have to respond to this."

"It's okay. I think we need a break. I'm going to go inside and find Conner. He is supposed to have a nap in twenty minutes, so I should be there."

"How did you know?"

"I emailed Peri last night. She sent his schedule," Gabi said. "Thanks for lunch and for that kiss."

She walked away and he watched her. She wasn't doing anything to turn him on, just walking away. But he couldn't tear his eyes from her body. Could barely make himself stay in his chair.

And that was as big a wake-up call as Hunter's text. Kingsley had come here for answers and for revenge. He needed to remember that.

Soon Conner would start school, and sooner or later it would come out that his father was an accused murderer. And he wanted better than that for his son. He didn't want him to have to deal with that.

And no matter how good Gabi felt in his arms, he needed peace of mind. He needed to clear his name and put the past to rest before he moved on. He knew that.

Hell, he'd never had any problem doing that until her. What was it about Gabi that shook him that way?

He picked up his phone.

Your timing could be better. How did you know I was with Gabi?

I know you. Is this still a priority for you?

Yes. I'm flying to the East Coast to meet with Daria Miller. She was one of Stacia's sorority sisters. I read a blog post she wrote about the college drug culture. I want to talk to her about her experience.

Great. I'm going to follow up on Coach. He's in the hospital.

Sounds good. Talk to you soon.

He put his phone on the table and looked at the empty spot where Gabi had been sitting. He wanted her. He was trying to—hell, he wasn't going to tell himself that lie. He wasn't doing anything but waiting for her. And he had to put that aside. Revenge and new relationships really didn't mix.

Gabi made sure Conner was sleeping before she retreated to her office. She had a video monitor so she could keep an eye on him, and according to Peri, Conner was good for a forty-five-minute nap. That meant she had just enough time to finish the draft of a speech she was giving next weekend to the Young Women's Business Association.

So why was she on the internet doing a Google search on Kingsley, Hunter and Stacia? But she knew why. He'd made her curious when he'd brought up college. She'd taken a break from college for a year shortly after Kingsley had been arrested and gone to Spain to visit her cousin Gui.

It had been nice to spend time with Gui and Kara. The escape from her real-life problems had been welcome, and when she'd returned home after spending time with her little niece, her mom had volunteered her to nanny for Mal and his family. She'd been too busy to follow the story except when Hunter and Kingsley had been released from jail. And then Kingsley had been drafted and went to New York to play pro football.

And now he was back. Why?

He'd said he was back because he wanted to raise Conner in the California sun, but Kingsley had grown up in Connecticut. True, given the past few winters it made sense that he'd want to be out here where they weren't snowed in for weeks. Her gut was saying there was more to it than that.

She read all the past articles on the original incident. She knew from her own memories of the night that the party had been wild. She'd been focused on Kingsley, having made up her mind that they'd finally have sex. So she really hadn't seen much of Hunter or Stacia.

Kingsley and she had left early. And that had been what she'd wanted.

"Got a minute?"

She minimized her search window and smiled over at Kingsley where he stood in the doorway.

"Sure. What's up?"

"I wanted to remind you that I'm going to be out of town for a week. I'll leave after Conner wakes up from his nap. I don't want to go without saying goodbye."

That was sweet. He was a good father. Was he a good man? That was the question that kept spinning through her mind. Every time she thought she had him figured out he did something else.

Like that lunch. He'd been funny, sort of sweet and oh, so charming. Everything any woman would want from a date…

She was afraid she was waiting for the other shoe to

fall. Experience had taught her that things never went smoothly with Kingsley.

"Okay. I will have to work around my schedule. I might need to take Conner to my office in Carmel a few days. I have a play area there. And it would only be for a few hours. But I wasn't planning to be away this long," she said.

"That's fine. I did spring this on you. We can work out a better schedule when I get back," he said. He handed her a business card with his contact numbers.

She took it, turned it over in her hand. Something was different.

Something had changed in him since she'd left the patio.

"Is everything okay?"

"Yes, why wouldn't it be?"

"Because you were all, *let's have an affair*, and now you're handing me your business card and dashing out the door," she said. "What's up?"

"I'm respecting your wishes. You said you couldn't do this while nannying my son."

She narrowed her eyes, watching him carefully and trying to gauge if he was lying to her. She had asked for the space. Just because she'd sort of counted on him not giving it to her was no reason to get upset now. Except, dammit, he'd kissed her. Gotten her turned on and made her believe that he was going to be pursuing her. Now he was turning it off.

Something had changed.

What?

Hunter. Hunter had called him earlier. Maybe there was bad news from his friend.

"Is everything okay with Hunter?"

"Yes. Why do you ask?"

She put his card down and walked around the desk so she could lean against the front of it. She noticed whenever she moved that he watched her hips and her legs. He'd always been a leg man. Though she was dressed conservatively, Kingsley's eyes on her made her feel as if she was wearing a micro-miniskirt and rocking it.

"You've changed," she said, crossing her legs at the ankles. The slim-fitting skirt pulled tight around her thighs. She noticed his gaze skim down to it before he looked away from her.

"What do you want?" he asked. "Did you say no so I'd push you? You know I'm not that kind of man."

She nodded. "I do know that. I wasn't saying no so much as…trying to see if you were serious or just toying with me. This feels like you don't know, either."

Talking about it made it all clearer. She did want him to keep coming after her. She'd gone to see him and bared her soul as a young girl and he'd rejected her. She hadn't thought that she was still carrying that scar around, but it turned out it hadn't faded as much as she'd hoped.

Instead she was afraid to be pushed aside again. She hoped that was it. Hoped it wasn't that some part of her wanted to reject him.

"We have a lot of history, Gabi, not all of it good. I am here in Cali for work but also to put the ghosts of the past to rest. I guess while we were having lunch I felt like the man I might have been. Thank you for that."

Her heart melted a little. While it was easy to focus on her feelings, it was harder to see things from Kingsley's point of view. He'd lost a lot the night he'd been arrested.

"You're welcome. I want us to at least be friends again," she said.

"Friends?"

She nodded.

"It's a start," he said. "But don't kid yourself. I'm never going to be satisfied being just your friend."

He closed the gap between them and kissed her with all the passion she remembered from that night so long ago. All the restraint he'd showed on the patio was gone. The kiss was carnal and then he pulled back, rubbed his thumb over her lips and walked away. She was shattered.

Kingsley stood in Conner's doorway and watched his son sleep. His dad had once said there was no greater joy and agony than having a child. Kingsley had simply heard the regret in his old man's voice and felt the guilt of his own failings. But recently he was starting to understand where the old man was coming from.

He wanted so much for his son. So much more than he could give him. He wanted to protect him and to give him everything he never had. But he'd had a lot of advantages. He wasn't sure how he was going to keep Conner from ending up in the wrong place at the wrong time as he had.

That fear was always in the back of his mind. He hadn't been a saint in college, but he'd certainly never pushed a girl to be with him—or drugged her. Both things were key in Stacia's death. The cold case had left open the option that maybe after a night of crazy drinking and drugging Stacia had taken her own life. But Hunter didn't believe it.

And neither did Kingsley.

He went into Conner's room, trying to shake off memories of the past. This little guy was the future. The driving force behind him being here. That and revenge. He wanted the person who'd tainted his future to pay for what he'd done.

He wasn't going to sugarcoat it. He wanted to ruin whoever had framed Hunter and him, and he knew that nothing was going to sway him from his mission. Not Gabi and her sexy legs. Not even Conner.

He needed revenge. His moral compass didn't always skew the same as most people's, but in this he was damned sure of his path.

Hunter was right. He was distracted with Gabi. But he also knew he wasn't going to send her away. To ask her to send another nanny so he wouldn't be…what? Conflicted.

Damn.

"Daddy?"

"Right here, buddy. How was your nap?" he asked, sitting down on Conner's toddler bed that was shaped like a race car. One of his friends was the F1 driver Marco Moretti, and Marco had sent the bed to Conner as a gift for his last birthday.

Kingsley rubbed the back of his neck. He had a good life. A life he'd carved for himself out of the ashes of that arrest. The only loose end was the person who'd done it and why.

He wanted to know why. Hunter needed it, too. He felt as if he was responsible for Stacia. And while Kingsley had Conner and a group of good friends, Hunter hadn't allowed himself to care for anyone since Stacia's death.

It had haunted his friend.

"Good. I like Gammi."

"Gabi, buddy, her name is Gabi."

"That's what I said. Gammi."

He rubbed Conner's head. He'd read an article that

said to gently correct speech mistakes but not make a big deal of them. Then the child would just struggle to speak. So he let it go. He had nicknames for many people in his life.

"I've got to go to a meeting on the East Coast. Gabi and Mrs. Tillman are going to watch you. Gabi might need to go to her office to work and you'll get to go with her."

Conner watched him with those serious little eyes of his. Sometimes Kingsley felt as though his son was an old soul. It was impossible not to look into that innocent face and those eyes and not feel as though there was a lot more going on in there.

Conner nodded and then climbed onto his lap, hugging him. "Can't I go with you?"

Kingsley hugged his son tightly to him. "Not this time. Gabi can't come with me and neither can Mrs. Tillman."

He nodded. "Will you call me?"

"Yes. I will video chat with you anytime you want and every night before bed."

"Okay, you can go," Conner said.

"Thanks," he said. He wondered if, when he was little, he'd been as sure of himself and his place in the world as Conner was. He'd have to ask his older brother. His parents had been distant since he'd been arrested. His marriage and providing them a grandson had mollified them somewhat, but they still weren't sure he wasn't entirely blameless.

"You're awake," Gabi said from the doorway. "I thought we'd go down to the beach after your daddy leaves. Sound good?"

Conner nodded. "I have to potty."

He jumped off the bed and ran to his adjoining bathroom and Kingsley stood up and looked at Gabi. She watched him as though she didn't know what he was going to do next. He wasn't sure, either. He wanted to pull her into his arms.

Say to hell with everything else and carry her down to his bedroom. But he wasn't going to do that. When he'd been a quarterback he'd been known as the ice-man. Nothing could shake him. And he channeled that right now.

He had to.

It was the only way he had been able to do what he'd had to on the field. Facing linebackers and rushers who wanted to punish the pretty boy who'd hurt a girl.

He had to put that in the past. Had to exonerate himself. Had to find a place where he could be the man he wanted to be for his son. And if he were being honest, for Gabi.

He wanted to get to know the woman she'd become without the big shadow of the past hanging over them.

"I'm not going to apologize."

"I wasn't about to ask you to. I'm still not sure what's going on between us."

"Good. I don't want to be managed by you. You'd probably draft up a plan like you advise parents to do and try to manage it."

She crossed her arms under her breasts and shook her head. "You're right. I want to deny it but I'm aching to plan this. To figure out what's going to happen next. But you won't let me."

"Good. You have become too rigid—too structured. You need a man to shake you up."

"I'm back," Conner announced. "And look what I did."

Kingsley turned to his son and noticed that he'd put

on his swim trunks and swim shirt all by himself. He felt a lump in his throat. His little boy was getting so big.

"Good job," Gabi said. "High five."

She squatted down to Conner's level and held her hand up. He gave her a high five and then skipped over to Kingsley and smiled up at him.

Kingsley ruffled his son's hair. "I'll watch him while you change."

"Thanks."

Gabi left the room and when she returned a few minutes later, he wasn't disappointed. She had on pair of khaki shorts that ended midthigh, showing off her long, tanned legs, and a loose-fitting off-the-shoulder white top that revealed her bikini strap and her tanned shoulders.

He wanted to cancel his trip and stay with them. And he promised himself soon he'd be able to do just that. He said goodbye to Gabi and his son and left for the airport, in pursuit of answers to questions still lingering from the past.

Six

Gabi fell into a routine, and she soon learned that like every toddler, Conner had his temper tantrums when he was hungry or unable to get his point across to her. But on the whole, he was a good kid.

What unnerved her were some of the mannerisms she knew he shared with his father. Watching him eat a bowl of ice cream was like watching Kingsley do it. Then other times he would give her a look when she made him laugh that also reminded her of Kingsley.

She missed him.

Silly, she knew. But there it was. The house was too big when he was gone. It had felt too small when he'd been there but now she realized it was his presence and not the house that was making her so aware of the space around her.

Kingsley video chatted with Conner every day at least once. Sometimes more. When she and Conner went for a walk on the beach and found an interesting piece of driftwood, Conner needed to send a picture to his dad and then talk to him. When Conner taught her how to play a racing video game, he wanted his dad to know. And every night after she finished reading him whatever book he'd chosen—his current favorite was *Good Night, Knight* after Gabi had told him she liked knights in shining armor—he had to call his dad and do their *One Fish Two Fish Red Fish Blue Fish* rap.

She knew that when the time came for her to go back to her house in Carmel and her regular life she was going to miss the little boy. But that didn't mean she was going to let his father walk all over her.

She and Conner had been to the beach, the park and had played video games but he didn't want to go to bed. She'd done all she could to get him ready but he wasn't having any of it.

She suspected it was because they hadn't been able to video chat with Kingsley all day. She got it—the kid missed his dad. She missed him, too, but he was in New York on business. And he'd warned them both that he might not be able to chat today.

"Let's try to call your dad one more time and then it's time for bed."

"Gammi, I can't sleep."

"You haven't tried."

"I just know I can't," he said with a big sigh.

"Your dad might answer," she said.

"I might get sleepy then."

She hoped so but she could tell by the way he watched her dial Kingsley's number from the iPad app that he was getting nervous.

She put her hand on his shoulder while they waited

for Kingsley to answer. "Do you always get to see your daddy before bed?"

This was the first night they hadn't been able to talk to him.

"Yes," Conner said, nodding. He wrapped his arms around himself and she stretched to reach his little stuffed pig and hand it to him. He pulled it close and kept staring at the screen.

Kingsley wasn't answering. On a hunch she hit the favorites button and noticed that Hunter was listed there.

"Would talking to Uncle Hunter help?" she asked.

Conner nodded. "Maybe he knows where Daddy is."

"Your daddy is fine. Remember he sent us that text around dinnertime? He said he'd be in a meeting until after your bedtime."

"I know. But maybe he got out early."

Gabi knew that men and women with demanding jobs couldn't pop out of meetings to talk to their kids. Intellectually that made perfect sense to her. So she could either text him that it was an emergency or come up with another distraction for Conner until Kingsley was out of his meeting.

"Want to roast marshmallows?"

"Yes! Like cowboys do when they are with the cows?"

"Just like the cattle drive," she said. They'd watched a video earlier that had depicted one.

She texted Kingsley to video call as soon as he was out of his meeting and helped Conner put his slippers on. He held his pig in one arm and the iPad in the other. She picked him up and carried him out to the patio area where there was a fire pit.

Mrs. Tillman had gone to bed in the guesthouse she lived in on the property, so it was just the two of them.

In the distance she heard the winds blowing across the land and the sky was clear tonight.

"My cousin Gui used to tell me tales about the stars when I was little," she said as she sat Conner in one of the chairs, taking a thick blanket from the storage bench and wrapping it around him while she got the fire ready.

"Like what? Unca Hunter says a man lives in the moon."

"Did he? What does that man do up there?"

"He watches over me. My mommy asked him to," Conner said.

Gabi had a hard time reconciling the playboy she knew Hunter to be with the man Conner knew. He was a good "uncle" to Conner and she could tell that Kingsley and he had each other's backs. That must be important to them both. After all, they were the only two people who knew what had really happened that night Stacia died.

She'd stopped thinking about it. Instead, she focused on her job of being a nanny to Conner and also trying really hard not to lust after Kingsley whenever he video chatted with his son.

But Kingsley had kissed her in a way that made it impossible to think of anything else. She'd wanted some peace of mind and hadn't even come close to finding it.

Not when he was here.

And certainly not when he was gone. It was as if…

What?

She liked him. She knew that. She wanted his body moving over hers—she admitted that, too. But another part of her, the woman who kept seeing signs of him in his son's face, wanted Kingsley to be something she thought she'd given up on wanting.

She wanted him to be her knight in shining armor. To woo her, and this time when he won her, to keep her.

Idiot.

She was too old to believe in fairy tales.

She got the fire started and they roasted marshmallows and told stories to each other until Conner drifted off to sleep. She kept his iPad open as she promised Conner she would and waited for a call from his father.

She finally acknowledged that Kingsley wasn't going to call and wondered what had distracted him from his son. She could think of only one thing. A woman.

She carried Conner to his bed and tucked him in before going to her own room, where she tossed and turned all night. She knew she had no claim on Kingsley. But she'd started to think he was someone else. A better man.

New York was too crowded and the party at the Kiwi Klub was too loud. Damn. He was getting old when he couldn't hang out in the club like he used to. But he was here with a purpose. Supposedly this was where he could find Daria Miller. She'd had her assistant text him the names of three different nightclubs she was checking out tonight.

"Kingsley Buchanan. I'm surprised you want to see me," she said, coming up next to him at the bar. She reached around him and took his drink—a scotch neat—and took a sip of it. "You know I'm a reporter, right?"

"That's precisely why I want to talk to you," he said, gesturing to the bartender for another drink.

Daria had short curly brown hair and a heart-shaped face. She was curvy and wore a pantsuit that accentuated her curves. Her eye makeup was understated and the look in her brown eyes was cautious.

"Finally decided to confess?" she asked.

"I already am on record with my story. I want to ask you about that night," he said. "What are you drinking?"

"Scotch," she said. "You really want to talk about that night?"

He ordered for her and when they each had their drinks he led the way to the VIP area. He found a quiet banquette toward the back of the roped-off area. Around them VIPs were partying but Kingsley wasn't interested in celebrity spotting. He wanted to know what Daria had experienced in college.

She sat down, crossing her legs. Her legs were nice enough but didn't hold his attention the way Gabi's did.

"What exactly do you want to talk about?"

"I read your blog post about people being drugged on college campuses and I wanted to know if anything like that went on at our school."

"Seriously?"

"Yeah. I know Hunter and I didn't harm Stacia, but someone did and I'm in a position now to find out who."

She leaned back against the bench and stared at him. He suspected it was her version of the truth stare. But he wasn't interested in lying about anything. He needed answers. And liars only heard more lies, in his experience.

"Convince me."

"Convince you? How about you just tell me what you know. I'm not really into talking people into believing me."

He'd missed talking to Conner and seeing Gabi to meet with Daria, and now it hardly seemed worth it. He put his glass down on the table and stood up. "Enjoy your drink."

"Kingsley, wait."

He turned around. She gestured to the seat he'd just vacated.

"Do you have something to tell me?" he asked. "I get that you might be curious given we went to the same school, but I'm not really here to satisfy that curiosity."

"I'll talk to you about what I know. Sit down," she said.

He did but left his drink on the table. He'd just ordered it out of habit. He wasn't really interested in drinking.

"I was surprised when you asked me about druggings on campus because your frat house was notorious for that behavior at parties. I know of at least seven women who went to parties there and woke up groggy the next morning with vague memories of sex and nothing else," she said.

"Date-rape drugs?" Kingsley asked. "I never knew anything about that. Did they have any idea who was involved?"

"I don't know. I wasn't working on the college paper back then. But I went through all the security records and found seven different girls over a four-year period."

"All the time Hunter and I were there?" he asked. He knew that he'd never drugged a girl. Since he was the star quarterback, panties had practically fallen off as he'd walked by women.

"Yes."

"Did the reports end when we left?" he asked.

She flushed and took a sip of her drink. "I never checked. I was determined to find out what really happened to Stacia, but the women who were drugged didn't run with you or Hunter so it was a dead end."

"Maybe it wasn't. What else did you uncover?"

Hunter and he had both been over the night a million times, but there were pieces that were missing. Things they'd never been able to put together.

"You are serious about this," she said again. "I'm shocked. I thought you had moved on."

"The ID channel is running a ten-years-later special on the Frat House Murder. They always do those re-enactments that make it seem like Hunter and I killed her. And I have son who's three, Daria. He's going to start school soon and the murder is always going to be a question in everyone's mind. But everyone still thinks I did it. Even you."

She leaned in and he had a feeling he was getting her reporter persona now. "Why? You have your life. You've been cleared of all charges."

"But everyone still thinks I did it. Even you."

She shook her head. "Touché. I think you might be changing my mind a bit."

"Would you mind sending me the research you did? I just want to see if there is something that you uncovered that will jog my memories of the night."

"If you uncover what happened, will you give me the story first?" she asked.

They would need someone to bring the story to light, and giving it to her wouldn't be a bad idea. "Sure."

"Okay. I'll send you what I have. It's not a lot. I mean, I copied the security reports and I have some videos and pictures that people took at the party that night."

"What were you going to do with them?" he asked.

"I'll compare them to see if the same people who were known to be at the other parties where the girls were drugged were there that night. There were no other reports of druggings the night Stacia died."

"Is that odd?" he asked. He couldn't wait to go through her notes.

"Sort of. Every other time it happened, there were a few women who reported feeling funny but who hadn't been attacked. Almost like the perpetrator had drugged a few women to see who would be an easy target."

"Interesting. I look forward to getting your notes," he said, taking a business card out of his pocket and handing it to her. She took it from him, dropping it in her purse before she got to her feet and left.

He might have gotten their first solid lead on who had harmed Stacia. The campus security hadn't been cooperative when he'd called them and no one wanted to talk to the guy they thought was trying to pin his crime on someone else.

He pulled his phone from his pocket and noticed he'd missed several calls from Conner's iPad. He checked the time but it was too late to call. He texted his son to say he loved him and then texted Gabi to apologize.

Now that he was on the path to figuring out what had really happened, it didn't seem too far-fetched to think about the future and Gabi waiting for him at home. He knew he needed to call Conner but it was after two in the morning, which was eleven in Carmel. His son would be sleeping and he'd wait until the morning to call him.

Gabi woke to Kingsley's text message on her phone. She rolled over in bed and stared at it. She had about ten minutes before Conner woke up. Her habit was to always wake before her alarm went off. Even as a teenager she was always awake before it.

Kingsley's text wasn't very explanatory; in fact, it was almost impersonal. She hoped he sent something more to his son. Conner was going to want to talk to him as soon as he woke up.

She texted Kingsley back to that effect and he returned her text saying he was waiting for Conner to call him.

She hopped out of bed and hurried into the bathroom, taking a few minutes to pull her hair back so it didn't look so crazy. She debated putting on makeup but that would look as if she was trying to impress him. So she settled for a quick swipe of eyeliner to define her eyes and then went into Conner's room just as "Everything Is Awesome" started playing.

He rubbed his eyes and glanced over at her with his stuffed pig in his arms. His hair was tousled and his gaze moved from her to his iPad, which she'd left propped open on his nightstand.

"I have to potty," he said.

"Go ahead, I'll keep my eye on the iPad."

He ran into the bathroom and then came back out a few minutes later. Just as he sat down on his bed again and was opening the app to video chat with his dad, Kingsley called him.

Conner hit the button and stared down at his dad's face. Happiness lit up the little boy's face. "Daddy, we missed you last night."

"I know, buddy. I'm so sorry. Tell me what you did yesterday."

As Conner talked, Gabi stared at Kingsley. It was just after noon on the East Coast. She was trying to see if he was in a hotel room but soon realized that he was in a car.

"Gammi didn't know about the man in the moon," Conner was saying. "But she did know some camping songs."

"That's good. So you enjoyed the campfire and then told her about the man in the moon. What else?"

"I fell asleep waiting for you. Was your meeting good?" Conner asked.

"It was. I might be done early."

"Yippee!" Conner jumped up on his bed and danced around on it. "Daddy is coming home!"

"Not yet, buddy. I'm trying to set up one more meeting before I can get back. I'll let you know at bedtime tonight."

"Okay. Love you, Daddy."

"Love you, too, Con. Go brush your teeth so I can talk adult stuff with Gabi."

"Okay."

Conner scampered off, his energy palpable now that he'd talked to his dad.

"What's up? Also, what kind of meeting were you at so late at night? Conner goes to bed at eight," she said.

"I wanted to let you know that I'm going to be leaving Manhattan and heading to Chicago. I will text you when my meeting's over," he said.

She noticed he didn't say what kind of meeting it was.

She felt a little angry because now she thought it might have been a date. And she knew she had no reason to be angry. They'd kissed—that was it. That wasn't a promise of anything except maybe another kiss. But Conner had been really upset that his father hadn't called last night.

"You know, it's fine if you want to go on a date. But Conner was worried about you. I almost called Hunter to calm him down. He wouldn't go to sleep."

"If it was a date, Gabriella, I would have said it was a date. I wouldn't have called it a meeting. I didn't mean to worry him. When Jade died in the car accident, he was too young to remember. He only knows that she was traveling. This hasn't been an issue before. I'll talk with him when I'm home," Kingsley said.

Gabi didn't feel that bad about assuming he was on a date. She knew lots of parents who claimed to be in meetings when they weren't. "I can help, too. We are going to be here all day today. We didn't discuss this, but how do you feel about me conducting meetings out of the home office?"

He rubbed the back of his neck. He looked tired and stressed now that she was really looking at him.

"I'd rather you didn't. I haven't advertised my address because there are people who post that information about me and Hunter on the web."

She had heard of those websites, had even stumbled on one when she'd done her Google search. He was listed on a blog run by someone named Captain Justice called *Presumed Guilty as Hell.* It had struck her as ironic that the blogger posted personal information about suspects who'd been wrongly accused but kept his own identity hidden.

"No problem. I'm still trying to figure out the logistics of working from here. A week isn't a long time."

"Wow, it's already been a week," he said. "Are you glad I blackmailed you into helping me out?"

"Glad? No, not really. But I do like this job and it's giving me a lot of ideas for my column," she said, smiling.

"I'm glad to hear that. Is there anything else I need to know?"

"I'm scheduled for a talk at a women's group a week from Thursday. Will you be back by then?" she asked.

"I will. I expect to be home either later tomorrow or the day after," he said.

"Conner will be happy to hear it," she said.

A minute later he was back in his bedroom. She scooted over so he could hold the iPad and talk to Kingsley again.

Conner leaned in close to the camera and gave his dad a big smile. "How's my teeth?"

Gabi had to laugh. She wondered how much of last night's upset had to do with being tired, because he was fine today.

"Perfect. See you soon," Kingsley said.

"Bye, Daddy," Conner replied, disconnecting the call.

She spent the rest of the morning trying to forget that moment when Kingsley had said he wasn't on a date. It didn't mean anything.

And during Conner's nap, when she came across pictures of him in a club on a society blog, she realized it really didn't mean anything. Except he'd lied.

Seven

"So this place is nice," Melissa said as she put a stack of papers in front of Gabi to sign the next day. "Doesn't seem like it's much of a hardship to be living here. I think I'd spend all day staring out the window."

Gabi smiled at her assistant. "Did I make the wrong choice when I promoted you?"

"Hell, no. Just saying. You weren't too sure about working here—"

"Not because of the location. Who wouldn't want to be on a cliff-top mansion with the Pacific Ocean stretching endlessly in front of them?"

"So how is the kid? Is he spoiled?"

Gabi shook her head. She turned away from Melissa, thinking about how sweet little Conner was. He was the kind of child that made being a nanny easy. She loved his attitude and the way he was well behaved. She tried to ignore the fact that a lot of that had to do with

Kingsley. Conner had his moments when he went into toddler meltdown, but King was firm with him. She'd seen the way he handled Conner's temper. He made sure Conner knew his behavior wasn't acceptable and always got him back on track.

She was impressed.

Not just with the three-year-old. But also with his thirtysomething father. Kingsley might have come back to California for reasons he wasn't being entirely clear with her on, but a part of her was starting to believe him when he'd said it was because he wanted Conner to have all the advantages of growing up in the sun and sand that Kingsley hadn't had.

"Conner is great. It's just that I haven't nannied in so long and I'm busy with the admin stuff. Thanks for driving out here today to deliver this paperwork. I'm glad we got the visas for South America out of the way. We also need to have proof of vaccinations before any of our employees leave for the rain forest."

"I'm on it," Melissa said. "I need some advice on something."

"Shoot."

"Abby is back. She wants to try another placement. I feel like she's taking advantage of our friendship," Melissa said.

Abby wasn't the best nanny; she flirted with a lot of the fathers so the moms weren't exactly keen to have her living in. "What did she say?"

"Just that she really needs a job and since I was in charge of hiring…"

"She can't go back into a house, but have you considered her as your assistant?" Gabi suggested. Gabi had a soft spot for Abby. She was a hard worker, and the kids loved her. And Gabi hated to think of anyone who was willing to work not working.

"I hadn't. That's a good idea. I will mention it to her," Melissa said. "Thanks."

"No problem. I get how hard it is to deal with friends and business."

"Wasn't that how you got started?" Melissa asked.

"Yes, Mal knew my parents. So when he mentioned needing a nanny…my mom said I would do it."

"What? She didn't even ask you?"

"Nope. She just decided I'd been figuring out my next move long enough and she pushed me back out into the world."

"That's funny. Were you mad?"

"At first, but it turned out to be the best thing for me. It gave me a chance to find a career I wouldn't have ever thought to try. And now it's a big business. I'd never admit it to her, but she's always known best."

"Moms are like that."

"They are. I think I've signed everything. I have a meeting tomorrow with the city planners about the playground that Kingsley's funding. I'm not sure if he will be back. If not, would you watch Conner while I go to the meeting? The housekeeper has a dentist appointment tomorrow."

"No problem. In fact, I don't have to be back to the office until two. Want me to meet him today?" Melissa asked.

"Yes, let's go."

Melissa put all the paperwork that Gabi had signed into her big leather backpack and they went down the hall to the sunny nursery where Conner was playing with his Duplo and Lego blocks. Mrs. Tillman was sitting on a chair in the sun reading on her Kindle.

"I guess my break is over," she said with a wink.

"Mrs. Tillman, this is my assistant, Melissa." The two women shook hands and chatted while Gabi went over to check on Conner.

"What are you building?"

"A space station," he said. "Want to help?"

"Sure. I brought Melissa in to meet you. She's going to watch you tomorrow while I'm at a meeting," Gabi said.

Conner looked up at Melissa, who'd finished talking to Mrs. Tillman and had joined them. She squatted down next to Conner.

"Hey, kiddo."

"Hello."

"Can I help with the space station? I went to space camp when I was a teenager. So I know a few things that they don't show everyone."

"Cool. Like what?"

Melissa showed him how to build an observation platform and Gabi stood up to straighten the room, surprised when she noticed that Kingsley stood in the doorway. He was back early.

"Daddy!" Conner yelled and jumped up to run over to his father.

Kingsley picked Conner up and hugged him tightly, kissing the top of his head.

"How have you been?"

"Great. I'm building a space station."

"I see that," Kingsley said.

"Will you be okay with Conner while Gabi and I speak in the other room?" Kingsley asked Melissa.

Gabi realized as he turned back to her and gestured for her to precede him out of the room that Kingsley was pissed. She could see it in his eyes. She wasn't sure what had happened.

She led the way down the hall to his home office and stepped inside. The shutters hadn't been opened and the room was dark and cold as she walked into it.

She didn't want to be alone with him now that she realized he hadn't been honest with her. She wished she could say that his lying to her would be enough to make her not want to kiss him and run her hands all over him, but that wasn't the case. He looked tired. As though his trip hadn't been a good one. She wanted to ignore what she'd seen, what she'd found out with a little internet digging and just open her arms to him.

Offer him comfort and whatever else he wanted.

Damn.

She was weak where he was concerned. She always had been and that was her problem. No matter how many times she thought she'd moved on, as soon as they were in the same room she was ready to believe whatever he said.

But she needed answers. And she wasn't going to be pacified by any half-truths. After first thinking he'd been on a date with the woman he'd been photographed with on the society blog, she'd remembered something. The woman looked familiar. So Gabi had done more research. She'd uncovered some things on the internet that led her to believe that Kingsley and Hunter might be back in California for, well, revenge.

And she had admitted to herself she simply didn't know him well enough to rule that out as a possibility. But she knew that if she'd been wronged the way they had...well, she would be tempted to find out who had set her up and then get back at the person, too.

"What the hell is she doing here?" Kingsley said.

"I thought I was clear that for what I was paying, you were to be Conner's nanny."

Gabi turned to face him. "Watch your tone, Kingsley. Melissa had to deliver some papers for my signature and since I have a meeting tomorrow that I can't miss and you weren't supposed to be back, she was getting to know Conner so that when she watched him at my office tomorrow he'd feel more comfortable."

He looked chagrined for a second, pushing his hand through his thick hair. He shook his head. "Sit down, Gabi. Let's be civilized."

"Why wouldn't we be?" she asked. "It's not like one of us is here for revenge."

"What did you say?" He stood up and walked around his desk toward her but she stood her ground.

"Just playing a hunch. Looks like I hit pay dirt," she said. "I thought that woman in the photo with you on the society blog looked familiar. She went to school with us. She was in my humanities class."

"What's that got to do with revenge?" he asked. His voice was low and controlled.

"Nothing on the surface. But she contacted me about four years ago and asked me what I remembered of the party that night. Had I felt drugged or anything."

Kingsley turned away from her and paced over to the window. "I didn't see your name in the file she gave me."

"Probably because I wasn't drugged and I didn't drink anything. I was focused on you. I didn't want to have any hazy memories or anything like that. I knew our night together was one I wanted to remember," she said. Saying it out loud reminded her that it was true. She'd thought she and Kingsley were special. She'd believed in happily-ever-after.

"I'm sorry. I wish I could have given you everything you dreamed of instead of having you wake up to that nightmare. I'm trying to make things right. Hunter and I heard some stories over the last few years of incidents that were similar to what happened to Stacia. We know we didn't do anything like that, so we're investigating. It isn't *revenge*."

Gabi closed the gap between them and put her hand right in the middle of his chest. His heartbeat was solid under her palm and he smelled good. That expensive cologne of his always made her want to curl up in his arms.

"I know you, Kingsley. You aren't someone who's going to be content to say, 'We found the guy who did this.' You and I both know that. Be honest with me."

He looked down at her, his eyes so cold and icy that she dropped her hand from his chest. Oh, yes, he was here for revenge. He was here to ruin whoever had crossed him all those years ago and set him up to take the fall for something he hadn't done.

Revenge. When she said it he didn't like the way it sounded. But he wasn't going to be swayed from his path, not now.

"You're right. I do want to find out what happened and make sure the one responsible pays," he said. "But that has nothing to do with you."

He took her hand and put it back on his chest. He liked it when she touched him. He was tired. Frustrated from all the dead ends he'd chased. Talking to women who thought he was guilty and had bought his freedom had left him with a sour taste in his mouth.

He'd gone to Chicago to speak with two of the women

mentioned in Daria's files, but they hadn't wanted to speak to him. He couldn't blame them.

He had no idea how he was going to make any inroads with his investigation. He'd reviewed the videos Daria had supplied, but most of them were shaky and he hadn't seen anything new. The pictures were also a dead end. He'd sent everything to Hunter to review, as well. But in terms of interviewing the women who'd been drugged, he doubted Hunter was going to get a warmer reception than he had, so they were stuck.

And vengeance and justice seemed even further away today than it had last week.

His body said the only thing that would relieve the stress and pain was Gabi. But he also didn't feel right kissing her. He felt tainted by the past and though nothing—absolutely freakin' nothing—had changed, it felt as if it had.

He lowered his head slowly, giving her time to pull away, but she went on her tiptoes, her hand pushing against his chest as their lips met.

This kiss wasn't the carnal dare the last one had been. This was all Gabi. She was the gentle breeze that circled his home on a spring day, thawing those frozen, broken parts of his soul that he'd always pretended didn't exist.

He knew he shouldn't do this. Any more than he should have kept dating her when she'd come to see him in jail. Right now, by asking questions, he was stirring up things people had forgotten about.

She bit his lower lip. Surprised, he drew his head back.

"What was that for?"

"For not paying attention to the kiss. What's distracting you?" she asked.

"I shouldn't do this. Before I started asking questions I felt like you and I could have an affair and there wouldn't be any repercussions, but now… I'm not so sure," he admitted.

He wasn't afraid to let her see the real man behind the confident swagger.

Gabi had always been the one person he felt he could let his guard down with.

"Let me be the judge of what's right for me. I'm a big girl now," she said.

But being a big girl had nothing to do with the ugly gossip that could come from nowhere. Even his wife had been painted with some ugly innuendo after they'd married. Jade hadn't allowed it to bother her, but she'd been used to ignoring the paparazzi and Gabi wasn't.

Gabi was a nanny who had spent most of her adult life taking care of wealthy children. There was nothing that would have prepared her—

"Stop it."

"Stop what?"

"Trying to tell yourself that I need you to protect me. I've gotten along just fine without you. I want you to see me as a woman. Not someone fragile creature you have to protect."

"I always see you as a woman," he replied. "In fact, it's been damn hard to see you any other way. Every night when I saw Conner on the video chat I couldn't help staring at you when he wasn't looking. I think I'm obsessed."

"Obsession isn't necessarily a bad thing," she said. "But I'm not an object you are watching from afar. I'm right here with you, and instead of talking about revenge and the past, how about we do something about it?"

"What did you have in mind?" he asked. Revenge was slowly being pushed to the back of his mind.

She eased her hands under his sport coat and slowly worked it off his shoulders and down his arms. He let it slide to the floor and then stood there waiting to see what she'd do next.

He liked Gabi like this. When she took control.

She went up on her tiptoes and twined her hands around the back of his neck. "Now, let's try this welcome-home kiss thing again."

"Oh, it was a welcome-home kiss?" he asked. Her breath was minty fresh and brushed over his lips when she talked. Her curvy petite body was pressed against his chest, and her fingers were fondling the back of his neck.

Shivers spread down his spine and he was suddenly very aware of every second since the last time he'd held this woman in his arms. He wanted her.

Blood pooled in his groin and his erection grew. He lowered his head slowly and this time thought of nothing but her full mouth and how she tasted when he kissed her.

She parted her lips under his, her tongue sliding deep into his mouth. He put his hands on her waist and drew her closer, rubbing his groin against her center. A soft little moan escaped her.

He was on fire.

He lifted her off her feet and turned to walk to his desk. He set her down on the edge of it without breaking the kiss and stepped between her legs. Now that she was seated on his desk, he was free to let his hands roam all over her. He caressed her back, squeezing her hips as he drew her even closer to his erection, rubbing against her as she deepened the kiss.

Her fingers tangled in the hair at the back of his neck and tugged as she bit lightly at his tongue.

He knew that he was going to have to stop soon. His son was just down the hall along with two women in their employ. This wasn't proper behavior—but he knew he'd never really given a crap about proper behavior.

And he certainly wasn't going to start now when he had Gabi in his arms and she was setting him on fire.

There was a knock at the door and he tore his mouth from hers.

"Who is it?"

"Mrs. Tillman. Sorry to interrupt, but Hunter is here and he says he needs to speak to you urgently."

"Kingsley—for God's sake, Mrs. Tillman, let me by," Hunter said through the door. Kingsley wasn't going to pull away from Gabi like an embarrassed lothario, but he didn't want Hunter to say anything rude.

"Just a minute, Hunter."

He kissed Gabi again softly. "Dinner tonight after Conner is in bed."

She nodded. He helped her off his desk and she walked out of his office past a stunned Hunter and a smiling Mrs. Tillman.

Eight

Driving from Kingsley's coastal mansion into Carmel wasn't a burden. The day was beautiful and she felt so good and happy.

Kingsley was back in town.

So different from how she'd felt when he'd walked in her door. A part of her was afraid to trust the way she felt about him. This was Kingsley Buchanan and he lived life on his own terms. Even before he'd been arrested he'd been his own man.

But this time…she couldn't help it. She was falling in love with him again. She knew it.

There was nothing else to explain why she kept grinning. And when she gathered her notes to go into the meeting with the community leaders, she couldn't help the feeling of pride that Kingsley was the man who was making this new playground possible.

Her phone rang as she was about to get out of the car. A glance at the caller ID showed it was her mom.

"Hi, Mom."

"Gabi, hello. You haven't called me in days. I was worried about you."

"Why were you worried?" she asked. "I told you I was working as a nanny in a client's home and that I would check in when I could. And I did text you last night."

"Texting doesn't put my mind at ease. Someone else could have your phone and send that." Gabi laughed and her mom started laughing, too. "Okay, so maybe I worry too much."

"You do," Gabi told her. "Why are you calling?"

"Are you free for brunch on Sunday? Your brother is in town and wants us to meet his girlfriend."

"Definitely. I want to meet her. Alejandro has been too secretive about her. I'm curious," Gabi said. "I might bring a date."

"Really? Both of my kids with a date. I won't be able to eat from all the excitement."

"Is that sarcasm? You'd think someone who was worried I might be in danger would be a bit nicer," Gabi said.

"Ha. Who's your mystery man?" her mom asked.

Gabi bit her lip. "Kingsley Buchanan."

"Kingsley? The boy from college? Gabi, now I really am worried."

"Mom, don't be. It's not like I thought."

"What about how I thought? That we were lucky you weren't dead, too."

"Mom! He was cleared of any charges."

"But no one knows what really happened."

"Kingsley does and he said he didn't do it," Gabi said.

Then she realized how that sounded. As though she

was grasping at straws to convince her mom of Kingsley's innocence. But she did believe him and she always had. But if her mom was this hard to convince, her father would be even harder. "Never mind. I'll come alone."

"Gabi, I'm sorry, but I just want what's best for you," her mom said.

"I know that. I have a meeting, so I better let you go," Gabi said.

"Not yet. Tell me why you like this—why you like Kingsley."

Why did she like him? It was always hard to put feelings into words and she worried that she'd sound like an idiot. But she closed her eyes and thought of Kingsley. Of how he'd looked when he came home from being on the road doing business.

"He makes me laugh, Mom. And he's smart and a good dad. His little boy is sweet and charming—a mini version of Kingsley."

"He has a son?"

"Yes. Mom, everyone knows he has a son. He also is a famous sports agent now that he's quit playing football."

"Oh, I didn't follow him after he left your life."

Gabi understood that. Her mom didn't dwell on the past—she was more of a shake-it-off-and-move-on type of person. "He's trying to move on for his son. And there are a lot of things about that night that make no sense. I think that's why the DA dropped the charges."

"Okay. I will talk to your father, but we'd love to have you and Kingsley and his son for brunch on Sunday."

She realized that her mom was going to be fair and give Kingsley a chance. For her. That meant a lot. "I'll have to ask Kingsley."

"Okay. Let me know. Call me later and I'll tell you what I've found out about Alejandro's girlfriend."

"I will," she said.

She hung up the phone and fiddled with her notes one more time before texting Kingsley.

Would you like to go to brunch on Sunday at my parents' house?

Do they know you are bringing me?

Duh. I asked if you wanted to go.

Conner too?

Yes.

Sure, as long as they are civil about the past.

They will be.

She typed in her next message and hesitated before finally hitting Send.

It never goes away, does it? You constantly have to deal with that night.

I am. That's why I want to put it to rest once and for all.

I can help.

I appreciate that. But I don't want you involved.

We can talk later. I'm off to my meeting now.

Gabi, I mean it. I don't want this to taint you at all.

Bye. See you at home later.

She wasn't going to let Kingsley tell her what to do. The affection she had for him was still growing inside her. When she thought of Conner and Kingsley she didn't want the two of them to continue to live with the aftermath of false accusations. She knew it was going to be hard. But she wanted to help Kingsley figure what happened so he could move on to a future with her.

"Go long," Kingsley said, and Hunter ran a pattern they'd done a million times before. Kingsley threw the ball and a few seconds later Hunter leaped in the air, caught it and started running, only to be blocked by Conner, who launched himself at Hunter's knees and brought him down.

Hunter rolled carefully, scooping up Conner with him so that he didn't hurt the toddler, and then sat up.

"I got you," Conner said.

"You sure did. You're pretty good at this. Thinking about being a football player someday like your daddy and me?"

Conner shook his head. "I'm going to be a knight."

"Wow, really? There aren't that many knights around these days," Hunter said.

"Gammi likes them," Conner said. "Daddy, I can be a knight, right?"

Gabi liked knights. Who knew? He was going to have to look into that a bit more. She seemed way too practical and too much of a twenty-first-century independent woman.

"You sure can," he said. "Modern knights are men who are polite and always treat a woman like a lady."

Hunter snorted. "Good luck with that."

"Thanks!" Conner said with a big grin.

Conner stole the ball from Hunter, jumped off him and ran the ball back to Kingsley.

"Want to try to catch it this time?" Kingsley asked his son.

"Yes," Conner said.

"Come here and I'll show you how to run the pattern," Hunter said.

Conner jogged back to Hunter and Kingsley watched his best friend and his son. Hunter would be a good father if given the chance. But not as long as the specter of Stacia's death hung over them both.

He had no idea what they would find next. He knew they were going to need some help. Most of the women who'd been drugged at the parties in college weren't interested in talking to him or Hunter. He toyed with asking Gabi to reach out to them. It would be the simplest thing. But he didn't really want her involved in the matter.

"You going to throw the ball or just stare at us?" Hunter asked.

He tossed the ball to Conner, careful to throw where he knew his son would be. He also didn't put the same force he would put behind a throw for Hunter. His son caught it and Kingsley felt a wave of love wash over him at the pure joy on Conner's face.

"Daddy, I did it."

"You sure did."

They played until the sun started to set. Hunter and he drank beers while they watched Conner playing with his toy set on the living room floor.

"I saw that Gabi is the head of the alumni committee," Hunter said.

"I noticed that, too. I'm not sure how that will help us," Kingsley said. They both were talking quietly. Conner seemed engrossed in his play, but Kingsley didn't want to take a chance on saying anything that his son would repeat later.

"Me, either. Just mentioning it. I have been over the files you sent me. I noticed that Mitch's name was in there a lot."

"You keep in touch with him?" Kingsley asked. Mitch had been a defensive back on the college team. And Kingsley hadn't really ever had a chance to talk to the man. Maybe once or twice but for the most part he was a stranger.

"No. But I think that Chuck has. I am going to take my Harley and drive over to the college and see if he will talk to me," Hunter said. "Want to come with me?"

Chuck had been a running back and now coached special teams for their former college. Kingsley and he had both played for New York, so he knew Chuck pretty well. "I might. I can't go on a bike if we take Conner with us."

"I was thinking that your nanny would be back by now," Hunter said.

"Well, she's meeting with the town council today. I think the meeting is going to go long," he said. "How about if we plan for tomorrow? Maybe we can drop by our coach's house, as well. His housekeeper might know when he's going to be back home."

"Good thinking," Hunter said. "I wasn't able to find out why he was in the hospital. But he is getting old. It's odd to think of the man who was such a tyrant on the field being sick."

"It is," Kingsley agreed. Coach Gainer had always been tough but fair. He had worked them hard every day they were on campus and it had paid off. He'd never resented those long grueling hours since they had brought him the results he'd wanted.

"Maybe we can get Gabi to help," Hunter said.

"I really don't want her involved in this," Kingsley said.

"Involved in what?" Hunter asked. "Women will talk to her. They aren't going to talk to us."

"That's precisely what I don't want her involved in," Kingsley said.

"Involved in what?" Gabi said from the doorway, surprising them both.

"Our investigation," Hunter said.

"Hunter, don't—"

Hunter was determined to ignore his wishes on this and that pissed him off. Gabi wasn't a pawn to be used by either of them.

"It's okay," Gabi said. "What can I do?"

"Nothing. As soon as you start asking questions, people are going to think you know more about that night," Kingsley said. "You can't have that. Your business will suffer."

Hunter didn't look happy but then he nodded. "King is right. Sorry, Gabi. I wasn't thinking about how this will look to your clients if you start asking questions on our behalf."

"It's okay. I have drinks with a group from my sorority once a month. I can ask if anyone remembers hearing stories from that night. I'll say that you are back in town and that's what made me think of it."

"Won't they talk?" Kingsley asked. Every instinct he had said she should stay away from questioning anyone.

"Not my girls. We're solid. And we're sisters. I'm happy to do it. Also, I could contact the women on your list, Kingsley, for an article for the alumni newsletter."

Kingsley didn't like it. He wanted vengeance on the person who had framed them, and that was something that was too…too dark for Gabi. He didn't want any of this to touch her, but as they looked through the new photos King had found together he realized it already had.

He had come back to fix this for himself but he realized now he had to fix the past for Gabi, too.

Gabi hadn't been on a date in about six months. It wasn't that she didn't like going out. It was simply… well, if Melissa and her mother were to be believed, she was too picky.

Picky.

That made it sound as if she had hordes of great guys to choose from, but the truth was she didn't meet that many men who were interested in her. Most guys her age were married or in serious relationships. And then the fact that she owned a nanny service made the men she did meet fear she wanted kids right away.

So it was slim pickings, as her dad used to say.

But none of that explained why she'd taken extra care with her makeup and hair after she'd put Conner to bed. Or the fact that she'd ordered a new dress from Nordstrom and paid Melissa double time to pick it up and bring it to her at Kingsley's house.

She knew the truth. She hated to admit it even to herself, but it was staring back at her in the mirror. She wanted this date to be a good one. She wanted the past mistakes between her and Kingsley to fade away. She wanted this to be some kind of over-the-top romantic date that she could use to replace the memories of their first one. A frat party that had ended in murder.

Damn.

She realized that all of her dreams of the future had changed that night. She had wanted a family. She had wanted to find what her parents had found when they were young. A partner. Someone to share her life with. She was staring down thirty. Honestly, by this time she'd imagined she'd have a family of her own. Not still be taking care of other families.

But none of that mattered tonight. Tonight was just a date.

Yes, her first in a while. Yes, one with Kingsley Buchanan. Yes, she wanted it to be perfect.

But she had that tingling in her stomach that warned her she was already in over her head. Heck, she'd known that when she'd defended Kingsley to her mother. When she'd come up with excuses as to why he'd been at a nightclub with another woman. When she'd carefully worded the proposal to the county commissioners so that Kingsley's name wasn't in it.

She was hedging her bets. Being careful to be on her best behavior. And it seemed that Kingsley was doing the same.

They were both pretending.

She knew it. She wondered if he did.

It would be so easy to pretend she wasn't. But she knew herself. She wouldn't lie; Kingsley was the one man she'd always had regrets about. The one man that she wanted a proper resolution with.

But she was afraid to trust in Kingsley and his real reasons for wanting her. Oh, she didn't doubt the power of the attraction between them. What she wasn't sure about was whether or not he'd still want her after she slept with him.

She put her lipstick down, braced her hands on the marble countertop and looked into the mirror.

There it was in her eyes. The secret fear that she'd been hiding and ignoring for too long—she was afraid to sleep with him in case it was like the last time when one night was all he spent with her.

She'd been cautious in her intimate relationships, always picking men who were staid and sensible. They weren't the most passionate of men, but they were consistent. But King wasn't. And he never had been.

He'd been the handsome, popular guy on campus and despite everything life had thrown at him, he still was. And it wasn't that she doubted her ability to keep his attention. She knew he liked her and had confidence in herself. It was just that the last time they'd slept together everything had changed between them. She'd be a fool to think this time would be any different.

Before she'd been a girl—no matter how mature she thought she was, she'd been a little bit silly and a lot foolish. But this time she was smarter.

Or at least she hoped she was.

Though already she liked him. And that was really too weak a word to describe what she felt for him. She knew seeing him with Conner had weakened her resolve. Hearing him talk passionately about needing to put the past to rest so that he could move on had made her dream that he'd move on with her.

But the truth was she was integral to the past. He needed her thoughts on—

"Stop it."

She spoke out loud to quiet her mind. Straightening her shoulders, she fiddled with her hair, put on her lipstick and walked away from the mirror and the woman in it who was afraid.

Six months. It didn't seem that long to be without a date until tonight.

She realized that her nerves had nothing to do with King or his intentions and everything to do with herself. She hadn't dated because she was tired of going through the routine of being someone she wasn't in the hopes that some guy would see through the ruse and like the real woman underneath.

So tonight…

Tonight she wasn't going to do it. She had nothing to lose with King. She knew that. The odds were already stacked against them really being anything other than lovers. She was going to be herself and if he didn't like it…well, that was too bad for him.

Because she couldn't change any more than she already had.

And she liked the woman she was. She forgot that sometimes when she was working, writing, mentoring Melissa. But she truly liked the woman she'd become over the years. The woman that the one night she'd spent with Kingsley had started her on the journey to becoming.

She opened her hall door and walked toward the dining room. When she got there a single rose waited on the table with a small note card with instructions to go to the patio.

She sniffed the rose as she felt that tingle of excitement in her stomach once again.

Candlelight flickered on the patio and flames danced in the large outdoor fire pit. When she stepped outside, her heel caught and she started to stumble, but King was there.

He caught her and she looked up into his eyes.
"I've got you."
He definitely did.

Nine

Kingsley had spent a good deal of time over the years thinking about this night. He'd never really imagined it would happen, but he'd always wanted it to. He wanted to make up to Gabi for all the mistakes he'd made. He'd been young and selfish the first time he'd taken her to his bed. He'd done his best to make it pleasurable for her but she'd always been the one woman to set fire to his veins. A fire that burned straight through his self-control.

Holding her in his arms reminded him that she still had that power.

"Now that you've got me, what are you going to do with me?" she asked. Her words were light but her tone was serious. She was nervous.

"Keep you safe," he said. But he was afraid that might be a promise he couldn't keep. Men focused on revenge had to be aware that there would be collateral damage.

"Promise?"

"Yes."

He knew he shouldn't have said that, but he couldn't help himself. He wanted to protect her.

She opened her mouth but he kissed her before she could ask for more promises from him. He didn't want to talk. Not about this. Not about anything serious. He wanted tonight to be something out of a dream.

He knew from Conner that she liked white knights. Men in shining armor who rode to the rescue of their woman. Damned if he wasn't a battered warrior in severely tarnished armor, but he still wanted to be her hero.

Her mouth was soft and she tasted of fresh mint and something else that was just Gabi. He took his time because it was a mellow California evening and he wanted it to last forever.

He wanted this night to be the start of something new between them. A beginning where he didn't let her down and she began to see him as…well, her hero.

He tangled one hand in her thick hair and let the cool, silky tresses play through his fingers. She tipped her head back and he thrust his tongue deeper into her mouth. She moved in his arms, her body undulating against his.

He put his other hand on her hip and drew her closer, wrapped his fingers around her and squeezed. She moaned and he felt everything inside his body clench. He lifted his head and looked down into her dark brown eyes. He saw the hope and the fear in them and realized that this night was more important than he could have ever imagined.

That tonight he was either going to make up for the past and start a new future with Gabi or he was going to put her forever out of his reach.

He knew what he wanted to happen.

He also had enough experience to know when he wanted something or someone this badly he often made mistakes.

He rubbed his thumb over her lower lip. God, he loved her mouth. It was full and lush and really he could spend all day kissing her. "Ready for a night to remember?"

"I am," she said.

He linked their fingers together and led her to the seating area in front of the fire pit. Mrs. Tillman had made them some appetizers and he had a pitcher of margaritas for them to share.

He seated her and felt the cool evening breeze. Gabi wore a sleeveless sheath made of white lace that showed off her tanned skin. He reached for the package he had placed underneath the bench before she got there and handed it to her as he sat down.

"What? You didn't have to get me anything," she said.

"I know. But I saw this while I was in New York and it reminded me of you," he said.

She gave him a sweet smile. "This is the first gift you've given me."

He knew that, as well. They hadn't dated long enough before his arrest for birthdays or holidays. He'd never had the chance to know if she was a slow present unwrapper or one of those who tore the paper off. Little things that seemed inconsequential until he found the right person.

Damn. This was a date. *Just a date*, he reminded himself.

Gabi was here. She was hot. And he had a lot to make up for from the past. That was it.

She carefully untied the blue ribbon and put it around her neck. His eyes followed the movement, noticing how long her neck was. He reached over to tuck her hair back behind her shoulder, pretending it was so he could see the ribbon better, knowing it was because he needed to touch her.

"Very pretty."

"Thank you," she said. "I love ribbons."

He'd had no idea. But he would remember it for the future.

She carefully unwrapped the box and set the paper aside once she'd folded it. She held the box on her lap, running her fingers over the Bergdorf Goodman lettering before slowly opening it.

Beneath the tissue was the scarf he'd picked out. It was multicolored and had crystals woven into it in a pattern. She pulled it out and held it up in front of her. Then she put it on her lap and traced the gems with her fingers.

"Thank you so much. It's gorgeous."

She stood up after setting the box to the side and put the scarf around her shoulders. She turned and glanced back at him over her shoulder.

"How do I look?"

"Beautiful," he said. His voice sounded hoarse and he knew that was because all the blood in his body had raced to his groin. He was hot and hard. Ready for her.

But when she smiled sweetly at him, he knew he could wait. Just barely.

This night had the promise of being more than sex. Of having all the romance that they had never experienced together.

He took the remote for the Bose speaker out of his

pocket and hit Play. The sultry sounds of blues guitar filled the patio and he walked over to Gabi.

"Dance?"

She nodded. He pulled her into his arms and danced her around the patio under the stars. And though he knew he'd done this all for her, he felt himself falling under a spell. He wanted to pretend that it was the trappings or romance that were making his heart beat faster, but he knew that was a lie.

It was the girl… Gabi was the one responsible.

The music changed from slow blues to "Smooth" by Santana and Rob Thomas. She'd loved that song when they'd been in college. Rob Thomas had been her first teenage crush. And she was pretty sure she'd mentioned it to Kingsley.

She tipped her head back and smiled up at him. "I like this song."

"I remember. You played it for me and made me listen to the lyrics."

"God, I was so annoying back then," she said. "Seriously, what was I thinking?"

"This song meant something to you," he said. "I did listen to the lyrics, and not just because kissing you made me hotter than I'd ever been in my life."

"That's saying something," she said with a small smile. "Why are you romancing me tonight?"

"I like you," he said simply.

"I like you, too," she said. "But that's not enough to warrant all of this."

"Why do you think I'm doing it?" he asked.

She studied him in the light from the flickering candles. His face was serene and as usual he gave away nothing that he was feeling. In fact, the only time she'd seen real emotion on his face was when he looked at Conner. Then she saw alpha dad in his eyes. Now, though, she wanted to see affection and maybe a little devotion, but she didn't see anything.

"I don't know," she said, pulling the gem-encrusted scarf closer around her shoulders as she stepped back from him. "You've got every detail planned, don't you?"

He shrugged and turned to the pitcher of margaritas, pouring each of them a glass. She took one from him.

"To old friends."

Old friends? That wasn't what they were. Maybe she'd been taken in by the house and the kid. Maybe she was pretending there was something more between Kingsley and her. Or was she?

"I'm so unsure tonight," she said. "That's not like me. I don't know if it's the past making me feel this way or you."

He set his drink on the table and came over to her. He took her glass and placed it next to his. Then he wrapped his arms around her and held her close, rubbing his hands up and down her back.

"Either way it's me. I'm trying to make up for everything that I took from you. We both know I never can. That night we were together I was your first. It should have been romantic and special. Not a frat party and then sex in your dorm room. And I knew it. Even then. I wanted to give you more, but I never had the chance. This is me making up for it. I know it's not enough. It will never be enough, but maybe this could be a start."

His words warmed her from the inside out. That cold dark place where the young woman she'd been cowered inside her was suddenly not so cold and definitely not dark. These were words she'd always longed to hear.

Words she'd never really thought she would hear.

Kingsley had wounded her deeply—not the night he'd taken her virginity, but the next day when he'd cruelly turned her away.

And she had to remember it.

"That doesn't help, does it?" he asked. He dropped his arms and moved away from her.

She had a choice to make. She could keep punishing him for the past—and she could come up with a million reasons to justify that. Or—and it was a big thing—she could forgive him and accept this.

She took a deep breath. Fear held her where she was. Fear held her tongue. Fear had her wrapped in an icy grasp. She could let it go.

She needed to let it go.

"It does," she said at last.

She heard him exhale and he turned back to her.

"Good. Now let's drink these margaritas and you can tell me about your favorite things," he said.

"My favorite things?" she asked, picking up her glass and going to sit down on the padded bench again. "Like what? You already know I love Rob Thomas," she said with a wink.

"Still?" he asked, sitting down next to her.

"Yes."

"What other music do you like?"

"Taylor Swift, Ed Sheeran and Kanye."

"Love Kanye. Got to meet him in a club in Manhattan about a year ago," Kingsley said.

They kept talking about music and he found that he wasn't listening to what she said so much as he was enjoying the lyrical sound of her voice. When she was happy it was easy to hear it. And when she laughed everything inside him came alive.

Mrs. Tillman served dinner and then disappeared back inside the house. They ate and talked about politics, books and movies. He found that subjects that had never seemed too important to him when he talked with other people now seemed very vital with her. She made him feel alive and passionate about things he'd never given much weight to before.

"My cousins in Madrid have a lot to say about politics, and every time I visit the dinner conversation is always dominated by the climate in Europe."

He knew she was related through marriage to the Spanish royal family. Her cousin was married to the infanta. "Do you go to Spain a lot?"

"At least twice a year. Mom loves to visit her sister. You know, that's where I went when everything happened with you."

"I didn't know that. I was a little preoccupied with..."

"Getting yourself out of jail," she said. "Tell me about that."

"That's the last thing I want to talk about tonight," he said.

She took his hand in hers. She knew she had little choice but to deal with this. She wanted to understand the man he'd been back then because it went a long way toward explaining the man Kingsley was today.

"I just want to know a little more about what happened," she said. "You have questions about that night—I know you've been talking to our classmates—but I want to know about what happened after."

Kingsley pulled his hand from hers. "I know you do, but that time just stirs up anger and fear. I will be happy to discuss it with you another time. Just know that entire summer I was wishing that I could be with you."

* * *

Kingsley didn't want to talk about that night. Not now. He spent all of his free time trying to figure out how to fix what had happened, but tonight he wanted to be a regular guy. The kind of man who could romance a woman he was interested in.

But that wasn't who he was.

Was he fooling himself that they could ever be more than this—two people with a white-hot attraction between them and too much history?

He didn't think of himself as an idiot. So why was he always taking missteps with Gabi? He saw hesitation in her now. She had wrapped one arm around her own waist and he felt it. Those damned chains of the past. He was never going to be free of what had happened.

Even being set free and having those charges dropped hadn't removed the stain. Were he and Hunter fooling themselves that finding the person responsible for Stacia's death was going to bring closure?

Until now, he hadn't thought so. He wasn't a defeatist so he refused to believe that this couldn't be fixed.

But tonight…tonight he'd been in a different head space. Now he was back to the world where doubt, vengeance and anger seemed to rule.

"I'm sorry. I didn't mean to bring that up," she said. "Why don't we go for a walk on the beach and pretend we are just like any other couple."

"Because we aren't," he said.

"No, we're not. But for tonight I was forgetting it," she said.

He could tell that she was sort of lying about it. But he let her get away with it because he wanted to pretend, too. Mrs. Tillman was in the house watching over Conner for this one night, so he knew it was safe for the both of them to be gone. He took her hand in his and she squeezed it tight.

For a minute he wished he were someone else. Anyone else. Just a regular guy with a normal job. Someone who maybe couldn't afford a nanny but needed a sweet, sexy woman like Gabi in his life.

Then the line blurred.

He was that lonely single dad. He had been for a while. Peri had made it easy for him to ignore the fact that his life had turned into all dad, all the time. Work was time-consuming, but most of the time he had staff to deal with the most demanding clients. He had the right people in place to help him with Conner. The only place where he was missing the right person was romantically.

Tonight he had been on the path to fixing that before the past had once again smacked him square in the jaw. And he was smarting from it.

He wanted to react the way he always did. Maybe carry Gabi into the house to his bedroom. Make love to her until he couldn't think anymore and then…then walk away. Get the hell out of California and give up on finding any closure. He would buy an island somewhere and homeschool Conner…except he wasn't a coward. He had never run from anything. He wasn't going to start now.

He led the way to the path down to the beach. "Why did you agree to this date? Did you feel like I owed you one?"

She watched her steps and when they got to a flat stretch of sand she stopped and turned to look at him. "No. I felt like I owed myself something. Everything that happened between us made me afraid to date guys I really liked. Made me think maybe I'd end up alone again. I never understood that I was trapped in that. I'm not saying I know what the future holds for us. But I'm not going to keep pretending that I don't want to be with you."

Her words humbled him. He'd told her his sin. Told her the truth that he'd been hiding from the world—and hell, from himself—for too long. But tonight none of that seemed to matter.

The sound of the waves on the shore lulled them as they walked slowly down the beach. She didn't speak and neither did he. He didn't want to. He just let the night close around them.

The breeze brought the scent of her perfume and sometimes stirred the long strands of her hair so that they seemed to dance around her head.

"If you could have one thing, what would it be?" he asked.

He wanted to build a bridge between the past mistakes and the future he was beginning to realize he needed with her.

"I don't know. I've never thought about it. I'm always busy looking at my next business goal or planning a family get-together with my mom. What about you?"

"I want the past cleared up," he said. His focus on that account had never changed. Gabi had a life. She might think she had been hiding from relationships—and maybe she had been—but the rest of her life had gone on. And why shouldn't it? She'd been a bystander in the Stacia matter. Not a real participant.

"I bet. As I said, I'd be happy to help you contact those women on the list," she said.

"I..."

"Let me do this. I want more dates like this, King,

and we both know that until you get some closure you're not going to move forward."

He hadn't had anyone on his side with this except Hunter. Even Jade hadn't wanted to know about it. She'd liked that other people thought he was dangerous. "Okay. But if I see any backlash toward you or your business, you stop."

"Agreed," Gabi said. She stopped walking and looked out at the sea. He stood there next to her.

She turned toward him, wrapping her arms around his shoulders as she went up on tiptoe and kissed him. It was a sensual kiss. The one he'd been craving all night.

Deepening the kiss, he put his hands on the small of her back and lifted her off her feet so that she was pressed along the front of his body. The night breeze stirred around them, wrapping her hair around his neck and shoulders.

He was surrounded by her. He wanted to be naked. To feel her pressed all over him and to be inside her.

He needed that. He lifted his head and switched his hold on her, carrying her back up the path to the house. She just kept her arms wrapped around him, her fingers toying with the hair at the back of his neck until he entered his bedroom and closed the door behind him.

He let her slide down his body until her feet touched the ground. Then he kissed her, taking his time because he knew he wasn't leaving her again.

Ten

Gabi had often thought about that one night with Kingsley. But she didn't want to tonight. She wanted tonight to be new and about the people they were today, not about the past.

She sighed.

"What is it?"

"I… I just want this to be good, you know?"

He cupped her face in his hands and tilted her head back so he could stare down into her eyes. There was something elusive in his gaze. Something she wanted to identify but couldn't.

"It will be better than good," he said, lowering his mouth to hers.

His kiss swept aside the doubts she had about the past. The fire that had slowly been building between them since he'd first walked into her office now blazed out of control.

He caressed his way down from her neck, his fingers tracing a pattern over her skin that made her feel alive in a way she hadn't before. She sucked his lower lip into her mouth and pushed his jacket off his shoulders. His hands left hers as he shrugged out of it and he broke the kiss. His lips were wet and swollen from her kisses.

She watched him as he sauntered over to the closet to hang up his jacket. The light from the closet spilled out onto the floor and he turned to face her.

"I didn't take my time with you when we made love the first time. I want to tonight. But you get to me," he said.

"You get to me, too. I promised myself this time—"

"You'd be smarter?"

Yes. But she didn't want to admit that to him. "I was pretty smart the first time. I got exactly what I wanted that night."

"Did you?" he asked as he toed off his shoes and pulled off his tie.

She nodded. He'd undone the top button of his shirt and his feet were clad only in socks. This was such an intimate thing, she thought, watching a man disrobe. Most of the time when she had sex, they were hurried couplings in the dark. No time to consider if she was making a mistake or not.

But tonight this felt right.

"I did. What about you?"

"I feel the same way I did back then—like a boy about to get lucky for the first time."

"It wasn't your first time," she said quietly, walking over to him and pushing his hands aside. She undid the buttons of his dress shirt, the backs of her fingers brushing against the warm skin of his chest.

He tipped her chin up and looked down into her eyes. "But it was for you."

She nodded.

She'd never tried to hide the fact that she'd waited until she was in college to have sex. And if she were totally honest, she would have waited longer if Kingsley hadn't come along.

He made her crave things she'd never really wanted before. That was why she'd thought she loved him. Why she'd thought…what they had was special. She shook her head, trying to dispel those thoughts.

His shrewd gaze seemed to see all the way to her core. To the doubts that were gaining traction in her mind.

"Don't. I screwed up afterward, but we were good together. And we will be tonight," he said.

Then he cursed and dropped his hands and stepped back from her.

"Unless you've changed your mind," he said. "I won't pressure you."

She hadn't changed her mind. She just wanted to keep it clear in her head that he didn't love her. The fact that he was clearly aroused—she could see his erection pressing against the front of his trousers—but would still walk away if she wanted him to told a lot about the man he was.

And that man was one she wanted in her bed.

"I haven't changed my mind. I just don't want to go all emotional on you."

"How about lusty?" he asked.

She laughed. "Sure."

"Good. Lusty I can handle. Tonight let's just be young and in lust. I haven't had that in a really long time."

She hadn't, either. Being this close to Kingsley reminded her of the woman she'd once been. She needed to find her again tonight.

"Okay, lusty, let's do this."

Now he laughed. And then he smiled over at her, the expression on his face so sweet and almost vulnerable. "You are the only person I know who makes me feel…well, normal."

Normal.

For tonight that was enough.

She closed the gap between them and reached for his buttons again.

He put his hands on her hips and slowly drew her closer. She barely got his buttons undone before his mouth was on hers, kissing her with carnal intent. She felt his hands at the small of her back, drawing up her dress until the cool night air brushed over her buttocks and thighs.

She pushed her hands under the fabric of his shirt and wrapped them around his back just as he cupped her butt and drew her more firmly against the cradle of his hips.

His erection nudged at her and he shifted his stance so that he was rubbing against her center. She caught her breath and her nails dug into his back as he thrust his tongue deep into her mouth while moving his hips in the same rhythm.

They were both still fully clothed but it was one of the hottest things she'd ever experienced.

She sucked on his tongue as he pulled her panties down and she felt his big, warm hands on her bare flesh. He squeezed her buttocks and everything inside her clenched. She wriggled her legs until her panties fell to the floor. He lifted her up with his arm around her waist and took a step backward until he was leaning against the wall.

He held her against him as their mouths and bodies moved together.

He tasted so good, felt so good pressed against her. She wanted to slow down, to savor this moment, but it felt as if someone else had taken over her body. A woman she hardly recognized as herself, but at the same time, it felt so damned right.

She reached between their bodies, scraping her fingernail around his belly button. He tore his mouth from hers, breathing heavily as he looked down at her. No man had ever looked at her with so much desire in his eyes.

If she wasn't already close to the edge of her orgasm, that look would have driven her there. He tangled his hands in her hair and turned so that she was pressed between his body and the wall. He captured one of her hands in his, drew it up over her head and held it shackled to the wall while his mouth came back to hers.

He plundered her mouth. Made her forget everything, even where she ended and he began. She was a creature of fire in his arms and he was something that fed her flame. Drove her higher.

She gasped as she felt his fingers against her most intimate flesh. He drew a teasing pattern over her and then slowly parted her and tapped his finger on her clitoris. She shivered and shook in his arms, struggled to breathe as sensation started to wash over her.

She tried to pull back but there was nowhere to move. He kept tapping on her until her legs were moving frantically against him. Parting to give him greater access to her feminine secrets. His touch on her changed; he cupped her intimately between her legs as his thumb now rubbed over that sweet spot.

She felt his finger tracing the entrance of her body and then slowly he pushed it up inside her. She tore her mouth from his, moaning his name.

He kept pushing his finger higher inside her, going as deep as he could, while his thumb rocked against her. Everything inside her clenched and stars danced behind her closed eyes as she came.

It was harder and stronger than she'd climaxed before. She turned her head and found his shoulder, biting him through the fabric of his shirt while wave after wave of pleasure washed over her. He kept caressing her until she stopped shaking in his arms, and then he lifted her up and carried her over to the bed. He set her down on the edge and she collapsed backward, staring up at his ceiling, which had Spanish mission-style exposed beams and a big ceiling fan that spun lazily above her head.

She was numb with pleasure, shock waves still rocketing through her body.

Kingsley pushed himself to his feet and stepped away from Gabi. He wanted her so badly he felt as if he was going to lose all control. He turned away and took a deep breath. The first time they'd had sex he'd been a college guy with lust on his mind. This time he was a man and he wanted to take his time.

She shifted on the bed, leaning up on her elbows. Her clothing was disheveled and he wanted her naked. He slowly pushed his shirt off and let it fall to the floor.

She sat up and reached toward him. He felt the coolness of her long fingers against his skin. She moved them up his body at a leisurely pace as she got to her feet. She traced the tattoo of Conner's name that was over his heart.

His muscles flexed under her touch. As she scraped her fingernail over the lettering, he felt goose bumps spread all over him. He wanted her. He was so damned close to losing all control.

She put her hands around his biceps. "I never told you, but one of the things that always attracted me to you was your arms."

"My arms?" he asked, struggling to make his voice sound normal and not guttural with need.

"Yes. I love how strong you are. Do you remember the day we met?"

"How could I forget it?" He'd stumbled into her after leaving the gym and almost flattened her. He'd grabbed her and rolled so that he was under her when they fell. And he'd been a goner. He'd had to get to know the woman who had turned him on with one brush of her body against his.

He lowered his mouth to hers, unable to wait another second. He didn't want to discuss the past. He wanted to get her naked and bury himself inside her. Get so deep that nothing would matter except the two of them.

She rose on her tiptoes and tightened her grip on his upper arms. He lifted her again, wrapping his arms around her hips before breaking the kiss and letting her slide slowly down his body.

She reached between them for his belt and while she worked at freeing him from his pants, he found the zipper to her dress and pushed it off her body.

He stepped back as the fabric fell away from her to pool around her feet. She wore only her high heels and a flesh-colored bra. She reached behind her and undid the fastening of her bra, shrugged her shoulders and let it fall to the floor.

She shook her head and her hair danced around her shoulders as she crooked her finger at him. “Come closer.”

He shoved his pants and underwear down his legs and kicked them off. He caught her with one arm around her waist and maneuvered them down to the bed, carefully keeping his weight on his free arm. She parted her legs and he settled between them. Her hands skimmed up and down his back as he pulled his hips back, reveling in the naked feel of her flesh against his.

Naked.

Damn.

“Are you on the pill?” he asked.

“Yes,” she said.

“Good.”

“Good?”

“Yes. I want to feel all of you, Gabi. Against all of me.”

“Me, too,” she said.

He lifted himself up on his elbows so he could look down into her brown eyes. He framed her face with his hands and stroked his thumbs over her cheekbones before slowly moving them lower. He followed the path of his hands with his mouth. Kissing her face and then moving down the side of her neck. He traced her collarbone and found a small scar right above her left breast.

He cupped both of her breasts and stroked his finger over one nipple while he sucked the other one into his mouth. He let his hands move lower over her ribs to her waist. He lifted his mouth from her breast and dropped kisses around her belly button, watching as she shifted against him, her legs moving restlessly.

He continued moving lower, placing his palm over her mound and rubbing before shifting his touch to her most intimate flesh. He traced the opening of her body, and her hips jerked upward against him. She opened her legs wider and he pulled his hand from her and replaced it with his erection.

He drew back his hips and slowly entered her. Grabbed her hands with his and stretched them up over her head as he fully seated himself inside her.

Their eyes met.

He felt that contact all the way to his soul as he started thrusting into her. He went slowly at first, feeling the way her body tightened around him each time. Hearing her gasps and how her breath quickened. He wanted the moment to last but felt his climax closing in on him.

He wanted them to orgasm together and pulled one hand free to reach between their bodies and flick his finger over her clit.

She cried his name and he felt her tightening around him as she arched her back and rocked her hips frantically against his. He buried his head in her neck and thrust harder and deeper than before, driving himself toward climax.

When they had both climaxed, she wrapped her arms and legs around him and stroked her hands up and down his back. She kissed his shoulder and rested her cheek against it.

He lowered his head to her chest, heard the hammering of her heart underneath him. He was careful to keep her from feeling all of his weight.

When he could breathe again, he got up and cleaned them both up. Then he tucked her into his bed and climbed in next to her.

"What are you doing?"

"What I should have done the first time," he said. "Staying with you all night."

She didn't say anything, just curled against him and fell asleep. He stayed awake, though. Knowing that his life would have been very different if he'd done this the last time.

Eleven

The county commissioners were mostly nice people who wanted to make the county better for the citizens who lived here. Her mom had served back in the early nineties and they'd done lots of good projects, like this playground that had been cutting-edge in the 1990s but was now out-of-date and sadly in need of repair.

But all of that was going to be taken care of today. She had the check from Kingsley in her pocket. The plans from the playground engineer she'd hired were in her bag. She had the feeling that she could do anything.

Sure, she was willing to admit the possibility that fantastic sex with Kingsley was partially responsible for her mood. But the truth was that she knew it was more than sex. When she'd woken in his arms this morning and looked over at his face and saw him watching her… she felt something electric pass between them.

Something.

Well, it felt like a hell of a lot more than lust. Was it love?

Love.

It scared her to think how all-encompassing the feeling was. She had to fight the urge to text Kingsley. Just to see how he was doing. Because she missed him.

She'd left his mansion at 7:00 a.m. and had been away from him for a mere three hours. But already she missed him.

Just a month ago she would have been happy to never see him darken her door again but now he made the day seem sunnier.

Damn.

This would be funny if it were happening to someone else. But it was her. And she knew that she wouldn't have it any other way.

She daydreamed about her life with Kingsley and Conner. Thought of them as a picture-perfect little family.

She wasn't really ready to be a mom. And things were complicated with Kingsley. No matter how many dreams she spun in her head, the reality was he was fixated on the past. A past that she was finally finding closure to.

She toyed with the sunburst charm on her necklace as it hit her that she might not have a happy ending with Kingsley. That these emotions that felt like love to her might just be a vehicle for her to move on.

She didn't like the way that thought made her feel.

"Ms. de la Cruz, please follow me. The commissioners are ready for you now."

Gabi followed the young assistant down the hall to the boardroom. She'd been in this room many times before. First as a young girl meeting her mom and then as an adult arguing for more funding for projects for kids and discussing the preliminary planning for the playground. She felt a little nervous as she smoothed her hands down the back of her linen skirt and then exhaled all those nerves out the way she'd learned from her mom all those years ago.

She had this.

Money had been the only stumbling block, and right now she had a check worth more than the commissioners thought the park and recreation center would cost.

"Good afternoon, everyone," she said as she entered the room.

There was a round of greetings and she took a seat after passing out her presentation books. She knew it was the digital age, but she liked paper. She made her presentation feeling the confidence of knowing that there was no way they could turn her down this time.

"Thank you, Gabi. The design you have come up with meets all of our criteria for incorporating the local landscape while at the same time making it a fun and exciting area for the community," Commissioner Ortiz said.

"I like that you've made the focus on children but also included facilities for adults, as well," Mrs. O'Malley said.

Gabi smiled at them. "And I've secured funding. So the only thing we are waiting on to take this project from dream to reality is your approval."

"Well..." Mr. Ortiz said.

"Well? Do you all have an objection?" Gabi asked. She couldn't think of a single thing that was standing in their way.

"We didn't realize that you'd secured funding from Kingsley Buchanan."

"He's a former college sports star and well-known. Why is that a problem?" Gabi asked.

Mrs. O'Malley looked at the other members of the board. All of whom refused to meet her gaze. Gabi felt an icy lump form in the pit of her stomach. Kingsley was their problem?

Finally Mrs. O'Malley leaned forward, leveling her steady gaze on Gabi.

"He's just not the sort of person that this town wants to name things after," she said at last.

"Football star? Single dad? Wealthy businessman? I don't understand your objection, especially since he doesn't expect you to name the facility after him," Gabi said. It was no longer about her playground, though she was still determined to see it go through. No, this was about Kingsley. Were these people honestly not going to accept his money because of charges against him that had been dropped more than ten years ago?

"It's about his arrest," Mr. Ortiz said.

"The charges were dropped," Gabi said. "He has been a free man for more than ten years."

"But many questions remain," Mr. Ortiz said. "And some in our community… Well, we just want the park to be unencumbered by any gossip."

She was angry but she kept her cool. Was this what Kingsley had to deal with? She had an inkling of why resolving the past was so important to him.

Mrs. O'Malley leaned forward. "I don't like it any more than you do, but the cold, hard facts are that several families that live in our city were affected by the frat-house murder and I think things would be better if his name wasn't involved."

"Very well. Thank you for your time," Gabi said, gathering her presentation booklets and walking out the door.

* * *

Kingsley didn't like the fact that he'd lied to Gabi, but telling her he was going to their old university to dig through witness statements made to campus security—well, he didn't think she'd approve. She had agreed to contact the women from Daria Miller's files, but he didn't want her involved any further than that.

A part of him wished he could drop it, but he couldn't.

It would be easier for Gabi if he did. She wasn't really involved in the incident. For her there were more traumas around the fact that he'd had sex with her and then left her.

He got that.

He knew that he had a lot to make up for on that front and he was willing to do whatever he had to in order to make that happen.

It surprised him how much she meant to him. He wasn't saying it was love—lust was about where he felt comfortable—but he wanted her to stay with him. He was looking forward to getting home and spending the evening with her and Conner, and then after Conner was in bed spending time alone with her.

Damn.

He had it bad and he knew it.

He pulled the huge archival box of witness statements closer to him. Better to focus on fixing the past. He liked the thought that he'd figure out what happened and fix it, enabling both Hunter and him to move on. Fixing things had long been something that mattered to him.

When he opened the box he was surprised to see how many statements were in there. He pulled a stack out and glanced into the box to see Gabi's name on one.

He hadn't known she'd made a statement. The DA hadn't mentioned her at all.

Maybe she hadn't mentioned him. So they wouldn't have known she and he had been together the night Stacia was killed.

He pulled her statement out and read it.

Well, this made no sense. Not only had she talked about him, she'd also said he spent the night at her place and she'd woken up to find him gone. Which wasn't what had happened.

He couldn't think of a single reason why she would lie unless she was covering for him.

He realized right then how badly it must have hurt her when he rejected her at the jailhouse. She'd come there ready to support him and help him out of a tight spot. And he'd gone into full protective mode, not wanting anything to happen to her. Not wanting her to be colored with the same brush that he and Hunter were.

He'd known that things were going to get ugly. Even his attorney—his own brother, Ben—had thought he was guilty and talked to him about cutting a plea deal. Gabi might be one of only two people to believe he hadn't been involved in Stacia's killing. Hunter being the other one.

Wow.

This changed things.

It made him see her in a different light. He'd always known the attraction between them was powerful, but this went deeper. This was a kind of attachment he hadn't let himself believe existed.

She had to have thought she was in love with him.

Kingsley divided the statements into two piles and was amazed at how big the file of statements he hadn't known about was. He skimmed all the ones he'd already read a dozen times. The ones that the DA had presented in order to have Hunter and him arrested. No wonder Ben had said to leave this alone. As he flipped through the documents he saw statements from people he'd thought were his friends. They'd told how he was always with another girl—not entirely untrue—and that he seemed to date each one for less than a month.

Gabi fit that profile, he realized. But he'd been planning to stay with her. Not that any of that mattered now.

He started reading through the statements that were new to him, and Hunter arrived when he was a third of the way into that stack.

"Did you know that Chuck gave a statement that night?" Kingsley asked once Hunter was up to speed on what he'd found.

"No. What did he say?"

"That we never left the common room after Stacia left. And we were in a corner drinking and laughing."

"Not sure that helps us, but at least he saw us there," Hunter said. Hunter pulled out his tablet and stylus and started making notes on it. "Have you sorted them at all?"

"Yes. These are the ones who all corroborate the DA's version of events, the ones we read at the archives. These are the ones that are different versions."

"Anything helpful like Chuck's?"

"Some. Some of them just mention that we were both at the parties where other girls had been given the date-rape drug. And Cassidy Freeman said you told her that you liked having sex with women who were passed out."

"Bitch."

"That's not helpful," Kingsley said. "Did you really say that?"

Hunter gave him a hard glare. "No. She was always

after me but you know I was into Stacia in those days. And I used to be a one-woman man."

Kingsley reached over and squeezed his friend's shoulder. So much had changed. These statements about himself and Hunter were about men he no longer recognized. They weren't the life of the party anymore… And he couldn't remember the last time he and Hunter had laughed together unless it was over something silly Conner did.

"Let's make a list of everyone who placed us at the frat house and those who thought we did it. Then we can contact them and see what they remember," Hunter said.

"What makes you think they will talk to us now?" Kingsley asked. He wasn't sure that they were going to get answers from people who thought they did it.

"I don't know. I thought… I had hoped this would be easier. That we'd find something that pointed the finger at someone else."

"Me, too, buddy," he said. "Let's just get this stuff sorted and then we can ask Daria to contact some of the people who think we are guilty."

"Good idea," Kingsley said. They both worked for the next two hours and when they were done, Kingsley had an idea why all of these statements hadn't been used. A lot of them were conflicting. He'd read two statements from people he remembered not being at the party. "Joe Falcone was in Detroit that night. I'm not sure I trust his statement."

"I know. This wasn't helpful at all. It clarified nothing," Hunter said. "We're no closer to finding out what really happened than we were yesterday."

Kingsley agreed. But he wasn't giving up. "Let's see if there is anything else that these statements have in common. I remember reading that Stacia left the party and came back. But I have to be honest, I'm a little foggy on when that was. I think I remember seeing her again. What about you?"

Hunter shrugged. "I can only recall the part of the night before you and I sat down and started doing shots."

Kingsley had the feeling that Hunter was hiding something. It was the way he looked past him instead of meeting his eyes. But just then, Kingsley's phone rang and he saw that it was Gabi.

"I have to take this."

Hunter nodded and Kingsley went outside to talk to Gabi. He needed something that was fresh and clean, not the murkiness of the past.

Gabi left the meeting with her hands shaking and got in her car. Instead of driving back to the office, she headed out to the Pacific Coast Highway. Without regard for speed, she drove the roads she knew like the back of her hand as if she was running for her life.

And she guessed she was. All those nice, safe thoughts that she had about maybe loving Kingsley and finding closure were gone. She realized that until he found Stacia's killer, the stigma of the past was always going to hang over him and by extension anyone who was associated with him.

It made her mad and shattered her illusions about the justice system. She'd always believed what the court said. She hadn't questioned their judgments because her father was a judge and she knew he was a good and righteous man. But today she realized that some people got their facts from the court of public opinion.

She pulled over and rested her head on the steering wheel. What was she going to do?

She picked up her phone and dialed her father's number without a second thought.

"Gabi, how are you?"

"I'm good, Papi," she said.

"What can I do for you? Your mother said you are bringing a man to brunch," he said.

"I am. He's the guy I dated in college. He's a single dad now and we are bringing his three-year-old son."

"Interesting," he said.

"What does that mean?"

"Simply that I always thought you had unfinished business with him."

"I do."

"You okay, princess?"

She smiled to herself. Her father was the one man she knew would have her back even if she was wrong. She realized she'd called him because she needed to dispel the anger and disappointment she'd felt after leaving the meeting. "Yes, Papi, I am."

"Good. I have to go, but look forward to seeing you Sunday."

"Me, too. Love you."

"Love you, too, princess."

She turned the car around and drove back to her office, where she found Conner playing with a pair of twins about his age. He ran over and gave her a hug when he saw her. She looked over at Abby, who was watching the kids.

"Where's Melissa?"

"In a meeting with the parents," Abby said. "They are looking for a nanny."

"When Melissa gets out, would you ask her to come and see me? Conner, are you okay? Do you want to come and help me work?" Gabi asked.

Conner looked up at her, his face so like Kingsley's. "I want to keep playing with my friends."

"Sounds good. My office is right down the hall. If you need me, come and get me."

He nodded and ran back over to the twins to keep playing.

She entered her office and drafted an email to send to the county commissioners. And then printed it out for Melissa to review. She was still angry and didn't want to say anything she'd regret. She needed an unbiased opinion.

She worked on her column until Melissa came down to join her. "Great news. I think I got my first clients."

"Congratulations. When do they want us to start? Mae is coming back on Monday."

"I know. I mentioned that to them and scheduled an in-home visit for then."

"Good job," Gabi said. Melissa didn't need her to micromanage things.

"Thanks. The twins and Conner are really getting along well and the parents—Daisy and Scott Banner—wanted to set up a playdate with him."

"I'll go and talk to them. And then I'll have to call Kingsley. I'm not sure how he feels about having other kids to his place."

Melissa led the way back to the playroom and Gabi talked to the parents of the twins. They were very friendly and clearly doted on their little boys. Daisy was a food blogger who had recently been approached by the Food Network to star in her own show and Scott was a champion deep-sea fisherman. Apparently that was a thing.

"I'm glad you're considering using our agency for

your sons. I understand you'd like a playdate with Conner," Gabi said after introductions were made.

"Please, Gammi, I really like Ty and Doug," Conner said, coming over to her.

She ruffled his hair. "I think it's a great idea. I have to check with your dad and then we can figure out the logistics. You keep playing while we do that," Gabi said.

Conner nodded and the boys went back to their playing. She overheard him telling them about how knights were fighters but did it for honor. One of the boys asked what honor was and Conner shrugged and said, "Something good." She smiled.

"Conner lives outside Carmel. His father is very protective of Conner, so I think the playdate would have to be at his place. Are you okay with that?" she asked.

Daisy looked at Scott and he nodded.

"Okay. Let me call Kingsley and I'll be right back."

Gabi went down the hall to her office and dialed Kingsley's number.

"Hey, you," he said by way of greeting.

"Hey. How's your meeting?" she asked. He'd told her he was going to meet with a prospective new client for his sports agency. It wasn't surprising to her that their old alma mater had another Heisman Trophy winner. Their school was known for excellence in all sports.

"Long and a little bit boring," he said. "What's up?"

"Conner has made friends with some twins and wants to have a playdate."

"How did he meet other kids?" Kingsley asked.

She explained the situation.

"I'm not sure I'm ready for my little man to be at someone else's house with parents I don't even know."

"I figured that. So I suggested they come to your place," she said.

"I don't want to advertise where we live, but Conner hasn't really played with his kids his age before." Kingsley hesitated. "Okay. I guess it would be fine if he had them over."

"Good. I will make the arrangements. Will you be home for dinner?" she asked.

"I will. It's been a long day," he said.

"For me, too. I'll be happy to be back at our home."

As soon as she said it, she realized that it was Kingsley's home and not hers.

"I'll be glad to be at our home too."

He disconnected the call and she had to tell herself that it was nothing. He hadn't just referred to his house as their home. But in her heart she knew he had.

Twelve

Kingsley got home to find a big bedouin-style tent set up in the backyard. He assumed it was Conner's big playdate, which made him a little nervous. His son had never really played with other kids and he wanted it to be perfect.

Gabi had certainly pulled out all the stops with the tent. He walked into the kitchen and found Mrs. Tillman playing her online bingo game.

"Hello, sir. Do you need anything from me?" Mrs. Tillman asked.

"Not at all. Are the other kids still here?" he asked. "What are our dinner plans?"

"There aren't any other kids here. Gabi has dinner covered and asked me to send you out back when you got home. She said you're camping out."

"What happened to Conner's playdate?" he asked Mrs. Tillman.

She shrugged. "I don't know the details, but Gabi did say that her agency wouldn't be taking the parents on as clients."

He didn't like the sound of that. He took his phone out of his pocket as he went into his room to get changed. There were no messages from Gabi so he would have to get the scoop from her once he was out in the backyard.

He changed into a pair of faded jeans and his old team jersey before heading out back. As he got closer to the tent he noticed that the fire pit had been moved from the patio and now sat in front of the tent area. There was a clay tagine suspended over the fire that emitted some delicious smells.

He pulled back the flap to the tent and poked his head inside.

Gabi and Conner were sitting on a mound of sumptuous-looking pillows in a scene that was straight out of *The Arabian Nights*.

"Daddy!"

Conner scrambled to his feet and ran over to him. He scooped his son up and kissed the top of his head before setting him back down.

"I told Conner he couldn't have his playdate tonight because you wanted to surprise him with this campout," Gabi said.

Kingsley looked at her and saw fire in her eyes. He was beginning to suspect that the other parents wouldn't let their kids play with his son once they'd learned who he was.

"I did. I hope you don't mind."

"Not at all. We've been reading about knights. But these are different than the ones I learned about before," Conner said.

Conner took Kingsley's hand and led him over to

where Gabi was seated. When they were both settled onto the pillows, Kingsley noticed an old-fashioned illuminated book on Gabi's lap. There were illustrations of knights with curved swords.

Conner climbed onto Kingsley's lap and Gabi went back to finishing the story they were reading, which was the tale of Aladdin.

"That was so exciting. I wish we had a secret cave," Conner said when she was finished.

"Me, too," Kingsley said.

"For tonight we do. In the trunk over there is everything you will need to go on an adventure like Aladdin. Go and check it out, Conner," Gabi said.

His son jumped up and ran to the other side of the tent. He opened the trunk and exclaimed excitedly as he started pulling out costumes, toy swords and a map.

"Why did you do all of this?" Kingsley asked.

"Because Conner deserved it," Gabi said.

"What about the playdate?" Kingsley asked.

"It didn't work out. The timing was wrong," she said, getting to her feet and walking over to Conner.

"What's this?" Conner held up a gossamer-thin piece of fabric.

"That's for my costume. I'm going to be one of those dashing ladies we read about. You and your dad are Aladdin and his band of thieves. Put on your costumes and meet me by the steps leading to the beach," she said. She took the pieces that made up her costume.

And Kingsley pushed aside his worries for the night and went to help his son get into costume. Conner talked excitedly the entire time. Once they were both dressed they went outside to find Gabi in her harem-girl outfit wearing a veil over her face.

Kingsley's breath caught in his chest as he looked

at her. And he was struck with the realization that he wanted her in his life. Forever.

He wasn't sure he could have her. He'd never really had a chance to figure out how to make things work in a relationship, and he suspected it might be due to the fact that he'd screwed up with her.

"You're gorgeous."

"So are you," she said. "Both of you. Conner, let me take your picture with your daddy."

"With our swords out," Conner insisted. They both drew their swords and posed next to each other as Gabi took a few pictures with her phone.

"Now all three of us," Conner said.

Gabi came over to them and Kingsley wrapped his arm around Gabi as she lifted Conner up between them. Kingsley extended his arm and got them all in the frame before snapping the selfie.

"Let's look at it," Gabi said. They stared down at the picture of the three of them.

"It's like we are a family," Conner said.

It was like that.

"But I'm just your nanny," Gabi reminded his son.

He could tell Conner didn't like that—and truth to tell he didn't, either—but tonight wasn't the time to get into it.

"Did you bring the map?" Gabi asked, changing the subject.

"I did," Conner said, pulling it out of his pocket.

They followed the map down the path to the beach and then got to a stone circle with a big X drawn in the sand.

"What now?" Kingsley asked.

"Now we dig," Conner said.

They all dug until they uncovered another chest, and

when Kingsley removed it he wondered what they'd find inside. Conner opened it and exclaimed. It was full of toy gold coins and trinkets just such as the ones the book had described.

Conner was over the moon with his treasure and Kingsley realized that the day he'd blackmailed Gabi into being Conner's nanny had been the most fortuitous one of his life. He'd found a treasure he hadn't realized he'd been searching for.

Brunch with her parents made her more nervous than facing an entire room of spoiled children and being told she was the one adult that had to get them in line. On the way there, Conner seemed fine in the backseat of the SUV and Kingsley… It was hard to get a good read on him. He had on his Wayfarers.

Kidz Bop music filled the car. To be honest, that might be part of her nerves. She was also still on edge over the canceled playdate with the twins. Once their parents had heard Kingsley's name, they'd pulled out. It bothered her.

She'd been really upset but Conner had taken it in stride when she'd told him that his friends would have to play another day due to the fact that his dad had planned a campout under the stars. She'd told a similar white lie to Kingsley so that he wouldn't have to know that the parents hadn't wanted their kids to play with Conner.

It all made her so mad.

They'd slept in the tent Gabi had brought over, a gift from a sheikh her cousin Gui knew. That summer she'd spent in Spain she'd met all sorts of interesting people. Even men who fancied themselves in love with her. But she had been too confused and scarred by what had happened to be any good to anyone.

"What's up?" Kingsley said.

"Nervous."

"Why?" he asked. "You like your parents, right?"

She laughed. She loved her parents. "Yes. My brother and I get along, as well. He has a new girlfriend. And it must be serious if he's bringing her home."

"Is it serious with us?" he asked. "Is that what's making you nervous?"

She leaned her head back against the leather seat, glad her large sunglasses concealed her eyes from him. She was serious about Kingsley. But she was seeing every day how much of a struggle it was going to be to live here where everyone knew his story and still be happy.

"Yes," she said. "Does that make you want to jump out on the side of the road and run for the hills?"

"Not at all. It makes me want to lock the doors so you can't get out," he said, reaching over to take her hand in his. He lifted it to his mouth and kissed the back of it, then put her hand on his thigh. "But if you're not nervous about brunch, that means you can only be nervous because you didn't tell me the truth."

"What?"

"I know about what really happened," he said. "I don't understand why you haven't said anything."

She glanced in the backseat and noticed that Conner had put his headphones on and switched on a movie.

"I didn't want to upset you. I was mad enough for the both of us. And really, there was nothing to be done to change their minds, so I just kept it to myself. I do think we made the evening a lot of fun for Conner. And I told Melissa we won't be taking them on as clients at the firm."

"What are you talking about?" he asked. "I meant

what went on at the county commissioners' meeting. I heard they don't want my money involved with the playground project."

"Oh, that," she said. "It was a rough day, Kingsley. First the commissioners and then the twins' parents. Until that moment I never realized what you lived with."

"It's not that bad on the East Coast or in big cities. But Carmel is too close to the campus."

"I was thinking the same thing. You should move back east," she said.

"Would you?"

"No. California is in my blood. It's my home. I couldn't live somewhere else and feel whole," she said. "Besides, I wouldn't want to let the jerks win."

He gave her a half smile.

"Me, neither. Which is why I'm here."

"You said revenge. And I honestly thought you should be more willing to let it go. That revenge never solves anything, but when I thought of how Conner would feel if he knew the truth…well, I get it."

She felt protective of Conner and not just because he was her temporary charge. She knew it was a mistake to get attached to Conner. There were no guarantees with herself and Kingsley, but she couldn't help it. Both of the Buchanan men had cast a spell on her.

She didn't want to break it.

"Tell me where you are in your investigation," she said.

Kingsley told her about all of the witness statements and how many there were that he'd never read before.

"I read yours," he said at last. "You lied."

She blushed and pulled her hand back. "I didn't. I just said that when I woke up you were gone."

"You and I both know that you were awake when I left your room," he pointed out.

"Yes. But…you know I fancied myself in love with you, Kingsley. I wanted to protect you in any way I could. But then—"

"I was an ass. I should have said thank you. I should have been nicer when you visited me at the jailhouse."

"Yes, you should have," she said. "Why weren't you?"

"Hours were going by and I was beginning to realize that it wasn't just a misunderstanding and the cops were definitely going to charge us. I didn't remember killing anyone and thought we were being framed. I still do. And I didn't want you anywhere near that mess."

"It was the only place I wanted to be. But perhaps you were right. I didn't need to be there."

He followed the GPS directions and turned in to the development where her parents lived. They had a sprawling Mexican hacienda-style house with a big circular drive. Kingsley parked behind a classic '69 Corvette.

He got Conner out of his car seat and took his hand as they walked up to the front door. Conner reached up and took Gabi's, as well.

She was struck by how they were a unit now. The past and future all disappeared and there was only the present and this little family she'd found. The family she'd always sort of wanted but never thought would be hers, which was why she'd frozen last night when Conner had called them that—a family.

Gabi's parents' house was elegant, sophisticated and very homey. But the fact that her father was a federal judge made Kingsley a little nervous. He shouldn't be, because his own brother was a lawyer and his father a CEO of a big conglomerate.

Maybe it came down to the fact that Javier was Gabi's father, not that he was a judge. Javier was the father who knew Kingsley had been arrested. The father who had seen his daughter upset and had to send her out of the country to recover.

Now Javier had invited Kingsley over to the grill for a beer and he suspected a serious conversation was coming.

"Your son is adorable," Javier said. "I remember when Alejandro was that age. They grow up fast."

The older man held a beer in one hand and a spatula in the other. The chicken had been dry rubbed with some sort of spice combination that smelled delicious. Not for the first time, Kingsley wished that he was just a regular guy enjoying a barbecue.

"Yes, they do. Seems like I was carrying him everywhere just yesterday," Kingsley said. He remembered the first time he held Conner in his arms. He knew then that he had to stop ignoring the past and fix it. Because he didn't want his son to deal with the repercussion of his actions.

"You want to protect him," Javier said.

It wasn't a question but a statement.

"Yes."

"That's the burden and blessing of fatherhood. My own father said this to me one time and I thought, *the old man thinks he's Cervantes*."

Kingsley smiled at that. "I get it. It makes no sense until you have your own kid, though."

"Exactly. I like you, Kingsley. I have seen you rise from the ashes of something that would have kept a lesser man down, but you just brushed yourself off and moved on. That takes *cojones*."

"Thanks." He wasn't sure where this was going. He heard the *but* in Javier's voice.

"Gabi is my princess. I know she's not perfect and that she has her flaws, but in my eyes she is faultless and I want her to have everything her heart desires."

"I want that, too, sir," Kingsley said.

"Good. If you hurt her, I'll visit the same pain back on you, and this time you will find it harder to rise from the ashes, understand?"

Kingsley nodded. "You should know I never would hurt her. I protected her the last time."

"I know. You sent her away. I wasn't sure if you did it because you didn't care for her or if you did it to protect her. I'm still not sure, but it was the best thing for her. It made her stronger."

"Papi, are you talking about me?" Gabi said, coming over and slipping her hand into Kingsley's.

"I'm warning him not to hurt you, princess," Javier said with a jovial grin.

Kingsley got the impression that Javier didn't hide anything from his family. Kingsley thought his parents would like Gabi's. The two families had a lot in common.

"Thanks, Papi, but I'm a big girl now. I can handle this."

Javier leaned over and kissed Gabi's forehead. "In case you can't, I've got your back."

She laughed but Javier leveled a very serious look at Kingsley. He wrapped his arm around Gabi and led her away from the grill and her father.

Conner was sitting on the big bench swing under the shade of a ponderosa pine tree in the corner of the yard. Kingsley led Gabi over there.

"I hope my dad wasn't too…too parental," she said.

"It's good. I can handle it. I'd be more worried if he wasn't protective of his kids," Kingsley said.

"He's definitely that," she said.

"Daddy," Conner said as they approached. "Will you push me on the swing?"

"Sure will, buddy. That's why I came over here," Kingsley said.

"Come on, Gammi," Conner said, patting the bench next to him.

Gabi sat by his son and Kingsley stood there for a minute feeling—overwhelmed. He wanted this family to be real. But right now he was distracted from the one thing that could bring him that dream.

He needed to focus on finding out who had killed Stacia or he was never going to have any closure. He was never going to be able to put the past to rest.

Anger like he hadn't felt since the night he'd been arrested welled up inside him. Whoever had killed Stacia and kept silent about it had stolen this from him. Had taken the life he might have had away from him.

He had been lucky to have Conner—God knew, that was the truth. But he could have had Gabi and maybe they could have had a few more kids. But now they couldn't—until the specter of the past was gone.

She wouldn't want to raise kids no one wanted to play with. Hell, neither did he.

"Kingsley?"

"Yes?"

"Conner asked if you wanted to sit with us. We can swing it together."

"Yes," he said. He sat down, more determined than ever to find the person who was blocking his second chance with Gabi and to make him pay.

Thirteen

Alejandro joined Gabi in the butler's pantry when she went to make more margaritas to go with brunch. His girlfriend, Eva, was funny, gorgeous and smart. She was a human rights lawyer who worked all over the world.

Gabi was proud of the business she'd built, but talking about kids and parenting issues after Eva had just finished telling them about the clean water campaign she'd spearheaded in Central America had made Gabi feel… Well, as though she should be sitting at the kids' table.

"What do you think of Eva?" Alejandro asked.

"Scary awesome," Gabi said. "I like her, but I think if I had to be around her too often I'd start to hate myself."

"Really?" Alejandro asked. "She told me she's jealous that you have your own business."

"She did?" she asked.

"Yes. She's tired of traveling all the time. She's thinking of settling down…"

It was funny how perspective changed things. Gabi's life looked good to Eva because it was very normal and Eva's sounded exciting to Gabi because…well, if she were being honest, because it would take her away from all the uncertainty she felt around Kingsley.

"With you?" she asked her brother.

"Yes. We've been dating for a year now," Ali said.

"Why are you just now bringing her home?" Gabi asked.

Ali shrugged and reached around her to dump lime juice into the blender. "You see what she's like. I met her when I was at Gui's last summer and we hooked up, but we were both on vacation, you know."

She did know. "So when did you meet again?"

"I called her from the airport when I got home and told her I wanted to see her again. I couldn't stop thinking about her, Gabi. I didn't know if it was just obsession or real affection," Alejandro said.

"How did you figure it out?" she asked her brother. He was eighteen months older than her and they'd always been close. She wanted to know if he had any insights into love that might help her.

She knew that Ali's situation was different than hers. Eva didn't have a past like Kingsley, but love…love was the great equalizer. She'd read that somewhere and it had resonated with her.

"I'm not sure. We've been living together for the last few months. Both of us still travel a lot but I know she's there."

"Is it convenience?" Gabi asked. "I feel like that with Kingsley, because I'm living at his place to be a nanny to Conner. Like maybe just living there is making me see us as something we aren't."

She dumped the ice into the blender and added the tequila but didn't turn it on.

"I see the way he looks at you, Gabs. Whatever he feels for you is intense. I'd say it was love, but I don't know him well enough," Alejandro said. "I know Dad warned him not to hurt you, but I don't think that was necessary."

She agreed. Kingsley would never intentionally hurt her. But he would do whatever he thought was necessary to keep her safe. And if that meant going after revenge or cutting her from his life, she knew he would do it.

She turned on the blender and moments later Ali poured the frozen margaritas into the pitcher.

"I'm glad you have Eva. Maybe I can come over for dinner one night and get to know her without Mom being all nosy."

"Ha. You'll report back to Mom."

"Of course I will. But it would still be nice."

"Sounds like a plan," Alejandro said.

They rejoined everyone on the patio, where Conner was "reading" to her mom and dad from his iPad.

Watching her parents interact with Conner made her realize that they probably wanted grandchildren. Yet they never pressured her or Ali to have kids. It was as if they knew that families couldn't be forced.

Of course they knew that.

"Margarita refills?" Gabi asked.

Kingsley turned and smiled at her and all the doubts that invaded her thoughts when they weren't together disappeared. Seeing him made her happy. Made her believe that whatever else was happening in the world couldn't affect them or hurt them.

"I'm driving, so no more for me," Kingsley said.

"I'm not, so, yes, please," Eva said.

"Me, too," Gabi's mom said.

After she refilled the glasses she sat back down next to Kingsley.

"You were gone awhile. Everything okay with your brother?"

"Yes. Just talking about how spectacular Eva is."

"I am, aren't I?" Eva said with a laugh.

"Yes, you are," Alejandro said.

"You're not so bad yourself," Eva said.

"To my brother!" Gabi said, lifting her glass.

Everyone lifted their glasses.

"What are you doing?" Conner asked.

"It's called toasting," Kingsley explained. "It's a way of saying good job to someone."

"To my daddy!" Conner said, lifting his sippy cup.

Everyone again lifted their glasses.

Conner then went around the table and toasted everyone who was there, including her parents' dachshunds, Gia and Marlow.

She glanced over at Kingsley as she heard him laugh. He had so much affection for his son. She thought again about the way the county commissioners hadn't wanted Kingsley's involvement with the playground and decided she was going to fight them. Because he was a good man. She saw that not only when he was with his son but with everyone.

He could have taken offense to her father's warning, but he hadn't.

Kingsley glanced over at her and she didn't look away. She saw the man he was with all his flaws and strengths. She wanted to accept him as he was.

"You're staring at me," he said.

"I like looking at you."

"I like it, too," he said. Lifting his hand, he twined

their fingers together and she felt as though they were on the same page. They wanted the same things from life, and together they would make that happen.

O'Hannigans was a California institution. Nestled on one of the curves of the Pacific Coast Highway, it afforded great views of endless blue sky and sun-drenched ocean. Gabi parked her car in one of the spots around back and pushed her sunglasses up on top of her head as she got out and walked into the restaurant.

It had been two weeks since they'd had brunch at her parents' house and she and Kingsley had grown closer—sort of. They were as close as two people who had white-hot sex every night and went their separate ways during the day could be.

He'd had to go to the East Coast for a client for three days, and when he was home, he and Hunter were locked in his office trying to piece together what had happened the night Stacia had died.

She hoped this meeting with her friends from college would reveal something—anything they didn't already know—about the case so maybe Kingsley would move on. And act as if he wanted a future with her. He was too obsessed with the past.

She scanned toward the left where she and her friends usually met. Dee and Marcy were already there and waved her over.

"It's two for one so we ordered you a pinot," Dee said as she hopped up to hug her. Marcy did the same and Gabi sat on one of the tall bar stools across from Marcy.

"Sounds perfect. Any word from Lena?" she asked as she took a sip of her wine. There was a fourth glass waiting for their other friend.

"She was stuck without a babysitter. Can you believe

she has a kid? The girl who used to get locked out of the sorority house every dang night," Dee said.

"She's matured a lot."

"Having kids will do that to you, or so my mom says," Marcy said.

"It hasn't hurt you being around kids," Dee said. "But you really don't nanny that much anymore, do you?"

"No," Gabi said. She hadn't told her friends about Kingsley or the fact that she was living in at his place.

Lena arrived and regaled them with how fabulous her nine-month-old son was. Apparently he was above the curve on every chart, which made Gabi smile. She could hear the love in her friend's voice when she spoke about her little boy.

"Now that everyone is here," Gabi said. "I wanted to ask you about something that happened in college."

"Is it about how many men I've gotten from the tattoo you talked me into and then chickened out of getting yourself?" Dee asked.

"No. But you're welcome for that," Gabi said, smiling over at Dee. Dee worked for an interior-design company and had been responsible for the decor in Gabi's office.

"Then what is it?" Lena asked. "Is this the best wine ever, or is it just that I haven't been drinking lately?"

"It's a nice vintage," Marcy added. Her family had been vintners in California for more than 150 years and now Marcy worked in their marketing department. "Stop interrupting and let Gabi speak. Does it have anything to do with the fact that you are nannying for Kingsley Buchanan?"

"Yes," she said, looking at Marcy. "How did you know that?"

"I make it a habit to know what my friends are up to," Marcy said. "But go on."

"You're back with Kingsley?" Dee asked.

"It's complicated," Gabi said. She should have anticipated that they would know about her working for King.

"Explain it to us," Lena said. "Because we remember how he broke your heart."

"I know. You all were my rock back then."

"We still are," Dee said, putting her hand on Gabi's. The other women followed suit.

"Talk," Marcy said.

"Well, Kingsley asked me what I remembered about the night that Stacia died."

"Other than the fact that he slept with you and then went to her?"

"He didn't do that, Dee," Gabi said. "He wanted to know if I remembered any incidents of girls being slipped date-rape drugs at other parties. That's the angle they are working for what happened to Stacia."

"Sorry, Gabi. It just toasts my nuts that you waited so long to sleep with a guy and then—"

"My God punished me?" Gabi said.

Lena laughed and almost choked on her wine. "Out-of-wedlock sex… Has that been a continuing trend with you?"

"No, thank you very much. Do you guys remember anything?" Gabi asked.

"My roommate had something happen about three weeks before…Stacia," Lena said. "She was at a football party, I think. Joel was there with her and managed to get her home safe. They both thought the drink was intended for someone else."

Joel had been one of the running backs on the football team, so Gabi made a mental note to mention it to Kingsley when she got back home.

"I can't remember anything, but to be honest I mainly just hung out with guys back then," Dee said.

Dee liked to have fun and thought life was all about sampling as much variety as she could. "Fair enough. Neither Hunter nor Kingsley remembers anything at the party after they started doing shots together. It was after he went back from my room."

"Really? I can't believe that. Hunter had a big fight with Stacia while you guys were gone, and when she came back, they got into it again."

"What?" Gabi asked. As far as she'd heard from Kingsley and Hunter, everything had been lovey-dovey between Stacia and Hunter. "They fought?"

"Yeah, I guess you would have missed it, and no one was really talking about it much after the arrest. But Hunter broke up with her earlier in the evening and she left."

Gabi didn't know what that meant other than either Kingsley had lied to her or Hunter had lied to him. "Who was she with when she came back?"

Dee looked at Marcy. "What was that guy's name? The one who always hung around you in the library? The sports-medicine guy."

"Garrett Keller," Marcy said. "Kind of a step down for Stacia."

"Definitely," Dee agreed. "That's when they had a second fight. Hunter took Stacia into the kitchen and all I heard was lots of yelling and then Kingsley went in there and dragged Hunter out. Stacia left a few minutes later."

"With the sports-medicine guy?" She'd never asked about any of this when she'd returned from Spain. By then, the charges had been dropped and Kingsley had moved on to the East Coast. She'd been trying to put it all behind her.

"No," Dee said. "He was talking with one of the players about an injury. I didn't see whom she left with. I thought she was on her own."

"That jives with what I remember," Lena said. "What about you, Marcy?"

"Yes, except I went home before any of that drama started. I had an exam to study for."

"Always hitting the books," Dee said.

The conversation drifted away from the past and into the present and Gabi tried to just relax and enjoy the evening with her friends. But she was worried.

It sounded as if Hunter hadn't been honest, and she really hoped he wasn't the reason why Kingsley's good name had been smeared.

When Gabi got back from drinks with her friends, Conner and Kingsley were playing games in the living room. It seemed like forever since she'd realized that he had come back to California to find closure to the past. She wanted to help him, especially after what she'd found out today, but it wasn't easy. Kingsley wasn't the kind of man who involved people in his business.

After putting Conner to bed and checking to make sure that Kingsley was in the media room watching the basketball game, she went into his office. The room was dark and not very welcoming as she entered it.

But that was probably just her imagination, since she knew she was sneaking where she shouldn't be. She went to his desk and using the flashlight on her phone started to look for anything that would give her a clue as to what he was looking for in the past.

Before she'd come home from meeting her friends,

she'd gone to her own office and accessed the public records from Hunter and Kingsley's indictment.

It had been pretty cut-and-dried. She was surprised Hunter and Kingsley had been released, since there were at least a dozen witnesses who'd seen them with Stacia at the end of the evening. It hurt her a little to think Kingsley had gone back to the party after he left her, but that was in the past.

She was snooping around now trying to find something that would show her he had some evidence he wasn't sharing with her. Something that would help her put the pieces together after what she'd learned today from her friends. Was he hiding evidence to protect Hunter? Could there even be something here that implicated him? What the girls had told her had renewed her suspicions, though she had a lot of trouble believing he would actually kill Stacia.

The door opened; a shaft of light spilled into the room and a dark shadow filled the doorway.

"Should I drop to the floor and hide?"

"Uh, no. I'd prefer you tell me what you are doing in here," he said as he entered. He hit the light switch as he closed the door behind him and walked toward her.

He didn't appear mad, which she thought was a good thing. She knew she'd be pissed if she caught him going through her desk.

"Looking for answers. You said you didn't want to talk about it. I respect that, but I reread the indictment today and I figure you must have found something, that there must be some evidence of a smoking gun in here somewhere."

She fiddled with her phone, turning off the flashlight as Kingsley reached her. He leaned against his desk, sitting on the file she'd been about to open when he'd entered.

"I've found evidence of an intruder in my office." He pulled her between his legs and kept his hands on her hips.

He was trying to distract her with sex.

Dammit, it was working, too.

She wanted to let it go. It didn't affect her. But she cared for Kingsley and Conner. She wanted the stigma of that arrest and release to go away.

"But—"

He brought his mouth down on hers. He lifted her off her feet and changed their positions so that she was seated on the desk and he stood between her legs.

He pushed the skirt she was wearing up and reached between her legs to pull her panties down, drawing the fabric slowly down her legs and tossing it on the floor.

"Do you really want to talk about the past? When the future is so much more exciting," he said.

She didn't. She tangled her hands in the hair at the back of his neck and drew his head forward, shifting her body against his hand as their mouths met. She channeled all her questions into the kiss, all her dreams and desires. She thrust her tongue deep into his mouth, letting him know that she wasn't passive. Not where this was concerned.

Whatever he was doing, she wanted to help him. And she would, but right now she wanted him.

He tore his mouth from hers, kissed the length of her neck and slowly moved down her body, finding her nipple through the fabric of her dress and bra and scraping his teeth over it until it hardened. She fumbled between them trying to find his zipper and found his erection pressed against his pants.

She stroked him through his jeans as he sucked her nipple into his mouth. She undid his top button, carefully lowered the zipper of his pants and then pushed his underwear out of her way.

He was hot and hard, and she drew him closer to her with a light grasp on his body. She stroked her fingers up and down his length and then rubbed her finger over the tip, making small circles.

He looked up at her as he drew her hips toward the edge of the desk and positioned himself to enter her.

But he didn't move any farther; the tip of his body remained poised at the entrance of hers. She wanted to outwait him but she needed him, wanted to be filled with him now. She shifted and forced him inside her and he drew back his hips and returned with a forceful thrust that drove him deep inside her; she arched her back and grabbed his shoulders as shudders racked her body.

She felt pleasure so intense she couldn't breathe for a second as he drew back and thrust again. Their eyes met and their kiss deepened as he continued to rock in and out of her body until they both orgasmed and cried each other's names.

He drew her close to him, wrapped his big strong arms around her and held her as their breathing slowed.

"I'm here for revenge," he said softly. "To make the person who stole you from me pay."

His words were quietly whispered and she felt them all the way to her core. She didn't know what to say to that. So she just held on to him and pretended everything would be okay.

Fourteen

Gabi tried to sleep in Kingsley's arms in his big, comfortable king bed. But his words kept circling around in her head.

Vengeance.

Revenge.

These were things that she didn't believe in. They had a justice system for a reason, and so far she hadn't seen anything resolved by digging into the past. Nothing new had been uncovered on this vengeance mission. Kingsley needed to let go. He needed to move on.

Sure, she was the daughter of a judge. She'd always had faith in the judicial system. Heck, even Kingsley, who was innocent, had been let go. Why would he pursue revenge?

Because Conner could be hurt. It wasn't just about ignorant parents who wouldn't let him have a playdate. This was the kind of thing that would poison Kingsley.

He thought he'd find something that everyone missed, but what if he didn't? Until he let it go they'd never be able to have the kind of future she knew she wanted with him.

She rolled away from him, staring at the clock on the nightstand. Time seemed to be moving so slowly.

She should have said something to him. Forced him to tell her what he really meant instead of allowing him to carry her back to bed to make love.

Love.

She'd been dancing around the word for days. Trying to figure out if she was just feeling the aftereffects of reuniting with her first love from college or if this was the real thing. She still wasn't sure. But she did know that a man who took justice into his own hands… She wouldn't allow herself to love a man like that.

"What's the matter?"

She rolled over and looked at him. In the dark room she could just make out his features. He was concerned. Rightly so: it was 3:05 in the morning. Most people were asleep.

"You said something earlier."

"I said a lot of things earlier."

He was being flip. She wished she could let this go. But then what? Would she just walk away and leave? The eighteen-year-old Gabi would have done that. But she wasn't that girl.

"Stop it. You know I want to talk about your quest for revenge."

"You know that I want to find the person who framed me and Hunter."

"I do. But finding him and getting revenge are two very different things," she said.

"I expect you to feel that way. Don't worry about my wrath. It won't hurt you."

How could he say that? "You don't really believe that, do you?"

"Yes."

"You're wrong."

"How do you figure? Once I have found the person I will alert the authorities and expose them for what they did."

That didn't sound so bad. "What exactly do you mean?"

"They lived free of the accusations and scrutiny that Hunter and I did. They have been walking around without any consequences while Stacia's murder has gone unsolved. I want justice for her. I will do whatever I have to that person. Once we find out who it is—"

"If you do that, Conner will live with the consequences," she said. "There's no way for you to do that and keep the source of the leak from the media."

"And I guess I'm supposed to just—what? What do you think would be the right choice? I'm happy to listen. But I am tired of living with the stigma of something I didn't do."

"Then let it go. Put it behind you."

"How can I?" he asked, rolling out of bed and striding over to his closet. He pulled on his robe and then turned to face her. "You had a small taste of what I put up with when the commissioners didn't want my money for the playground. But that's just part of it."

"I know. I'm sorry. But how will getting revenge help?"

"It will make me feel a hell of a lot better," Kingsley said.

But she doubted it. "Whoever it is…"

"We don't know yet. Chuck remembers seeing our coach at all of the parties where the women were drugged. And Hunter has been trying to talk to him but he's sick. Coach Gainer—he wouldn't have been drinking at the parties, so he would know something. He used to stop by to congratulate us when we won."

She put her head in her hands. This had been a mistake. Why couldn't she just have stayed quiet?

There was a chance that Kingsley wouldn't get his revenge at all, because finding out who had killed Stacia was proving harder than they'd ever anticipated. And she'd been looking for just a short time. He'd been doing this for years.

"Come back to bed," she said. "I'm sorry I started this tonight."

"I'm not. I know it's on your mind," he said.

He stayed where he was.

"You have a point about the past. Maybe we should end this now. Before you are affected any more by it than you already have been."

She was tempted to say yes. To get out of his bed and walk out the door. It would be easier. But the truth was she'd been affected by that incident for her entire adult life. If Stacia hadn't been killed, and Kingsley hadn't been arrested, they would have dated and probably broken up. She would have graduated and gone to do something else. Without that incident, without that one night that had changed everything, her life would be different.

Not better.

Just different.

"I don't want to leave."

"Are you sure?"

There was something in his voice that warned her things were about to change.

"Yes."

He didn't move and she got out of bed and padded lightly over to him. In her heart she knew that she wanted to fix this, but was beginning to believe that she'd never be able to.

He had to let go if they were going to move on.

She put her arms around him and rested her head against his chest. He stood there stiffly for another minute and then wrapped his arms around her. He rested his head on top of hers and she thought that this should feel more like coming home, but in her heart of hearts she knew the truth. This felt like goodbye.

Kingsley's dreams were troubled nightmares where he was left alone. He rolled to his side and jerked awake when he felt Gabi next to him.

Everything was unraveling out of his control and he knew it was only a matter of time before she left him. He couldn't see a future for them. In fact, he never had. Not really. Only now could he admit it.

He'd thought he'd come back to her for answers and to care for his son, but as he pulled her into his arms, he knew he'd come back to her for himself. Because he wanted to feel like the man he'd once been. A man who wasn't jaded by the life he'd lived.

But that man was gone.

And the only thing that came from holding on to Gabi would be to bring her down with him.

And he wasn't going to do that.

"King?" she asked in a sleepy voice.

"Yeah, baby?"

"Are you okay?" she asked.

No.

He was pretty sure he was never going to be okay again, but right now he didn't want to think about that. Instead he wanted to make love to Gabi one more time. To use a little bit of the California sunshine she'd brought into his life to illuminate the dark parts of his soul. Just one more time.

He kissed her. He wasn't shy about it, thrusting his tongue over her lips and teeth and then deep into her mouth. Her tongue slid against his and her arms came up to wrap around his shoulders.

He looked down into her eyes as he kissed her. Their gazes met, and he realized she could read his intent.

She knew this was goodbye.

Tearing her mouth from his she started to speak, but he put his finger over her lips.

"No more talking tonight."

She nodded, her hands caressing his chest. Tracing over the tattoo of Conner's name. She leaned forward and kissed it. Traced the line of hair on his chest down past his belly button. She ran her finger around it and then pushed it into his belly button before going lower.

Wrapping her hand around his erection, she stroked him. He hardened even more as he reached for her breasts, cupped them and then rubbed his thumbs over her nipples.

She looked up at him again and he closed his eyes against the questions in hers. He rose up to his knees and tugged her up on her knees, as well. He turned her around so that her back was toward him and wrapped his arms around her. Held her pressed to him, burying his face in her neck as he rubbed his hands over her torso.

His erection nestled against her buttocks and she undulated against him as he bit the nape of her neck. He felt her shiver in his arms as he reached between her legs and parted her intimate flesh.

He rubbed his finger over her clit in that swirling motion he knew she liked. Then he whispered dark, sexual words in her ear and heard her breath quicken. He leaned her forward, bracing her hands on the headboard as he pulled back, kissing his way down her back.

He took his time, biting gently as he moved down her spine. He kissed the small indentation right above her butt and then cupped the cheeks of her ass. He squeezed them and heard her moan in response.

Her legs parted and she looked back over her shoulder at him.

Her hair was wild and her eyes no longer held questions. Now he saw need and fire and demands there.

"Take me," she said.

Her words were like a hot glove brushing over his body. His blood felt heavier in his veins and his heartbeat pounded loudly in his ears.

He put his hands on her hips and shifted until he felt the opening of her body with the tip of his erection. He drew his hips back and slowly drove them forward until he was fully embedded in her.

He stayed there for a moment, reaching around to pluck at her nipples until she thrust her hips back against his, and then he slowly drew back before slamming forward again to fill her completely.

She arched her back and he continued thrusting into her until he felt that shiver of sensation down his spine and knew he was going to come.

He reached between her legs and flicked his finger over her. He drove harder and deeper into her until she arched frantically against him, her body tightening around his and driving him to his own climax. Her body continued to squeeze his, milking him of everything he had to give.

He wrapped his arm around her waist and put his hand between hers on the headboard to support himself as his breathing slowed. He rested his head in the middle of her back between her shoulder blades. He kissed her gently and then pulled her down onto the bed into his arms. He cradled her to him and rubbed his hand up and down her back until she drifted off to sleep.

He couldn't find sleep. Instead all he found were images of a future where he did the selfish thing and kept Gabi until her life slowly became sullied by his. He knew he had to let her go. And after all the things he'd walked away from, all the people he'd told himself he could live without, all the people who didn't matter, he realized she did. Walking away from her was the one thing he wasn't sure he was strong enough to do.

But he also realized he had no choice.

He'd meant it when he'd said he'd protect her. Even though he never realized he'd have to protect her from himself.

He got out of bed before dawn, showered and went down the hall to Conner's room. He got his son out of bed and dressed and then left a note for Gabi on her pillow in her room.

He got in his car and drove with no destination in mind. Conner was quiet in the backseat, not sure what was going on, and for once Kingsley knew he had no answers for his son. He only knew that he couldn't tell Gabi goodbye in person.

Gabi woke up alone in Kingsley's bed and knew before she got down to her own room and found the note on her pillow that he was gone. He'd said goodbye to her without words last night. She left the note on her pillow and went to take a shower.

He was letting her go. She had to be honest: she wasn't sure she was ready for that.

Hell, she thought as the hot water pounded down on her, she knew she wasn't ready. She'd spent the last month and a half falling in love with Kingsley. He was complicated and stubborn and way too fixated on the past, but she'd been confident she could change him.

Fix him.

Dammit.

She turned off the shower and toweled herself dry. She got dressed in a pair of linen pants and a long tunic shirt before blow-drying her hair. She took time with her makeup because focusing on that made her feel as though she was busy. But her mind just kept circling around and around.

He had rejected her again.

This time it hurt far worse, because she knew it was final. And she had loved him as a woman, not with the first crush of infatuation as she had before.

She took as long as she could in the bathroom and finally went to sit on her bed and opened up his note.

His handwriting was scrawling and masculine. She ran her fingers over it without really reading the words. Just putting off the inevitable a few moments longer.

Finally, she settled in and read.

Gabi,

Thank you for all you have done for Conner. You truly deserve all the accolades you've received from parenting blogs and magazines. But then I'm not surprised, since the woman I knew had a kind heart and a happy smile. I'm so glad to see you haven't lost those.

Our time together, as lovers, healed wounds I didn't know I had from the past. I thought that we had said everything we needed to that day at the jail, but I realize now that we hadn't.

Saying goodbye is hard. Harder than anything I've done before, and so I took the coward's way out and put my words here in this letter.

You were right when you said there was no way to put aside the past and not have it affect my future. And I see now there is no way to protect you, either. Well, there is one way, and I'm doing that now.

Please take good care of yourself and know I wish you only the best.

Kingsley

That bastard.

He was leaving like this to avoid…what? Her? The truth of the emotions between the two of them?

She wouldn't let him do that. If he wanted to dump her, he was going to have to do it to her face. None of this leaving a note.

She grabbed her purse and walked through the house, finding Mrs. Tillman in the kitchen drinking coffee and playing that game on her phone she loved.

"Have you seen Kingsley?"

"No. He was gone when I arrived," Mrs. Tillman said.

"I'm going out, but I will be back later. When he comes back, would you mind asking him to call me?"

"Not at all, Gabi," Mrs. Tillman said.

She got out to her car and dialed Hunter's number

and got his voice mail. "It's Gabi. I'm looking for Kingsley. Can you call me?"

Then she drove to her office in Carmel. Abby was sitting at Melissa's old desk and smiled when Gabi walked in. Melissa had moved into an office now that she was assistant manager. Gabi went down the hall to her own office and pretended that it was a normal day. She wrote her column. But she was distracted. Where was he?

Did he really just think she would walk away without talking to him?

Her intercom buzzed.

"Yes, Abby?"

"Mr. Ortiz and Mrs. O'Malley are here to see you."

The county commissioners? She was surprised. Though she had expected a response to the email she'd sent them.

"Send them down."

A moment later her door opened and she stood to greet her visitors.

"Hello. What can I do for you today?" Gabi asked, gesturing for them to take a seat in the guest chairs in front of her desk.

"We thought coming to see you might be better than sending an email," Mr. Ortiz said. "I wanted to apologize for the way the meeting went."

"Me, as well," Mrs. O'Malley said. "We've had time to discuss Mr. Buchanan and his generous contribution to our city in some detail after we received your email. The committee feels we might have been too hasty in our judgment."

Gabi crossed her hands together. "I'm glad to hear that. What changed your minds?"

"It was something you said in your email, that we

all must let our actions speak to the type of person we are. Mr. Buchanan has never had another incident like the one in college, and when we pulled up his charity work, well, we were embarrassed by the way the committee reacted," Mr. Ortiz said. "If you and Mr. Buchanan are still interested, we'd love to go forward with building the playground, and we'd even like to name it in his honor."

Gabi swallowed hard against the emotions welling up inside her. This was the kind of gesture that Kingsley needed to see.

"I will discuss it with him and let you know later this week. But I'm sure he will be happy to move ahead with the project," Gabi said.

She showed the commissioners out and texted Kingsley that they needed to talk.

He texted back that he'd said all that needed saying.

And she clenched her jaw and sent him one more message that she deserved the chance to say goodbye to Conner in person.

Kingsley simply responded that they'd drop by her office later in the day. She wondered what he was going to do? Had he just left the house to avoid a messy goodbye or was he leaving the West Coast permanently?

She wasn't pleased with the way he acted. But at least she'd have the chance to see him again and maybe make him admit that he cared for her. The committee had changed their minds; perhaps time was all that was needed to heal the wounds of the past. Or at least she hoped it was.

Fifteen

Kingsley pulled into the parking lot of Gabi's office and sat there for a long minute. He'd taken Conner to the Redwood Forest and his son was worn out from walking and talking. His lie that Gabi had a full day of meetings had worked on his son.

Conner couldn't wait to tell her about everything they'd done and it made Kingsley a little sad that Gabi would no longer be a part of his life. But they were fine before she'd become part of their family and they would be fine again.

He knew what was required to keep Gabi safe and also, if he were being honest, to protect the two of them. There were no guarantees that they'd ever put the past to rest. What if she stayed in his life and then one day had enough of it? Better to end things now.

He got Conner out of his car seat and took his hand as they walked to the office building.

Abby was seated behind the desk talking to Melissa when they walked in.

"Hey," Conner said.

"Hello, kiddo," Melissa said.

"We're here to see Gabi," Kingsley said.

"She asked to see you alone first," Melissa said. "I have a new book on knights if you want to read it, Conner."

"Daddy?"

"It's okay, buddy. I'll be right back," Kingsley said.

He didn't want to be alone with Gabi. He wasn't sure he trusted himself with her. He wanted her, but this thing between them had grown way past young lust. He wasn't sure it had ever been just about lust.

He knocked on her door.

"Come in."

He took a deep breath before he opened the door. He had chosen his path and nothing—not even Gabi—could shake him from it.

He walked into her office and closed the door behind him. She looked much the same as she had the first time he'd come to see her here. Very poised and professional, sitting behind her desk and watching him with a guarded expression in her dark chocolate eyes.

"What's up?" he asked.

"Are you kidding me right now?" she asked. Her words revealed that the serenity she projected was only on the surface. Something deeper simmered underneath and he had the very real feeling that he wasn't getting out of her office without a few burn marks.

It was okay. He could handle it.

"No, I'm not. I thought my letter said everything that needed saying."

"Well, it didn't. I didn't get a chance to tell you how I felt," she said.

"Is that necessary?" he asked. "I think we both know there is no way of moving forward."

"No way? What happened? Was it what I said last night? Because I'm not going to apologize for that. I mean, I know it was the middle of the night when doubts are strongest, but in the clear light of day—"

"I realized that you were right. Doubts aren't just clearest in the middle of the night, Gabi, they are also revealed to be the truth. You were right when you said I'd never be free of the repercussions of revenge, but you didn't mention the other item. The past. I'm never going to be free of it."

"That's not true," she said, getting up and coming around her desk. "Today the county commissioners stopped by and apologized. They are honored to have you sponsor the park."

"That's nice. But I'm sure it was financially motivated and it changes nothing. People are always going to remember the headline arrest and the truth—whatever it is—will hold no sway over them."

Gabi reached for him but he stepped away. He wasn't sure he could handle her touching him right now.

"Really? Is that the way things are between us now?"

He looked into those eyes, the same ones he'd avoided last night, and knew that he didn't want it to be over. He wanted to find a way to have her and keep her and protect her. To create the family he'd been searching for with her. The family he wanted for Conner and for himself, too.

"Yes."

"Bastard."

He nodded. Better to end it now and like this. So

he'd never be tempted to come back and try again. "I'll bring Conner in to say goodbye."

"If that's what you must do. I'm not sure why you are cutting me out of your life. I thought this time we were being honest with each other and building something real."

"I don't know how I lied."

"When you invited me to have dinner with you and we walked on the beach. You seduced me with romance and I let you because…well, it doesn't matter. Why did you do that? Was it just a game to you?"

"No. It was never a game," he said.

"Then why?"

"The reason no longer matters," he said.

"Figures you'd say that," she said.

"What do you mean by that?"

"Just that you've been covering up for Hunter, so I guess I should never expect the truth from you about anything."

"I haven't lied to you," he said. "What the hell are you talking about with Hunter?"

"He and Stacia broke up the night she died. I find it hard to believe you didn't know that."

"I didn't."

"Well, maybe you should be cutting the people who have hurt you from your life instead of the ones who are just trying to help you," Gabi said.

"How were you trying to help me?" he asked. He'd figure out the Hunter thing later.

"By loving you, Kingsley. But a man like you is too hard, too locked away in the past to let something like love lead you out of it. And frankly, I'm tired of trying."

She walked out of the office and down the hall to Conner. She hugged him and told him she had to start working for another family. And the smooth, professional way she handled it made Kingsley realize she'd said goodbye to children before.

He wondered if she even cared for his son, but when she stood up and turned her head he saw the tears glistening in her eyes and realized that she did.

He wondered if he'd made a mistake. She was making him question things he'd always thought were true, but it was too late to go back.

Kingsley was angry. Gabi's arguments made a certain kind of sense, but surely Hunter hadn't been lying to him the entire time. He texted Hunter to come over to his place, and they met there twenty minutes later.

He looked haggard. His friend wasn't dealing with being back in California well at all. His family had never really believed in his innocence and Kingsley didn't want to heap onto him the same accusations as they had.

But there were questions that needed answering. And he needed those answers now.

"What's up? Did Gabi find out anything useful?" Hunter asked. He walked straight to the sideboard and poured himself two fingers of scotch. He downed it in one gulp before turning to face him.

Kingsley couldn't speak for a second. This was a man he thought he knew better than anyone… Did he really know any person at all?

"She did. She found several witnesses who saw you and Stacia fighting the night she died."

Hunter cursed and poured himself some more scotch. "Okay. So now what?"

"Is it true?"

"Yes."

"Why haven't you ever said anything about that?"

Hunter put the glass down and shoved his hands through his thick blond hair. He stared at the floor for a long moment and then looked up. His gray eyes were dark and there was something in his gaze that Kingsley had seen only one time before—when they'd both been locked up in the holding cell.

"I was afraid you'd think I was guilty," he said at last.

Kingsley walked over to his friend and clapped him on the shoulder. "You know that you're not."

Hunter didn't say anything and Kingsley dropped his hand. "You do know that, right?"

"I don't. I mean, the entire night is hazy. I've never been violent. You know I can't even go hunting or anything. But I've never really been able to remember what happened. And it's only been by searching for the truth that I hope I will find it."

Damn.

This sucked. Majorly sucked. He'd been on this path believing they were wrongly accused. He'd been prepared to ruin another man's life because of Hunter. Because he believed that they were both innocent.

"Why the hell haven't you said anything before this?" Kingsley asked.

"You were the only one who had faith in me. You're the only person in the world who looks at me like I'm a man and not a monster, King. I couldn't give that up."

He got it. He knew what it felt like to have the entire world staring at him as if he were a monster.

"What do you remember?"

He needed to get to the bottom of what Hunter had done that night. Maybe if they were able to match it up with what the other witnesses saw…they could both be satisfied that Hunter wasn't guilty.

Hunter walked over to the French doors that led to

the patio. The patio where Kingsley had that first date with Gabi. That night had changed things for him. Made him believe that once he finished this investigation he could move on—have a future. But the things she'd said tonight…well, maybe that wasn't truly in the cards for them.

"I have been over it a million times," Hunter said.

"Not with me. So we were both at the party, drinking, dancing—I left with Gabi. What happened while I was gone?" Kingsley asked.

"Stacia and I went up to my room to be alone. Things were so intense between us and I knew things would change once I was in the pros, so I wanted to cool it down…but I couldn't. She was… She was in my blood, King. I mean, I told her I thought we should cool it down, but she thought I was joking. And for a second I let her believe that but I knew I wanted to enjoy being young and a football god so I had to break it off with her."

"Football god?" Kingsley asked.

"Yeah. You know how cocky I was back then. Anyway, we fought. She got mad and said she didn't need me and left. I stayed in my room for—I don't know, maybe twenty minutes, and then Chuck came up and dragged me back to the party."

"I got back about then," Kingsley said. "You and Chuck were at the keg, right?"

"Yes. But I wasn't in the mood to drink," Hunter said.

"Beer. You weren't in the mood to drink beer, but we both started doing shots."

"Yes. When Stacia came back in, she was with all those guys. I didn't like it, but knew I couldn't stop her."

Things were starting to become clearer for Kingsley. They'd been doing shots when Chuck got up and left. Then someone had brought over the next round… Kingsley searched his mind, but it was hazy. He'd been conflicted over Gabi. But it was beginning to come back to him, how Hunter had been pouring his heart out once they'd gotten a little bit drunk. How Kingsley had been consoling him.

"I remember now. You were telling me that you loved her but she was better off without you. That you weren't ready to be tied down."

Hunter looked up. "I said that?"

"Yeah."

"Damn. Then I didn't kill her, did I?" Hunter asked. "I mean, we were too drunk to do anything."

"We were. Remember I spilled the bottle of Jägermeister and someone brought us another one… I can't remember who, do you?"

Hunter tipped his head back, staring up at the ceiling, and then shook his head. "No. Did Gabi get anything else from the witnesses?"

"Just that most people were too drunk to remember much and one girl—Amber Riley—was passed out in the corner," Kingsley said.

"Coach," Kingsley said. "He came in at the end, didn't he? Warned us to get out before the cops came."

"Yeah. I remember that. I didn't see Stacia again," Hunter said.

"Did you get to talk to him?"

"No. He's still in the hospital, but one of the nurses told me he's going home. That's why I'm back. I'm going over to see him tomorrow."

"Maybe then we can find out what happened. But one thing is for sure," Kingsley said. "You didn't kill Stacia, Hunter. Don't torture yourself with that for a moment longer. We were together and with Coach."

Hunter nodded. “I wish…”

“We both do.”

He clapped his friend on the back. A few minutes later Hunter went to the guest room that Kingsley kept for him and Kingsley went into Conner’s room. He stood over his son and remembered all the reasons why he was here. Why he had decided to stop running.

It didn’t matter that he had screwed things up more than once. He always—always—made them right. And he knew that he was going to have to figure out how to get Gabi back. He needed her.

Gabi had contacted Mrs. Tillman to find out when Conner and Kingsley would both be out of the house. And then she and Melissa had gone over to pack up her stuff. Conner, she suspected with Mrs. Tillman’s help, had left her a printout of the photo of the three of them dressed up for their Aladdin adventure. She should have realized then that saying goodbye was going to be hard.

She had warned all the nannies who worked for her not to get too attached, because nannies weren’t part of the family, but she’d forgotten that rule and now she was paying for it.

“That’s the last of the office stuff. I’m going to head back unless you need me for anything else,” Melissa said.

“No, that’s okay. I’ll probably go home from here, so I’ll see you tomorrow,” Gabi said.

Melissa gave her a sympathetic smile before turning to leave. She finished packing up her closet and the bathroom things she’d left behind. She had been so sure that she’d outmaneuver Kingsley and force him to realize that they were meant to be together.

But she should have remembered he was very good at getting his way.

She was zipping her suitcase closed when she heard music coming from down the hall. It was an old Matchbox Twenty song, "If You're Gone." She followed the sound of Rob Thomas's voice to the open patio door, where she found Conner dressed like Aladdin waiting for her.

"Princess," he said formally. "We have been waiting for you. Come with me."

"Conner, I don't think this is a good idea. Your daddy and I—"

"Please, Gammi," Conner said. "Please."

She nodded and slipped her hand into his. He led her to the garden area, where a brass lamp waited on a table.

"That's for you," Conner said.

She looked around, having expected to see Kingsley here somewhere. "Thank you. I will put it on my desk so I can see it every day."

"No. You have to rub the lamp," Conner said.

She looked at him standing there watching her with anticipation, a serious expression on his face.

She knelt down next to him. "Should we both do it?"

"Just you," Conner said.

She rubbed the lamp and was surprised when smoke started to rise from it. Just a small burst. She looked at Conner, but he was staring over her shoulder. She turned around and saw Kingsley standing there.

He was dressed only in a pair of loose linen trousers and had his hands on his hips. He had two big brass bracelets on each wrist.

"What is your wish, mistress?" he asked.

"Uh, I'm not sure what's going on," she admitted.

"You've uncovered the magic genie of the lamp," Conner said. "You get three wishes."

Her heart was beating so loudly she thought that everyone could hear it. She wasn't sure what this was all about but had the feeling that Kingsley wasn't saying goodbye.

"What should I wish for?" she asked Conner.

"I'd ask for you to be in my family," he said. "We miss you, Gammi."

"Is that true, Kingsley?" Gabi asked.

"Yes, it is. I'm sorry for everything that happened. I wanted to protect you and thought…well, I thought you'd be better off without me, but my life is dull without you. I want you back."

"Me, too," Conner said.

She hugged Conner and got to her feet to walk over to Kingsley. "Why the genie outfit? I don't want magic tricks. I want the real man."

"I know that," Kingsley said. "But the truth is I love you and I will do whatever I have to in order to make you feel the same way."

"I love you, too, Kingsley, but that was never the issue. Can you let me be a part of your life? Trust me to stay by your side?"

"I can. In fact, that's why I'm your genie. I'll be by your side granting all of your wishes."

"And if I wish for you to give up on this revenge idea?" she asked.

"Then I will continue to help Hunter—we have to talk about that later—but will not be involved in taking justice into my own hands," Kingsley said.

She looked into his eyes, searching for the truth, and it was there for her to see. He wasn't hiding from her or from his emotions anymore. He loved her.

She couldn't believe it. It was what she'd wanted from the first time they met. A schoolgirl's crush had developed into a true and deep love. She hadn't dared to hope. Had thought he was too caught in the past to ever make a real commitment to her, but she was glad to be proved wrong.

She threw herself into his arms and he caught her and swung her around in a circle, kissing her.

"You've made all my wishes come true," she said.

"As you've done for me. Wishes I never dared to dream I could have," Kingsley said.

"If Gammi isn't going to use all her wishes, can I have one?" Conner asked.

Kingsley started laughing and Gabi reached for Conner's hand.

"What do you want?" Kingsley asked, striking his genie pose again with his hands on his hips.

"A family. The three of us to be a family," he said.

"I want that, too," Kingsley said. "Will you marry me, Gabi?"

She looked at these two men who meant the world to her and realized that she hadn't dreamed she could ever be as happy as she was in this moment.

"Yes, I will marry you."

"Yay!" Conner yelled, dancing around them.

Kingsley drew her into his arms and kissed her. She put her hands on his face and looked into his eyes, remembering the first time she met him and fell for him. She'd thought she'd found her true love and now she realized that the love she had for Kingsley was deeper and stronger than ever before.

He dropped to one knee and pulled a ring from his pocket.

"What are you doing, Daddy?"

"Asking Gabi to marry me," Kingsley said to Conner.

Conner came over and knelt next to his dad and Gabi felt as if her heart couldn't get any fuller. Kingsley reached for her hand and when she gave it to him, Conner reached up and held it too.

"Will you marry me, Gabi? Will you be a part of our family?"

"Will you, Gammi?" Conner added.

She knelt down in front of the Buchanan men and wrapped her arms around them both. "Yes, I will."

Kingsley drew back and took a ring box from his pocket. He opened it up and Conner put his hand on his dad's arm and lifted the ring out. He held it out to Gabi and King helped Conner put it on her finger.

They spent the rest of the day together, and when Conner was safely tucked in bed for the night, Kingsley made love to her. He held her close all night long and promised her she'd spent the rest of her life by his side.

* * * * *